Cruel Souls

By
Jacey K Dew

Content Information

Please visit the link below for a specific content information guide, leading to pages, numbers, and brief nondescript summarizations should you decide to skip those pages.
https://jaceykdew.ca/books/content-warnings

Published by Crimson Notebook Publishing
crimsonnotebook.ca

Hardback ISBN: 978-1-998486-00-7
Paperback ISBN: 978-1-7387710-9-7
eBook ISBN: 978-1-7387710-8-0
Audio ISBN: 978-1-998486-05-2

To my wonderful children; Emily and Jeremy.

You make me so proud to be your mom.

I love you forever and always.

XOXO

The Story So Far...

Alexa Brenner

Finds out her boyfriend (Darius) is a vampire when he kidnaps her niece (Rayleen) and takes Alexa to a farm (base of operations) on the day of the attack.

Friends kidnap Alexa and turn her against Darius (to hurt him and destabilize his region) by showing her that he's on the wrong side (causing war, death, and destruction to take over the world). Miles (accidentally) gets captured and Darius forcing Alexa to hurt him ensures that process.

Once rescued, they make it to James' house (Magic Folk Council Leader) and start collecting people and land for a rebellion. Making friends with the dwarves in the Rocky Mountains (by tree nymph travelling) to get weapons and armour made.

After a couple of detours, they and the dwarves end up at the mall with a large base of people (allies – Nikki's group).

Darius attacks the mall to kidnap Rayleen and Alexa again, but Sandra has other plans. She kidnaps Nikki, suspecting she's from a long line of Dreamers (visions of the future in dreams).

They go to the farm and try to rescue Nikki. But, Rayleen is kidnapped. Sandra and Darius ride away with Rayleen and Nikki on the back of a dragon.

Alexa is a mess. They leave the farmhouse once they recover. They run into Jaiden and then travel south.

They stop in Fort MacLeod and are welcomed into the old-time village while James follows a lead by himself. When James comes back, he's found a new lead.
They go to a jail, then Jaiden says they have to go to Banff. They make it to Banff by night and stay at a hotel on the edge of town.

They go rescue Rayleen and Nikki, then make it through the torture forest to a hotel for the night. Darius visits Alexa to invite her to join him, He'll be back tomorrow for her.

They go to town and try to find supplies. They are attacked by a dragon, then go to Nikki's Uncle's house. Jaiden interrupts Darius coming to get Alexa.

Alexa escapes to the castle hotel to find Darius with Rayleen but is thrown in with other prisoners along with Rayleen.

They are let go and rush down the hall. But, someone shoots at them, it's Nikki (accident). Alexa manages to get Rayleen out and down the mountain. They end up at the Uncle's house, as Jaiden is getting fixed up.

Taylor is shot (on purpose and killed) and they go into hiding.

Daniel accepts Alexa's apology and moves them houses. Rayleen sings a song about Christmas.

A bear is in the backyard. There is a meeting of people and Alexa follows a boy to a shop for supernaturals and helps bring supplies back to them. She and Rayleen make it back to their house unnoticed.

During the blizzard, a cerberus is outside, and people go out to kill it. The boy, Cam, defends the cerberus with magic and is kicked out of the house. They get a note for a human-only meeting the next day. They move out.

Rayleen practices her magic. Bruce gets angry so they leave the house. Darius gets Alexa alone to tell her to go to the farm for a present. They join Dominique and Jaiden's convoy out of town.

Once they make it to the farm, Alexa convinces Rayleen to go for a walk to search for Crystal (but really for the mysterious present). They only find Crystal when they make it back to the farmhouse.

Daniel, Rayleen, and Alexa leave with Crystal. They go to Alexa' house, then Daniel's house.

Once back in Banff, they find out Darius attacked and killed most while they were gone. So they leave again with survivors, planning to go to B.C.

They make it to a house in the rain and stop. Ghosts kill a bunch of people, then they decide to head back to Red Deer on a new majority vote.

In Red Deer, they get Rayleen a new magic teacher and they work for their keep. They have to stay away from the rest because of being human.

Daniel isn't happy with Margie (magic teacher) and complains to get Rayleen to stop seeing her, but it doesn't work.

While taking Crystal out to pee, Daniel is killed and Rayleen is kidnapped by Darius.

Alexa falls into a depression. Jaiden forces Alexa to get out and start looking for Rayleen with Dominique. Alexa gets annoyed when it looks like they are just running errands.

Jaiden takes Alexa out for breakfast, hoping Darius had a spy there. He did, and meets them where they search that day. He promises to bring Alexa to Rayleen, but Sandra kills him and shows Alexa a blood vision of her killing Rayleen.

Alexa goes back to her room, cuts herself, drinks alcohol and takes sleeping pills. She dies (accident) after her heart slows too much.

Nikki Marshall

Skipping work to go to the mall with friends (at the insistence of Shawn - an elf who would have prior knowledge of something coming) on the exact wrong day (supernatural uprising) ends with them stuck inside a dollar store (having dodged doomsdayers on the road and supernaturals inside the mall, and collecting some people from the army store upstairs).

They scout out and secure the mall while finding people (including Tyler) and host a party at the end of the world. The atmosphere tenses eventually when rescue doesn't come and they can't agree on how to proceed.

Nikki and her friends go out to find their families but are found dead or missing. Finding no point in staying out, they go back to the safety of the mall.

Some want to continue partying under Tyler's lead, while others turn towards long-term survival. Nikki's friends group is split at the reveal that Shawn is an elf.

Nikki's group relocates to the theatre when Tyler's group ransacks the mall. Then Nikki rescues some people from the hotel.

Kelly and Miles come. It's put to a vote to go or stay. The majority votes to stay at the mall. But, they agree to be allies.

Tyler's group attacks Nikki's and some are killed on both sides. They agree to split the mall and not enter each other's territory.

Kelly returns quickly as James' house was attacked and Nikki prepares for refuge and takes in people from James' house.

Once James arrives, he plans for an attack on the farm. Nikki saves Rayleen from Daniel (Alexa's new human boyfriend) after he violently rages toward her age-appropriate temper tantrum. Darius attacks the mall, and Nikki is kidnapped on the back of a dragon. She's quickly rescued and then kidnapped again, but this time Rayleen is kidnapped as well.

They land at a jail and are taken inside. Nikki is separated from Rayleen and tortured until she agrees to help them by telling them visions of the future (that she's going to have to make up).

Nikki attacks a guard before being led away with Rayleen. Shale tells Darius that he'll watch them to keep them safe from the others.

Sandra and Darius move Rayleen and Nikki via dragon to Banff.

After a meeting with Sandra and Darius (ending with them fighting), Nikki runs back to Rayleen, then takes her out to the torture forest. Narrowly avoiding traps, ends with them captured and Nikki knocked out.

Jaiden and the group rescue Nikki and Rayleen, and they go to a hotel for the night, then down to the town, and eventually to her uncle's house.

James leaves. Nikki takes the opportunity to go up the mountain and find her Uncle. She brings him back, and many of Banff return.

They figure out Taylor is the spy and put her up in a room by herself so she won't hear anything else.

They attack the castle hotel with Banff residents. Nikki accidentally shoots at prisoners. Jaiden stops her in time, and Nikki is taken down the mountain by others. Hotel collapses.

Taylor is shot, and Nikki helps defuse the situation.

Nikki goes to a meeting with Bruce and Banff residents. Bruce and Nikki disagree about Taylor and Jaiden.

They prepare for a blizzard. After being shut inside for so long. They think that they should use the generator for a movie night. Something to look forward to like holidays.

With the snow melting Dominique wants to search for family. Jaiden agrees to pack up and go.

On the way, Dominique figures out Jaiden knows her family is dead. Dominique stops and rides in another car to the farm.

They leave the farm, to go to Dominique's house (Shawn and Steph don't want to go to theirs). People raid the house and Steph is killed.

Dominique and Shawn escape and take a long detoured route back to Banff (mostly from getting lost).

Once back in Banff, they find out Darius attacked and killed most while they were gone. So they leave again with survivors, planning to go to BC.

They make it to a house in the rain and stop. Ghosts kill a bunch of people, then they decide to head back to Red Deer on a new majority vote.

In Red Deer, Dominique works as a waitress in the lounge. She's mad at Jaiden for keeping the secret and decides to confront her by sneaking on a delivery with her.

They get kidnapped by vampires, and then rescued. Back at Jerry's, Dominique starts making the rebellion public. Rallies people.

When Rayleen is kidnapped Dominique tries to go after her but loses her quickly. John and Dominique stay out looking, and on their travels, they find a man injured. They bring him back to Jerry's.

Dominique goes out daily to search for Rayleen. The group she's with kills to keep Jaiden safe. They find a farm (making it into a new outpost) and find a few places with supplies.

They find the Bower group at a mall and invite them to be allies. Find out that Jerry kills people to gain their territory and supplies.

While out, Darius finds them. Sandra kills him and they think Rayleen is dead.

Jaiden figures that Rayleen's alive and figures out that she's at a school (through details in the blood vision), and sends them to rescue Rayleen.

Dominique and the rest rescue Rayleen. They bring people back to the hotel for rest, healing and sorting.

Rayleen starts screaming. They discover Alexa dead and Rayleen screaming. They take her to the hospital.

Jaiden figures out that it may be because of a soul transfer. That Alexa's soul is transferring into Rayleen.

Dominique yells at Alexa to give up to let Rayleen live.

Jaiden Kensington

Gets a vacation from her regular life when the world is attacked and spends a week alone and relaxing.

This ends when people break into her home. She decides to go to grandma's house because she's having visions of her sister.

Gets to grandma's to find only strangers. They have a set of werewolves captured and show her as proof of a demon takeover.

Jaiden separates from them on a walkabout and finds her sister's ex-boyfriend, who brings her to his family farm (pack of werewolves).

They rescue the werewolves and Jaiden finds out that the group had killed her whole family (assumes Dominique is alive from visions and not seeing her in the pile of bodies). Jaiden decides to go back home and figure out the next steps.

Calli (succubi) takes her to a grocery store with a bunch of people. They are sent on a mission to the hospital and are attacked. Ostracized from the grocery store, they (along with Lucas) go south.

Calli brings them to Jerry's (bar/hotel/delivery service for supernaturals). Calli wakes Jaiden saying they have to leave (another attack). While running from an ogre, they run into Alexa's group. They take refuge at a house.

Jaiden finds out the group is trying to rescue Nikki (who is also Dominique).

Jaiden spends time at Fort MacLeod trying to learn what she can about old-timey solutions. She finds out Sara gave her a working phone.

James comes back with a new lead. They go back north, to a jail, where Jaiden tells everyone they moved to Banff.

They save Nikki and Rayleen, then go to a hotel, main street, and then Dominique's uncle's house.

Jaiden catches Darius in Alexa's window, and he leaves. She tells James. He leaves. Alexa leaves with Rayleen.

Jaiden follows Nikki up the mountain to find her uncle. They return with many people from Banff.

They figure out Taylor is the spy and put her up in a room by herself so she won't hear anything else.

Jaiden stops Nikki from. killing innocent people accidentally and sends Nikki down the mountain before the hotel collapses around Jaiden. Jaiden calls a truce and everyone alive goes down to the town.

Taylor is shot, and they go into hiding.

Jaiden is stuck at the house because of her leg, but ends up leaving to go to the ruins to help, and is sidetracked by a Cerberus.

Back at the house, Christmas comes and goes. Jaiden is asked to go to a meeting with the supernaturals of the hotel to advocate for them. She talks to Bruce about them after asking for things for them, like blood.

They prepare for a blizzard and now have a generator (from Bruce who was hoarding them for the humans, on the condition it would be for his house).

With the snow melting Dominique wants to search for family. Jaiden agrees to pack up and go.

Dominique figures out Jaiden knows her family is dead, stops the car, and goes to another car. They drive to the farm.
Jaiden and Leah go through the house. Everyone is dead, but they take their supplies. They find Darius did it through a bloody note (his gift to Alexa).

On their way back to Banff, they detour to Leah's family. The vampires in Banff are starving and out of sunblock. The family thing goes south and they don't get anything.

Once back in Banff, they find out Darius attacked and killed most while they were gone. So they leave again with survivors, planning to go to BC.

They make it to a house in the rain and stop. Ghosts kill a bunch of people, then they decide to head back to Red Deer on a new majority vote.

They pick up John and Sara on the way.

In Red Deer, Jaiden makes a deal with Jerry to stay at the hotel. Jaiden starts planning a rebellion.

When trying to do deliveries, Jaiden discovers Dominique stowed away. They talk, then get kidnapped by vampires. They get rescued by Chad's group.

Back at Jerry's, Jaiden gets fed food that Jules cooked. She has a breakdown in her room.

Jaiden finds out Dominique has started auctioning the rebellion. Jerry corners Jaiden and she makes new deals to keep them alive.

Jaiden deals with Alexa spiralling, rebellion started, and moving people to the hotel across the street. They start expanding.

They discover a group at the hospital and make allies when Jaiden holds a baby succubus.

Jaiden goes around organizing new people into new places. One group doesn't cooperate and reveals that they killed a family. They are killed, and people are brought as meat to Jules.

Henry makes leaps to get a market started up.

Jaiden takes Alexa out for breakfast, hoping Darius had a spy there. Things don't go to plan when Sandra kills Darius.

Back at the hotel, Jaiden talks to Alexa and figures out Rayleen is at a school (because of details in the blood vision and her own vision). Jaiden sends everyone out after Rayleen.

The Bower group escorts Jaiden to the school when they show up randomly. Jaiden takes the injured to the hospital.

Jaiden figures out that Rayleen might have transferred Alexa's soul into her. Reveals she has gotten ahold of James, who confirms it's possible.

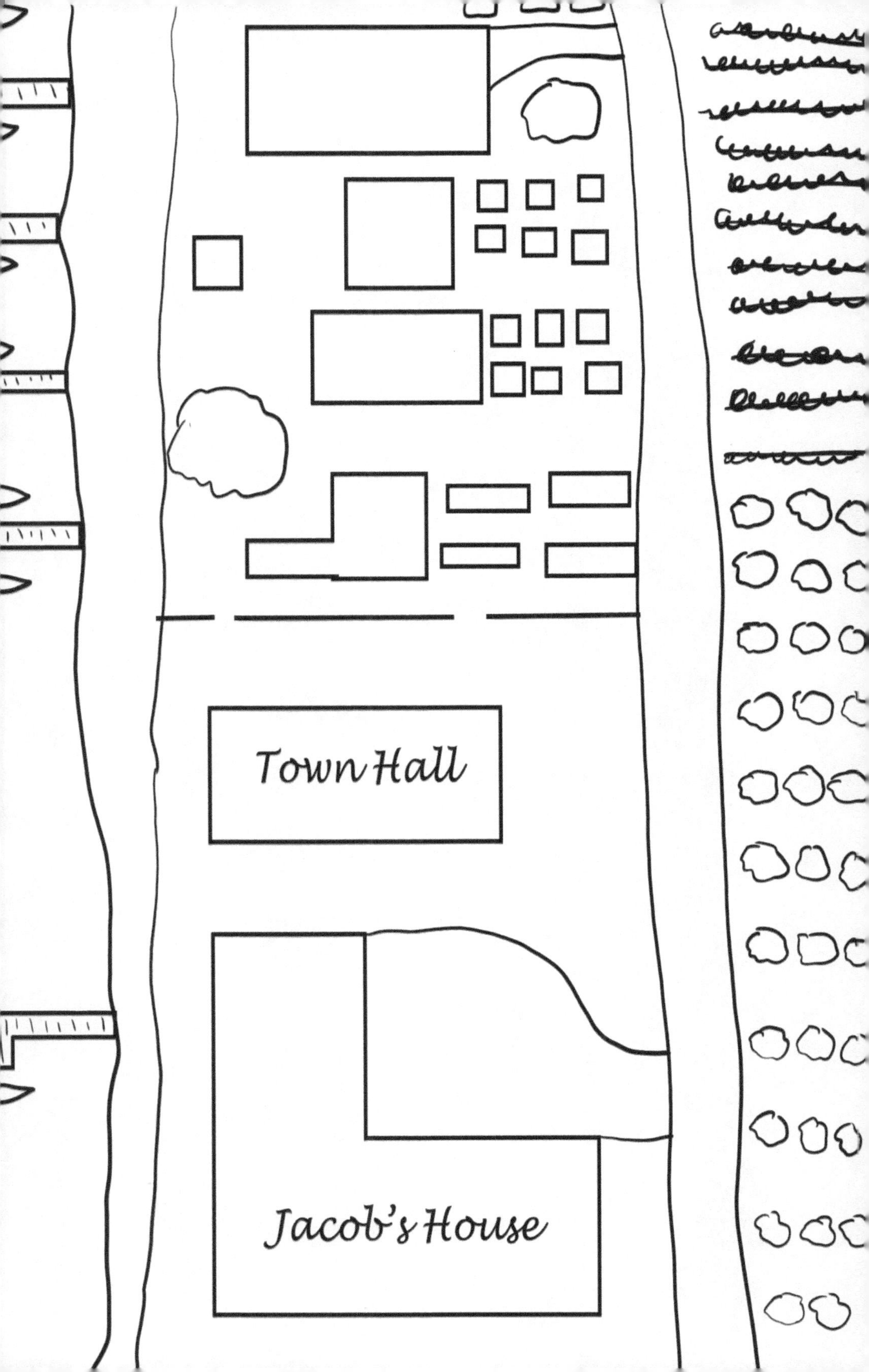

Town Hall
Jacob's House

Chapter 1

It starts as a poke in my chest.

Hot sharp pain increases and spreads every time I breathe. The growing heat makes the cold room freeze worse. It feels like someone is pressing ice cubes against the skin of my entire body. But, I know that they aren't

Feverish wetness drips from the back of my neck.

Short, quick breaths hurt a little less than normal breathing, but not for long. Something squeezes my chest; making it harder to catch some air.

While waiting for it to pass, the pain spreads to my tummy and back.

I curl into myself as much as allowed. Being pressed up against Alexa stops me.

"Alexa," I whimper. A little louder, I say her name again as I squish her arm. "Alexa."

I didn't wake her when I found her. She was sleeping peacefully and I didn't want to wake her. Alexa needs her sleep, and you shouldn't wake someone up unless it's an emergency.

This feels like an emergency. But, is it enough of an emergency?

It hurts too much. I feel sick. I'm so cold. Something is wrong.

Definitely, something is very wrong.

"Alexa!" I yelp as the pain increases.

My eyes squeeze shut in the darkness.

I scream in pain; not wanting to. Not able to stop myself anymore. Noise doesn't help my pain go away.

I scream in the hope that Alexa will wake up and help me. My whole body is on fire in the frozen room.

"Alexa!" I beg.

Wake up!

A door thunders into the wall. People rush in and around.

Spotlights wave around before settling on blinding me. I close my eyes to protect them from the bright pain; it's little relief. The light is still too bright through my eyelids.

"Rayleen, what's wrong?" A woman asks. I know that voice but I can't begin to think who it is.

Hands roll me onto my back. A wave of nausea stops my scream in my throat from searing pain.

I feel like I'm going to throw up.

They hold me so I can't curl back up.

"Alexa? Alexa!? Wake up!" A male voice shouts. "Turn on the lights." But, we're not supposed to use power for lights. We're only supposed to use it for necessities; light isn't necessary.

The lights flip on. Even with my eyes closed, it's too bright. My eyes ache with the peach flash.

I don't feel right.

"Is she dead?" A woman questions quietly.

Dead?

Rayleen's dead.

Wake up.

"Check for a pulse." She murmurs. Her voice is far away.

I don't feel right.

Maybe if I stay still it'll help. My muscles feel disconnected from my brain.

The world turns out of focus and swirls despite knowing I'm still. My eyes keep swimming while closed.

My chest aches as my heart races.

My arm refuses to place upon my chest.

My breath goes in and out in sync with my heart; never enough air makes it through my shrinking throat. My mouth and throat dry out, and I'm sure I'm about to throw up. But, my muscles loosen.

I feel myself sinking in.

I don't feel right.

A cold hand relieves some pain, but only for the moment it touches my forehead.

"Rayleen's burning up."

Where's Rayleen?

She's dead.

No. She's burning up.

I open my eyes to look. Dominique has her hand on my forehead. As it lifts, pain explodes. I screech as every inch of my body sears. My heart sears as something tears it apart.

"What's wrong with her?" Dominique asks.

"I don't know." He answers.

The word, "hospital," breaks through a scream; my scream.

I'm hoisted into arms and jostled around as the person carries me out to a vehicle.

I open my eyes to see how close we are when the breeze outside takes the edge off the burning.

John opens the door. Nikki lifts me into the front seat of a large vehicle. She leans me up against the seat, buckles me in and shuts the door.

I want Alexa. I hurt too much. I want it to stop.

It hurts. Am I going to die?

I can't move. My muscles burn more when I try to move.

The back door opens and people get in. In the mirror, I see someone bouncing up and down. I screech as the vehicle moves. Each bump and movement hurting me more.

I curl up in hopes that will help alleviate the extra pain caused by the movement.

Dominique slams on the brakes in front of the hospital. I reach for the door release but can't reach it. Dominique opens the door and undoes my seatbelt.

She wraps her arms around me. I seethe as she pulls me out. Nikki turns around to the people leaving the back.

Alexa is uncannily still. A wave of terror jumpstarts my heart.

No, I…

Nausea.

Chest aching.

Can't move.

Suffocating.

Sinking.

My heart pumps pain from my chest, out to the rest of my body. It's quickly overwhelming my senses.

I know she's dead. Part of me knows that; starts preparing me for that. But, we're at a hospital. They'll help. They can bring her back to life.

She won't be dead anymore.

Dominique places me on a bed as instructed by a doctor. The jolted pain unleashes a bottled-up howl.

Questions blur into each other. Nothing processes beyond my ears. Hands and instruments examine quickly.

The bed jerks. We roll further into the hospital; taking some twists and turns.

We settle into a room with curtains for walls, but they aren't pulled far out.

Someone tells the others to leave and to let the doctors work.

Mumbled words swirl around.

I make out the name Jaiden, then more words come into focus. "Dominique, go find Jaiden, now!"

I don't want her to leave me, but I can't find the voice for anything except pain.

Alexa's moving bed is rolled up a little ways away beside mine. I choke on my breath.

Someone is on top of her pressing rhythmically against her chest. They do that in doctor shows when someone is dead.

The doctors aren't leaping to help her. They are more concerned with doing things to me. Their hands and tools are burning cold against me.

I don't understand.

She's dead. She's worse. She needs help more than I do.

Help her.

Please, help her!

I can't find the voice to tell them. The words stick in my throat.

A doctor tells someone to stop performing compressions. When they do and get off of her, the doctor checks a couple things in just a few seconds. "She's dead."

"There's nothing we can do."

"Wake up," I say.

"Wake up!" I scream.

Something pinches in the back of my head. Darkness circles the outer edges of my vision; closing in.

"I'm dead," I whisper.

Overwhelming pain fills my chest and head. Screaming rips up my throat.

I use all my energy to try to get to her, but I'm held down with much stronger hands.

The curtain between us is pulled sharply. I can't see her anymore.

Everywhere hurts; especially where they touch me.

My eyes grow too heavy to keep open.

Chapter 2

"Stop blaming yourself," I tell Jaiden as I watch her fiddle in place; bouncing her heel against the ground. She rubs her finger against the opal ring; back and forth.

She's not paying attention to anything outside of her head; just staring blankly into space.

"Jaiden." She looks over to me in a quick startle. "Stop blaming yourself," I repeat.

Her brows crease slightly. "No, I'm, I'm going over the conversation with James. It doesn't make sense. Because I-eh um."

Jaiden sits up straighter in the hard chair and squares up her body to talk to me directly.

She takes in and lets out a quick breath. "Okay, so souls are different ages, not usually based on the body's age; unless it's a brand new soul. A baby could get a soul that's already a thousand years old or it could be new.

So if children don't survive, then maybe it's the body that doesn't survive. Maybe the body isn't strong enough for the process.

If the body lives and it's the soul that dies, it has to be whichever soul was stronger, that won, that takes control.

But, that wouldn't necessarily be Alexa's soul just because

Alexa was older. Alexa's soul could have been weaker than Rayleen's.

And, we could be talking about stronger souls taking control rather than a soul death, because of the elder Magic Council Reps. All their souls get transferred into the new Council Rep so that they can have all the knowledge and memories of past Magic Council Reps. In theory, the amalgamation of all the previous souls should always be stronger than the new one.

But James is James, he has to be or else whoever is the new Magic Rep would end up dying when chosen and becoming the amalgamation, so maybe it's a choice the souls can make to relinquish control.

Or, the host is always the host and absorbs the rest of the souls and memories.

Unless James isn't James. I don't know who he was before the Council and if that changed after the soul transfer. But, that would cause trouble with Magic Reps just being the same person over and over, in a different body. It would cause issues with accepting being a Magic Rep because it would be accepting that the person you are, is going to die.

Unless, they don't tell them beforehand, and that's another issue.

Then, it can't be a soul death that happens in the transfer, it has to be a melding or absorption, or both souls existing in the same body. Because otherwise, how would the life extension happen and the memories be transferred if it was just pure death; unless it's like an eating thing with memories and aging being the nutrients absorption?

Either way, Rayleen and Alexa, neither can be gone completely. Because a death would completely get rid of the memories, and you wouldn't get the age extension if it just died.

Unless, it's an absorption-type event, and you reason it dies that way.

Which all brings us back to it's the body that can't handle the process.

Which, kids are resilient. I've read stories about them surviving things adults likely wouldn't have.

And, a hundred souls going into an adult seems like it would be a much bigger issue than one soul going into a child. So if James, as an adult, can handle a hundred souls transferred, all at once, then why shouldn't a kid be able to handle one soul?

Unless, there's something in the process that we're missing to help the exchange along, that James purposely left out.

But, there are circumstances of accidental transfers and people surviving, so maybe it's not that; or that item helps but isn't necessary, but does help the survival rate.

It could be a medical thing, like a sickness. You take medicine not to cure the sickness, but to treat the symptoms so your body survives. So like Chief said, he'll just treat the symptoms, and maybe that's all Rayleen needs to survive.

I don't know. It just doesn't make sense, and I'm trying to work it out still. I don't have all the information I wish I had. Sorry. That was… a big ramble. Sorry." Jaiden deflates a little. Her shoulders slouch and she bites her lips together once. She drops her eyes and goes back to fiddling with the ring.

I nod while taking all the information in. She talked fast and twisty, and brought up more questions than answers.

But, at least she's working through thoughts that don't include Rayleen just dying.

In all, she brought up a few possibilities and issues. I go over them quickly from the points I remember.

The boys, John, Cole and Connor, stay quiet. I don't think they have anything to input. Or, maybe they're going over the mass of information too, before they answer.

Out of all of us, I would think they should have more answers.

They grew up in the supernatural world. They were raised on this stuff, or at least what the Council told them. Which could be part of the problem. If the council suppressed soul transfer information, then they'd be just as clueless. Or, they might only have incorrect or vague information.

None of the boys look like they are about to answer Jaiden. They've all gone off to look elsewhere; gone back to their previous waiting modes.

I start first with the points that stick in my mind. Jaiden and the boys look over at me when I start talking. "Okay, so if it's the body, we're in a hospital, so that gives Rayleen the best chance that way. If it's a choice, then we have to convince Alexa to give up. We can't help anything else, so we'll deal with what we can, when we can."

I decide to hang on to the possibility that it's a choice. Standing abruptly takes everyone by surprise. Connor looks ready to jump out of his chair.

"Relax." I wave my hands palm down to the floor. "I'm going to check on Rayleen. See if I can find someone who can give me an update."

John gets up and follows me out. I wonder if it's for solidarity, or because he suspects an ulterior motive.

Maybe I'm just being paranoid because I do have an ulterior motive.

Busy halls have turned quiet. The darkness intensifies the lack of sound. All I can hear are my footsteps. My boots squeak a little now and then.

I peek inside as I pass an open door. The two beds inside have people sleeping peacefully.

I rub my arms for warmth or comfort. The cold of the hospital never leaves, despite the heaters they post here and there.

Everyone has been seen, at least, once. Those who had minor injuries have been sent to wherever Jaiden told them to go.

Those who were worse off, have been given beds here for the night; if they survived.

Doctors and nurses still go in and out of rooms to check on patients, but major events aren't happening; many are sleeping. Their footsteps join mine and John's, as they pass us making the rounds.

Rayleen's room isn't far. I look at the empty bed space. They wheeled Alexa out of the room. I don't know where they took her body.

What does the hospital do with their dead? I doubt they'd let them rot in the morgue.

I shake my head and divert my vision to Rayleen.

I'm glad to find her sleeping, but scrunched eyebrows and a frown reveal the turmoil going on inside of her.

She looks so fragile in the large hospital bed. Phantom beeping monitors join the image; pulled from a distant memory of a TV show I used to watch. I wish it was just a scene in a show. The director would call cut, and Rayleen would spring to life.

But, this isn't that. Rayleen's life is in danger, and the props in this hospital are about as good as TV props.

Though these doctors are real, I'm not sure how much they can do given what they have to work with.

How well can they work without all the monitoring equipment they used to have? How well can they diagnose or treat without being able to use diagnostic imaging machines?

Would everyone be willing to sacrifice their power for the hospital to be able to use their power-sucking equipment, if it meant someone could be saved from death?

I tuck Rayleen's sprawling hair down to lay neatly near her shoulders and pull up the covers to her armpits. I make sure to be careful of the IV they have in her hand.

Walking around to the other side of the bed, I grasp her free hand and kiss her forehead. Both are chilly. I don't know if that's good or not, but I'm relieved her fever has broken.

I wish there was a chair, I could pull up and sit in. A light I could turn on to see her better. Machines that work, so I can hear that she's still alive.

I don't know what to say, or if she can even hear me, but I have to give it a try. "Alexa, if you love Rayleen, you have to let go. Let Rayleen win control. Stop fighting her. She is going to die if you don't. She doesn't deserve that.

You have done what you can to protect her, and now you have to do that again. Protect her, by letting go and letting her live.

I'll be here for her. I'll protect her for you going forward. I swear I won't let anything happen to her, for as long as I live.

Let her have control. She will die if you don't."

"You aren't supposed to be in here." A nurse comes around me to check on Rayleen and her IV. She forces me to move by invading my space. "You need to leave."

I wasn't doing anything wrong. "I was just-"

"Out now." The nurse flicks on the light behind the bed. "She needs to rest, and you were told to stay in the waiting room." Her stern voice is enough to get me up and moving. I look back at Rayleen when I leave. The nurse clicks her tongue and softens her tone. "I know you're worried, but you need to let her rest. We're doing everything we can to help her, and I will let you know if anything happens."

John and I thank her to be polite. We weren't doing anything wrong. I could've stood there in silence if they had a problem with me talking.

John puts his hand against my shoulder blade to nudge me forward and back to the waiting room. I wrap my arms around myself in slight comfort. It hurts to have to leave her there.

"You couldn't have known." Cole or Connor's voice floats out of the waiting room door.

A different man's voice cuts. "As the one in charge, she should have known about the woman having heavy sedatives. At the very least, she knew she was suicidal. She should have put her on suicide watch here at the hospital instead of leaving her alone. This is what happens when little girls are put in charge, they make terrible judgement calls."

I step inside of the room. Jaiden is the only one to notice. Her eyes meet with mine. I shoot her a questioning look. She breaks eye contact to rejoin the other conversation.

"She took precautions for what she knew about. There was no reason to believe Alexa was suicidal. No one knew she had the pills." Red shirt, Connor says.

"There are warnings on the bottles not to mix them with alcohol. She died because her heart slowed too much. Even just one pill mixed with alcohol can cause it." The male doctor advises. "Obviously, she wanted to die."

I haven't seen him before or, at least, I don't remember him. Maybe he was in the room when we brought Rayleen and Alexa in, but I don't remember; it was such a blur.

"If Alexa knew and did it on purpose, then it was suicide. If she didn't, it was an accidental death. We have no way of knowing for sure, so it's best not to torture the living with guilt for something she ultimately had no control over." Blue shirt, Cole says.

"Jaiden did what she could with the information she had," Connor adds. "Her age has nothing to do with anything."

"I knew she was out of sorts, and she has had a history of cutting. If I had stayed, maybe I could have gotten her to the hospital sooner." Jaiden looks down to the ground. Rage fuels, knowing she's taking this blame to heart.

"You got Kelly involved to watch her, so if anyone is to

blame, for not noticing sooner, it was Kelly. Don't blame yourself and don't let others blame you for Alexa's mistake." I sharpen my tone. "And you. Shut up and get out of here before I tell Chief about your horrendous bedside manner."

I cut him off as he opens his mouth. "Get out!" I boom and point toward the door. He huffs but ultimately leaves.

Jaiden exudes a sullen countenance. She draws into herself; frowning and biting her lips.

If she wasn't blaming herself before, she certainly is now.

I walk over to hug Jaiden, before drawing her out to arms reach. Keeping my hands on her shoulders to reassure her. "It's not your fault. You couldn't have known, and you did what you could with the information you had.

And, if it wasn't an accident, you couldn't have stopped her. If it wasn't the sleeping pills, then it would have been cutting or hanging; something. She would have found a way. You couldn't have watched her forever."

"Not forever, just a couple of hours. Once she saw Rayleen was alive, she would have been fine." Jaiden points out.

She is right. If it was intentional and situational, then knowing Rayleen was alive and well, and returned, it would have kept her will to live.

However, there's more to it than just the here and now when it ultimately comes down to it.

"Until the next time, she's captured or killed. Or maybe Rayleen being alive wouldn't have mattered. Maybe the guilt of everything else would have gotten to her. Or, maybe she would get into a frame of mind, where she thinks Rayleen is better off without her.

Alexa needed therapy, deep therapy, and you aren't a therapist." I try to reassure her.

There's so much unknown about the situation, and too many

ways it could have played out. We have no way of knowing what the future would have been.

I stiffen. But, Jaiden sees the future. Maybe she saw things that are now weighing on her, more than what happened.

If she had visions of Alexa having died, then didn't save her or couldn't save her, then she'd blame herself worse.

But, I don't know if that would make sense. If she knew Alexa died, and how she died, then she never would have left her alone. Or, would have done more reassurance to make sure.

Or, something.

Unless, she didn't know how or when. Maybe she didn't know it was happening then and thought she had time. Thought it could wait the few hours until Rayleen was back safe.

If she had visions of Alexa only being alive, but then had interactions with her that could have led to her death; the heavy guilt she would have would be unbearable. Knowing she should have lived-

Jaiden takes a deep breath in the dead silence.

I soften a little. "I'm choosing to believe that it was a tragic accident that nothing could have prevented it, and I suggest you do the same. Nothing you could have done differently would have changed anything."

"Yeah." Jaiden nods. "It was an accident and not my fault."

"Now say it like you believe it." I jest, hoping to lighten her up a little; make the point get across better.

"It was an accident and not my fault," Jaiden repeats. She breaks out of my grasp. "I should go though. Lots to do. Lots of other people to check in on, and I can only get so much done through walkie-talkies. You stay with Rayleen, and let me know if anything happens."

Jaiden avoids the eyes of everyone as she sets off to leave the room. My heart pulls off in her direction. I want to tell her to stop and reassure her, but I don't think it would help.

I wave for the twins' attention and once I have it, I point at them, then point at Jaiden. Red shirt, Connor, chases after her. Cole stays with us.

I look over to John and give him a look. He pulls his mouth tight to acknowledge with a short nod. Jaiden needs to be watched and reassured.

She's blaming herself for Alexa's death.

Chapter 3

"You were supposed to be here hours ago." Jerry scowls.

So much for hoping I wouldn't run into him. I was putting off Chad's delivery until I had all the other local stuff done. I knew Jerry wouldn't be pleased, so I waited until he should have been inspecting an incoming delivery.

After I left a briefing with the Chief at the hospital, I checked on the people at our hotel with Ted and the people at the market with the security team. I checked in with Henry and Bower, and walkie-talkied with DeAngelo to make sure he didn't need anything immediately.

I figured I could get the delivery done now, and spend the evening at the farm.

With an apologetic smile, I lighten my voice and start apologizing. "I am so sorry. I've just been so busy. There was a raid last night and we discovered one of their bases and Rayleen was there. And so, we rescued Rayleen but Alexa ended up dying. So, I was dealing with that.

And, there were a bunch of injured people that were at the base. So they had to get fixed up and we had to find places for them to go. And I've been dealing with a whole bunch of stuff to deal with that.

But, I am sorry that I did not get to Chad's delivery yet. I am about to go do that. I'll explain it to him and I'll make sure he knows it was my fault." I rattle off an apology, the reasoning behind it, and reassurance that I'm going to do what he wants. A nicely packaged assurance that I take responsibility and that I feel bad about it.

If that's not enough to placate him, I don't have the patience to deal with an argument. I move as quickly as possible past him, hoping he'll leave it alone.

"Chad's delivery is tomorrow," Jerry states.

I stop and spin around to look at him. He's smirking, but I can't tell if he's joking or serious. "I was sure it was today."

His regular schedule would dictate that the delivery would be today; I'm sure of it. I even double-checked two days ago, to make sure nothing was updated.

"No. Tomorrow. You can check with Hectre if you want to confirm." Jerry ends his part of the conversation by walking down to the hallway and towards his room.

I look to Connor for his thoughts. "I guess we get a car and go to the farm then." He says.

"We should double-check with Hectre. Make sure Jerry isn't setting me up to fail." I'd wait for a response, but Connor is already leading the way to the kitchen.

I've had that happen before, a few times, with different people. They tell me that something is cancelled or postponed, then when I missed the deadline or appointment, or whatever it was, then they tell me they were just joking and that I shouldn't have taken them seriously. That it was so obvious that they were joking. Yet, I still faced all the consequences of trusting that they were telling me the truth.

It's always possible that Jerry would tell me it's not today, so that Chad starts questioning his loyalty to me. It would benefit Jerry if he could deal with Chad directly.

But, what's stopping him from changing the schedule in the books and getting Hectre to go along with it? Hectre already helped him once.

Hectre is at the till ringing up a few drinks. The lounge is fairly empty, but a new guy is strumming on a guitar in the corner. A little section was carved out for him to have an open stage. I wonder if he's new staff or just a customer taking liberties. The stage part is new.

"Hey, Hectre. You have anything sweet to drink? Jaiden hasn't eaten since yesterday, and she didn't sleep last night, but she hates caffeine and won't stop to eat." That's not what he was supposed to say. A tinge of betrayal gets overridden by embarrassment.

Connor glances back at me with a smirk; he's just like Cole.

I lift my hands up on either side of my head; making a W shape with my body. "Connor."

Connor lifts his finger up to tap towards me before he turns to Hectre. "Oh, and Jerry said Chad's delivery isn't until tomorrow, but she thought it was today, so we wanted to double-check."

"Definitely tomorrow. We had supply issues, so things got delayed by a day. Chad knows and we're compensating him for the delay. You can relax." Jerry very well could have explained that himself. Hectre motions to a bar stool near us. He backs up a couple of steps to crack open the kitchen door. "Jules, Jaiden's here and forgot to feed herself again. But, she's busy and in a hurry so could you-"

The door rips out of his grasp. Jules barrels out of the kitchen and beelines for me. Their arms reach out and engulphs me in a hug. The hug is consuming. A lump forms in my chest. "I'm sorry about your friend. Sounds like you had a rough night. Are you okay?"

Tears force themselves out in a quick attack. My chest hurts and my eyes sting. A few tears fall down my cheeks as Jules pulls me away to look at me.

"Sorry," I say in a panic.

They try to pull me in again, but I break it off. I need to get out of here. People can't see me cry. I don't want to make a scene. I have to get this under control.

I maneuver around Jules and Hectre, and into the kitchen; the closest way out. I close my eyes and focus on breathing evenly.

Shame heats my cheeks.

I can't believe I just cried in front of people. That can't happen. They'll think I'm weak. They won't want to have me around if they think I'm going to cry all the time. I don't want to make them have to comfort me just to be nice. They shouldn't have to deal with that.

The three of them come into the kitchen just as I wipe away the remaining tears.

"I'm so sorry. If you just give me a moment I can stop this." I motion to my face. "I just need a moment."

"It's okay to cry. It's okay to not be okay." Jules trying to reassure me is the opposite of what I need. The tears and heat start up again.

I wasn't even good friends with Alexa. I don't know why I'm crying.

"I just need a moment. My eyes started stinging for some reason." I smile to show them I'm okay.

"Must have been some onion juice in my shirt or something. I'm sorry." Jules apologizes. I feel bad they are taking blame and guilt, but it's better than everyone thinking I'm a weak crybaby.

Though, they might just be making the excuse. I don't know if that makes it better or worse.

"Oh, that's alright. Don't worry about it. I'm all good." I try to reassure them by waving it off.

Jules politely shoves Hectre out of the kitchen to deal with customers but allows Connor to stay. I focus on what they are doing, to forget about the sadness, guilt, regret, frustration, and anger swirling near the surface.

Jules cuts a slice of bread and then grabs something from the warming tray. They put them together, one on top of the other, then hands it over to me.

"Hotdog; sort of. You can eat it fast and on the run, but it gets some food in your belly. You need to start remembering to eat better. Here," Jules pauses to grab something from the freezer. "Have a water too."

I take the bottle while thanking them. "We'll see you later." I dismiss myself. Connor says his goodbyes, and we wave at Hectre on the way out.

I eat the sausage and bread on the way back to our hotel while Connor walks beside me. He has both hands shoved into his jacket pockets, and glances over to me frequently.

I imagine he's wishing that he could read me; Cole does the same thing. But, I'm still glad that he can't. Well, at least without using regular observation.

"How are you doing?" He finally asks as I finish off my last bite.

"I'm good. Thanks for mentioning food. I forgot I hadn't eaten." Wait. "You didn't eat?"

"Wasn't hungry yet, besides I ate breakfast." He dismisses. "Do you want to take the bikes? Would save a bit on gas, and I don't think we have to cart anything back and forth?"

I'm not entirely keen on the idea of bike riding. It seems like so much more effort than riding in the car. And, it's still a bit chilly outside, which gets colder when moving around at higher speeds on a bike.

However, we are getting low on gas. The all hands on deck, every vehicle to the school and running people to and from had depleted much of what we had left. Jerry's fuel is too expensive to waste; or buy in the first place.

"Yeah, I guess so." I relent.

"Hey," Connor says before taking off inside the hotel. I follow quickly, anxious about what had him taking off unexpectedly.

"Hi." Connor greets the patient guy; I don't remember his name. I'll have to wait until someone says his name, so I don't appear rude for not remembering it.

He's up, out and about, which is better than he has been. Even partially healed, he's been sticking inside his room and keeping to himself.

"You said I could help myself to food." He quickly jumps to the defensive. He was alone in here; maybe that's why.

"Yeah, of course." I smile sweetly. "Just glad to see you up. How are you feeling?"

"Better." He cuts off quickly. He continues off to where he was headed before our interruption, the food table.

"Good," Connor says. "Do you feel up to telling us what happened yet? Who attacked you? Was it Jerry or one of his people?"

He grabs a couple of granola bars to shove in his pocket, then turns to look between us, cautious on how to continue. "Aren't you his people?"

"No, we were only there temporarily. We're distancing ourselves from him. We've recently heard of some terrible things he's done." I try to reassure him without revealing too much. Maybe he'll feel safer knowing that bit.

"We've all done some terrible things." He deadpans.

"Not like that," Connor says.

"Exactly that." He frowns.

"Were you one of Jerry's people?" I push a little for information. It would make sense why he would be afraid of

Jerry. One of the reasons, anyway. The other is that he was an enemy or someone Jerry attacked.

"I worked for him from before and continued after. But, I didn't realize he'd do anything like that. He killed anyone who got in his way. I tried to get away and did for a bit. But, someone survived one of the massacres. He found me and talked about how we'd killed his family. So, he would kill me. Almost did." His body remains tense. He looks around for escape if needed.

"Then Dominique and John found you. We didn't have anything set up here at the time, so they took you to Jerry's to see the doctor there." I explain to fill in the gaps.

"Am I free to go?" He asks.

"Of course. You aren't a prisoner." Connor reassures.

The tension immediately releases from his body. He turns his side to use and continues picking up items off the table. "I have to go. Jerry can't find me or I'm dead." He means leave, leave.

"He didn't seem to recognize you at the hotel," I say.

He turns to look at me. He opens up the wrapper in his hands. "I always enjoyed my human mask better. He never saw me like this, and I was pretty beaten up, but give him a good look at me and he'd know." He takes a bite of a granola bar.

"We have somewhere else further away, if you want to stay with us." I offer, without giving away the location. It might be best if he doesn't know that, if he's leaving.

His face tenses. "Absolutely not. I'm leaving. Getting as far away from here as possible."

"Are you sure? We've got lots of-"

He cuts me off. "Stop. I don't want to hear a pitch. I want to get out of here, and as far away from you and Jerry as I possibly can." He calms a bit. "Sorry, thank you for saving me. But, I need to leave. I don't trust anything connected to Jerry, and that includes you by proximity. Thank you for what you've done for me, but I'm leaving." He grabs a couple waters from the counter, then takes off for the entrance without another word between us.

His leave is abrupt and everything turned at a snap. He seemed like he was relaxing, but then he got scared again.

Was it something I said? Something I did?

"Well." I fill the empty space.

"Yeah."

"What happened?" Connor shrugs. I look to the door then back to Connor. "Do we have anything to worry about with him?" For a moment, I forgot he wasn't like Cole; they don't have the same powers type.

Connor looks at me. He tilts his head to the side and back in pointed thinking. "That's not an entirely unreasonable reaction. We've been worried about Jerry attacking us. He knows firsthand what Jerry can do. He's likely going to do what he said, and leave."

"We should get to the farm. It's a long bike ride." I sigh. And, it's going to be an even longer ride back home later.

Chapter 4

I gasp for air as I startle awake. I grasp my chest to stop my heart from leaping out of my chest.

My arm is heavy and doesn't want to move. My legs feel the same way when I try to pull them up.

"Rayleen!" Dominique leans into my view of the dark ceiling above. "You're awake."

Further away, I hear a man shouting, "We need a doctor!"

I sweep my eyes around the small room. Why am I in a hospital?

"Are you okay? Do you feel okay? Do you hurt anywhere? What happened? Are you, you?" Dominique starts in on a bunch of questions.

Any response is stuck as a lump in my throat.

I don't know how to answer or what to say. I barely know what she asked.

My brain feels like it's slowed in a heavy fog. Weights pull my eyelids closed, but I force them back open. I just want to go back to sleep, but there are too many unanswered questions.

I look around. I'm in a small room with a light-coloured blanket for a wall on one side of my room. There are some medical things to the left of my bed.

Dominique leans over from a chair she has next to the bed. There's another person partially in view behind her, but I can't tell who it is.

Someone else rushes into the room.

"Don't overwhelm her. Give her a moment." A woman takes Dominique's place. She's wearing the doctor clothes that look like pyjamas. Scrubs, the word comes to me.

She looks down at me with a smile. "I'm Nurse Jenny. You sure have beautiful hair. We'll have to get a brush and some ponytails, and I can braid it, if you'd like? I used to braid my sister's hair all the time. She liked to have fishtail braids. Have you ever had fishtail braids?"

I shake my head. I don't know how to braid well. No one ever taught me.

Nurse Jenny holds up a stethoscope and starts an examination. We wait in coached silence as she listens to my chest.

She goes to a cart and pulls out a thing she wraps around my arm. She explains each step before she does anything.

"They're fancy braids that are supposed to resemble fish scales, I suppose." Nurse Jenny continues on from where she left off. "Very tricky to do, much more than French braids, but I miss doing them.

It's funny, the things you miss as you get older. I used to complain whenever she'd ask for them because my fingers would be stiff by the end.

But, if you'd like, I could braid your hair. Then you could see what a fishtail braids looks like. I think it would look marvellous in your hair. It's such a pretty colour. You don't have to answer now, we have plenty of time, and the offer is open any time."

She brings out a light to flash into my eyes and makes me follow her finger around.

"Are you hungry? I'll go get you something to eat. If you have to go to the washroom, let Dominique know. She should help you get up. Your legs might be a bit wobbly. I'll be back soon." The nurse quickly nods and smiles at me before she leaves. I take that to be a good sign.

"How are you?" Dominique asks softly.

"Tired." My throat aches. "Sore." My whole body still feels like it's asleep, or wants to be.

"What do you remember about last night?" She waits with bated breath. I scrunch my eyebrows in slight confusion.

I try to think back.

How did I get to the hospital?

Why did I have to come to a hospital?

A pinch grows between my eyebrows and at the back of my head.

Memories flash through my head in half moments.

A blade runs along my leg.

"That's enough Jaiden! She's dead!"

A burning drink.

Swallowing a pill.

Laying down.

Nausea.

Sinking.

I don't feel right.

I swallow the lump in my throat when the memory flashes stop coming.

I know Nikki wants an explanation. "I was sad and hurt myself; drank vodka. But it wasn't working fast enough so I decided to sleep. I took some-" I stop myself as something shifts in my head.

Other memories push to the front of my head.

I swallow hard. "No. No, I was in the dark. I was in the gym. Sandra and Darius took me. You saved me. I-"

I don't feel right.

I close my eyes, but the memories keep coming. My head and hands meet in the middle to cover my ears.

I want it to go away.

I need it to stop.

The scenes keep pushing their way to the front of my brain.

It's not fair.

Why would Sandra kill Rayleen? How could she kill a little girl?

She's a monster.

Rayleen is dead.

Just enough light to see, but not clearly. Rayleen's hair looks darker, she's dirtier, and wearing an angry bobcat crested black shirt. Her hands are tied in front of her. She sits with them between her crossed legs.

She looks up to me. My hand pulls out Sandra's blade. Drawing down, the blade buried into Rayleen's chest.

Her dying scream chills my blood.

The silent and still body kills me.

No. I shake my head hard.

Sandra only threatened me.

I sit against the cold floor with my hands crossed in my lap. Sandra comes up to me out of the darker darkness. She threatens me, "If you try to escape I'm going to have to kill you."

Words get stuck in my throat, so I nod.

Tears fall, but I hold in the cries. They don't like it when I cry loud.

Sandra jumps towards me, but stops when she gets close.

I scream in fear.

Rayleen's dead.

No, she's not.   No. I'm not.

A bunch of people went out to a school nearby; to look for Rayleen. We think that the shirt might've been a school shirt. And, we think she might be alive.

I don't feel right.

Is she dead? Check her pulse.

A doctor tells someone to stop performing compressions. When they do and get off of her, the doctor checks a couple things in a couple of seconds. "She's dead."

"There's nothing we can do."

"Wake up," I say.

"Wake up!" I scream.

"I'm dead," I whisper.

Alexa's dead.

No, she's not.   No, I'm not.

Opening my eyes, John and Nikki have moved to each side of the bed. Worried expressions harden their faces.

I sit straight up, while letting my hands fall. They lean back slightly to allow me room.

"Where's Alexa? I want Alexa."

Their concern for me turns to sadness. Frowns drop their mouths. They look between each other and me.

"She's-" Dominique doesn't have to finish her sentence; she doesn't finish her sentence.

She can't.

She doesn't have to. I already know.

A deep pain explodes from my chest. I throw myself down into my pillow. Screaming out my pain as I wrap my arms around it.

Where is she? I want Alexa. I need Alexa. She can't be dead.

A hand touches my back. I snap away from it.

"NO! I WANT ALEXA!"

Chapter 5

Cole walks in and sits down. The colour is drained from his face, or maybe it's the terrible lighting. We wait impatiently for him to tell us what he's learned.

We did as he asked and gave him some time alone with Rayleen to read her mind and concentrate. Now he owes us what he figured out, and it doesn't look promising.

Cole intertwines his fingers and rests his chin on them. His elbows dig into his thighs.

He takes a deep breath when he collects himself. "It was an accident. Alexa was depressed and just wanted to go to sleep when other vices weren't helping."

"That's great, but what about Rayleen?" I try to move him along. I realize it sounds insensitive, but Alexa's dead and we already half assumed it was an accident. That knowledge isn't going to change anything.

Except, maybe, take some of the guilt off of Jaiden.

"It's Rayleen in there for sure." Relief floods through me. "But, she's got all of Alexa's memories. But also, every now and then, there seems to be moments of Alexa, yet not quite."

"They're both in there," John says.

Cole shakes his head. "I don't know. It seemed more like echoes of Alexa and confusion, rather than two minds in one."

"What does that mean, exactly?" I ask.

"So, it's Rayleen and Rayleen's mind, but she's six years old. Alexa had three times the amount of life and experiences. So, Alexa's memories are overpowering at times.

Like, Alexa's recent memories are fresh and potent, and are recalling lots. There were two moments where Rayleen started panicking about Rayleen being lost, before correcting herself and thinking that she's here and not missing.

All of Alexa's memories keep popping in and out." He explains.

"And you don't think Alexa's in there too?" I need to know for sure. The dread is back and settling in my chest. Even if she's not in there too, Alexa is still overwhelming Rayleen.

"Not the way you're thinking. Not two people in one body. Not a battle for control of who gets to control the body.

It's still a theory, an uneducated guess. But, it just seems like a very confused little girl who suddenly has more memories of being another person than she does of being herself. Which, I guess, one could argue that makes her partially Alexa now.

Then again, I could be wrong. I've never dealt with this before." Cole sits back further in his chair, and rests against the back.

"So either way, she's going to be more Alexa, than she is Rayleen." John summaries when I can't.

"Until she properly sorts it all out." Cole sits back up straight and addresses me specifically. "She's going to need you to parent her and guide her. She's attached to you. At least her feelings towards you didn't change to Alexa's."

"Yeah, good thing." I scoff.

Cole stares through me. "I mean it. She's attached to you. She trusts you. You're going to have to help her sort herself out. Figure out who she is now, and guide her so she's not a complete wreck."

"Yeah." I bring both my hands up to my face and pull them down my cheeks. "Can you update Jaiden? I'm going back to Rayleen."

Cole agrees and I leave the room. I stop in the hall, out of view, to lean against the wall. I look up towards the ceiling and wrap my arms around myself.

A deep pit has worked its way into my heart and my mind is heavy. Whether it's Alexa's mind in Rayleen's body or Rayleen becoming Alexa through an overload of Alexa's memories, Rayleen will never be the same little girl.

I put a hand over my mouth to stifle a cry. It's not fair. Alexa made her mistake, and now Rayleen is paying for it.

John comes around the corner. When he sees the state of me, he wraps me in a tight embrace. I set my chin on the crux of his neck.

I mourn Rayleen because who she was died in the soul transfer. She never had a chance.

Squeezing him tightly, I wait for him to respond the same way. We part at my cue by releasing my arms.

I wipe away the wetness on my cheeks.

"We'll get her figured out. Rayleen is still in there." John tries to reassure me, but I'm not so sure.

I nod and turn to get back to Rayleen. Pulling in a deep breath, I then let it out slowly. I don't want to let her see how upset I am. She doesn't need more to worry about.

As I come through the door, Chief gives Rayleen a white stuffed cat. "What are you going to name her?"

Rayleen scrunches her lips in thought. "Snowy."

"That's a lovely name." He comments.

"How's she doing?" I ask.

They both turn, now knowing someone else is in the room with them. Chief puts his hands in his lab coat pockets. "Medically, she is well. Tired and sore, but there's nothing else I'm concerned about. Though I must admit, it's a little out of my purview."

"When can she leave?" I ask. That's always the best sign of whether or not a doctor truly feels like a patient is getting better.

"Tomorrow, maybe." He says.

"But, you just said she was fine." I push. I want the truth.

Chief shrugs. "I don't have a medical reason to keep her, though with what happened, I would like to keep her for observation for a little longer."

"I wanna go home. I hate hospitals." Rayleen's input is important. It seems to sway the Chief's decision.

He softens and gives Rayleen a charming smile. "I think the only people who like hospitals become doctors and nurses. It's just about time for sleep anyway, and there's not much to be done while you sleep. So, I'll make you a deal. If I let you go home tonight, can you come back in the morning for a checkup?"

Rayleen's eyes brighten up. She smiles with a big toothy grin. "Yes!"

"Alright, I would just like to talk to Dominique outside the door here, and we'll get you going real soon." Chief taps Rayleen on the shoulder.

I take that as my cue to lead the way out the door. I turn around when I figure we're out of earshot, but still close enough to the room.

Chief stops in front of me, but looks back towards the room as he speaks. "I'd like you to remain vigilant in watching her. I can't imagine what might come with a soul transfer, but now that we're over the physical symptoms, the mental ones are going to need dealt with.

I need you to watch her like you would do a suicide watch. Someone needs to be with her at all times. Look for anything physically wrong with her. Talk and listen to her. And, if she starts saying things that are concerning or depressing, then I need you to bring her in for a check-up."

"I don't think she's going to commit suicide." She's a kid.

Chief stands taller and looks down at me. "Rayleen might not have, but can you say the same about Alexa?"

He doesn't know; I realize. "She didn't though. Cole learned it was an accident."

"Even so, it's not just suicide we're worried about. Her only remaining family just died, and she absorbed her. We need to worry about survivor's guilt and depression. We also worry about any sort of relapse of her physical condition."

"Right." I get it now. He was drawing a parallel. He's not worried about suicide. He needs us to take watching Rayleen seriously and constantly. "I'll make sure to watch her, and I'll bring her in for a check-up tomorrow morning."

He nods. "We'll see you tomorrow morning then." Chief puts his hand on my shoulder and gives it a comforting squeeze. He leaves to go into another room.

"I'm ready to go!" Rayleen jumps out of the room. She speeds towards me and stops too fast. She wobbles before catching her balance.

I look over at John, he's got a big smile on. "Let's go, Kiddo." John points the way out of the hospital.

I can't help but stare at Rayleen as she and John play along the way out. Her burst of energy is a good sign. The childish play is a good sign that part of her is still a kid; I don't know how much though. That concerns me.

Rayleen stops skipping and drops her shoulders. "I'm tired."

"When we get back, we'll get you straight to bed," John tells her.

A feeling nags in me that if a doctor sees that she's tired, they'll force her to stay for the night. Though, I admit to myself that I might be a bit paranoid about that.

We get outside after saying goodbye to the guards. The truck is still in the middle of the road, right where we left it. At least we had some presence of mind to shut the doors; unless someone else did that for us. I don't remember shutting them or not.

We all get in the front seats. I look behind. The scene of Alexa dead in the back is seared into my brain; an imprint of her is still there forever in my memory.

Rayleen leans into my side. I pull my arm out to wrap around her, and use the other hand to swipe the hair out of her eyes. We ride quietly back to the hotel.

We avoid everyone on the way in. They are all set about getting supper, so we slip through the hall and stairs relatively unnoticed.

Rayleen starts to go to Alexa's room. My heart skips a beat. She can't stay in there. "Wait, you'll be staying with me in my room now." I open the door for her. "Right in here."

She doesn't say anything about the move. I get her to change into some of my clothes for bed; not wanting all that mess in my bed. We should have thought to grab her some of her clothes to change into at the hospital; should have moved her stuff into my room before now. I don't want to pull up bad memories trying to get her things now.

She leaves the bathroom, and goes straight into the bed. John pulls the covers over her. "I want Alexa," Rayleen whispers.

I kneel down to be at her face level. "I know sweetie. Alexa is a part of you now and forever. She's inside of you and your heart. So, she's going to be with you always."

"I miss her. I want her." Rayleen says sleepily.

"I know. I'm sorry." The empty air is thick.

Her eyes shut and I'm relieved that she is so tired. She might not even remember my pathetic excuse for comfort. I don't know what to say to her. Alexa isn't just dead. She's dead and inside of Rayleen. I don't know if that makes grief better or worse.

John and I wait until we're sure she's sleeping before sneaking out of the room. I walk across the hall and open Jaiden's door.

"Shouldn't you knock first?" John hesitates.

"Knock. Knock." I say as I walk through the open door. Jaiden jumps, shrieks quickly, and drops her phone.

"If only there was an early warning system used the alert someone of your intention of entering their private space." I nudge John for his snark. He smirks back at me, knowing he's right. I should have knocked; I guess.

"Sorry." I apologize to Jaiden.

She gathers her phone and places it on the bed beside her. "That's okay. How's Rayleen?"

"Chief let us take her home, but everyone is worried about her mentally. He's also worried about a potential physical relapse." I inform her. "Thanks for getting my room back."

She nods. "I got ahold of James and caught him up."

"He expected her to die but she didn't." I remind her.

A heat flares in my stomach. He could have helped but he didn't. Jaiden shouldn't be telling him anything. James doesn't deserve to know anything.

"Yeah, but he's been through it. He knows a lot more than we do. And, since it's forbidden, there isn't anything I could find online." Jaiden pauses briefly. "He gave me a bit more to go off of since she did live. This isn't something done to children; he had no way of knowing for sure.

But, right now, we need to focus on Rayleen. It's going to be confusing for her. She's going to claim all of Alexa's memories as her own. You have to separate her from that. James said it can be hard at first. It takes practice.

He said his therapist told him to imagine boxes inside his brain, and each person's memories go into a different box. Eventually, it becomes easy to distance yourself and compartmentalize.

He did say that even still, someone's something gets through. Like a year ago, he saw the grandson of the previous leader and it took him a good minute to remember that the guy isn't his grandson.

I think the hard part is going to be dealing with the emotions and irrationality of a six year old. James was lucky as an adult with a fully developed brain, knowing what was happening and being able to rationally sort things out.

It's going to be a huge fight to get her to understand that the things she remembers and experienced, aren't actually things that she's done."

I push down wanting to disregard anything he says to note the therapy advice. It might help. It also might help to know that it's for sure Rayleen with Alexa's memories added to hers.

"At least she's already gone through her teen years as Alexa, maybe those won't be so bad this time around." John chides.

"No, she's going to be worse because her teen years are going to last way longer. From six years old, to however long it takes her to age up now. James said to expect a varied slow down on her aging process." Jaiden says.

"She's not a teenager though." She's six, I add in my head as an afterthought, not a teenager.

"Alexa was." Jaiden reminds me, as if that wasn't the whole issue, and I had forgotten. "Rayleen is still six, but she's also got memories of schooling up to grade twelve, and drinking alcohol, and dating, and all the abuse Alexa took, and all the freedom through parental neglect that Alexa had. And, maybe Alexa had a job or knew how to drive, or whatever.

Rayleen has all those memories and experiences built into her now. You can't treat her like she's six years old and hasn't experienced anything yet. You have to treat her like a six year old genius who was supposed to graduate grade twelve this year, and has a load of trauma to deal with."

I stare at Jaiden as I think about and process what she says. I swallow a lump in my throat. Poor Rayleen. She'll never be the same. She doesn't have a chance.

"She's going to hate when we give her a bedtime curfew." John jokes. I look back at him to stick him with a glare. I wish he would take this more seriously. I'm not in the mood.

Irritations fade a moment later. He's trying to use humour to get through it; to help me through it. He's just trying to lighten the stress load a bit, and I can appreciate that.

"Maybe, probably, but likely we'll have huge issues in every decision that has to do with personal freedom. Alexa's used to all the freedom and doing everything on her own terms. But, Rayleen's six and should have an adult with her at all times. And probably shouldn't handle sharp knives." Jaiden pauses briefly. "I don't know?"

"Sharp knives?" I repeat. That's the example she decides to use.

"I don't know. My parents were terrible examples of parenting. I don't know what's normal or not for childhood; just that the more I talk about my own childhood, the more people tell me that what I experienced wasn't normal."

"Like what?" I question; a snippet of relief comes to me. A subject change might be a good distraction, whatever that might be. This one might give me some insight into Jaiden's childhood; she never says too much about it.

Jaiden shrugs. "No kids' shows or normal kid play stuff

because they couldn't stand them. I walked myself to and from school almost every day since kindergarten. With the different school locations, it took at least a ten minute walk. Up to a half hour when I went to the junior high. Through winter too; didn't matter how cold it was.

Or, how my mom would kick me out of the house during summer vacation at eight in the morning, and I wasn't supposed to come back until around supper time. She did buy me a summer pass to the pool to keep me occupied, and I had a library card. Both were about twenty minutes to a half hour walk away, and that started when I was five.

They also had this thing about, if I was physically able to do something, it was now my responsibility to do it. Like, I've made my own breakfast and lunch as long as I can remember.

Because, as soon as I was physically capable of pouring myself cereal, that was my job. Not even milk. One of my earliest memories is me eating dry cereal because I gave up after I physically couldn't lift the milk out of the fridge. And, I didn't want to risk spilling milk or asking for help.

Although, my earliest memory is me practicing riding my bike, a two-wheeler, when I was two years old. It was raining and I was alone. And, I was determined to ride a bike, and no one would teach me, so I knew I had to teach myself.

My mom would tell that story as a crowning moment of my genius daughter learned how to ride her bike when she was only two years old. She was so determined to learn that she didn't stop practicing for anything, not even the rain.

Funny how people can twist those things around."

I'm stuck in silence. Mournfully mulling over everything she's said.

After a moment of silence, John encourages her. "Go on, I'm learning so much about you."

Jaiden nods and searches her brain for other points. "Um-One time, when I was about five. Mom had a friend over during supper, and she had a daughter who was two years older than me. And, her daughter kept calling her mom to get her things and do things for her, and I thought it was magic; basically.

So, I perfectly mimicked her voice, tone, and inflections. When her mom showed up, I said sorry it was me. And, she was so sweet and told me that she would of course get me whatever I needed. And, it was magic and made me feel so special that a mom would get me something if I asked."

"What the fuck?" Jaiden's smile disappears with my outburst. Those three words burst out after repeating in my head. "None of that is normal. What the fuck? How could they treat you like that? I am so sorry."

"It's okay." She answers quietly, then smiles sweetly.

Rage enflames a sharp heat within me. "It's not though."

John puts his hand on my shoulder. "It's really not. But, I feel like this explains so much about you." He says. "I also feel like, maybe you should end it there for the night. Before this one decides to go hunting for your dad."

Jaiden shrugs. "He's probably dead anyway, and we know Mom is dead, so no point in hunting them down." She stands up and comes closer to me. "I'm sorry I upset you."

Why is she apologizing? "No, don't be. You're just telling stories about your childhood. It's not you, it's your parents who should apologize. We should go anyway. I don't want to leave Rayleen alone for too long." I make an excuse.

"Of course."

I close the space between us to give her an encompassing hug. Jaiden tries to hug and let go immediately, but I hold on longer. Fury melts into sadness and a need to help.

I had always just thought she wasn't the hugging type. Especially, when she said that her family aren't huggers.

But, now I realize, she might be uncomfortable with hugs and touch because she was never hugged or touched. She's uncomfortable, not because she doesn't like it, but because she's not used to it.

I let go when I feel like I've hit a turning point between a good long hug, and possibly turning her off of being hugged.

"Good night. I love you." I tell her. She flinches as I swipe a wayward hair behind her ear.

"Love you too. Good night." Jaiden answers automatically. It feels robotic. Like, she's had to repeat for the sake of repeating her whole life or she'd get in trouble. Not, like what I've previously assumed, that she's just awkward.

I hear a quick 'night' from each John and Jaiden as I leave the room. A rush of exhaustion rolls over me.

I glance down the hall towards the exit. A quick thought enters then leaves just as quickly; to go outside for a night stroll and talk with John about everything. I need a venting soundboard.

But, I don't want to talk about it with John tonight. I just want to go to sleep. Besides, we shouldn't leave Rayleen alone for too long. Across the hall is one thing, leaving the building is another.

I quietly open the door. A quick chime of relief rings when I see her sleeping peacefully in the bed still.

I change for bed, then come out of the bathroom to see John changed as well. I set the upper lock on the door, and we climb into the other bed.

John softly whispers, "Goodnight".

I echo, "Goodnight".

His hand finds mine; fingers intertwine. John pulls our hands up to his mouth and sweetly kisses the back of my hand. I squeeze his hand twice in gratitude. He resettles our hands beneath the blankets.

Another thing I have to talk with him about, officially. I don't know what this is, but we've settled into comfortable small gestures and now sharing a bed; albeit not romantically and with a child in it too.

He keeps pushing more and more into romantic relationship territory; settling into old routines slowly.

I've accepted all of them. It's comfort and comfortable. But, a nagging pain still remains from our break up. It's confusing though; knowing it wasn't entirely his choice. A choice made with no good options is presented.

John's soft snores start a minute later. I have no such luck. While my body craves sleep, my mind keeps thinking about Jaiden.

I cycle between anger and sadness, with a persistent ache in my chest throughout.

Dad was going to fight for custody, but he didn't want to disrupt her perfect life. We thought she had the perfect life.

She's rich. Doing amazing in school, and could go to the best universities on a full ride.

Her dad is rich and famous, sort of, and owns his own company. Jaiden was set to inherit the company and millions.

She never gave any indication that they were neglectful and abusive. Though now that I know, it spins some of the things she has said around. Turns some of her quirks and independence into something sad.

Fuck her mom.

Fuck her dad.

If Dad knew about Jaiden, we could've saved her from all of that.

Or, at least, helped give her the option for something better. Tried to fight for her, and show her that her family would fight for her.

Cruel Souls

But, then we might've all been at Grandma's.

We all would have died at Grandma's.

Chapter 6

"I'm here."

It takes me a moment to register the words James speaks through the phone. They aren't, at all, what I was expecting him to say.

I wasn't expecting him to call me at all. We haven't spoken since my last update about Rayleen; that was days ago. "What do you mean?"

"I'm here." He repeats.

"Where?" I ask.

"At your hotel." My eyes widen. He means literally, he's here here.

Abandoning my paperwork, I dash out of my room and down to the lobby.

Scanning the room quickly, I can't find him.

I ignore a wide assortment of looks.

The secret of my phone is completely out in the open. But, I guess there's no taking that back. I mentally kick myself, but also, I don't think it could be helped given the situation.

"Where?" I go to the windows and look through them. I don't see him out there either, but it's rather dark. Still, there are no vehicle lights or people close by.

Working streetlights would be nice for moments like this.

"In the lobby," James says.

"Where?" I dash to look around the corner, then back to the door.

"In the lobby." He repeats.

It doesn't make sense. He's not in the lobby.

A realization hits me.

"Which hotel?" I panic.

"The big one."

No! I shout the word loudly in my head.

I grab the door nob and swing it open quickly. "We're across the street. Go outside, and I'll be right there."

And, hopefully, no one saw you. Especially, not Jerry. Especially, not anyone who would tell Jerry.

I look at the phone at the tone of silence and lack of response. He hung up on me. I shove the phone in my pocket.

I sprint across the street and wave when I see him walk out. He's drawn a crowd around him.

Given the situation, I would have thought he'd keep a low profile. Given the other situation, I would have preferred he kept a low profile.

James shakes two hands, pats a guy on his back, and leaves the crowd to meet me on my approach. Word is bound to reach Jerry soon; unfortunately.

"Hi. Welcome. I didn't know you were coming." I rush the words out before drawing in large breaths. Whether in the panic or the sprint, I winded myself.

"I thought it best to keep that to myself. Now, I'd like to see Rayleen." James gets straight to the point.

But if you had told me you were coming, then I could have

told you exactly where to go. I could have been prepared for your arrival.

"Of course," I answer. It's why he's here. "But, I think she's already gone to bed for the night. It's pretty late for a kid."

"Wake her up. I came all the way here to see her." James prevails.

I don't see him changing his mind, so there's no point in me trying. I just have to hope Dominique can change it, or that Rayleen hasn't gotten to sleep yet.

Hopefully, she won't get too mad. She's never been the biggest fan of James in the first place.

"Right. Of course." I sweep my arm to motion him to continue towards our hotel. He starts walking. I take one last look at the crowd; it's dissipating quickly.

I catch up to walk beside James. It's a quick trip, but I try to fill the silence with niceties. "Did you have a good trip?"

"It was uneventful," James announces.

"That's good." I have no follow-up questions. This has never been my strong suit.

I wave off the people who have lined the window. I must've drawn a lot of attention running out of the hotel like that.

I shake my head and I hope they get the message to back off.

We quickly go inside and ascend the stairs. James says a quick hello to nosy people in the open doorway.

I knock on Dominique's door softly; maybe she can talk him out of waking Rayleen up.

Dominique opens the door sharply. I don't have to see her glare to know she's annoyed. She looks over me, behind me, at our company.

"James is here. He would like to see Rayleen." I say softly.

Her face scrunches. "You can wait until tomorrow. She just

got to sleep a few minutes ago."

"I travelled all this way and risked my life to get here, so she can wake up for a couple of minutes to talk to me." James insists; loudly.

Dread fills me. James' entitlement is going to battle against Dominique's protective stubbornness.

"She's exhausted. You won't get anything out of her." She starts to try to reason with him.

John comes up behind Dominique and stops her with a hand on her shoulder. "She's awake anyways. Come in."

Dominique huffs out a quick breath. We must've woken her with either my knocking or our talking.

Dominique holds open the door off to the side to let us in.

Rayleen is sitting up in bed. Her eyes are still shut, but she rubs them, then slightly opens them. She yawns without covering her mouth.

"Alexa," James says. I open my mouth to correct him, but Rayleen answers instead.

"I'm Rayleen. Alexa's dead." Rayleen says sleepily. I prepare for a tearful outburst, but none comes. Maybe she's too sleepy to quite fully think about it.

"Interesting," James mutters. "You're right. My condolences. Do you know what happened to you?"

Rayleen straightens her back a bit and frowns as she looks at James. "I absorbed Alexa. She lives inside of me now."

"You told her?" James questions me.

Dominique sneers and answers for me. "We weren't going to lie. How else were we supposed to explain what's happening with her?"

James ignores Dominique's question to continue where he left off with Rayleen. "You're right. Her memories are a part of you now."

Rayleen yawns. "I'm tired."

"We'll just talk a little longer. Do you remember when we first met?" James asks.

"Mmhmm." Rayleen closes her eyes and slouches.

"Tell me about it." James pushes.

I see what he's trying to do. He's trying to see if Rayleen can separate the memories. Or, see if one set of memories is more prevalent than the other.

It might be better that he's doing this while she's half awake and half asleep. She doesn't entirely have her fully alert brain to think about everything before she says it. He might be getting truer answers, and a better look into her thoughts this way.

He's testing her for his own curiosity. He's never met a kid who has done a soul transfer. The last and only person James has met who's done one was his predecessor.

The Council forbid soul transfers under threat of death because people were abusing them; to prevent more people from finding babies and small children to transfer into at the end of their lives. They needed to stop forced transfers to extend lives of the host body.

It's why it's important that people don't know what happened. Or, if they do, that it's a complete anomaly she survived. He had hoped she wouldn't.

"You tried to get me to explode a marshmallow," Rayleen tells him something from her memories.

"Do you remember anything else?" He asks.

"You told me I didn't have powers, and that I must've gotten it from my dad's side. And, you made the food and dishes fly." Rayleen answers.

That must've been from Alexa's memories because he wouldn't have told witchy Rayleen that she doesn't have powers. Perhaps the latter was from both. I heard the stories from Alexa and their group about James' magical house, and the tree travelling.

"Curious. Her speech pattern has changed." James' observation has me questioning what he noticed. I hadn't noticed a difference in how she spoke, yet he had. Her speech pattern changed. Was it the words she used? Or how she spoke them?

Or, was it just because he hadn't seen her for a few months, and the speech pattern change is normal childhood development that happened without the soul transfer?

"Stop talking like she isn't right in front of you." Dominique outbursts. I jump at the suddenness.

Jerry barges into the room, I jump again. "Hello Councilman Ellesworn, I'm so sorry that I missed you while you were at my establishment. If you'd return, I have someone preparing our finest room for your stay and some dinner. I'm certain you're tired and hungry after your long trip."

Jerry holds his hand off to the side, to guide James out of the room. James doesn't follow the silent instruction or the verbal implication.

James looks at me. I hesitate for just a moment.

He should be staying here, but I don't have a room available that wouldn't come without roommates. Except Alexa's, but I don't think he'd want to stay in a room that someone just died in; a bed someone just died in.

I could give up my room; I guess.

James looks over and tells Jerry. "How thoughtful. I will need a place to stay for a bit."

Jerry's eyes beam with glee. If James stays there, Jerry has every opportunity to kill him. "You can stay as long as you wish."

"Thank you."

Jerry doesn't skip a beat. "You must be hungry after a long journey. I have my chef preparing you something. It'll be ready shortly."

"That is appreciated," James says. I feel like such a bad host with the alternative plans made for, what should be, our guest.

"We should go soon, so it will be warm for you. So, if you're done here. We should leave." Jerry swings his arms to wave James out, again.

James looks over to Rayleen, then back to Jerry. I think he's decided he has finished their conversation; for now.

"Jaiden come." James orders as he starts moving.

"I'll go too." Dominique starts.

"Just Jaiden. I insist." James cuts off Jerry's protest with a look as he's still opening his mouth. He places his hand on my back and sets me to walk in front of him. He turns his head to stare down a proceeding Dominique. "Stay with Rayleen. Get her back to sleep. I only require Jaiden's presence."

Dominique and I exchange glances, but we leave the room without more dispute.

Along the way, Jerry has no problem holding small talk by himself; even with James' curt responses. He starts with James' trip, admiration of James, and being glad it's spring, then once inside the hotel Jerry moves on to a glowing summarization of everything he's ever done.

We sit down at a table. The lounge has been cleared out. Jules immediately comes out with two plates.

They place the plates in front of Jerry and James. Jules looks at me. "I'll be back with something for you." They place their hand on my back for a half second. I nod, and prepare a thanks.

"She'll have this. No reason she should wait." James places Jerry's plate in front of me. I want to argue, but I don't want to go against James and whatever power display this might be.

He's not doing it to be nice, I get that much. Those who eat first, are the most important people in the room. Many cultures, traditions, and dynamics have some sort of version of that. You don't eat until Dad has taken his first bite.

He's telling Jerry that I'm more important than he is. That Jerry doesn't eat, until I am able to. Jerry is the one that should have to wait; sit in his hunger until more food is available. Or, maybe I'm over thinking this.

Jerry's smile tightens. I'll pay for this later; I'm certain of it.

"Be my guest." Jerry stares at me. I look down to avoid his eyes but thank him. He quickly moves on; he has to. "To mark this occasion, we should make a toast. James, if you don't mind, I have superior liquor in storage and I would be honoured if you'd choose tonight's drink. Something more to your taste."

Jerry gets up and swings his hand to wave the way; it feels aggressive, though it might not appear that way.

James obliges. "Jaiden, you should come too." He insists. I feel like I should either way.

I get up to follow after them. My nerves creep up my neck. The air feels colder than it should.

Jerry, true to his word, brings us to the storage room with racks of dusty bottles of alcohol.

I place myself beside Jerry as James peruses the labels. I glance between them.

Jerry catches my eyes with his and smirks. He reaches for something at his waist, and swings it up and around.

I push James from behind. He narrowly avoids the blade aimed at his neck, as he falls into the wine rack.

The hand with the blade falls near my hand. I grab Jerry's wrist with both my hands. My body gets in front of Jerry for a better angle.

A boom cracks through the air. My body pulls in on itself, trying to duck out of the way of whatever made the sudden loud noise.

My hands automatically let go of Jerry to cover my ears. A sharp pain rings with the pitchy screech in my ears.

Remembering what was happening, I throw my hands back out to grab at Jerry's wrists, before the knife finds me. But they've dropped to his side.

I look up at him. A hole has appeared in Jerry's forehead. He crumples down to his knees and then leans into me. I stick my hands out to catch his shoulders before any of his blood can get on me.

I push him off to the side and get out of the way of the dead body.

The blood drains out of his head, I move closer to James to avoid getting blood on my shoes.

"Good thing you're short," James smirks.

I look back at James and see the gun in his hand being placed back into a holster.

"You had a gun," I state.

I keep further accusations to myself. He shot above my head. What if he missed and hit me? What if my hands went up too high at the last moment?

James nods once. "It's efficient and effective. You knew he was going to kill me. "

"I-" I panic. I need to deny it. He might kill me too.

"Thank you." He says.

I automatically respond, "You're welcome." He's not mad.

It hits me. He thinks I had a dream. He thinks I saved him because of a vision, not because I knew Jerry was conspiring against him.

Jules then Hectre are the first to rush in; many follow in quick succession. A gunshot is bound to draw attention. That's why Jerry was using a knife.

No one says anything. It's clear by the hole in his head and the growing blood puddle, that there's no helping Jerry.

"This treasonous man tried to kill me. I would be dead if Jaiden hadn't noticed him trying to stab me." James speaks loud enough for those out in the hall to hear. "If anyone else tries the same, I will kill you too. Everything Jerry had, now belongs to me and the Council. You now report to Jaiden, who will report to me."

And, just like that, James takes over Jerry's whole operation.

"I was promised the best room in the hotel, does anyone know where that is?" Ziam puts his hand up. "Good. You will take me there. Jaiden, get this cleaned up. Find me in the morning."

I watch him go. Some people stand in awe, wonder, and shock at what they stumbled upon. Some people leave.

I'm in charge of clean up. I don't know how to clean up from a dead body; all that blood. I didn't handle blood cleanup before.

I only know the first step. "Jules, can you use this body?"

"Yes." They say. Hectre taps on the shoulders of two others and recruits them to take the body to the kitchen. They lift him up by arms and legs. Hectre grabs a box to hold under the dripping blood.

Jules holds out a hand to help me get on the other side of the blood. I grab the hand and step into the space where Jerry's body was.

Jules pulls me to the side, closer to the door. "I will deal with the blood; I'm used to it. You should go."

"Are you sure?" I ask. This feels like something I should help with, even though I don't want to. James told me to clean it up.

"Yes. It's called delegating tasks. You need to get used to being able to hand jobs off to other people." They assert while herding me through the door. "And, take your food with you. You might not be hungry now, but you will be later. Don't let it go to waste."

"Okay. Thank you." I say.

I do as they say to and go to the lounge. Hectre passes me, without a glance, on his way back to Jules. He'll help Jules.

I grab my plate. It doesn't look appetizing. The thought of eating pulls bile up. Maybe, later.

For now, I have other things to do. I make my way to Jerry's room and to his safe. The key works to open it, and to my delight, the contents still relatively look the same as they did when Jerry showed me it.

I take the information treasure trove and my food, back to my room to go through and make a plan for the morning. This might not have been how I thought this was going to go, but it's how it is.

With James backing me, a takeover won't fail. But, I'm also not the one in charge. James is, but I don't think he'll stay; he doesn't seem to stay for long.

There are dozens of papers to go through.

I have a lot to do, and I know I won't be able to sleep any time soon. Too much has happened, and there's too much unknown to be able to slow my brain enough.

My thoughts creep back to Jules and Hectre, were they just trying to get rid of me? Are they mad at me for Jerry being dead? Are they going to be mad at me for making them clean up Jerry's body?

I shake my head.

Jules said it was fine, so I have to believe they were telling me the truth.

Cruel Souls

I have a lot to do.

I need to focus on what's in front of me.

Chapter 7

I wish Jaiden never suggested that James meet Margie. All I wanted to do was practice magic, but they haven't stopped talking.

First, Margie just wanted to talk to James about James, then they talked about different advanced magic they've done and how things used to be.

When they finally got around to me, it was just about how weird I am.

James called me an anomaly.

"Don't bite your nails." Margie chastises me when she glances over at me. Hot shame fills me.

I hadn't realized I was biting at the skin around my thumb. I drop my hand into my lap.

I shouldn't be doing that. Everyone always yelled at Alexa when she did it.

James frowns from behind his teacup. "That's something Alexa used to do. I've never seen Rayleen bite her nails before."

That's because Rayleen never bit her nails because Alexa always got in trouble for it. And, I shouldn't be like Alexa because Alexa does bad things.

A wave of guilt hits then passes through me, cooling the

shame instantly.

Guilt for biting my nails when I shouldn't.

Guilt for always being gone.

Guilt for not wanting to be like Alexa.

Guilt for being Alexa.

"Interesting. This is the first time I've seen Rayleen do it." Margie says.

They both stare at me; examine me. At least the other adults talk about me when I'm not supposed to be around or awake.

James continues on the same conversation from before they were distracted. "It's a different world now. We're under different protocols. The strength she has with being able to survive a soul transfer; she might be a great asset. But, she's far behind where she should be at by her age. I don't know if we could catch her up."

"We'll catch her up. Don't you worry about that. She's a fast learner. I'm sure she'll work hard enough to advance quickly.

Having absorbed Alexa might be a blessing on that. The memories, of years of learning how to study properly, might help her out.

We won't have to explain things to her like a small child. It's much easier teaching older people how to do things, they understand more. Know how to behave properly during lessons." Margie assures him.

I don't know about that. I don't know if I know how to study properly. I don't know what that would mean.

How does someone study properly? How does someone not study properly?

I've never had to study before.

I wait for memories to pop up. This is usually about when they would push forward into the front of my head, but nothing happens.

Maybe Alexa didn't know how to study properly either. I don't ever remember her having to study for things.

Sometimes Andy would stare at his book, and tell me he was studying.

Is studying just reading books? In that case, I guess I could read some books. But, I don't think there is such thing as magic books, or someone would have shown me a spell book by now.

Why has no one read from a spell book? They don't talk spells like in the movies. Maybe no one has spell books because of that.

I look behind me to see if there's anything on the bed that I will hit. There isn't. So, I lay down.

The white ceiling is about as boring as this conversation.

I don't know how they're going to catch me up when they aren't teaching me anything at all. They could have at least set me up with something to do before they started talking.

"It's a shame her father chose a human wife," James tells Margie. My ears perk up. I look up at them, at the mention of my dad. "When her parents died, her father's family decided to abandon her in the foster system."

I didn't know there was other family who chose not to take us.

No one could take us, so we went into the foster system.

But, it wasn't like that; not really.

No one wanted us, so they left us in the foster system.

Margie shakes her head. "Then they should have notified the Council. We don't leave our children to languish with the humans."

I drop my head back to the bedding.

No one wanted us.

They didn't want me.

"It's likely, they had personal issues with their son having a baby with a human, and if I had to guess, the son never told them she had magic." James continues after a small pause. "It was quite common despite being illegal."

"Maybe they didn't know yet. My youngest took nearly a year longer to show his magic than my oldest." Margie mentions. "Do you know how they died?"

"Plane crash. She was just a baby." James says.

"There was a plane crash. I'm sorry honey, but they died. They aren't coming home." A chilling scream echoes after those words pull up inside my head. My lungs lose air. My throat closes tightly, and a heavy weight blankets over me.

Suddenly missing the people, I never really knew. He used to toss me high into the air and zoom me around the house. She would let me taste-test chocolate chips when we made cookies.

No, I shake my head hard. I was a baby when they died. They didn't do anything with me. I never knew them.

I choke on a sob as tears form and fall. My chest hurts. I curl my arms around my legs.

"What's going on right now? What's going on in your head?" Dominique asks softly. She's close to me now.

She had stayed silent from just after our arrival until now. I had almost forgotten she was sitting in the corner chair.

I shake my head. "I don't want to think."

"It'll get easier to sort. Just push away Alexa's memories and eventually they'll stop coming without you wanting them to." Margie says.

"Remember, put Alexa's memories in a box with a lid and close up the lid," James adds annoyed. "You aren't hurt, you shouldn't be crying."

"I think it's time to let her have a break." Dominique stands up. She pulls me up to stand and tucks me into her side.

"She hasn't done anything yet." James counters.

"A mental break. Besides, we've been here for twenty minutes and neither of you have asked her to do anything yet. At most, you've observed her like a freak show attraction. She's clearly upset, and it happened right after you talked shit about her dad." Dominique counters.

"Go for your break. We'll say what we need to while you're gone and come up with a lesson plan, so we can get right to work when you come back." James lines out. "Be back in fifteen minutes."

Dominique tugs me along out of the room. She lets go once the door has shut.

We walk down the hall a little ways.

"Sorry about them. I think they're so old they forget what it's like being a kid, and you've got a lot going on right now. They had no right to talk about your family like that." Dominique says.

I stop. My chest hurts too much to continue walking. Dominique notices quickly, stops and turns around.

"I was just a baby. I remember now, though. We were being babysat. An old woman told me the plane crashed and they all died. It hurt so much."

"That must make it hurt like it's fresh again. It's a new memory for you, so it's like it's happening for the first time." Dominique says.

It makes sense.

I nod, unable to get out any more words through a lump in my throat. Dominique leans down and sweeps me up. I wrap my arms around her and let go of the sobs I was holding.

"We don't have to go back; not if you don't want to." Dominique offers.

I nod.

Chapter 8

James spent the morning successfully taking over Jerry's business without a fuss. He took a break to meet Margie and talk shit about Rayleen around lunch. Then, he spent the afternoon overtaking Jerry's rivals.

Jaiden seemed to quickly hand everything over to him. She had done all that work to set up a takeover for Jerry's, and then she gave him all the information to do it seamlessly.

Jaiden has been attached to his side for everything except lunch. He insists on having her with him for every possibly dangerous meeting.

James knows about her visions and is using her to make sure nothing happens to him. I just hope nothing happens to her while she's doing it.

I would feel better about it if Cole was allowed to tag along with them, but James declined saying they don't need a bodyguard.

I have to admit, James is efficient. Though, now that he's taken out all of the competition, I can't help but feel like we're next; or were we the first to fall?

The supernaturals all automatically respond to James; it's like Jaiden and I don't exist as leaders to them anymore. The humans are more likely to hesitate, but most go along with it when they see Jaiden cooperating or hear who James is.

They haven't gotten to Bower or Chief yet; I wonder how they'll take to James?

I stare down at the makeshift long table; James is at the end with Jaiden around the corner to his left. Others, who had arrived before me, had picked up all the closest spots they could.

James closed the lounge to show the other leaders what he has; unrestricted electricity, a feast and drinks.

I seemed like a last-minute invite; Jaiden's doing, I'm sure. James didn't greet me like he did the few who came after me. Jaiden, however, smiled the first and last true smile of the night.

Her shallow dimples only appear when she's smiling big and true. It's the biggest telltale of when she's truly happy about something.

James cleaned up, put on a dark gray business suit with maroon accents, and put on cologne. He looks and smells out of place with everyone else.

I realize that's part of the image he's creating. Join me and you don't have to live in the dark and dirt.

It's working.

That, or his reputation and power position is.

Everyone started off hesitant about the situation, but now all the leaders are fully on board with James' every word.

The wine and champagne might've had a bit to do with it as well. Possibly the food too, if the others aren't used to Jules' cooking.

Conversation has died. People are done eating and are in the process of leaving politely every so often. James gets up to escort them out when they do go.

The last batch leaves one after another; no one wants to be the last to leave and overstay.

Jaiden yawns. She's been so busy running around today. She's always so busy running around. And, I don't think she's sleeping well enough.

Now that everyone is gone, I get up to sit beside her.

I'll leave when she leaves. I won't let James push me out. It's too late for her to stay for much longer.

I nudge her with my arm and she nudges back. We look at each other with silent messaging.

James gets back and sits in front of us. He takes a long stare at me. I stare back. He breaks first, to look at Jaiden. "I hadn't realized the reach and strength here. We could take back the entire city in a few days."

"Would we be stretching ourselves too thin that way though?" Jaiden asks. That's a worry I've heard from her before.

"Not at all." James waves it off. It irks me that he's so dismissive of her without any thought. He could at least explain a bit why he thinks that way.

"Don't you have enemies after you?" I ask. "Isn't that why you were in hiding? Is it wise to draw all of this attention to yourself? Are you going to have to go into hiding again? Are they going to attack us to get to you?"

James mulls over my questions as he takes a pointed sip of his wine. He taps his wine glass towards me. "If you're going to use the Council Emblem to fuel your rebellion, then you need a Council member in charge."

Shit. Maybe I should've waited before doing that. Sara had reservations about using the emblem, and I guess this is the consequence.

I change the subject with another question; maybe he'll actually answer this one. "Are you planning on striking now, since Darius is dead?"

"Sandra would have just taken over immediately," Jaiden says.

James shakes his head. "Seth wouldn't allow that, or else she would have been in charge from the start."

"Do they not get along?" Jaiden asks.

James shrugs. "When you're as old as Sandra is, you don't really get along with anyone in charge."

"How old is she?" I ask.

Jules reaches to clear the dishes in front of me. I move over slightly to help give her a little more room. She piles the dishes onto a cart, then moves to the next spots.

"I'm not sure exactly. I've never asked." He pauses. "A couple thousand years; probably."

That's old. I wonder how old different supernaturals can get? What is Sandra, that let's her be two thousand years old?

"So, what's your plan now?" I ask.

"Simply?" James states. "We get Red Deer up and running as a prime example of the future. Then we get the word out."

"What about when Sandra comes to attack us?" I ask. Or, the other people trying to attack James?

James changes his focus to square purely on Jaiden. "We'll know ahead of time and have time to prepare. Speaking of, you need to get off to sleep. You need to get a proper rest if you're going to dream up anything useful."

James gets up and leaves abruptly. I guess that's it.

Jaiden and I exchange glances, stand up, and push our seats back into the table.

It's our cue to leave.

As soon as he's out the door, and out of hearing distance, I sneer. "You know he's using you, right?"

"Yeah." She says quietly.

"You lied to me." I turn to see Jules with her arms crossed, looking at Jaiden with an eyebrow raised. "You're a seer."

"Yes, I am," I answer almost immediately. I know it's wrong

the moment it comes out. There's no saving the reveal James started.

Jules swipes her hand in Jaiden's direction. "No. Jaiden is. She's the one James is treating like an all-seeing bodyguard."

"Yes, sorry," Jaiden admits.

"A dreamer too?" Jules pushes. Jaiden affirms with a nod. "Cool. But, the rest of what you told me, truth or lie."

"True," Jaiden assures. "It was just that that I lied about."

Jules sighs. Her taut expression relaxes. "Alright, it's fine. I get it. But, be careful. The Council has a long history of using their seers to the point of death; especially dreamers."

Jules grabs some more dishes and takes them to the back.

Jaiden starts to leave. I follow her out of the hotel. Waiting for the right moment to ask, needing the slight privacy to talk.

"Can we trust Jules?" I ask.

"Yes, not that it matters. I've come to terms with the fact that everyone's going to find out sooner or later." Jaiden breathes out heavily.

"Do you have a problem with that?" I push for more information.

"I'm scared, but I guess it might be time to embrace what I am. I'm not human. I'm supernatural. I'm a seer; a dreamer." Jaiden says.

"Would you be half?" I ask.

"No." She backtracks. "Depends on the social circles. Some consider it a yes or no answer. Human by textbook definition is a lack of supernatural abilities. So there isn't meant to be a half. You either are or aren't. But, there are some circles that take the percentage into effect, saying it's diluted blood, diluted powers, so on and so forth."

"Of course there is." There are always some varied views

depending on who you talk to. "Do you trust James?"

"Yes and no. I think that he's got the same goals in mind, and has more status, connections, and experience to get us there; faster too. But, I also think he's also willing to sacrifice me in order to get it, and if things go south, he'll run away again." Her deductions are fair enough. I'm glad she's not blinded by him. She sees what's going on behind the curtain.

"That's why he doesn't want Cole around." I vocalize my realization as I have it.

"Can you imagine the intel Cole could find out from someone like him?" Jaiden says. It means he doesn't have a block like Jaiden does.

We stop talking as we get into our hotel. We climb the stairs and get outside our rooms. Jaiden says a good night, then goes inside her room. I echo as she is closing the door.

Slowly opening my doorknob, I crack open the door quietly. But, the ruckus inside tells me the quiet sneaking isn't needed.

I close the door behind me. "I thought you'd be in bed by now."

Rayleen stands on top of the bed with Snowy in hand. John stands closer to the window. I imagine a game of toss was happening, but it could have been other things. I don't have the energy to ask.

"Rayleen didn't want to go to bed without you here," John answers for her.

"That's fair," I know I've stayed up late waiting for one parent or another. "But it's late. Into bed now. I'll get ready for bed, then tuck you in. Sound good?"

"Okay." Rayleen sounds disappointed. His shoulders drop before she bum-drops to the bed.

I don't think she wants to go to bed yet. She might still be too riled up from the game they were playing. But, exhaustion is pulling me down.

I change into my pyjamas in the bathroom and brush my teeth. As I get ready for bed, the tension leaks out from my shoulders. I didn't realize how stressful the dinner had been, until now. Sometimes, stress doesn't hit you until you get a moment to relax again.

"Did you have a good night?" I ask once I get out of the bathroom.

"Yeah," Rayleen says from her spot at the edge of the bed.

"How was dinner?" John asks, already on his side of the bed.

"It was good." I go through getting Rayleen into bed and tucking her in as I continue. Sitting beside her when done. "We had dinner. Some meat, pasta and vegetables. We had some nice drinks. I got to see and meet a lot of different people who have storage houses and supply trails, and communities. There was a lot of boring talk and some interesting things said."

"Like what?" Rayleen asks.

I decide to give the most optimistic outlook on the conversation. No sense in unloading my worries on a six year old. "Like, James wants to make Red Deer an example, and because of that, he wants to bring people here and build it up to be like how cities used to be. So if we wait long enough, we should have running water, heat and electricity. Plumbing, too. And, shopping and schools.

He thinks he can make it safe, so everyone can live in peace.

He also plans to make it better, and healthier. Build the world back better. So it'll be interesting to see how he plans to do that.

But, probably the most interesting was some of the people there. A lot of them were Jerry's contacts, so we learned a little about them, and a lot about what they have and have to offer. Lots of people. Lots of little communities. Lots of warehouses full of things for us to use and survive on."

I trail off when I notice Rayleen's eyes have closed. When she doesn't reopen them or make a comment about me stopping talking, I assume she's fallen asleep.

I turn off the light and crawl into bed. I swallow the urge to vocalize how chilly the bed is. I know it'll warm quickly. "Goodnight."

"Goodnight." John murmurs.

His hand finds mine and holds onto it as we fall asleep.

Chapter 9

I cover my mouth from yet another yawn. I couldn't get to sleep easy last night, and instead of being able to sleep in, James made sure I was up to follow him around again.

For someone who wants to make sure I have visions by sleeping, he sure won't let me sleep in to have the visions.

Henry crosses his arms as James unties Shale's rope bonds. His facial muscles shift slightly as he contains shock and scowl. Clenched fists turn white.

James didn't have to untie Shale completely; he's making a statement about the binds. Whether to Henry, Shale, or the rest, I don't know. But, it certainly makes a statement.

James could have just undone the rope latching Shale to the metal support beam and led Shale off. But, he took the moment to untie the rope around Shale's wrists; in front of everyone else. He takes it one step further, in calling the binds, unnecessary.

While he hasn't vocalized it as such, Henry is a bit out of sorts with James' focus on the market today; despite James not having changed anything, yet.

I certainly didn't help when I asked why the prisoners were tied up; it wasn't something we agreed on. Henry's simple response stating that they're prisoners, didn't help his case.

At the least, James doesn't seem to agree. Or maybe, the statement is for me, in some weird and twisty way.

I don't know.

From the beginning, James had asked for a tour and explanations of everything. Henry started to turn sour the moment James started asking too many questions and giving suggestions.

Henry's movements have slowly become strained and sharp. His speech is hardened and succinct.

Henry wanted to end the tour with the market, but I had already filled James in on the prisoners. James wanted to see them and discuss things with them.

Once we got up here, that's when we noticed they were tied up to beams, and sitting on the cold floor.

James asked for an interrogation room, which Henry reluctantly supplied. A room far enough away from eyes and ears, but something close enough so it isn't an arduous trek each time.

When James and Shale start making their way over, I start walking too. Being closer, I'm the first back in the interrogation room; an old manager's office. The natural light gives enough light for the whole room.

The room has been stripped of everything but the giant dark wood corner desk. It takes up three-quarters of the room, so the room barely looks empty.

Shale follows with James right behind him. James spins quickly and shuts Henry out of the room; locking the door, so he can't barge in.

With no way to see Henry, I can only just imagine him fuming from behind the door.

At least that's an upside to this; James can deal with Henry and the same sorts. While they may be willing to bulldoze me over, they can't, or won't, with James. And, if they try, James will push back by any means necessary.

Shale leans up against the wall running his thumb along the reddened skin around his wrists, until he gets to one area that he pokes with a glare. It's possibly a particularly sore spot.

"Are you healthy?" James asks.

Shale holds up his wrists, twisting to show both sides, in silent complaint. "Henry's been withholding blood rations for bad behaviour, but otherwise-," he trails off. I imagine he's also sore from sitting on the cold hard floor, with the unnatural pose of having his hands tied together.

Shale pulls the ponytail out of his unkempt hair. This is likely the first time in days that he's been able to fix it properly.

He gathers his hair together at the back of his head. Finger combing the hair gets it relatively smooth.

"Otherwise?" James pushes for more.

"Fine enough for a prisoner of war." He wraps his hair in the ponytail, but a snap stops his progress. The remains come out of his hair as a short line. Shale lets go of his hair to try to tie the elastic back together.

I pull off my extra hair tie from my belt loop and hand it to him. He needs it more than I do. I have a few in my room, that I can replenish with later.

Though, it's going to be annoying to have to have my hair down the whole day now. Unless, I can sneak off to get one at lunch.

Shale says a quiet, "Thanks," and finishes tying up his hair into a bun.

"Don't be dramatic." James scolds. "I need a list of prisoners that would integrate well."

"And, the rest?" James doesn't respond. "I see."

I didn't connect the dots before, but now my brain jumps to

the worst-case scenario; we kill them.

But, we wouldn't just kill them, would we? I'd like to think that we wouldn't, but I don't think we have the time, resources and patience to deal with prisoners.

That seems to be what the Council does with anyone who causes trouble; they eliminate them and the issue in one fell swoop. I guess I should have figured it out by now.

James hands Shale a pencil and paper. He writes against the desk. I watch as he writes four names on the list and then hands it to James. I wasn't able to glean the names he wrote. The angle is off from where I'm at.

Shale instructs, "These are the ones to do away with. The rest would integrate well."

"Appreciated," James says. He folds the paper up and puts it in his pocket. "Do you know where Sandra is?" He quickly moves on to his next question; like a succinct checklist, he's making his way through.

Shale shakes his head, as he sets back to lean against the desk edge. "No. Last I saw her, she had just learned that Darius kidnapped Rayleen and kept her a secret from Sandra. Then, Darius had just ran off to go collect Alexa again. So, she was pretty pissed.

Obviously.

I mean, she'd frequently threaten to kill him, but I don't think she knew she was going to do it until she heard Darius went off to collect Alexa. Maybe not even until the moment before she did it."

"What about after?" James asks.

"She fled; abandoned everyone right after she killed him. Ram disappeared when he heard. I'd bet they had a meet-up point prearranged; in case anything happened." Shale absent-mindedly rubs at his wrists to soothe the sores.

"Do you know what she could be planning?" James asks.

Shale shrugs. "I could give you educated guesses." James waves his hand for Shale to continue. "She had one comment with Darius about how ridiculous it was for you guys to use the Council Emblem. That it would be easy to discredit you and turn it against you. She didn't say how, exactly.

She would make comments to Darius about hating living in the dark ages, and that if she knew that's how they'd be living, that she would have fought against the rebellion. And complained to him about when would he get it together and fix basic necessities. So, she might try to get some of those up and running.

I know that she's going to move fast and hard to get this region in order and to get enough support behind her, so that Seth has no choice but to keep her.

I think she has a good chance at that. People were more loyal to her than they were to Darius. There's already been infighting before this, from people who wanted Sandra in charge and wanted to get rid of Reckless Darius.

I know that there are plenty of spies planted in your community, but I don't know who. I might recognize some; maybe. There were just so many people, and I never met most of them. But, you should assume anyone could be a spy."

James interrupts Shale with a point to me. "Jaiden, that'll be your job. Figure out who the spies are and stop them before they do anything." James orders.

"Okay," I answer.

I want to back out. I want to take back my agreeance. I have no qualifications or know how to catch spies. I don't know what would be involved.

I don't want to leave it on the off chance that I have a vision; they aren't exactly reliable for important situations.

James addresses Shale. "We'll need to act discreetly. We'll

pull each person one by one and take them to my hotel to get food, then find homes for them. I'll dispose of the ones on the list along the way."

He did mean that he would be killing them; I confirm with myself.

His plan sounds like it would take a while. Processing everyone one by one, might make people less suspicious, but would take a while.

Or, they might be suspicious about us dividing them up into manageable bits. They are less likely to win a fight two against one. Especially, with James added into the mix.

Either way, it could take hours.

"You wanted to meet with Bower and Chief still today?" I remind James while questioning him at the same time.

He shakes his head. "This is more of a pressing issue."

"We told them we would meet with them today, though." It would be rude to cancel. Our relationship with them is already thin.

"They're already your allies. Do you have reason for concern?" James questions.

I don't want him to get the wrong impression. "No, just they might get offended if we don't show up."

"We'll reschedule. There were extenuating circumstances. I'm sure they'll understand." James assures.

"Okay." I won't push it further.

James pulls his hand up to tap his finger at me in the air. "In fact, that's what you will do. Go tell them that we had something come up and we'll have to reschedule to another time, once our issues have been dealt with and we know a better time to meet."

"Okay," I add it to my internal to-do list.

"You may leave." James dismisses me suddenly.

I want to argue, but I don't know what I would even say. I feel like I'm being punished for something.

Did I offend him or do something wrong? I think back through the entire interrogation, then the whole marketplace, and finally through the rest of the morning. I find multiple points where I possibly could have offended James, or done him wrong in some way; maybe I inserted myself into the conversation too much.

I leave while working through it. The guards return my polite goodbyes on the way out. Henry is nowhere to be found. He's probably off having a tantrum about James.

I don't want to be a part of killing the prisoners. Relocating people is tedious. But, contacting Bower and Chief will also only take a couple of minutes; assuming I get ahold of both of them on the walkie-talkie immediately.

I decide overall, it's a good thing it worked out this way. I can take a nap, then start working with Cole on the spy thing. I have low hopes that my dreams would catch anything useful. But, Cole might have some suspects with his numerous brush-ins, or he can start looking for signs.

So long as James actually lets me be away from him for long enough to get this task on the way.

I call Bower and Chief on my walk back. Both answer and each show concern for our sudden problems. But, I assured them it wasn't catastrophic, and that was that.

I feel guilty for not explaining the real reason, but nothing good would come from it.

The lobby is empty for once, so I don't have to sneak in or deal with anyone.

Taking the chance, I decide on a whim to grab a can of peaches for a quick snack on the way back to my room. The sugar will help my need for some energy.

I put the half-empty can down on my desk, then sink into my

inviting bed.

The bright room annoys me. I grasp blindly for the sweater I had thrown onto the bed earlier. My hand hits the different fabric, and I pull it up to drape it across my eyes.

I wait and breathe.

I don't dare turn on a light. Thankfully the moon is bright tonight and the large windows let a lot of the light inside.

I tiptoe across the room to the fridge. Mindful of any and all noise, I do my best to make as little noise as possible. I wouldn't want to wake anyone and get in trouble.

Opening the bottom freezer door and grabbing out the tub of vanilla ice cream, I then close the freezer.

The cold tub pulls goosebumps to my arms and legs. I move my hands to grasp the lid more than the sides, but a moment later, I set it on the counter anyway.

I pull open a drawer but find the stove utensils instead.

You'd think I would know where everything is by now.

I close it up and open the drawer next to it. Taking a spoon out of the drawer and closing it behind me.

Next, I find a bowl in the corner cupboard too far out of my reach; it's a terrible spot to keep bowls when short people are around. I climb the counter as quietly as possible to get it. Settling the bowl on the counter, then easing myself back down to the floor.

The lid of the ice cream tub makes such a loud noise, that I momentarily regret my decision of a late-night snack. Hopefully, I won't wake anyone and this will be worth it.

I scoop out my ice cream and put the tub away. The counter still has the canned peaches from earlier, so I decide to put some of those on top of my ice cream.

With one last touch left, I go into the pantry to the spices.

I pull out my phone and press the power button for a little light to skim the labels. Taking the cinnamon for a quick sprinkle, then putting it back exactly where I had found it.

Bowl in hand, I go to the other side of the counter to the raised ledge and high chairs. Settling in, I take my first bite of my sundae. The concoction tastes like all the best parts of a peach pie.

The white walls look gray in the dark. The wooden counters appear darker, though I supposed everything does in the dark.

"Couldn't sleep?" My body jumps at the sudden intrusion. My heart jumpstarting at the possibilities.

"Sorry." I apologize immediately. Swinging around in my spot, I see that I'm not in trouble.

"Don't apologize. I'm sorry. I didn't mean to scare you." Dominique continues as she walks closer. "Sorry, I couldn't sleep."

"Neither could I," I tell her. I turn around to grab a bite of my ice cream.

Dominique flutters around the room, much more noisily than I had, but still at a usually reasonable sound level. I cringe at each peak noise, waiting for someone to come out and scream at us for being too loud and waking them up. Then yelling at us for getting ice cream in the middle of the night.

Once she's got her own ice cream, she comes to sit next to me. I make sure to add a mental to make sure everything is placed back exactly as I had found it, before I go back to bed.

She leans over and points at my food. "What's that?"

"Canned peaches and cinnamon."

"Oh, you genius." She gets up and adds those two ingredients to her ice cream before settling back beside me again.

We eat in relative silence. The only noises are coming from our eating.

After a couple minutes, I relax. No one is going to come out and discover us stealing a midnight snack. The noises that we made didn't wake anyone.

Dominique leans over, her arm touches mine. She looks over at me and smiles for a moment before grabbing another spoonful.

I tilt my head to rest it a moment against her shoulder. She leans her head against mine.

Chapter 10

"Slow down, before you choke," Dominique warns me.

I chew and swallow the spoon full of warm chocolate cake a bit more slowly, and slowly take another piece. A bit more mindful to savour the treat, like Jules told me to.

Chocolate cake was a treat, even before the war. My foster parents made it a special birthday treat; I wasn't allowed cake if it wasn't someone's birthday. No one gets cake for no reason at all.

James asked Jules to start making desserts for customers. At a premium price due to scarcity; I was told. I'm the lucky customer who gets to taste-test her latest creation; it's amazing. It makes my mouth so happy.

I wish I could have a whole cake all to myself, but there was only enough for a tiny square.

There are a few people in the lounge, but it's not busy. There's no one interesting to watch. Nothing to eavesdrop on. The adults are talking about boring things.

I wish there were other kids to play with.

I put the last bite of cake in my mouth and hold it there on my tongue. I'll make it last as long as I can.

Jules quickly comes by to clear my plate. "How was it?"

I hum my delight and smile as big as I can without opening my lips.

"That's great!" She asks, "Does anyone need anything else?"

"No, we're good; thanks," Shawn responds for the group.

Jules leaves us be again.

I look around. It's bright outside. The snow is gone, but Dominique isn't convinced it's going to stay gone yet. We're all hoping for an early summer though.

The farm will get busy as soon as the ground is thawed and the last frost has gone. I'm a bit excited to help with planting. I've never planted a garden before.

There's no one outside doing anything interesting right now though. Some people walk around from place to place, but that's about it.

I turn my attention inside again. Dominique, John, and Shawn talk around me as they talk about nothing at all; catch-up talk.

 Three other tables have two to three people at them. They are eating off their plates of food and talking to whoever they are sitting with. One person leans over to talk to another person at a nearby table.

Two people walk into the lounge.

Kelly takes in a deep breath. Her eyes turn darker; a trick of the lighting perhaps.

Watching Kelly's movements carefully, I try to figure out what she's going to do. Her hand comes up and quickly swipes against my cheek, then goes back to her side.

I see an opening to swing a punch of my own. She grabs my arm, twisting it around my back. For just a moment none of my limbs are touching the ground. My back hits the floor and my breath escapes my lungs.

She attacked me.

I shake my head. No, she attacked Alexa.

My heart starts pounding in fright. I need to go.

Giving him my right hand, he takes it in one of his. He places my hand palm side down on his hand and then puts his other hand in between my thumb and pointer finger. Miles then squeezes the area right in between those two fingers.

My mind focuses only on the warmth of the hand under mine and the pressure in my hand. The two feelings combined start a sort of electric tingling.

Miles held my hand. He made me feel safe. No, he made Alexa feel safe.

The man smiles. I remember him. He's one of Alexa's friends. He saved me before. "Are you okay?" I shake my head. The tears keep falling.

I want Alexa. I want to say, but I can't.

He holds out his hand. "Alexa will be alright. She just needs sleep right now. James just wanted to make sure she gets the rest she needs. He didn't mean to shout and hurt your feelings."

He made me feel safe. He wouldn't let anything happen.

Miles is chained from the ceiling; blood oozes from wounds on his naked back. Horrified by the image, I freeze. Darius comes from behind Miles. A bleeding knife is held in his hand

He turns and brings his hands up to Miles' head. One hand fixes on the top of his head and the other under his chin with the blade.

Finding a bare spot on his stomach, I hold the knife there for a moment. A tear rolls down the side of my face. I mouth the word 'sorry' to him, as I ensure the knife cuts a shallow horizontal groove. More tears fall as the knife leaves his skin.

No, I couldn't. I wouldn't. Not me. No. Alexa, she did it.

Miles and Kelly walk towards the counter.

I curl in a flinch and look down at the table. My heart runs. I hope she doesn't see me. I hope he doesn't see me.

How could I do that to him?

No, it was Alexa.

The black in Kelly's hair isn't there anymore. She must've cut it. A darker colour is growing from her roots.

Miles, it's been so long that he's healed from Alexa attacking him. Why would she do that? Why did she help Darius hurt him?

I can't look at him without seeing the wounds I made.

I swallow the warm lump of cake mush.

"Can we go see Margie now?" I ask.

Dominique doesn't hear me, but John does. He points to me to get Dominique's attention.

"Sorry, what did you say?" Dominique asks as she turns her head to me.

"Can we go see Margie now?" I ask again.

"This is probably boring for you, eh?" John asks.

"Yeah," I say.

"Alright, let's go." Dominique agrees.

I scoot out from the booth and walk towards the exit. Dominique stops for a moment to say her goodbye.

I wish she would hurry.

Kelly and Miles are at the till, so I feel like I should be safe enough from her.

She always freaked me out. I didn't know that she attacked Alexa too.

And Miles, I didn't know Alexa hurt him. He was always so nice to me. Why did she do that? The answer doesn't appear.

I get to the open doorway before I look back again. Miles and Kelly are at the counter. Dominique is following me. John is getting up from his seat at the table. He starts cleaning up the table with Shawn.

I turn around and see a face that cuts fear into my heart. His brown eyes line up with mine.

I sit against the cold floor with my hands crossed in my lap. Sandra comes up to me out of the darker darkness. She threatens me, "If you try to escape I'm going to have to kill you."

Words get stuck in my throat, so I nod. Tears fall, but I hold in cries. They don't like it when I cry loud. Sandra jumps towards me, but stops when she gets close.

"SANDRA! ENOUGH! Don't take it out on her."

That was him.

That was me.

I run. My name is shouted behind me, but I can't stop. Bounding by people and doors as fast as I can until I find the right one.

I usually knock, but I know Margie keeps it unlocked when she's awake inside. The doorknob turns and opens.

I run inside and open the closed mirror closet; shutting it behind me. I sink down near the shoes, with my knees to my chest. Holding my hands over my ears dulls loud name calls.

It's safer in here. It's safer when no one can find you.

My breath cuts short when Margie opens the door. She pulls my hands from my ears and holds them. I'm not strong enough to pull away.

"What is wrong with you child?" She scolds.

My breath returns at a quick pace. "Why is he here?" I breathe out.

Margie frowns. She looks behind her to see only Dominique rushing into the door. No one else is with her. "Who?"

"I don't know." His name pulls up in my head. "Shale."

"He's here?" Dominique asks.

"Who's Shale?" Margie turns to Dominique to ask her.

"Is Sandra here?" I ask Dominique.

"No." Dominique chooses to answer me. Her eyes go wide and she holds out both her hands. "No. No. No. No. No, Sweetie. Shale is here because he's free now too. Sandra was keeping him there with her, like kidnapping but different. But, we got him free." Dominique kneels down beside Margie. "Did he do something to you?"

"No." I shake my head. He's never hurt me. But, he was there when I was captured, at the jail, in Banff, then at the school.

He didn't stop me from hurting. But, he did stop people from hurting me.

"That's good," Dominique says. "Remember, he helped make sure we were safe, while we were at the jail."

"He helped me," I admit. "He stopped Sandra from hurting me before you rescued me."

"That's great. See, he's good." Dominique says.

Margie shakes her head. She gets up from her spot to disappear into the main part of her room. Dominique scoots over to be more centered in the opening of the closet doors.

"Alexa liked him." Dominique opens her mouth but stops before she can make a sound. "He was her friend," I tell her.

I look down to the ground. The carpet sticks up near the wall. I pick at the edges, but can't make the carpet come up anymore.

"Did he seem nice as her friend?" Dominique asks.

"Yes. And, he gave me Crystal." I remember. Alexa wasn't there.

Crystal reaches her paws out and stretches like a feline. She comes closer to us. Rayleen struggles, so I let her down. The redhead walks over to the creature. Bending over to pick her up, Crystal jumps into her arms. Rayleen stands up and shifts her arms to get a better hold of her new pet. She turns to face me and comes closer.

Crystal looks like what the legends say a griffin should look like. She has a head of an eagle and a body of a lion; though miniature in size due to her age. At her size, the lion part of her looks like the body of a cat with oversized paws.

Fine feathers starting at her feline ears become finer and slowly form into short golden fur down her back. On her sides, tucked into her, are two feathered wings. Her tail tucks around her as she brings her beak around to tug at the tuff on her hair at the end. The griffin lets go of her tail and looks at me. Her ocean-blue eyes look into mine.

Opening her beak, a noise escapes; something between a squeak and a roar chimes into my ears.

Rayleen gives a short giggle. "That means she likes you. You wanna hold her?"

Darius snarls as he comes for me. His hands reached out to grab me. He's fast. Too fast for me to do anything. I freeze.

Crystal squawks and folds out her wings as she guards me. His foot stomps down on her. She releases the most awful squeak.

"Where's Crystal? Did she die?" I know she did. But, I need to know.

"I'm sorry." Dominique starts. That's how they always start when they have bad news.

A sob escapes my throat. I throw my upper body back towards to wall behind me. The deep hurt in my chest is back.

"I think it might be best for you to take her home. I can't train her like this. Who knows what damage she could cause with her emotions going wild like this." Margie tells Dominique.

"What about the soul stuff?" She asks.

"I don't think there's anything I could do. She doesn't seem confused. She needs to stop crying, and she can do that somewhere else." Margie tells her.

Dominique pulls me up and lifts me. "Alright, let's go home." She says softly.

I curl into her and let her carry me home.

Chapter 11

I close the door quietly and cautiously. Holding the doorknob in an open position as I connect the door to the door jamb, then slowly unroll my wrist to connect the latch.

After all that, Rayleen passed out; and I'm glad for it. Her uncontrollable sadness is heartbreaking.

It must've taken a lot out of her.

On this one, I'm betting it was the powerful emotions that took their toll, rather than any sort of medical thing. I'm hoping so, at least.

I take a deep breath to calm myself, then pull away from the door.

Is there anything else we forgot about, that we should have told her? Anyone else died?

Shit. Daniel. Did anyone tell her about Daniel? Alexa knew, but has that memory hit Rayleen yet? Would she care?

This stuff is confusing and difficult to manage. It's hard to know what Rayleen knows and what she doesn't.

The memories seem to trigger from things said and what she sees and does, rather than her knowing everything ever that happened to Alexa.

I'm thankful for it in many ways, but when the memories hit, they seem to hit hard. Especially the traumatic ones, but that's no wonder. It's like these things are happening in the moment, and for her, they might as well be.

Letting out a deep breath quickly helps calm me. There's nothing I can do about it now. We'll have to deal with that later. And, have another emotional moment later.

The hits just keep coming for her.

I should find something to do while I wait. I can't just stand here awkwardly for however long her nap is going to take.

I decide to go down to the lobby. There's always something going on down there; if not there are always snacks.

People sit at one of the tables. I don't recognize them, but that doesn't stand for much now. We've grown so much in so little time.

I make my way to the snack table and start choosing from the variety of pantry items.

"Hello?" I turn around instantly at the word. A tall man with red hair and a red beard watches me purposefully. He kind of reminds me of a lumber jack, with his red and black checkered jacket.

"Hi," I respond politely. He gets up from his seat and looks lost towards me. "Do you need something?"

"Yes, sorry. I'm Dave and this is my family, Winston, Claire, and Roy. James said to come here and Jaiden would find us a new place to live." He emphasizes Jaiden's name.

"James told you this?" He nods to confirm. I switch immediately to more of a customer service voice. "Hi, I'm Dominique." I put out my hand to shake with his. "When Jaiden's not around, you are welcome to come to me. We're co-leading, and she's currently running errands for James. Anyway, I can get you sorted out, and find you a place to live."

"Great. Thank you." Dave responds.

"So you'll want to stay together, so we'll need at least enough room for four. And, preferably not sharing housing." I go to the board and look for the housing placement list. Scanning through the messy board, I finally find it underneath another paper.

"Yes, sorry." Dave apologizes for his interjection. "James mentioned you needed a vet. I'm an elf and I grew up assisting my dad. He was a vet. And, Claire grew up on a canola farm. She had a horse; that's how we met."

"That's amazing. Yes, of course. We'll get you near the farm to help with the animals. You'd be so useful there. I'm glad you're here." That's great news. I know Sara's been worried about how the animals are going to survive.

"Yes, of course. We'll get you to the farm." Ted says as he comes out from the stairs. He walks over to me and takes the housing list. He snidely mutters. "Any idea how many people James offered housing to?"

Claire and Dave exchange worried glances.

"No, sorry." His abrasiveness surprises me, but not as much as his stating such right in front of Dave and his family. "Is it a problem?"

"Not at all. Just would like a heads up." Ted releases the tension in his shoulders. "A dozen families showed up today, and I imagine there's much more to come." He pulls on his mouth in thought. "I have another three families to settle in on the other side of the hospital right now, but I could come back after that to get you over to the farm, and introduce you to DeAngelo."

"I can do it." Wait, no I can't. "I mean, I just got Rayleen to sleep, but if I can find someone to watch her, then I can do it." I shrug to Dave. "It'll be faster than waiting for him."

"I don't mind waiting a bit for you. Rayleen your kid?" Dave asks.

"Sort of." I guess she kind of is now. "She was recently

orphaned, and I've been taking care of her."

"Oh yes, sadly a story I've heard too many times in recent months." His frown turns into a smile. "That's good of you, that you are willing to take care of her. Everyone needs someone looking out for them."

"Thanks." I look back to Ted. He shrugs, grabs some papers from the counter, then leaves. "I guess I'll see if someone here can watch her. I'll be right back."

I realize too late that he left with the available housing list. I guess we'll have to get Sara and DeAngelo's help when we get there.

I go to Jaiden's door first and let myself inside. She isn't here.

I move through the rest of the upper floor doors; knocking on each door. Not even Kelly is in her room, but she might just be ignoring me.

My door opens slowly. I let out a huff of air as my chest drops to my stomach.

"Sorry, did I wake you?" I apologize. I know I did.

"Yeah, why were you knocking on the door?" She rubs her eyes. The noise from the knocks must've travelled through the walls.

"Sorry Sweetie. I was trying to get someone to watch you while you slept. I have to go to the farm." I walk over to her and swoop her hair out of her face.

Rayleen immediately perks up and brightens. She bounces a little. "Can I go with you?"

"Sure. Yes, let's go." I point towards the exit door. When I cross over to her, I herd her with my arm wrapping around her back. A small push gets her going.

We get to the lobby. "Guess who woke up?" I chime. "Rayleen, this is Dave, Winston, Claire and Roy. We're going to escort them to the farm." I point to each person as I say their name.

"Oh, she woke up," Dave says.

I explain. "Yeah, I accidentally woke her trying to get someone to watch her. But, this way, we all get to go on an adventure."

"That's sounds amazing." Dave takes on a childish exaggerated animation many parents have when they talk with smaller kids. "Are you super excited to show us around?"

"Yeah," Rayleen responds quietly. She tucks in behind me. Claire smiles sweetly while watching Rayleen.

"Awesome." I grab a set of keys for a truck before we set out. "Let's go."

Dave and his family follow us in a blue car to the farm. I park on the road out in front, and they park behind us.

Sara comes out of the first building immediately, making her way quickly to greet us. I wonder if she watches the roads, or if this was a coincidence.

I make note of the cute pink, orange and yellow plaid shirt she has on. Combined with the jeans, it helps her look farm chic.

Rayleen and I get out and meet her between the vehicles.

"Hey." Sara greets me. She looks between us and the new people, waiting expectantly for an introduction.

"Hey," I say. "This is Dave and his family; Winston, Claire and Roy. James invited them from elsewhere to come to live here."

"Really?" She pushes for more information subtly. I guess they haven't really been inundated by the new people yet.

"Yeah, he called us the other day and asked for us to move here. He said he was making it safe and stable, and that you could use our skills." Dave relays.

"That's us; safe and stable," I note a hint of a joke when Sara and I cross eyes.

"He's an elf and a son of a vet. He used to help out. So, we figured he'd be best off here. Oh, and his wife grew up on a canola farm. And, had a horse." I list off the information they had relayed to me; the stuff that would be useful for the farm.

"That's great. We're going to need your help. If you go into that building," Sara points to the first house-like building; the same one she came out of. "DeAngelo is in there. He's handling the housing; he has a system and I apparently mess it up when I try to do things. So, you're better off talking with him about it."

I toss out any thoughts of assisting. DeAngelo sounds like he has a system going; and he's particular about it.

"Sounds good. Thanks." Dave and his family take their suitcases over to where directed. Sara and I watch them leave in silence.

An empty space begs a question to be answered; now what? This didn't take as long as I had thought, and there was no tour to be had. DeAngelo will handle all that.

I look around and take in the sight of it. I haven't spent much time here.

There are a few different buildings inside a chain link fence.

One looks like a classic old red barn, while another looks like an old farmhouse, and yet another looks like an old church/schoolhouse.

There are closed and open structures that look like they have a variety of purposes. Those I knew about from the first time we came here, but they look refreshed.

I know the farm goes bigger beyond the closer buildings. It looks like they've been digging up the ground in a few areas; probably to add gardens. I can't see how far back they've dug up.

"Do you have horses?" Rayleen breaks the silence, and my

look around.

Sara puts her hands on her thighs and bends a bit to get down to Rayleen's level. "We have one horse. Would you like to see all our animals?"

"Yes, please!" Rayleen bursts. She looks to me for approval, so I nod.

Sara stands up, to look at me. "If you guys have time. I probably should have asked first."

"No, that's fine. We have time." I answer.

I tread lightly and stop myself from explaining, not wanting to restart Rayleen's tears.

"Let's go." Sara helps set Rayleen off in the right direction.

Her excitement has her setting a pace that is increasing with each moment. She keeps looking behind herself to us and waits when she must figure she's gone too far.

"Thanks for the distraction." I make sure to speak a little quieter, on any off chance Rayleen can hear us from her distance. "Rayleen got out of magic lessons because she remembered Crystal died."

"She was quite upset?" Sara comments in a question.

"Quite," I answer.

"Well, hopefully, the animals don't remind her," Sara says.

"Oh no." I hadn't thought about that. "Hopefully, not."

Sara and I exchange glances. We both hope this goes well. You never know with kids, how they're going to react to something.

Rayleen's situation makes this particularly complicated. She's already had a burst of emotions today, so she might be particularly raw emotioned from that already.

We can just hope for the best.

There's a bunch of people walking purposefully around to and from different buildings. As we come around the corner of a building, I can see many more working in groups on a variety of projects, encircling and inside a giant soil rectangle.

Some are up on roofs installing solar panels, while others are gathered around some farming equipment. Fencing is being torn down, and put up in other areas. Landscaping and spring cleaning yard work is getting put into a large wooden bin.

A fire is going, with many benches and lawn chairs surrounding it.

It's refreshing to see so many people working together to help with projects for the community.

It makes me realize how isolated everyone is at the hotels and surrounding areas. Each person does things that only benefit them, or they trade for it. If they even visit with others at all, not that I've seen much of that; except for the lounge. But, even then, most keep to their small groups.

We're so busy expanding and surviving, that we haven't reached a level of working towards a future yet.

The market is a collection of hoarded items in a dark guarded building that's now also being used as a prison. It's an uninviting nightmare.

The dining building isn't ready for large amounts of people yet, because only two people have been setting that up and running it. They aren't quite equipped enough to satisfy a large amount of people.

The closest thing we have to a community gathering spot is Jules' Lounge, but that's for paying customers, and Jerry was an issue.

We need to work towards *this*.

I'm glad Jaiden put Sara and DeAngelo in charge of the farm. They're doing much better than we are.

When they get set up, and running fully, we should ask them to implement some of their things in our area too. A secondary community area would be great for morale.

A second farm might be good for more food, and for if anything ever happens to one plot, we still have the other.

I note to ask them for advice on how they're getting so many people to work together later; when we're ready for it. It's certainly something we need to work on. I wonder if Jaiden's noticed.

I wonder what system they have in place for things, or if it's truly just a bunch of people working towards the greater good for all?

"So, how's things going?" Sara breaks through my thoughts.

"It's gotten a bit stuffy at the hotel," I say politely. She waits for me to continue, but with so many people around, I don't want to bad mouth James or the hotels.

John's reminded me quite a few times about those with extra hearing. That I need to watch what I say because you never know who might be listening with better hearing than a human. It takes time to get used to the larger range.

After a few moments, Sara catches on that I won't be saying more. A look exchanged, a twitch of the corner of her mouth, and a nod, she lets me know that she's reading between the lines.

She suggests. "Maybe you should come live here. The fresh air is great for the soul."

"Yeah, maybe." It's a good thought, but Jaiden's declined it before. I don't want to leave her alone at the hotel; with James.

"It might benefit Rayleen." She offers. "Less triggering memories here."

"I'll think about it. But, you're probably right." It feels different here; a good different.

Cruel Souls

Something I don't want James to corrupt.

Chapter 12

I wait, hopefully, undetectably anxious for the video call to turn on.

The icon keeps circling. James has the phone propped up on its side against some books, to get the camera to capture the both of us.

We sit closely, but not touching. There's enough space for a bit of elbow room.

I make sure I sit straight and proper, with my hands folded in my lap. I'm not sure whether or not anyone can see us yet, and I don't want to be caught doing something I should be embarrassed about.

I don't say anything for the same reasoning.

When he said he wanted me on a conference call with the Council, I didn't think it would be a video call. I was fine with a voice call, because then I could hide silently forgotten in the background, but with this, I'll need to actively participate or they'll see if I'm not.

There is a constant reminder that I am with them.

A man pops up on the screen. He's shrouded in darkness. I can barely make him out.

"Niklas." James greets. "You could turn on a light."

"I'd rather not." His accent is heavy; Russian maybe. "Wouldn't want to give away my location, should someone recognize something in the background."

Is this not a secure line? You'd think they'd want to make sure they conduct business on a secure line. If anyone could be watching, then we'll need to watch what we say.

But, that defeats the purpose of trying to conduct important business on a conference call.

"You can trust the Council." James insists.

Oh. Is Niklas worried about the Council, rather than someone hacking the call?

"Can I? We're in this because we were betrayed." Niklas reminds James.

I understand his trust issues a bit more now. He's holding onto the betrayal of two close colleagues; friends possibly.

James scoffs. "That bunker is going to your head."

Niklas sneers. "You're a fool if you think you couldn't be betrayed again. I suggest you get back in your bunker before your experience ends with you."

The small screen divides into six rectangles, effectively stopping Niklas and James from continuing.

"Hey James, Niklas. May I present to you Interim Elemental Councilman Ariela and Interim Nocturnal Councilman Claudia. Aleena and I are spectating. And, Aalayah still hasn't come to her senses." They each wave shortly at their names; I try to remember them all but I know I won't be able to.

It doesn't help that only the first one has a different background from the others.

I would bet most of them are in the same building; possibly adjacent conference rooms.

They don't echo, so likely not the same room, but the same fake wood panelling can't be a coincidence of design.

The text for their names is too small to read properly. I can barely make out some of the letters. But, between trying to remember the names and the vague sense of letters, it helps me, sort of, figure out who each person is supposed to be.

"Alright, we're all here now. James, let's hear it. How's America?" Niklas asks with a hint of a sharp edge from their previous confrontation.

"It's been a rough transition," James answers politically.

The first introduced woman chuffs. "It's been a dumpster fire."

"Not everyone can be New Zealand, Ariela." The one who introduced everyone else responds. She never said her own name. I can't make out her name, except that it starts with an A, and is sort of long.

Ariela shakes her head once and leans a bit more into the camera. Her blue eyes swirl on camera. "I'm not saying he has to be. I am well aware of the great privilege we've had here, but sugarcoating it does no one any good.

It hasn't been a rough transition, it's been a dumpster fire, and it's still burning."

"You're right." James pauses for effect. When everyone's attention is on him, he continues. "I'm not meaning to downplay the severity of our situation. It's been terrible, but we have made some headway in our position. Alberta lost its regional leader."

"And, gained a worse one." Niklas sneers.

"I hear Seth is going rabid about it." Claudia smiles in her amusement.

"It's created a brief reprieve, which we have taken advantage of." James pulls the conversation back.

"We saw your pictures. While it does look promising, what makes you think Sandra will leave you alone?" Ariela asks.

"Sandra, unlike Darius, is not unreasonable. She won't be

controlled if her goals don't align, and she can be reasoned with; which is why Seth is upset.

We use that to our advantage. While they argue and Sandra tries to rally people behind her, we create a stronghold utopia and an army big enough to make them question attacking in the first place." James explains his thought process.

I hold my tongue.

There's more to it.

Now that Darius isn't alive to be obsessed over Alexa, there might not be a reason for Sandra to bug us at all. Not unless we threaten her, and her goals.

And, she might not attack us so catastrophically once we get up power and water. She might not be willing to damage infrastructure so unnecessarily.

Niklas says. "Sandra isn't going to let you-"

"She will." James interrupts him. "Intel says she had issues with how Seth and Darius ran things.

That she wants to return to a simpler, more comfortable life. But one where supernaturals are still above all others. She's not going to destroy the electricity grid, because she doesn't want to live without electricity.

Darius didn't care as long as the humans suffered."

"Is your intel reliable?" Ariela asks.

"Yes," James responds.

Ariela points to the left of the screen. "I was asking her."

All eyes focus on me.

"Oh," I panic. So far, I've evaded involvement. James didn't even bother to introduce me. Suddenly being asked a question catches me off guard. Especially, for something I had nothing to do with. "I wasn't the source of that intel."

"What's your purpose here then?" Niklas asks; his arms come

up for emphasis.

I look to James to answer, because I'm not entirely certain of the right answer. "This is Jaiden Marshall. She's my permanent shadow now."

I don't want to correct him in front of the group, but I'll need to make sure he knows that Marshall isn't my last name.

Though, he could know already. He might be using that last name to quickly explain things.

"That's why you're so confident. You got yourself a secret weapon." Claudia surmises.

James nods in response to her statement, then moves back to the previous subject. "The best we can ask for is that Seth and Sandra take each other out. Then, we can enact a vote to officially and permanently replace Seth."

"We all know Sandra would win that battle." Niklas chides.

I don't know Seth, but would Sandra be any better? Would Sandra be in charge of it all, if Seth wasn't? If she's the one who took him out?

Claudia would likely be the next in line for the Council position itself; I assume with her being in charge in the interim. But, maybe they don't follow that line of succession.

That brings us back to a more important question; does Sandra want to be in charge of the whole rebellion?

What would she do if she was in charge? Would it be better or worse than it is now?

If Seth and Sandra don't get along, would they run things differently? Do they have different ideals, and goals for this takeover?

Could we get back to a fully running society quicker, if someone else was in charge?

Whether that means negative things for the humans, or not, would be another question.

"There should be some law that allows a vote to happen under our circumstances," Claudia says.

"We've been under split circumstances before. We can't just vote each other out because we don't agree with other's beliefs." James bites out. "The Council majority has been on both the sides of good and wrong before, and it will happen again.

We need to have a foothold in the Council when good is the minority. That only happens when you can't vote someone out for disagreeing with you."

"What about actions? This isn't just a disagreement; they've cost lives running into the millions." Claudia responds.

"Any vote of such magnitude has to be unanimous between Council and Elementals, or it could be abused. And, it can't be done by interim leaders looking to take over the position. We all know Aalayah could hold a grudge until the next changeover." Ariela reminds them and advises me. "The only way he's getting out is if he dies.

That's the best-case scenario because his listed replacement automatically gains power at his death. We don't need Aalayah's cooperation for that."

Ariela puts an end to that topic.

It makes sense that only a unanimous vote could vote out a leader. If the interim leaders can't vote, and you can't convince those in official power to vote to oust a leader, holding a vote would be useless in the first place.

In order to vote Seth out, Aalayah would have to agree. In order to vote Aalayah out, Seth would have to agree. Since they've partnered up in their revolution, they're not going to do that.

That's not even counting, if you could get the others to agree to vote them out. James might not vote yes to a change, based on his words and the principle of the matter.

"How'd you find a Marshall? None of them survived the

attacks." Niklas asks.

"She wasn't reported to the Council; raised by human parents," James informs them.

"No one knew she existed, so Seth couldn't send anyone to kill her." Ariela surmises.

A question pulls to the forefront of my mind.

"Sorry," I interrupt. "The people that killed my family at the farm near Alberta Beach, did Seth send them?"

"It is speculated; yes. Many prominent prophetic families were assassinated at the start of the war, and in the months leading up to it." Aleena's soft voice confirms. "I'm sorry for your loss."

They systematically got rid of anyone who could potentially warn the Council ahead of time and thwart the revolution. It makes sense.

But, why wait until the moment of, to get rid of my family? Would they not have had visions, and be able to warn the Council? Unless, they truly were more on the outs with the Council than I had thought. Could they have secretly favoured the revolution?

"Thank you," I say.

But, the culprits were human; weren't they? I suppose they might not have been. Or, maybe a couple were supernatural and the others were human and following their unknown supernatural leaders.

They never admitted to killing my family. I was just told that they did it. I saw bullet holes and assumed the guys with the guns had done it; that they must be human.

Maybe, it wasn't them. And, assumptions were made.

Or, maybe it was, and they didn't make the connection. And, that's why they didn't kill me. Or, maybe by that time, they had regrets or ulterior motives figured out. Maybe, they couldn't kill a kid.

James used a gun. Supernaturals aren't above using guns to kill. Why should they be? Guns aren't inherently just a human thing.

"Should we get her to a bunker or headquarters? We should think about preserving her bloodline." Niklas says.

"Not only that, but she looks like she's still a child. How old are you, Sweetie?" Aleena questions.

I always hate this question, because the answer always makes people treat me differently. "Fifteen."

"She's old enough." James tries to justify his actions. "She's already saved my life. I've been told multiple stories of her heroics. She's capable and knows what she's doing."

"You can't put children on the front lines, James!" Ariela scolds. "You're breaking Marshall's Law; her family law."

"I'm not forcing her to do anything. She's old enough to make the decision for herself. And, she's decided to help." James' response confirms my earlier conversation position with Dominique.

There's never been a conversation asking me if I want to do this. He just encircled me into this role after I saved him.

He's willing to sacrifice me to get what he wants.

He's willing to sacrifice me to win.

It's not going to really be my decision.

I have to keep reminding myself of this.

"It sounds like James needs all the help he can get. Maybe a Marshall is what he needs to turn the tides." Claudia adds another angle to help James.

The screens drop down to five. A few questions about what happened come from the speakers before Ashlynn, I can now read her enlarged name tag, speaks. "Niklas must've lost connection again. We'll have to reconvene later."

"If I may," Claudia starts.

"We cannot continue discussing Council matters, without all Council members present. We will reconvene tomorrow. I will send you the invites. Goodbye, Everyone." Ashlynn crosses her arms and waits for others to drop off the call.

James sighs as he grabs the phone to disconnect us from the chat.

I have some lingering thoughts and questions from the call. Now that we're alone, I have to ask them. "What did they mean; we can't all be New Zealand?"

James gets up to move to the other side of the room. He looks out the window. "At the start of it all, when we passed the point of no return, the New Zealand government held a conference recognizing supernatural existence and everyone just accepted it. They never had war. They just shut their borders to avoid fall out from other countries at war and continued on with life."

"Hm, wish we all had it that easy." He doesn't say anything else, so I continue. "Why didn't the Council explore doing that everywhere?"

"Not everywhere experienced it like we did. New Zealand isn't the only place that never went down; it's just the prime example.

Some places only went down a few days, up to a month. Others are like us, still in the midst of the fallout." James avoids the question to comment on my comment.

He turns around to look at me. "We may have been in control of supernaturals, but we were controlled by the upper echelons of the governing powers of the world. We existed so long as we upheld peace, and part of that peace was contingent on supernaturals pretending not to exist.

The human governments of the world insisted supernaturals would never survive if we revealed ourselves; that we'd go to war and die. The Council was required to ensure this never came to be.

If New Zealand had tried that at any other time, they would have been wiped out by a natural disaster. There would have been a systematic witch hunt; so to speak.

We've done it before; many times."

"It could have been done peacefully. If they had done it everywhere, all at once..." Just like their plan for war. They didn't have to take over. They could have just all revealed themselves.

"There wouldn't have been a way to contain it all." James finishes for me. "But, we were afraid of this outcome either way; or worse.

Human governments twisting a supernatural reveal to give an excuse for a world war. Either right away, or after some real or faked tragedy blamed on supernaturals and staged as a declaration of war."

"I'd like to believe we'd be beyond that as a society," I say.

"Clearly not when half of us are capable of destroying the world like this." James throws one hand in the air, motioning vaguely to the outside.

He didn't understand me correctly. "I meant us humans automatically resorting to oppression and war." I clarify.

"You're not a human." James reminds me.

"I forget sometimes." He knows, but I don't think he truly understands or realizes my situation. "I was raised by a human family. My last name's actually Kensington, not Marshall.

The Marshalls didn't know about me until less than a year ago. I met them last summer. And, they certainly never said anything about my ability or the supernatural world.

In my head, I'm still human. I just so happen to have dreams that come true sometimes."

I feel human. I don't feel like a supernatural being. Nothing changed with my discovery, so I don't feel like I'm any different. Other than having vision dreams, I'm not any different from a human.

"You should go by Marshall. It's a well-respected name." He changes the subject adjacently.

I don't know. I don't know how I feel about it; using a different last name; one that has such a history and reputation behind it. One that I feel, I'm not entirely connected to. "How can I be a secret weapon, if everyone knows who I am?"

"Touché." James walks closer to me. He swoops his hand upwards. "Well, let's get you set off home. We won't start until after lunch tomorrow, so you can get a good sleep. Then, we'll take some pictures and videos."

I stand up and head towards the door. "To send to the Council?"

"No. I post it on my SuperData page. You should get one." James suggests.

I stop and turn towards him. "I'm not one for social media." I make in a quick excuse. Remembering too late, that he knows I use Sara's. It's how I got in contact with him in the first place.

"You should be. If for nothing else, it's good for spying and collecting information. But, people should know you exist. Knowing a Marshall is on our side, would give some people hope." James explains.

Spying is kind of like what I've already been doing already. Much easier to hide behind Sara's profile, than it is to get my own. At least, so far.

I open the door and watch what I say. You never know who could be listening in.

"I'll consider it," I tell him, as I leave the room. He closes the door without a goodbye.

I will consider it, but I don't think I will; not any time soon.

Cruel Souls

I can't even agree on a last name to use.

Chapter 13

"I have a few things to get done, so I'll pick her up in a couple of hours," Dominique announces as she herds me through Margie's door.

We discussed this along the way over. Dominique needs to meet with another leader and has to get back to contributing to the daily leadership tasks again. Not everything she needs to do, can be done with a kid attached at the hip; or is too dangerous to have me tag along.

I'm safe with Margie. Dominique trusts Margie. I trust Margie.

She'd be able to protect me if needed. Not that it should be needed. There isn't much danger to happen while stuck in a hotel room going over the basics of magic.

Dominique planned a drop, quick explanation, and run approach because Margie specifically asked Dominique to remain during training.

"I'm not a babysitter." Margie tries to argue.

"Okay, well, I have too much to do, to sit here and do nothing for two hours every day. Things James needs me to get done, so you're going to have to step up and do this by yourself. I'll be back later." Dominique doesn't leave room for further arguments, by walking away.

I let myself in all the way as Margie watches after Dominique. Careful to avoid her gaze, I take off my shoes and jacket and tuck them away into the closet; quickly and quietly. Then, I move further into the room to start my lessons.

Margie quickly forces air out of her mouth. The door shuts sharply. I jump a little. I wasn't watching anymore, so I couldn't prepare myself.

She's annoyed, so I need to make sure I'm careful not to make it worse. I don't want her taking her frustration out on me. It's best if I am on my best behaviour while with her.

Margie looks at me with a slight frown when she comes down the short hall. "I'm not a babysitter, so you better not act like a baby while you're with me. None of that bullshit from yesterday. I won't stand for whining and crying."

"Okay, I promise." I nod. My chest tightens. Crying won't be tolerated. It's nothing I haven't heard before.

Margie sighs. She walks over to her desk to drink from a mug. She turns around to look me over, then passes by me to go into the bathroom.

I wait for her to tell me what to do, but she seems lost. I sit on the bed and watch her. She goes back and forth for a bit doing small tasks. I wonder what she has planned for today, and when we are going to get started.

When she looks more like she's tidying, rather than getting things ready for an interactive lesson, I start wondering if we'll ever get to it. But, I don't dare ask.

I sit on the bed bouncing my legs to pass the time somewhat patiently.

Margie finally announces, "It's time for lunch." She goes to the closet to grab out her purse. "I want you to go downstairs and go get us two soups. Do you think you could handle that?"

I don't dare mention that I already had lunch. I don't want to make her angry. She's trying to do something nice for me, and I don't want to be ungrateful.

"Are you not coming with me?" I ask.

Dominique wouldn't let me go by myself.

Alexa wouldn't have let me go alone.

"No. You're old enough to handle this. You need to grow up and learn responsibility." Margie takes two coins out of her purse and hands them to me. "This should be just enough to cover the soups. I expect you to go right there and right back. No dawdling."

I nod and squeeze the coins in my hand tightly. I don't want to take any chance of losing them. Margie would be really mad if I lost her coins.

"I'll be super quick," I promise. I pop up, put on my shoes, and leave the room in a jog.

Margie might be angry if I take a while. I don't want to take any chance that she thinks I took my time doing the chore.

She'd already be annoyed if she knew I already ate lunch. I don't want her offer of doing something nice for me to be turned into me being rude to her.

Keeping pace the whole way, I get to the lounge and order the soup to go; paying the man the money.

He goes into the kitchen and comes out of the kitchen almost immediately with two bowls on a tray. "Would you like me to help you carry this?"

"No, thank you," I say. I don't want to disappoint Margie by having to get help.

The tray is quite heavy when he hands it to me. I watch the soup carefully to make sure I don't spill it the whole way back.

I'm glad I ran the way there because of how long the walk back takes.

When I get back to Margie's room, I pause. With how heavy

the tray is, I need both hands to carry it. I don't think I could open the door without spilling the soup. But, it would be rude to shout at Margie from beyond the door.

I kick the door to knock.

Margie opens the door moments later. "No trouble?"

"No," I add with a beaming smile. "It was fun."

Margie takes the tray from me, and we go inside to the desk. She sets down the tray. "See, that's what you need. A little bit of freedom. You aren't just a little girl; you're special. More grown-up than people will accept. You just need a little more freedom to grow."

I agree in a hum. A warm feeling runs through me when she calls me special. I want to make her happy and proud.

Margie grabs her soup and spoon. She sits down at the desk chair.

Nodding towards the other soup bowl, Margie starts my lessons. "Let's see how you do, cooling down the soup by moving cold air over it."

Chapter 14

Bower waits outside with three other tall men around a newly set up metal fire pit. They've pulled up a truck and put down the tailgate to sit on.

I'm surprised he's out and about. For all the times we've passed by here, he's never been out before. Maybe he feels freer now that Jerry is dead.

I wring my hands with trepidation. He asked for a meeting, but wouldn't say anything more over the radio. It's not the best for privacy, anyone could be listening in, so I don't blame him.

John places his hand on mine after he parks and turns off the vehicle. The warmth pulls away the antsy tingle and replaces it. I pull out the bottommost hand and place it on top of his to sandwich his hand between mine.

Unfortunately, we have to get out of our truck before it's weird and suspicious. I'd like to stall a little longer, but Bower is staring directly at us.

I smile briefly at John, before taking my hand back. We get out of the truck and greet Bower.

He nods an acknowledgment of our hellos. "Are you having any troubles with supply runners coming back?" Bower gets right into it.

I'm caught off guard for a moment. I thought we'd get through some small talk first; or at least quick greetings. He dove straight into the point of the meeting.

No one has complained about supply runners not coming back, or being injured. Though I'm not even certain if we even have anyone directly going out for supply runs lately.

James cornered that market, by getting Jerry's suppliers to agree to supply us. And after that, I don't think any of us have gone out.

I suppose James or Jaiden would be the ones to ask about it, or their supplier leaders. We could also ask Sara or DeAngelo, but Sara likely would have mentioned something when we dropped that family off.

I look at John questioningly. He shakes his head negatively. He hasn't heard anything either.

"No, why?" I ask for more information. He's asking for a reason. The leading theory is the obvious answer; his aren't returning. But, I need to hear it from him directly and get more details.

"Couple days ago, four runners went out and never returned. They should have been back before dark; we have strict rules about it.

When they didn't return, we figured they would hunker down and come back the next day. But, nothing.

We wanted to check in with you before sending a party out to search for them. In case you were having issues too." Bower says.

"No, nothing. I'm so sorry. But, we can help you look." I look to John briefly to see if he's in on that idea. He nods once. "Do you know exactly where they were searching?"

"South, always south," Bower says. Jerry was to the north, so south makes sense. "Take Dan with you. He can show you where they were last headed off to. They likely would have been around that area. It would be as good of a starting place as any."

A balding man steps forward and walks over to us.

He's dressed differently than the others. Bower and the two other men look like they took their clothes off the rack today; shoes too. The white of Bower's runners are too white.

But, Dan's clothes are worn. Dark stains line the cuffs of his grey sweater. The one knee of his jeaned pant leg has rubbed out. His boots have mud encrusted around the bottom edges.

I'd bet, they planned for this. Dan would be going out, with or without us; but they planned for him to go with us.

He's dressed ready to go for a supply run, or a rescue mission. The others are dressed to stay in their cozy mall for the day.

The expectation is for us to go now.

I guess we don't have anything else to do, and we did offer. But, we don't have anything with us, if we run into any trouble then we won't be able to do much.

"We'll check in before dark if we don't find anything by then," I assure Bower. That's their rule, and we have an unwritten similar rule like that too.

"Good luck." Bower wishes us before we are dismissed with a wave.

We escort Dan back to our truck. John drives and I sit beside him, with Dan on my other side.

I explain my thoughts, as I have them, to the guys. "We should ask Jaiden about it. See if she's had anyone contact her about supply runners having disappeared. She'd have the contacts to talk to about it. And, maybe we should grab Sara and maybe some others for extra backup; just in case we run into anything out there."

They both agree quickly. John turns out of the parking lot to the right; towards the farm.

The farm is big, and Sara could be anywhere. I should call her and see where she's at. I think otherwise about it; maybe a text instead. That way I can explain a bit more, while also not alerting others.

"Can I get your phone? Give Sara a heads up?" I ask John. He digs into his pocket and hands his phone over.

I quickly text Sara on John's phone to explain the situation and ask her for her help. We aren't far off from the farm, so it's not much of a heads-up, even if she gets the message right away. We're not even a minute away.

"Maybe we should've asked for something for you to smell?" I ask John.

"I'm not a dog." John scrunches his face with displeasure.

That's not what I said. "Can you, or can you not, track through scent?" I ask to make my point.

His face softens and the barest smile peaks through. "Can."

"Would it have helped?" I ask.

"Maybe." He flashes a quick smile at me before turning his attention back on the road. "I'll grab Sara when we get there."

I check the phone for any incoming messages, but there aren't any. "Should we take a few people; just in case?" I wonder out loud.

"Expecting an attack?" Dan interjects.

"What if it's Sandra?" I answer his question with a question.

"I doubt she's still around," John adds.

"But, what if she is?" I insist.

"Who's Sandra?" Dan asks.

I forget not everyone has had to deal with Sandra; and Darius for that matter. "She's the one who was in charge of that school that had all those people kidnapped in it."

"Ah." He nods in understanding. Dan looks out the window.

We park at the farm, not too far away. John leaves to collect

Sara. He heads straight for the backyard area.

A few moments later, they come back with two others I don't recognize.

John gets back into the truck, while the others pile into the back truck box. There's no more room in the cab for them.

"Where to?" John asks.

"Back to the mall. We take the main road south from there." Dan guides John down the road past the mall.

Bower is still out at the fire pit. He and the two others watch us go by. I bet they're wondering what we were up to. But, they might guess it from seeing that the others have joined us.

We turn down the corner of the mall; south. North, would take us straight back to the hotels.

Not long after, Sara knocks frantically at the back window. John slows the truck quickly, yet smoothly. We look behind us to Sara. She points over to the right.

John starts up the truck again and drives down the road some more.

It takes me a moment to see it, but prominently displayed on a high billboard in the slight distance are four severed heads on poles and the Council emblem painted in black spray paint behind them.

John screeches to a halt.

"Shit!" Dan mutters under his breath. He covers his mouth with his hand.

"Whoever did it, made a show of it," John says.

"Could it have been one of yours?" Dan asks breathily.

"No, of course not." I defend.

Is that what he's been thinking?

"Someone who thought we were you then? Sending you a

message? Sandra?" He questions angrily, trying to find some reasoning to explain this; trying to find anything to explain this senseless display.

"Maybe," I say. I don't have a definite answer; I wish I did. "Maybe someone new."

This is jolting and terrifying. Who would be capable of doing something like this? What type of person? No one we'd want to be dealing with.

"We should tell Jaiden. Maybe she'll have an idea." John suggests. Jaiden sees and talks with a lot more people than we do. It's a good idea.

Dan averts his gaze to his lap. This must be harder for him to see. He would have known those people. "I've seen what I need to. Can you take me back?"

"Of course," I say.

John rolls down the window to talk to those in the back. "We're going to take Dan back to the Bower Mall." He turns the truck around, and we travel back the short distance to the mall.

"Thanks for the help. I'll tell Bower." Dan leaves the truck and stumbles over to Bower. They frown, knowing nothing good could come from our quick return alone.

"Should we go with him?" I ask.

"No, probably best to let him tell them," John says.

I watch them as John drives us out of the parking lot. It nags in my brain Dan's line of questioning. Surely, he won't think to blame us in some way.

Dan stumbles stiffly over to the other three. Bower gets up from his seat but stays where he is.

Dan detours to keel over beside the truck and vomits. Bower goes over to put his hand on Dan's back.

I look away. Swallowing the nauseating lump in my throat, I detach the walkie-talkie from my pocket. She always has the radio on and attached to her.

"Jaiden?" I wait for a response with my fingers off the button. "Jaiden?"

"Don't say anything over the radio. Just ask her to meet us. We don't want to freak anyone out." John tells me.

I nod. "Jaiden?"

"Here." She finally answers.

"Are you busy?" I ask.

"Not especially. Why?" Jaiden sounds suspicious.

"Where are you?" I ask.

"J-James' Hotel." She fumbles over the first letter. I wonder if she was going to say Jerry, and caught herself.

I look at the buildings around us. "We'll be there in a minute. Meet us out front. We're kidnapping you for a bit."

"Okay." She emphasizes the O by dragging it out.

When we arrive at the hotel, Jaiden comes out in a quick walk. She must've been watching for us from the windows.

Jaiden opens the passenger door after a quick wave to Sara. "What's going on?"

"Get in," I tell her.

Jaiden gives me a hard look but does as I said and shuts the door.

"You're being weird. Who died? What happened?" She looks between the both of us, waiting for one of us to spill.

I look at John, not sure what to say. How does one just come out and say that people have been beheaded and displayed on a billboard?

"It might be easier to show you." He says. Jaiden does up her seat belt as John lurches the truck forward.

Wait, no. I don't know if I want her to see it. She doesn't have to see it. Maybe if I explain everything before we get there, she can be prepared for it.

We drive back to the scene as I catch Jaiden up. "Bower asked for a meeting this morning. We met up with him and he said he had supply runners go missing, and asked if we've had any supply runners go missing. We went looking for them and found them. They're dead."

"Did you tell Bower yet?" Jaiden asks. Just as we pass Bower Mall. The men don't appear to be outside anymore.

"Dan said he would. He was one of Bower's guys. He had come with us to search. But, it's the way they were killed and displayed; you'll see." John finishes.

We come up to the display moments later.

John stops the truck, and Jaiden gets out while she keeps her eyes on the display.

She slowly creeps forward.

Maybe this was a bad idea. Should we have just told her, so she didn't have to see it? This is going to give me nightmares, maybe I should have spared her this.

John shuts off the truck and we get out of the cab. Sara and the other two join us near Jaiden.

"Shale said that Sandra was looking to discredit us using the Council emblem." Jaiden breaks the silence.

"This kind of showy violence would be bad PR," Sara says.

"Dominique, go back to Bower. Assure him that we're going to handle clean up, and see if we can find out exactly who did this. Make sure he knows none of us did this. That it was likely done under Sandra's orders." Jaiden orders me.

She's trying to get rid of me. There's no reason that has to be done right now. "No, I'm staying with you. I can talk to Bower again later, but Dan said he'd tell him it wasn't us. I'm not leaving you alone with that." I gesture towards the gruesome display.

"I'll be fine. We need to make sure our relationship with Bower isn't tarnished because of this." Jaiden says.

"He'll be fine. What if you get attacked while I'm gone?" I ask, making any excuse to stay.

"I've got help." Jaiden motions around herself at the other people.

"I'm staying." I assert heavily, before lightening up. "Besides, we haven't seen much of each other lately. And, I need some sister bonding time."

Jaiden finally takes her eyes off the billboard to frown her eyebrows at me. "You want to bond over severed head disposal? That's a bit odd."

"You've been avoiding me." I accuse.

Sara's eyes widen dramatically. She looks over away from us and our small family drama. I try not to laugh. I remember doing the same thing when friends would have tiffs with their parents while I was over.

"Have not. I've just been busy." She says.

"Whatever." I brush it off. If she's not going to tell me, then I'm not going to force her to. She likes her secrets. Maybe she's telling the truth too. She's been busy, but it still doesn't mean she couldn't have fifteen seconds to say hi, how are you doing?

"No, seriously." Jaiden looks deeper at me. "I'm not avoiding you. I've just been busy. I haven't had much time for anything. I'm sorry if I made you feel like I was avoiding you."

"Chill. I was joking." I change the subject. I didn't want to make her feel bad. Maybe she hasn't been avoiding me; it's fine either way. "So, how do we investigate this?"

There's no forensic team in the apocalypse.

"There's an allied group near here, across the road, we'll ask them if they saw anything. I'll tell Cole about it too, and have him start asking people if they heard about some missing people. Just enough information, that a guilty person would immediately picture this. Or, Connor could catch someone in a lie.

Not enough to cause a huge panic.

We'll talk to other supply leaders too. See if they might know anything.

I don't imagine we'll find much here, but we can see if there's any clues dropped nearby." Jaiden lists off some things she's come up with for a plan of action.

I have nothing to add.

"You heard her. Let's make this quick. Those heads are freaking me out." Sara orders the other two. John goes to help. The four of them walk off towards the billboard.

They scour the ground for clues as they go.

"James made it my job to figure out whatever Sandra was going to do to discredit us and stop it. He's not going to be happy about this. But, it might help us catch someone." Jaiden tells me quietly.

"Why is that your job?" I ask. Not to be mean, but she's not exactly qualified by any means.

"I don't know." At least, she knows this too.

Jaiden walks over to the billboard ladder. She reaches her hands up to grab the metal. My stomach drops.

"No. Absolutely, not." I scold Jaiden. It jolts me a little, how much I sound like mom. How many times had she said that to me? Exactly in that tone and in that way?

She quickly stops and turns around. "What?"

"You're not going up there. What if you fall?" I press.

"I'll do it." Sara volunteers.

"It's fine. I can do it." Jaiden insists.

Sara pushes her lightly out of the way and starts to climb the ladder. "If I fall off, I stand a chance of not even breaking a bone. If you fall off, you die."

"Sara." Jaiden chastises her with her name.

"Relax. I'll do the hard work. I'll throw the heads down, and you guys can catch them." Sara jokes.

"I'm not catching anything." John puts up both his hands and steps backwards.

"No one should be catching anything," Jaiden adds. "Just throw them to the ground."

"You guys are no fun," Sara shouts as she gets to the top of the ladder. She climbs to the billboard walking ledge.

On her knees, she pulls up on the pole from where it's stuck into the walkway. It takes a couple tugs before it gets free. She tosses it down.

The head lands first with a thud, kicking up dust. I grab Jaiden and pull her away from the blast zone. The others follow us out further away.

We wait until Sara pulls out all the heads before the boys go to collect them. Jaiden and I watch as Sara crawls backwards to the ladder, and makes her way down.

"What do we do with these now?" Sara asks.

"Find a dumpster?" Jaiden asks more than tells. She's unsure.

"Bury them?" I suggest. "Does Bower want them back?"

"Would you?" Jaiden answers. She obviously wouldn't, but I can't say the same. It would depend on the person. He might want them back.

The boys decide to find a dumpster for holding purposes and walk off with the poles in hand.

"What happened to the bodies?" Jaiden asks.

"Probably eaten," Sara says.

"Sandra had a dragon," I add. "They'd need to feed it somehow."

"Sandra probably took the dragon with her. Shale said she bolted after she killed Darius. She's got too much to do, to stick around here." Jaiden explains. "It might be someone else."

"Should we get the emblem cleaned up?" Sara asks.

"No. Without the heads, it should be fine." Jaiden says.

Chapter 15

It started with happening upon one picture on SuperData. A picture of me grabbing two plates from Jules. We were in the lounge a couple days ago having mystery meat and cooked canned vegetables.

I remember the moment, but not the picture. Not that I was looking at the camera.

In fact, when I clicked on the source of the shared photo, James' page, I found all sorts of pictures of me not looking at the camera. A slew of photos James has taken to show people what he's creating, and many have me featured.

He's taking credit for it all, however, and showing the shiny version of everything. Like taking a selfie with a chocolate cake Jules made, that Jules could only make a couple of because they didn't have the cocoa powder for more. But, there's a caption stating, 'Can't wait to eat more of this later!'

I can't place how I feel about being in so many pictures; especially with so many people liking the posts. People aren't talking about me in the comments, and James doesn't say anything about me in the captions. But, James also didn't ask if he could post me on his page to his one million-ish followers.

I've never had much of a social presence in the first place. Posting a couple times when I first set up an account, then forgot about it or lost interest.

There wasn't anything to keep me on it. I wasn't interested in playing non-sense time-wasting games for hours, or knowing people's thoughts on their day-to-day on-goings.

It's a bit different now, just because people's thoughts are mostly on current news. I'm finding out what is happening in the world beyond just here.

I jump up at the light bang on my door. It clicks softly before it swings open. "You ready to go?" Dominique barges in.

At least she knocked this time. "Yeah." I bound up from my seat on the bed. Putting my phone away in my pocket, I follow Dominique into the chilly outdoors.

She drives us across the highway to Gasoline Alley; the quintessential truck stop neighbourhood. It has seen many a trucker stop by, but also families stopping through on their way to Calgary; at least when they were coming from Leduc and area looking for a halfway point to stretch their legs.

The windmill parking lot is nearly full. Jesse likes doing his business inside the old donut shop.

I kind of wish they still made the donuts. Maybe they've got a recipe they could revive one of these days.

For just a moment, I could pretend that Dominique and I are on a road trip. We heard about the legendary donuts at the windmill and just had to stop on our way to Calgary.

The illusion is set easily from the outside. The parking lot is busy, just like it would have been.

Though, with the freshly falling blanket of snow, it doesn't feel like a summertime road trip. Maybe, there's a wintertime event at the zoo we planned to visit.

I wonder what happened to the zoo, and all the animals? They would have already been winterized when everything happened. Some of the zoo keepers might've stuck around to help some of the animals survive. Though it might've started getting hard to feed some of them.

Dominique shuts off the parked vehicle and quickly gets out. I follow suit, after her to the entrance of the shop. She opens the doors ahead of me, letting me through first. I open the second set of doors, go through first, and hold it open for her.

The moment I step through the second set of doors, I hear a loud greeting of my name. "Jaiden!"

Immediately, I pinpoint Jesse at a table in the corner. I give him a short wave and start over that way. "Hi, Jesse," I say when I get close.

"How are you?" Jesse asks just as boisterous as the rest of the crowd.

"Good, personally." I specify. "How are you?"

"I'm well, thank you. What can I do for you this chilly afternoon?" Jesse leans back, stretching his arms out to lie against the back of the bench.

I tell him. "One of the other leaders had some people go missing the other day. We found them across the highway, and they were beheaded and the heads were lined up."

Jesse picks up before I can finish my whole thought. "With the Council emblem, yeah. We came across that too. Didn't know it was your people, though I suppose it's all our people now, isn't it?"

"Yeah." I ignore the likely jab attached to the question. He might not have meant it that way; benefit of the doubt. Then again, the comment was a bit out of the way of linear thinking.

Jesse answers the question I didn't get the chance to ask. "No, we haven't come across anything like that before. But," he taps his finger at me, before folding his hands together to rest on his elbows. "I'll be honest with you, since you seem to be in the business of investigating missing people, we've had people go missing all winter.

We had assumed it was Jerry, but another couple of people have been missing for two days. Always the same, they go out for a supply run and we never see them again. Sometimes we find their truck, but no sign of them."

That's the same day the others went missing.

"I wonder if some of the people we rescued from the gym were from here?" Dominique asks me.

"None of them have mentioned anything. And, those who chose to leave would have probably been back here by now. Or, they would have taken one of the offers to return them to nearby homes." I reason. If they had been from here, they would have returned by now; if they wanted to return.

I don't know anything about Jesse, other than he's loud and boisterous. So, I can't speak to whether he's a kind leader, or not.

"Could be Sandra?" Dominique suggests.

"No, she was spotted back in Edmonton around that time," James said he saw a post about it. That Sandra was spotted back in Edmonton two days ago. The timeline on that would make her innocent. Though theoretically possible with a dragon, I don't see her doing these things while running back and forth.

"But, that doesn't mean that everyone following her left," Dominique adds.

I ask Jesse for more information. "Where have you been finding their vehicles? Is there any pattern?"

"No pattern we could figure out, but you might have better luck. The last one was found in a housing community just north of us. Take Jack and Cassie with you. They can show you where." A man and a woman come up to the table holding hands; I assume Jack and Cassie. "And, show them some of the other areas we know the others should have been around when they disappeared."

"That would be great; thank you. Maybe we can find some answers for everyone." I say.

I tap Dominique on her arm to signal her to get out. She gets out of the bench so that I can too.

"It would be nice if people stopped disappearing," Jesse says.

"Yeah, that would be nice." I commiserate.

Jack and Cassie follow us out to the parking lot. Jack points to an orange beat-up truck. "That's us. Let's take it, so we save on gas. It's about five minutes from here. Not far, but why waste."

"Sounds great," Dominique agrees. We get into their truck. It's tight to fit us all into the one seat, but we manage.

Jack starts the truck. We pull out of the parking lot.

While we haven't had that much of an issue with our people disappearing, it seems that other groups have. Those groups now belong to us, so it means we now have an issue with it.

But, with Bower having people disappear and Jesse saying he's had people disappearing all winter, we could have a bigger problem.

Jerry's hotel was too transient to really know if people were disappearing. And, we grew too quickly to grasp if people were disappearing or just leaving. Maybe some of ours have disappeared and we didn't know it; people we figured had just decided to leave or we haven't realized disappeared.

I'll have to check with the other leaders to find out if they've also had people disappearing, and if people are still disappearing.

Some we could write off as Sandra and Jerry, but if it's still happening we could have a bigger problem.

And, that bigger problem is likely multiple problems.

The differences in circumstances are far too different to likely be the same person doing it. The same person making people disappear without a trace all winter, isn't likely going to be the same person who decided to decapitate people and make a showy display out of them.

That makes at least two separate issues. If not, more.

People disappearing from multiple locations around the city could be the work of multiple separate people, animals, or creatures.

"Do you have any leads?" Jack asks.

"No, sorry." Dominique answers.

I debate answering but ultimately decide to keep quiet about my theories. Speculation won't do anyone any good.

Chapter 16

I try to see the air flow like Margie suggests. See the air wrapping around the paper airplane, as I push it around. But, I can't see anything.

I can't do it.

Every time I fly passed the window, the airplane sharply turns in whichever direction I'm trying to fly it.

I lose control and it crashes.

I growl in frustration.

I don't want to be in here practicing my magic. I want to be outside. I can practice outside, but Margie doesn't want to take me out into the cold and snow. Or rather, Margie doesn't want to be outside.

Why would you want to be outside in this weather? She had asked in that tone adults use when they're trying to mock your dumb idea without saying that it's a stupid idea.

Why would you not want to be outside in the snow? I would have asked, but I didn't want to risk back-talking and getting in trouble.

She's old. She doesn't understand that this is the fun type of snowfall. The last snow of the year when everything had previously melted is the best type of snow. The type of snow you know isn't going to hang around for more than a few days at most.

This isn't like the snow that comes in January when you are already sick and tired of the cold and snow.

You need to take advantage of it while you can, before snow doesn't come around again for five or six months.

"Rayleen, again," Margie says from behind her book.

"Can't we just go outside for a few minutes?" I plead.

Margie puts her book down on her lap with a finger in between the pages; a look of scorn creasing every edge of her face.

"I'm bored, and I wanna play in the snow." My foot picks up and stomps down.

"That's enough!" Her voice booms thickly. "I know you're bored. Learning isn't always fun, but it's something you have to do. You are far behind what you should be doing at your age, and you won't get caught up if you don't take this seriously.

Do you want to lose the ability to do magic? Because that's what happens when you don't exercise your magic muscles."

"We've been doing this for hours and I don't understand why I can't just take a small break," I add.

"You've only been at it for an hour. Do you think you deserve to have a break after only an hour of learning?"

"Yes," I say.

Margie opens her mouth. Her shoulders rise with a sharp intake of air, before falling as the air is pushed out quickly. "I'm done. I can't deal with you today. You don't want to be here, fine. I'm not going to force you, because I don't want to deal with you.

I'm trying to do something nice for you and teach you magic so James will be proud of your progress, but you're just focused on playing in that damn snow.

So go for a walk. Go play in the snow. But, you have to be back in a half hour, long before Dominique comes to pick you up.”

“A half an hour?” I ask. That’s a long time.

“Yeah, go.” Margie thrusts a finger up to point at me. “As long as this stays our little secret. Dominique doesn’t need to know, or she’ll stop letting you come and won’t let you learn magic. And, you’ll have to stay with her all the time, even though all the boring stuff she does.”

I’m a bit nervous, but I don’t want to lose my chance.

I leave out Margie’s door once I get my jacket and boots on. Taking a final look at the door while closed, and it’s done.

I don’t know exactly what to do with myself now. I start walking down the hall.

I wonder what would be more boring; training with Margie or going with Dominique? I think it’s more of a matter of danger. That’s why I have to stay with Margie.

She seemed much nicer when I was first learning. When Alexa was bringing me. Before, when James was watching. Or, even when Dominique was watching.

I don’t know what I did to make her not like training me.

The lounge is a bit busy. Music comes into the lobby from the open doors. They’ve decided to play disk music today.

I pass by quickly, hoping no one I know is in there. Not only do I have to avoid Dominique, but anyone else who might tell her that they saw me out and about by myself.

I slip through the hotel doors. Immediately, the chilled air washes over me. The cold air fills my lungs in a pleasant hug. It brings a smile to my mouth.

Snow covers everything. It’s only been snowing a few hours, but the snow is thick enough that I can’t see the ground underneath. The flakes fall big and fluffy from the grey sky.

I walk over to one of the cars and brush my fingers against the snow on the hood. Four hills swiped into the otherwise perfect blanket.

I point my finger like a pencil and carve my name. Then, a heart, a star, and a kitten.

I draw until my finger is too cold. I cup my hands together and blow hot air into them. The cold air quickly takes away the warmth.

A thought hits me and I wonder.

I breathe three hot breaths into my hands, concentrating on the flow of my breath. The air swirls around in a ball in my hand, holding the heat for longer.

I try again and hold it for longer.

My smile grows, and a heat swells inside my chest. I'm doing magic and it's fun.

This is how it should be.

I try again. Moving the air faster holds the heat longer. I concentrate on speeding the warm air faster.

I squeak when pain registers on my hand. The fast air turned too hot to touch. I throw my hand into the snow to quickly cool it down.

"Are you alright?" A man asks suddenly. I jump at his question.

"Yes," I say.

He looks around. "Where's your parents? You shouldn't be outside by yourself."

"Dead," I answer his question blankly.

"Sorry." He frowns. "The people taking care of you, they're in the hotel, yeah?"

"Yes," I say.

"You should get back inside then. You never know what's lurking outside these days." He turns his body to stand off to the side a bit. He watches and waits for me to go.

My shoulders drop. I guess my fun is over.

I don't want to get in trouble, so I go back inside the hotel. But, just barely. I know I haven't used up my whole half hour yet, and I'm not in a rush to return.

Off to the side of the doors, are some benches built to line the windows. I sit in a spot, to watch the snow fall.

Curling up my knees, I rest my arms onto, and my head atop them. My back rests against the wall.

The grey skies pour the snow onto the city, and people rush to get inside buildings or vehicles from other vehicles or buildings.

"Wake up," Margie exclaims. I jolt off the bench and up to standing, nearly knocking into her. "You were supposed to be back twenty minutes ago. Thankfully, Dominique didn't show up early, or you'd be in deep trouble. Falling asleep; what were you thinking?"

"I'm sorry." I apologize. "I didn't mean to sleep."

I didn't realize I had fallen asleep; I'm still not sure that I did. It only felt like a blink.

I follow Margie back to her room. She doesn't talk the whole way back, so I make sure I don't talk. Every now and then, I think I hear a grumble.

I know I'm in deep trouble, and I don't want to make it any worse.

I take off my coat and boots, and put them away. I rush to the desk and wait for Margie to finish getting settled back in.

She goes back to her seat and book.

"Maybe, since you got a nap in, you'll be able to focus better." Margie pauses. I don't know what to say, if I should say anything. "You'll resume lessons until Dominique arrives. Start with the airplane; right where you left off."

Margie goes back to reading her book, and not paying me any attention.

Chapter 17

"This was where we found their truck, but there was no sign of them." Cassie points ahead of us on the snowy road.

There's no longer any truck there. They must've brought it back already.

"We'll drive around the neighbourhood. Look for any tracks. If something is out there, we'll find them." Jack tells us.

"Only if they've moved around since it started snowing, and if the falling snow hasn't covered them up." Cassie reminds him.

"True." They smile sweetly at each other. He puts his hand over into her lap palm up. Cassie smacks down to hold his hand.

Jack continues up the road three houses. The truck sharply pulls to the right.

"Fuck!" Jack sharply exclaims. He pulls his hand away from Cassie to put it on the steering wheel as he breaks hard.

He shuts off the truck and tells us, "Wait inside." Jack gets out, and Cassie follows a moment later. The cool air fills the truck.

I decide to get out too. It's just a flat tire. I know that sharp jerks of a vehicle usually mean that, and that we probably have a long walk back.

Maybe we should have taken two vehicles.

I scoot over to the driver's side and leave the truck.

Making my way over to the other side of the truck, my foot kicks against something on the ground. I look down and see something sticking out of the snow. Moving the snow around it with my foot, I see a jagged piece of sharp metal. That must've been what we hit.

I pick it up and toss it into the back of the truck. No one needs to be stepping on that. I'm glad I didn't step on that.

I get around to the other side of the truck and confirm the flat. The tire rim lies nearly flat against the ground. A piece of metal like that would put a large gash in a tire.

Jaiden stays inside for a moment more before she decides to get out too. She quickly stops to pick something up; another piece of jagged metal.

We need to be careful where we step. Who knows how many of those are out here hidden in the snow?

"Do you have a spare?" I ask Jack and Cassie.

"No. I used it last month. Fucking snow covering debris." Cassie rubs her hand against his back. He takes a breath in and out. "Well, I guess we scavenge a tire."

"Did Bailey put the jack back in the truck?" Cassie asks.

Jack stares at Cassie for a moment before dropping his shoulders. "I guess we are also looking for a jack."

"Might be quicker to walk back and get help?" I suggest.

"Yeah, maybe. We'll do that if we don't have any luck out here. Cassie you go with Shorty, I'll go with her, that way, if we find anyone we can recognize them. And, they can recognize us." Jack suggests. He points to the right of the road for them, and the left for us.

"Yeah," Cassie says.

"Sounds good," I say.

I partner up to follow Jake. We go off to the driver's side of the road.

I scan the ground but don't see any footprints, or any disturbances in the snow. I keep in mind the jagged metal; there might be more.

Too bad there wasn't snow on the ground when the other group broke down, would've been easier to track down what happened to them with a trail.

"Did you search much around here when you first discovered the truck?" I ask Jack as we go through a gate.

"Yeah, we looked a little. But, there wasn't anything to go by." He informs me.

"Was it a blown tire as well?" I ask curiously.

"No. No, it was a hose issue." Jack says. "None of that debris was on the road a couple days ago. Not that I remember seeing, anyway."

It was probably there, he just didn't see them before.

"Okay, well, I'll check the house for the people. Do you want to check the garage for what we need?" I ask.

Jack turns around. "Honestly, don't bother looking too hard. Don't tell Jesse I said anything, but I don't think they're alive. I'm out here because Jesse asked, and that's all.

The guys who disappeared weren't amateurs. I've never seen anyone as good with a knife as Frank was, took down quite a few rogues by himself. And, Randy, once took a bullet to the chest and kept going, finished his supply run, got back, and had a drink before he'd let anyone go near him to properly fix the hole in his chest. Just those two alone, they aren't guys that wouldn't come back for no reason at all. If they don't come back, even if they got hung up the night before, because they didn't come back the next day, it means they're dead.

Jesse holds out hope because he is very much a man who

doesn't leave anyone behind. It's against his code. So, until we find proof, one way or the other, he's not going to let this go.

He's got a list of names of people who have disappeared without a trace, and at least once a week he's setting up a new mission to see if we can find those people.

But, you can use your brain too. Four capable guys, disappear without a trace; except for a broken-down truck with no supplies in it. That means, they either broke down early in the run, my bet, or they didn't find anything at all for however many hours of searching. Or, they were killed and robbed.

We're, what, maybe a twenty-minute walk from home. Guys who wouldn't get lost, and are stubborn as hell. And, capable fighters and survivors.

If those guys don't come back from a mission, you assume they are dead, right?"

It would make the most sense. "Yeah, probably. Or, taken. We've had quite a few people taken."

"Even taken, what are the chances they come back alive?" Jack asks.

"I did. Rayleen has twice now. It's not entirely impossible." He stares. "Sorry, to play devil's advocate."

Jack shakes off the stare. "No, sorry, I was processing. Um, I'm sorry you were kidnapped. I had no idea. None of our people have ever come back."

"Not something I like to advertise. But, I'm just saying it's not entirely impossible that they're alive and are going to make it." I add. "But, I do get what you're saying as well."

He smiles with his mouth shut and nods. "You want to check the house?"

"Sure," I say. I go to the door of the house, as he goes to the garage.

The white wooden door is locked. I knock on it a few loud

times. Waiting, hopeful that the door will open, while listening for any commotion inside.

When nothing happens and no noise sounds, I look in through the windows.

There's no sign of anything going on inside; no movement through the open curtains. Dust gathers on the cabinet beneath the window, with nothing looking like it's moved in months.

Glass shatters. I jump in place and whip my head towards the noise. Jack has broken a window with a rock. He clears out the pane, before reaching inside to unlock the door. He opens the door and goes inside.

Should I also break the glass to get inside? No, I think just a moment later. If it doesn't look like anything is happening inside the house, then there may be no point.

Right now, the house is sealed to the elements and creatures. Any break in the window could destroy anything valuable inside if left open like that.

If the guys were inside the house alive, then they'd be alerted by my knocks. They would check us out in secret, then come out when they see Jack.

Besides, assuming the house has been locked since the beginning, they too would have had to break in too. There's no sight of that on this side of the house, nor in the front.

I leave the small porch to go inside the garage.

I brush off collecting snow from my hair.

He pulls out a small cylinder jack from a shelf. "No good. Not big enough for the truck."

"It's not big enough?" I ask.

Jack keeps looking around the garage as he explains. "Nah, our truck is higher than their car. I'm going to need, preferably a floor jack. I was hoping they might've had a truck that's just not here, but guess not. We'll try at the next house."

"WHO ARE YOU?" A voice booms from the doorway. I jump and turn around. A manly silhouette blocks some of the light coming into the garage. He steps in further, becoming clearer and more of a person with each step inside.

The old man holds a hunting gun up from his black puffy jacketed chest.

"Who are you?" Jack asks. He slowly shuffles over to me. The gun follows Jack's every move, as he moves himself to the front of me.

The man tilts his gun up and to the side, his other hand coming up. It gives a false sense of safety. I know at any moment, he could shift it again, and shoot.

"I don't want any trouble. Is that your truck with the flat?" The man asks.

"Yes," Jack answers.

"What were you doing in the area?" He asks.

"Looking for someone who disappeared around here a few days ago. Did you see anyone?" Jack asks.

"No, but my wife might've." The old man's voice loses all roughness and drops down in octaves. The quick change is a surprise, but I realize that he wanted to intimidate us until he figured out why we were here, and if we are a danger. "She's always got her nose out the window. We can go ask her. Come. We've got a fire going. Might have some food to share. Get you out of this storm for a bit." We hesitate. "I might have a spare tire you could use. God knows, I don't use my truck anymore."

"Do you have a floor jack?" Jack asks.

"Yeah, of course. Don't have a spare kit?" The man asks.

"Not anymore. I used the spare tire last month and forgot the jack at home. I've got the tire iron with me, but that's it." Jack explains.

"Good. I used to use an impact, so I didn't have a use for a tire iron. But, I doubt there's battery left."

"Cool," Jack says. "We've got two others with us. They went looking across the road. We should let them know."

The old man nods. "The more the merrier."

The man leads us back out to the road. Cassie momentarily lights up with excitement when she initially spots us, before it's doused out. I think, when she realizes it's not anyone we were looking for.

"Hi." She gives a short wave as we meet in the middle. Cassie looks at Jack expectantly; waiting for an introduction.

Jaiden follows cautiously behind. Standing a few feet back as she silently checks over the older man.

"I'm sorry, I didn't get your name." Jack apologizes.

"I didn't give it. But, it's John." The man says.

"John says he has a possible tire for us to use, and a jack. He's also got a wife at home, who might have an idea about our missing friends." Jack catches Cassie and Jaiden up.

"Oh, that's so nice of you. Thank you so much!" Cassie beams again.

"No thanks needed. It's just nice to see some lovely faces around here. You know, it's been months since I've talked to someone who isn't my wife." John says.

"That must be lonely sometimes." Cassie commiserates.

"Not at all. Don't tell the wife, but she talks enough that I should never need to talk to another for as long as she lives." John smiles at his own joke.

"That's good. It sounds like she likes to chat." Cassie says.

"She'll be excited to see you. I'm not much in the way of being a good conversationalist." John leads us down the road a little bit to a house a few houses away. He must've seen us, or his wife did, from the window.

I line up to walk beside Jaiden. She ducks in behind me when we get to the footstep-carved walkway in the snow.

John leads us inside through the front door. "Leave your shoes on. Too damn cold in here to take them off. Don't mind the mess."

"John." His wife scolds him with his name.

"Mary." John tries to mock her tone. "These are the people who belong to that truck. No spare tire and no jack. Lovely people."

Mary loosens up and smiles. John must've gone out to make sure we weren't murderers or pillagers. "Come in, you must be cold and wet. Like John said, don't mind the mess. Leave your shoes on. We stopped taking ours off shortly after the power went out."

They usher us in through the tiny entry area to the living room. Jaiden stays behind to stomp off as much snow as possible from her boots.

"Sit. Get comfortable. Now that you're here, you might as well take a moment. Must've been quite the fright to have your tire blow like that?

The cold and snow doesn't help. You must be freezing. Normally, I'd have hot water ready to go, but no one was expecting the snow, and we moved the fire pit outside. The snow put out the fire, would you believe that? But, it would take no time at all to get something going."

Mary excuses herself to disappear around the corner. I hear a few things clanking in the kitchen. John sits down in a recliner chair, and gets comfortable nearest to the roaring fire.

Cassie sits down in a huff on their couch. I decide to sit on the other side of the couch. Jack sits closer to Cassie.

"Are you sure you don't mind? We don't want to put you out. We could quickly go get the tire and be out of your hair." Jaiden suggests.

"Not at all. We could use the company. It's not often anyone comes around anymore." John waves her off.

I lean back to get comfortable.

Jaiden stands awkwardly where she has entered the room. "Jaiden, have a seat." I urge her softly.

She does but sits delicately, yet stiffly, at the very edge of the couch.

Mary comes back into the room with a glass container. She offers the contents to Jack and Cassie first. "Moose jerky? John makes our own. We have a smoker out back. Helps to keep the meat fresher longer."

Jack and Cassie each take one, thank her and take a bite.

"That you complained about when I first bought it." John reminds Mary.

"It stayed in storage for the first five years we had it. I told you you weren't going to use it." Mary gestures the canister towards me to take one, but I shake my head. "It took the end of society for you to finally use it."

"No, thank you." I politely decline. I'm not really hungry, and I've never really liked beef jerky anyway.

"I use it now." He reminds her.

"You do. And, it's delicious." She tilts the canister towards me again. "Take one dear."

"No, thank you. I'm a vegetarian." I decline with an excuse.

"No, you aren't." Mary accuses.

"I am." I insist.

"Impossible." She insists.

"Leave the girl be, she's trying to politely decline our food. If she's not hungry, she doesn't have to eat. Sorry, my wife has this thing about feeding people." John tries to assist.

"That's okay. I mostly live on canned fruits and veggies, and granola bars these days, so I get why." I continue with the ruse. I will eat meat nowadays. I started up during the winter after a nurse insisted I start up before I became nutrient deficient. I'm not going to starve myself and deteriorate just to not eat meat. The world isn't built for vegetarians right now. But, I still try to limit meat consumption; especially mystery meat.

"What were you doing out in this storm?" Mary changes the subject as she offers a jerky to Jaiden. Jaiden takes one. She lightly thanks her and takes a bite.

"We were looking for some people who went missing a couple days ago. Have you seen anyone around?" Jack asks.

Mary frowns momentarily. "No, I'm sorry. I wish I did."

"That's okay." He insists.

"If you don't mind me asking, what are you still doing here; in your house?" Jaiden asks.

"Our kids were born and raised here. We plan on dying here." John explains stubbornly.

How did she know it was their house? The answer comes quickly as I look around the room. Plenty of pictures on the walls feature a man and a woman who look very much like younger versions of our hosts. Others, are featured by themselves or with other people and with one or both of our hosts. I imagine the others are their children and their family.

Mary explains. "When everything started happening, we couldn't get ahold of our children. I figured, that if they were still alive, and we stayed here, then they would know where to find us."

"Did they?" Cassie asks.

"No." Mary quickly pushes out.

"Sorry." She says.

"Oh, don't be. I still hold hope that they're alive and well somewhere." Mary says. "What about you?"

"We live in a hotel, with lots of people. A community." Cassie explains.

"What about your homes, your family?" Mary asks.

Jaiden interrupts the topic. "I'm sorry, do you have a bathroom or something I could use?"

"Oh, of course, Dear. Follow me." Jaiden gets up to follow. "The plumbing doesn't work, you'll have to excuse that. But, we have a bucket." Her words trail off when they get too far to hear. I make a note to make sure that I don't have to go to the bathroom while here.

"So, you have two sons and a daughter?" Cassie asks.

I look on the TV stand and see a few pictures of the same assortment of people. The daughter has a couple kids of her own and a husband. But the sons, twins just appear with each other, alone, or in family portraits.

John glances over to the portraits with a small smile. "Elizabeth, she was our little princess. She went to school to become an accountant and met a doctor at University. She quit school to be a stay-at-home mom after they got married and had Kayla. He became a prominent foot doctor.

The twins were little shits. Clark and Joey. Growing up, those two were always in trouble."

"The trouble didn't stop when they were grown." Mary continues as she comes back into the room. "It just changed from painting murals on the wall with their poop when they were two, to putting hair dye in conditioner or whatever new prank idea they had next."

"Do you remember when they toilet-papered our house?" John asks.

"The school had an officer come to their school to tell them not to toilet paper people's houses for Halloween, but it backfired. Just gave the boys the idea to do it to our own house. Can't face charges when it's your own property." Mary shakes her head. "Grounded them for a month though, and they had to clean it up."

"I'm just glad it was toilet paper and not eggs," John says.

"Could you imagine the smell come summer?" Mary asks the room rhetorically. "We'd of been hosing down everything as soon as spring hit."

Mary pauses and then continues with another story. "I still can't believe they got that car into their school gym.

In high school, they had a shop class to learn about cars. By the end of grade twelve, they were experts in taking the car apart and putting it back together. So, they enlisted help, never told anyone who it was, but they stayed late at school, told us they had a school-sanctioned sleepover, and disassembled the shop's car, and relocated it into the gym.

The boys were so proud of themselves and bragged about it. School was good-humoured, and didn't suspend them."

"Suspending them could've risked them graduating. They didn't want to risk them having to redo a semester." John points out.

"Hey, sorry." Jaiden apologizes for interrupting again. "I've got to go grab something from the truck, I'll be back really quick."

"Something wrong, dear?" Mary asks.

"Girl problems," Jaiden explains.

"I'll go with you." I offer. "You shouldn't go alone; never know what's out there."

Jaiden nods. "We'll be back soon."

We leave the house in a quick rush of cold.

"How did you know it was their house?" I ask to fill the void. I know how, but I hadn't thought to notice those details until it came up.

"They had pictures of themselves, and probably their kids, everywhere," Jaiden explains.

"Did you look for it, or did you happen to notice?" I ask.

"I looked for it. I was curious about who we might be dealing with." Jaiden says.

So, she looked for clues to who they were. And, made sure the story lined up.

"You didn't have a bag or anything with you." I realize. "What would you need to grab from the truck?"

Jaiden looks over her shoulder quickly. "Ah, nothing. I just needed a way to get their address, that wasn't suspicious."

"Why?"

"Just in case." She explains simply yet vaguely.

"Just in case of what?" I push. Did she see something? Did she have a dream about them?

"Nothing." Jaiden tries to stop there, but I look hard at her. "I just, have a weird feeling. And, I thought I heard some howling noises coming from the vents. Got spooked."

"It's an old creaky house. It's bound to make noises. There's wind. Wind can make howling noises." I try to help.

"Which, is why it's probably nothing, and I'm just being paranoid." She reasons.

"Yeah, you are. They're cute. They're a nice, sweet old couple. They don't have a mean bone in their frail bodies. What are they going to do?"

"Like I said, paranoid. But, I'd rather be paranoid and have John know exactly where we are, than not paranoid and we become the people who disappeared with only a broken down truck left behind as a clue. Besides, old people always creeped me out." Jaiden's last note surprises me.

I chuckle as I ask. "What? How?"

"I don't know. But, old people have always freaked me out. And, they're usually mean or weird."

"You know you're going to get old one day." I remind her.

"Probably not."

"Jaiden!" I scold.

"The chance we make it long enough to be old and frail is slim to none." She insists.

"Aren't you the pessimist?"

Jaiden points with a tap of her finger. "I prefer realist. Because statistically, I'm right. This world, has no place for someone who can't take care of themselves or defend themselves. Let alone, if you have dementia, a stroke, or a heart attack. Or, fall down and break a hip. You're relying on other people to take care of you, and they will only do so for as long as they want, or have the sympathy to, or have the physical capability to. Given the people around us, and cultural norms from before, who'd be willing to do that?"

"John might," I say before I can think it through.

"As he grows old and frail with us. You guys are going down first. I'm the youngest."

I look over to her in fake shocked dismay. "Maybe our kids will take care of us. Be a good auntie, and maybe they'll take care of you too."

"Are you back together?" Jaiden asks.

I look ahead of us and take a deep breath. How do I explain what we are when I don't even know what we are? John and I haven't had that conversation yet. And I don't even know what I want. The words had just slipped out without much thought. "I don't know. It's complicated."

"But, you're thinking about kids together?"

Kids went with the joke. I hadn't read that much into it. "It's complicated. Don't tell him I said anything."

"I won't," Jaiden promises. "But, back on track. I needed the address, so I can text it to John. I texted them while I was in the bathroom the general area, just in case, but I wanted them to know the exact address. So, I'll send that off when I get inside the truck, and I told them I'd text them if we needed a rescue."

Jaiden gets inside the truck and texts John, while I wait outside. She's quickly done, and we go back to the house.

As we approach, I see Mary in the window, watching us. Has she been there the whole time? That's sweet that she wanted to watch out for us.

We make it back inside. Cassie and Jack are gone, but Mary and John are still here.

"Did Jack and Cassie go to the garage?" I ask as I sit back in the same spot as before, while Jaiden kicks off the snow from her boots.

"Tires were no good. Cracked and blow from sitting for so long. Jack said they'd run home to grab a vehicle, and come back for you." John explains.

Jaiden gives me a pointed look as she comes around. I turn my head to ignore her, before her gesture becomes rude. Weirdo.

"Well, that's great, thanks for letting us know," I say.

"I'll be right back. Just have to go to the washroom again." Jaiden says. I watch her go.

"It's nice having some company. You don't realize how lonely it gets." Mary says.

I go to respond, but end up yawning. "Sorry."

"Do you drink tea?" Mary stands up.

"Yes, I do." More so now, than ever before.

"Great! I'll put on some tea. It'll help warm your bones and get some caffeine in you." Mary leaves down the hall.

Chapter 18

My eyes slowly open to dark blurs. I try blinking away the fuzziness, and while things do sharpen slightly, the world view is still blurry.

I can't move my hands to slide my glasses up my nose. They are stuck behind my back with something biting at my wrists.

Where's my glasses?

A piercing ringing lowers until it disappears. Nausea waivers with it.

My head hurts in multiple spots and in multiple ways.

Thoughts move sluggishly through resistance in my head, like walking through an ocean.

"Hm. Looks like we didn't hit this one too hard." A smooth male voice jests.

A large figure comes in front of me. I see him reaching for me, my glasses focusing into view in his hands. I hold still so he can put them on my face.

Once he's clear, I recognize him. He's one of the twins from the pictures upstairs. He has dark wet stains down the front of his apron.

Beyond him, is his duplicate. The light is over near the other twin. A lantern creates a bright glow in one spot around the room.

My eyes adjust and bring focus slowly.

Cassie hangs from the ceiling. A hook protrudes out through her mouth. Blood covers half her face.

My own mouth slack jaws open with surprise and horror.

The twin in front of me notices where I'm staring. He backs away and off to the side to give me a fuller view. "This one had to die, because he would put up way too much of a fight."

The other twin smacks down a massive knife. He grunts as he separates the elbow. He uses the forearm to point at Cassie. "She was an accident. Idiot whacked her too hard."

The one closer to me shrugs. "It's been a while since I've had to keep them alive."

"Don't worry. We'll keep you alive. We have plenty of meat to last us a few months. It's better when we can eat you while you're fresh." He chuckles. "Actually, funny story. All of this was an accident.

If you hadn't of left the house, we wouldn't have come upstairs thinking everyone left. We had enough meat, from a bunch of dudes we caught the other day, to last us a long while. So we really didn't need you guys, but, oh well. Guess we're keeping back stock now."

"Might become family before we ever end up needing to eat her." One says to the other. "Either way, she won't go to waste."

A door pulls open sharply. "Boys!" Mary yells down the stairs. They jumpstart and sprint up the stairs.

Dominique.

I look around quickly. Much of the basement is in dark shadow. The windows seem like they are covered lightly from the outside; maybe just the snow. The only measurable light comes from a fire lantern on the cutting table.

But it's enough that I can figure out that she's not down here.

Feet pound against the ceiling. One thump hits larger than all the others.

I pull at the tight restraints on my wrists, but they don't budge. My ankles are tied together too. I scoot my butt flush against the pole holding me sitting upright.

Trying to twist enough with hips and hands to reach the phone in my pocket, fails. I lean over with my shoulder on the ground. My wrists scream in pain, I twist and try to reach the top of my phone case, but it still doesn't work.

I pull myself back upright.

The world spins around my head. I feel like I'm going to pass out. Breathing in and out deeply, I focus on staying still and staying awake.

Survival could depend on me staying conscious right now.

I glare down at my pocket. It's so close. If I could reach it, I could call for help.

John got the address message I sent him in the truck. A vibrate against my leg while we were walking back to the house told me that he answered back. That's why I was going to the bathroom again. That, and to keep up my girl problem ruse.

I told him not to come; before I sent the full address. But now, if I could only send him another message. Get a call out while they are distracted, so I could keep my phone.

It's too quiet upstairs now. I hope the big thud wasn't Dominique.

I huff. Yelling won't help. We're out numbered. I'm out, so it's Dominique against four people, unless there's more of them hidden somewhere.

If I live, if she lives, I'm going to ask Dominique if she still thinks that old people are cute.

I hope she gets out. She could get help. She would be safe.

It sounds like they plan on keeping me alive; at least for a while. Maybe I could be rescued before anything permanent happens.

Chapter 19

Alexa is dead. But, she is still here; inside of me. Not alive, but her memories are alive. They are part of my memories now. I just need to separate her memories from mine, and I will be fine.

I sigh internally. I think Margie just wanted some quiet time, and made an excuse to have mindful meditation. She told me what to think about, and I have, but it's boring and nothing new.

My mind runs through her words and nothing else. She told me to find memories and separate them, but nothing comes up.

I want Dominique. People were saying she disappeared with Jaiden. But, no one knows where. James isn't concerned. He said they'll be fine, but it's been hours.

Dominique was only supposed to be gone for an hour or two, but I feel like it's starting to get close to supper; not that I want to ask Margie. But, it's dark outside.

She has been getting crankier and grumpier as time has passed. "I did my time with my own children. I'm fine with training but I'm not a free babysitter. They can't just dump you on me anytime they want, and run away." She has said, amoungst many other things.

"I'm done." Margie's sudden outburst brings me up to lean on my elbows to look at her. I keep my mouth shut. "You're basically eighteen, you have the memories of one anyway. So why are they treating you like you're two? There's no reason why I have to be the one to watch you. It's basically your bed time anyway, right? So, I'm going to send you home, and you can go to bed. Alright? Up you go."

I don't know what to say. I feel like this is going to get me in trouble with Dominique. I was supposed to stay with Margie, but she's telling me to go back. She's in charge. We have to listen to adults; they always know best.

I get up and put my boots on near the door. Margie comes out to the hall with me, and to the lobby doors. We go just outside.

"Go. I'll watch you go back to your hotel, to make sure you get there safe. You go straight to bed." Margie points at me and points to the hotel.

I want to argue, but I know it won't help. And, Margie hates it when I whine.

"Thank you. Good night." I say. I walk back to the hotel. Before I cross the road, I look back. Margie isn't there.

A chill creeps up my back.

I dash across the road and into the hotel and up the stairs. I go inside Dominique's room and finally feel safer. Yet, not entirely. No one is here. I get ready for bed, like I should.

Curious, I go out into the hall and look around. No one is around, though I know I heard people in the lobby.

I go into Alexa's room; my room. I crawl into the bed and smell the blankets. They still smell like Alexa. I wrap the blankets around me tightly, just like a hug.

For a moment, I can pretend. It won't hurt anyone to pretend she's alive and with me.

Chapter 20

Jaiden should've been back by now.

She only had to pretend to go to the bathroom, right?

To stick to her story?

I don't have a clock; wish I did. For the first time in months, I wish I had my phone or a watch. I had gotten used to going without.

I look around the living room, but the only clock is a glass one on a shelf. None of the hands have moved, so the 2:14 time displayed is unreliable. Must be broken or out of batteries.

It's hard to know exactly how much time has passed, but it feels like it's been too long.

Maybe, I'm being paranoid now.

Jaiden put thoughts into my head. She's probably just texting John, and he's responding, so it's taking a bit longer. Maybe she's convincing him not to show up without being needed.

And, he won't be needed.

These people, Mary and John, are such a lovely old couple. They are couple goals. They've been together for their whole adult lives. They have three kids. And, they playfully bicker at each other. And, they reminisce about their wonderful life together.

But, I can't shake the growing dread gnawing away in my stomach.

"I'm going to see if Mary needs help," I tell John as I get up.

"Nonsense. She knows how to make tea." John says. "Sit down." His order comes out a bit too gruff and insistent.

"I also have to use the washroom, but I thought helping out might be a more polite way to excuse myself." I flash a bashful smile.

"Down that way, through the kitchen, then second door to the left. Holler if you get lost, and I will show you." John instructs.

I follow where he says to go.

Mary isn't in the kitchen. I wonder if she's making the tea over a fire in the back.

I go beyond and find the open doored bathroom.

No Jaiden.

Do they have another bathroom she would be using? Maybe a bathroom connected to one of the bedrooms?

As I peer over to the other doors, I spot something out of place. A bat lies on the heavily stained carpeted floor by a decorative table. I pick it up by the handle. There is something dark on the hitting end. I poke it and smear it. A bright red glistens from the thinner spots.

My heart drops.

Jaiden.

All my senses rise up in defence.

Methodically, I sneak my way into each of the other rooms on this end of the house. Bat held at the ready to beat anyone if I need to. But, no one is there.

Where is Mary? She must be with Jaiden.

But, where?

Maybe, a basement or a garage?

I track back to the kitchen. The yard is out back, in view of the big kitchen window above the sink.

I walk closer to see down to the yard. Six fires burn with smoking racks full of meat strips hanging from them. That's too much meat.

A metal door creaks as it opens and shuts. I hop into view of the back door. Mary jumps with eyes wide.

"Where is she?" I demand.

Mary reaches for an adjacent wooden door and pulls it open. "Boys!" She shouts down the stairs.

Boys? My brain stumbles for a moment. They said they were the only ones here.

I hear thumping coming up the stairs.

My heart drops at the likely probabilities. I swallow a lump in my throat and push down bile.

Jaiden.

Boys, means multiple. Mary and John plus boys; on a quick count, I'm severely outnumbered. I can't help Jaiden if I get captured or killed.

Spinning around, I sprint for the front door.

John breaks my speed as he blocks the way. He grabs the bat in the middle. I put my other hand on the other end and twist to wrench it away from him.

The motion sends him off balance to the floor. I bolt around him and out the door.

I sprint out towards the truck. I don't know exactly how to find Jesse, but I figure I can backtrack my way out of here well enough, from the route we took to get here.

Jesse is my best bet. He's the closest. I can run back, get help, and we can raid their house with his army of truckers.

No, I should go back to get Jaiden. Who knows what they would do to her while I'm gone? It would take way too much time for all of that.

Maybe it's not too late, if I go back now.

My heart and brain are torn. I stop and turn.

Two large men come barreling towards me from the house.

I spin and sprint.

Those would be the boys; the twins they said weren't home. They're much larger in real life, than they were in the pictures.

I don't know if I could take them. Maybe if I got them separated first, then I'd have a chance.

I could probably take on John and Mary separately too. They might go down easier than their sons would.

At the end of the street, I veer to the left.

A horn honks behind me.

My legs trip up with the sudden scare. I lurch forward and crash hands and knees to the ground. My main body hits second. Pain jolts through my whole body. Cold shocks my face and hands. Hair falls in my face.

I let go of the bat in the fall and it rattles away from me.

I screech in anger at my pain; at the truck and the men chasing me. Scowling at my only weapon for leaving my hands. Using my anger, I pop up off the ground and grab the bat, spinning on my heels to see how close my assailants are.

The truck, the twins, and I stand in the T roadway. The twins have stopped; their eyes watching the truck.

I wipe the snow off my face and flick the wet clumps off my hand. The snow starts melting against my legs. My jeans stick uncomfortably against my skin.

John, DeAngelo, and that guy who showed us how to get to Jerry's hurry out of the truck and close the distance between the six of us. The other guy has a gun, he aims at the twins.

A blast of relief runs through me. They're here to help.

I'm not going to get run over by more of their children, or friends.

"Is there a problem?" DeAngelo booms.

"They did something to Jaiden. She's in their basement. There was blood on this bat found near where Jaiden should have been." I explain what I know.

Two shots pierce the air. Two bodies collapse to the ground. The other guy shoots them on little confirmation of what they've done.

John comes rushing up to me. His eyebrows furl before he glares at the bat. He grabs the bat and smells it closely. "That's not Jaiden's blood."

John looks at me with questions unasked.

Brief relief washes through me, before other thoughts catch up. "We were with two others; Jesse's people. They said they walked back home."

What did they do to Jack and Cassie?

Who's blood is on the bat?

"Jaiden's message said they were an old couple. Did they shapeshift? An illusion?" John asks.

"No, the boys were hiding in the basement. We didn't know they were there. The old couple is still there; in the house." I realize she is still there; they could be doing something to her. "Jaiden."

I sprint back to the house.

Letting myself in through the front door. Each of the other men comes in directly after me.

My feet slide against the floor as I hit the smooth flooring. My arms come out to stabilize and prevent another fall. I catch my balance.

Old man John meets us. A kitchen knife plunging towards my chest. My John knocks it away with the bat.

Old John gasps in pain. He grasps his wrist.

Mary shouts, "John!" from her place by the front window.

With both of them accounted for, I run towards the kitchen.

Mary screams as a few more thumps hit. She stops suddenly.

The carpet wicks away some of the wetness on the bottoms of my boots, so I don't slide when I hit the smooth floor in the kitchen.

I reach the top of the stairs.

"Jaiden!" DeAngelo calls out as he comes up behind me.

I stop and spin. I hold out my hands.

DeAngelo stops as he reaches my hands, then backs up a step.

This stops the two other men from entering the kitchen.

"I think she's in the basement, but," I swallow a lump. Silence burns in place of terrible thoughts. "The twins were down there with her; alone.

We split up. She went to the bathroom to text you," I point my whole hand towards John, "but she was taking so long to come back.

I don't…

I need to go down first. I don't know what they were doing to her."

"You're not going alone." John insists.

"I have to. If…" I trail off. I don't want to say it out loud.

The other guy puts his hand on John's shoulder. "If she's alive, if… she's not going to want us to see her that way. If she's alive, she needs someone to be with her as soon as possible. And, we're wasting time arguing."

I take that as my cue to leave, whether John is going to agree or not. While I've got a moment's head start.

"She's not going to care if she's severely injured." I hear. "Seconds could matter if it's life or death."

I open the door to the basement and go down the stairs. I know the boys will be following any moment.

Straight ahead, Cassie hangs strung up from the ceiling, and Jack lies on a dripping table of blood with pieces missing. My heart stops, my breath catches in my throat.

I raise my hand to cover my mouth, and the scream that wants to escape; to stop the instant nausea from coming up.

"Hey." Jaiden chirps.

"Shit." I curse. My head whips around to follow her noise. She's tied up against a support pole. "Are you okay?"

She looks okay. Her hair is a bit messed around, and a couple of strands fall in her face; pulled out from her ponytail. Her glasses look off-kilter. Her clothes are on and in the regular place. Nothing looks broken or bruised.

"Yeah, I'm fine." She looks over at the bodies. "Relatively speaking."

The boys come barreling down the stairs. "Behind you!" Jaiden shrieks, but a moment later she realizes who it is. "Oh, hi." She cheerfully greets them.

"What the fuck?" John exclaims as he takes in the scene.

"Can someone untie me, please?" Jaiden asks.

The other guy goes over with a pocket knife and cuts the rope bonds. Jaiden rubs at her wrists. He cuts the rope around her legs next.

DeAngelo and John go to the bodies. I cover my mouth to push back a wave of nausea.

Jaiden stands up on her own; ignoring the held out hand from the other guy.

I rush over as she wobbles. She throws a hand out to the pole to catch herself. My hands support her under the armpits.

"Sorry, head rush." She closes her eyes hard and breathes in deep controlled breaths.

"Are you okay?" I ask at the same time as two other voices.

Is this because of how she was tied up?

Did she get up too fast?

Is something else wrong?

Did they hit her with the bat, or just the other two?

Jaiden opens her eyes and smiles at all of us. "Yeah, I'll be okay. Just give me a moment."

"Looks like they were getting ready to eat them," DeAngelo says. He blocks the way of an open fridge.

"They were cannibals?" John asks.

A terrible thought crosses my mind. "The beef jerky. They have meat over fires in the back. You don't think the missing people-"

Jaiden turns out of my grasp, keels over and throws up on the floor.

When she stands, I can see the same thoughts cross Jaiden's eyes. Her face turns even paler in the dark. "They admitted to keeping me alive because they had plenty of meat to last them a long while, after the people they caught a few days ago. I'd be fresher if they kept me alive until they needed me."

All this time we were staying with the very people who had kidnapped and killed the ones we were looking for.

People who welcomed us into their home, gave us shelter and food.

A cute old married couple, and their troublemaker sons have been eating people all winter.

I look around. Where John and DeAngelo are, it looks like I'd imagine a butcher cellar to look like. And, the hanging meat outside. They were making jerky out of them, and the others they caught.

My stomach jumps to my throat. Jaiden ate the jerky. I could have eaten it. I feel hot and faint from the thought.

My stomach lurches. I can't keep anything in my stomach. I bend over, and my lunch comes up my throat. My eyes shut themselves as tears stream out.

I can't believe, Jaiden; she ate people. Those people ate people. They were going to eat her.

My stomach finally empties. I get control over my dry heaving until I look down. The vomit is all over; even on my shoes and splatter drops on my pant leg.

I'm finally able to control everything. I look up at Jaiden, she's covering her mouth and doing everything she can not to look at me. She's probably trying to keep from throwing up again. She bends over and dry heaves.

I wipe my mouth dry with my sleeve. I can't stop the tears going down my cheeks. I choke up and a whimpering noise comes out of it. Deeply breathing in, I hope to not start hyperventilating.

"Let's go," John says softly.

He pulls me backwards while pushing my shoulder to turn me.

"You alright?" The other guy asks Jaiden.

"Fine." She says.

I look back at her. She starts walking.

I turn around to go back up the stairs. We go through the kitchen and into the living room. Mary and John are dead in piles of their own blood. I step around the liquid.

I try to clear my eyes from all the tears blocking my sight and blurring everything. It's hard to see where I'm going but I manage through shapes.

I think I may know a bit about how Jaiden feels without her glasses.

I swallow the growing acidic lump in my throat.

We leave the house, and I speed up. I can't get away from this place fast enough.

"Are you alright?" I stop and look over my shoulder; following through with the rest of my body when I see DeAngelo with his arms around Jaiden.

"Just tripped a bit. All good." Jaiden says.

"No. Did you get hit in the head?" DeAngelo says. His hand goes to her head. "You're bleeding." She grimaces as he touches her head.

I rush back to her.

"Yeah, they knocked me out," Jaiden says.

"With the bat? But, you said the blood wasn't hers." I question John accusing him of missing Jaiden's injury.

"It wasn't her blood. She's not bleeding." John says.

He dives in to check her head too. Quickly, there are four people towering over her at her head, and in her hair.

A raised elongated bump is discoloured in blues and purples at the right top back of her head. We move her hair around to get a clearer look. There's blood, but it's not hers.

"We should get her to the hospital." The other guy says.

"I'm fine." Jaiden brushes off our worry. "We don't need to go to the hospital. It's just a bump. I feel fine."

"Listen to the adults. You're going to the hospital." The other guy orders. "Let's go." He scoops Jaiden up.

Her feet accidentally brush against my stomach. I step back to give them room and get out of the way.

We encircle Jaiden back to the truck and get inside. I watch over her as we drive to the hospital.

Jaiden adjusts her glasses, bending the nose clips and pulling the frames until she gets everything straight again. Although, the glasses still look a bit off as they rest on her face.

She touches her bump gingerly a couple of times. Feeling around it more. Jaiden rubs her fingers along the perimeter checking her skull.

I knock off the urge to tell her to stop touching it. But, she would know best, if she felt something truly wrong.

She should have told us she got hit in the head. We would have gotten her out of there sooner; rushed her to the hospital sooner.

What if- I stop the thought.

John parks the truck out in front of the entrance. This feels too familiar in a cursed way.

I follow Jaiden out while holding my arms out to catch her if she falls.

"I'm gonna stay with them. Can you get the truck back?" John says to the two left behind, as he gets out of the driver's door.

I nudge Jaiden along to get her into the hospital quicker; she lacks the urgency the situation calls for.

I shout the moment we step through the doors. "She needs to see a doctor. She was hit in the head with a baseball bat."

A wheelchair is rolled over to Jaiden with orders to, "sit."

"I can walk." Jaiden objects.

"Hospital policy," he insists.

Jaiden relents, and sits in the rolling chair.

"Were you playing baseball?" He asks as he starts taking her deeper into the hospital.

"No, she-" I start to explain.

He interrupts me. "I was asking her. I need her to talk." The way he says it, it clicks in my head that he needs her to talk for medical reasons.

We quickly speed up to a quick-paced walk.

"We were out looking for some people who were kidnapped, and we met an old couple who invited us back to their house because we got a flat tire on our truck and it was snowing, and they offered to help. But, they ended up being the kidnappers, and hit me over to head with the baseball bat." Jaiden explains quickly.

"Did you fall unconscious at any time?" He asks.

"Yeah, um, I was upstairs near the bathroom when I got hit. When I woke up, I was tied up to a pole in the basement." I frown further. Jaiden hadn't mentioned any of this. She should have told us that she passed out.

Though I guess it makes sense. How else would they get her to the basement without her shouting for help?

But, she still should have told us. The throwing up, head rush, and loss of balance all twist for the worse when you know they could stem from a brain injury. I had made excuses and written them off to other things because she didn't say anything about all of this.

"Minutes, hours?" The nurse asks.

"Minutes." I blurt. How would she know how long she was unconscious for? "She didn't come back from the bathroom so I went to check on her, no more than five minutes. I tried to get to her, but, maybe another five minutes, and when I finally got to the basement, she was wide awake."

"I was awake when the twins were called upstairs. Not long

before that." Jaiden clarifies.

The nurse stops in the hall as we pass near another doctor. "Hey, do you know where Sally might be?"

"She was getting Calli's bottle not long ago." She says.

"Thanks." Our escort starts pushing the wheelchair again, through the dark and winding halls.

Soon enough, we hear a baby crying and follow the noise into a room.

A doctor is holding the end of a bottle and trying to pop it into Calli's mouth. She's propped up with blankets. Little hands swat the bottle as it comes close. Her head turns and screams if the bottle makes it in, then pops it out.

"Come on Calli," Sally begs.

"Sally, I have another patient for you. This is Jaiden. Hit on the head with a baseball bat in a fight with kidnappers, lost consciousness for five to ten minutes. She's fully coherent and remembers the incident in detail." He explains.

"Wheel her closer to Calli." He does as Sally says. "Grab her and feed her."

"But, she-" The man reaches his hand out to stop her.

"She's that girl that can touch Calli without dying," Sally explains. He takes his hand back.

Jaiden takes Calli into her arms and pushes the bottle at her. Calli opens her eyes in surprise, then latches her fingers into Jaiden's sweater. Her crying stops and she angrily sucks at the bottle.

"See." Sally goes up to Jaiden. She pulls out a flashlight and shines it at the top of Jaiden's head. "Get an ice pack for this."

"No abrasions, but it's swollen. Looks like they gave you a good whack." Sally prods around the raised edges.

"Yeah, I guess I got lucky. They hit Cassie too hard first and killed her. So they knew to hit me less hard." She swings her head. "Can you call Jesse? We need to tell him about Cassie and Jack, and what happened to the others."

"That's what you're worried about?" I ask incredulously.

"He deserves to know, and the world doesn't stop just because I'm hurt." Jaiden reasons.

John squeezes my hand. "We'll go see him in a bit. Focus on the doctor." John tells her.

The doctor moves around to Jaiden's front. She flashes the light into her eyes and gets her to follow her finger. Then she moves on to examine the wrist holding the bottle up. "I was tied up," Jaiden answers the unasked question.

"Oh and, ah," Jaiden stumbles with her words. "James heard back from a family of succubi who are going to come here; live here. They're on their way. He said they don't mind adopting Calli, or in general, helping her. Whichever we need, and are comfortable with."

"That's wonderful. Did you tell Chief yet?" Sally asks.

"No, not yet. I just found out today." Jaiden says. "Before the kidnapping."

The man comes back into the room and holds the ice pack to Jaiden's head. The doctor moves on to collecting Jaiden's blood pressure while they maneuver around Calli.

Sally steps back and folds her arms. "Alright, physically and mentally you don't appear to have deficits. You're handling Calli just fine, and you're coherent. Now you just need to tell me what I can't see."

Jaiden doesn't miss a beat. She interrupts whatever Sally was going to say next. "I have a dull headache all over. There's a dull throbbing pain here, and a sharper pain here." She points to the bump on her head first, then to the opposite side of her head last.

She moves her hand to rub two fingers up and down against the back right of her neck. "My neck has a dull ache here.

I threw up after I stood up in the basement because the world felt like it was spinning around me, not that I was spinning. I tripped and waivered a couple times because of that too. It felt like the ground was slipping out from underneath me.

Also, my jaw has a dull pain here." She points near her ear. "I'm pretty sure I have a concussion. Maybe some whiplash too."

"I agree. I should have just had you talk first. Sounds like you had it all figured out." Sally jests.

Rage bubbles over with Jaiden's grin. "Jaiden that's not fine. You said you were fine."

"I didn't want to worry you. And, they can't do much for a concussion. And, I figured that if something traumatic was happening, they wouldn't be able to fix it anyways. The apocalypse is short on sterile environments and equipment for brain surgery." Jaiden reasons.

I stare at her and shake my head in disbelief.

"It would not be ideal, but we would try if the alternative was certain death." The doctor counters. "And, I'm not completely ruling out something worse is wrong with you, at this time. I would like to keep you for monitoring.

And, there are special care instructions for concussions, that you need to make sure you follow. That you might not know about, and those who will need to watch over you will need to know about."

"We're taking her for a CT," Chief announces as he comes in.

"We don't know if it's life or death yet," Sally argues. "She's not showing any alarming signs."

"We're not taking the chance," Chief says. "Besides, it gives us a real chance and excuse to test the generator limits and scan protocols, and whether or not the machine still works."

A CT scan would make me feel better. That way we know for certain what is going on. We can know for certain if she's going to die.

Chapter 21

My hand itches to grab my phone again.

"No phones!" The doctor's angry shout echoes in my head and stops my hand. I hold hands with myself and weave my fingers together.

I huff out a quick breath of frustration.

No phone for forty-eight hours after the concussion; doctor's orders. I can only have it near me for emergency purposes.

No thinking.

No braining.

I get to sit in the dark and do nothing.

I'm supposed to rest, and sleep, and eat, and drink water, but that's it.

My visitors have been severely restricted. Probably, because Dominique kept talking to fill the silence, and berate me for not telling her, and asking me for constant updates.

I mean, she's probably right, but I didn't want to worry her for something no one could fix.

They even took Calli away when they saw me flinch at her cry; the sudden noise was sharper than expected. I don't think that's entirely unusual even under usual circumstances. But, they don't want to take any chances.

At least the CT showed us I'm not a dead man walking; no brain bleeds or significant swelling to worry about.

I'm guessing that's the only reason they let me sleep through the night last night. I remember concussion advice about waking a concussed person every two hours, but they didn't and didn't seem concerned to.

Though, I did have an early morning wake-up to check everything. The nurse doing the morning rounds was nice enough, but I don't know what advantages there could be to waking up your sick patients. Especially, those with traumatic brain injuries who get in trouble if they aren't resting enough.

Unless, the brain injury is why I was woken up.

That could be it. They'd want to see if they can wake me. If not, it could mean my brain swelled too much through the night, or something.

But, she did mention she was on her morning rounds. That would suggest she's checking on everyone at the same time.

A light knock alerts me to the door. It opens quickly after.

"You have a visitor." Chief lightly announces. He walks ahead of James to the end of my bed.

"How are you doing?" James asks loudly. His voice stabs at my head. I flinch and my eyes blink hard automatically.

"Try to speak quietly. She's a little sensitive to loud noises." Chief advises.

"Of course," James speaks slightly quieter. "I just brought Calli's new family to meet her. They're moving into a house near the farm."

"That's great!" I say. It doesn't seem enough to just say that, but I leave it there. I'm so happy for her.

"Are you certain, we can't move her?" James asks Chief. "I'm certain she would be more comfortable at the hotel."

Chief tells him. "She's still under observation."

James cuts him off. "We can watch her, and get her back if needed. If she can't work, I at least need her to observe on-goings."

"Right now, she needs to rest her brain; physically and mentally. If you don't allow her this, she could suffer long-term effects of brain damage. And, once we do release her, she'll need a lightened workload for two weeks, and no physical activities that could risk another concussion for at least a month." Chief already explained this all to me. James, however, seems to take it worse than I did.

James asks through tightened lips. "Could you at least put her to sleep?"

Taken aback, I miss controlling the scowl before it crosses my features. James misses my look, but Chief doesn't.

"No," Chief answers James directly; hard with a bit of a booming strength behind the word.

James stares blankly at Chief for a moment. He turns his attention to me; seeing as he's not going to get anywhere with Chief. "Then you're going to have to try to sleep as much as you can, so this time isn't wasted. Find me when the doctors release you." James dismisses himself, walking out the door.

Well wishes for lots of sleep could be taken as compassion, but I know better. He just wants me to have as many visions as possible, while I'm here, so I'm not wasting his time by only existing.

I'm useless if I can't be useful.

I'm a waste of space if I can't have visions of the future.

Chief watches in silence as James leaves, and a few moments beyond.

"I was going to let you sleep in your own bed tonight, as long as you continued to be well, but now I'm thinking of keeping you longer." He confesses, then turns to look at me.

I get that.

It's actually a bit sooner than I was expecting. On the shorter side of things, I was thinking they'd keep me for a couple nights. On the longer side of things, I figured it might be a week.

"He's," I try to find a nice way to put it, without putting James and Chief's ally relationship at risk, "goal orientated."

"He doesn't seem concerned with keeping you alive and healthy." Chief bluntly captures the dynamic. He's more observant than I would like; to make it easier. But, James didn't really make it that hard to figure out just now.

"Only so much, as long as I'm fit to work," I admit nothing more than what Chief would already deduce.

Chief takes a deep breath in. He runs his fingers through the top of his hair. "If that's their highest leadership, I can see why the supernaturals revolted like they did."

"They didn't see another way to change things significantly enough to make a difference. Especially, with the threat of being wiped out at even the thought of telling humans they exist." I say. It's easier to see how the rebellion came about when you start looking into the history.

Chief takes the information in. He nods. "Alright, rest, and stop using that big brain of yours."

A light knock at the door gets our attention. One of the nurses comes a bit inside the room. "Sorry. Calli's family is here. They wanted to see Jaiden and thank her. Is she able to take visitors?"

"Quickly and quietly." Chief assents. "Jaiden needs her rest as you can imagine."

The nurse waves a couple into the room. They come up to stand near the side of the bed.

A tall dark-haired man smiles wickedly. "Yeah, the stories are circulating. Someone tried using your head as a baseball."

He's elbowed by a small woman holding Calli. It's striking, and relieving, to see her held by someone else; skin touching skin. "Keith. That's a terrible joke. Don't make them regret letting us come."

If anyone did risk holding Calli, they held her decked head to toe in gear, and often like she was a bomb ready to go off at the slightest jostle. There weren't any cuddles or closeness.

This is nice.

"She's smiling." He motions towards me to make his point. "She gets it. Some people cope with terrible circumstances with equally terrible humour."

"It's fine." I wave it off. It's a bit funny, though that's not why I was smiling. "It's nice to meet you. I'm so happy you're here to help Calli. Thank you, so much for coming."

"No, Sweetie. We're here to thank you. There's not too many of us left. And-" She stops and takes a deep breath. Keith puts his hand on her shoulder. "We could never thank you enough for saving her."

I didn't save her though. I didn't really do anything. They're here because of James. They are the ones saving her. What have people been telling them?

"You'll have to come visit often, or else she'll miss you," Keith adds.

"Of course. I'd miss her too." I make a mental note to visit them; the offer seems sincere; though it might not be.

"We thought we'd name her after you. I understand you named her Calli. We decided her middle name would be Jaiden; to honour you." She says.

"That's so sweet. Thank you." Calli Jaiden doesn't really roll off the tongue, but I get the sentiment, and I'm not going to be rude about it.

"I think we're getting the signal to leave," Keith tells his partner. She looks over to Chief.

"I'd hug you, but we'll hold that off for later." She wipes tears from her eyes and chuckles to herself. "Sorry. Get well soon, please."

"Take care." Keith echoes the sentiment, and I echo his farewell.

Chief and the nurse follow them out. He closes the door behind him, and I'm left to the relative darkness by myself once again.

With nothing to do but rest.

Chapter 22

"Girl! Wake up!" I pop up in a jolt. My heart racing to find out what's happening.

Margie stands at the side of the bed scowling. Her voice is heavy and rough, and loud. "You're lucky I found you. What were you thinking? Sleeping in here? You're just lucky I saw the name on the door and thought to check."

Margie rips the blankets off me. "Get up! Dominique is returning. We have to get you to your own room. This is highly inappropriate. What were you thinking?"

She pulls on my hand to pull me up. She grips my wrist until we get in front of my bed in Dominique's room.

"Get into the bed. Go back to sleep. Make sure you don't tell anyone I let you wander alone; especially Dominique. She'll never let you out of her sight again, and she won't let you learn magic if you tell her." Margie lists all the consequences of telling our secret.

I want to be able to wander alone sometimes. I want to have some time away from Dominique now and then. I want to learn magic. So, I have to make sure that I don't tell Dominique that Margie let me go outside by myself.

Margie sits down at the edge of the bed.

"It'll be our little secret." She states again. "Go to sleep. She won't be very happy if she finds you still awake this late."

I don't want Dominique to get upset with me.

"I promise. Goodnight." I tell Margie.

I walk over to the side of the bed and peel back the blankets. I scoot over to the middle of the bed; my spot between John and Dominique.

The bed is freezing. Raised bumps appear on my arms and legs as I settle down in a comfortable position on my stomach.

I close my eyes and wait for sleep to come, though I doubt it will so soon. My heart still pumps fast.

Margie's breathing distracts me when she huffs out a few sighs. She sniffs up some snot.

I hear her get up, but I don't dare try to move to see what she's doing. Some things rustle behind me for a minute, then she moves to the other side of the bed and does the same thing.

She moves again, down near my feet. A drawer grinds open and closed, then another, then another.

I realize what she's doing. Margie is snooping through our things. She must think I'm asleep and she's curious, and wasting time.

There's nothing interesting in any of our drawers, something I think she realizes fairly soon. I hear the chair creak as she sits down on it.

I wait for sleep to come. Trying better to sleep again, now that Margie has settled down. Less distractions will help me sleep; I think.

The bed has gotten a bit warmer now, but it's still not a cozy warmth. I want to run my legs against the sheets quickly. The friction helps warm them a bit, but that would let Margie know that I'm awake.

The door clicks open. The quiet noise ticks in my brain.

"Is she sleeping?" Dominique whispers. I stay still on Margie's warnings. I stay still because I don't want Dominique mad that I'm still awake.

"Yes. She was tired. Felt more comfortable sleeping in her own bed." Margie tells her in a hushed voice.

She's right. But, she doesn't tell Dominique that I went to Alexa's bed first. I make sure to keep that a secret too. I wouldn't want Dominique upset about it.

"Thank you so much, for watching her. We didn't expect to be gone so long. Got kidnapped by cannibals, and had to take Jaiden to the hospital." Dominique explains quietly.

What are cannibals? I ask internally. The answer pops up almost immediately. People who eat people.

I flinch at the horror. People were trying to eat Dominique. Is everyone okay? Is she okay? She sounds okay.

But, she said Jaiden had to go to the hospital. I hope she's okay.

"Well, that certainly sounds like a long story. I'm glad you're well. But, I am tired, and wish to retire." Margie yawns.

"Right, of course. Thank you, again." Dominique whispers.

"Of course. Any time." Margie tells her, but I wonder if she really means it. She complained so much about having me stay, that she can't really mean it.

A round of good nights is said before the door closes.

"You alright, Rayleen?" John asks.

"She's sleeping." Dominique scolds.

"No, she's not," John tells her as a matter of fact.

Since they know I'm not sleeping, I take the moment to take my chance. I don't want them mad at me.

I sit up and launch myself at Dominique. The tears start the moment she wraps her arms around me.

"I thought you weren't coming back," I admit. Knowing that someone kidnapped her in order to eat her, fuels the hurt inside.

"Oh, Sweetie. I'm so sorry for scaring you. I promise you, I'll always come back. Is there anything I can do for you?" She asks.

Nothing comes to mind. I don't know how to fix this. "I don't know."

"Is there anything you want?" Dominique asks.

All I want is for this, right now, what we are doing. "I just want a hug."

"Okay." Dominique hugs me tighter. She picks me up and carries me back over to where I was in the bed.

She pulls my arms off of her and pushes gently to get me to settle back into the bed. "Please don't leave me," I say when she takes a step back.

More than anything right now, I don't want to be alone, without her.

Dominique bends over and rubs my shoulder. "I'm just going to change out of these clothes, brush my teeth and comb my hair, then I'll come cuddle you. Okay?"

I nod and wipe my tears away.

Chapter 23

Rayleen tears apart her bread into chunks, then tears those chunks into pieces.

She doesn't seem too interested in eating, despite complaining about starving ten minutes ago, and twenty minutes ago, and a half hour, and more.

Since about nine o'clock, only an hour after she ate breakfast, she's been saying she's hungry. But, now that we've sat down to eat, she doesn't seem to be.

We even decided to have lunch early because she was super starving.

I wonder if it's something she's thinking about. Or maybe, it's food that she doesn't really like. Or, maybe she just wasn't that hungry in the first place, and something else was going on.

A thought dawns on me. I look around the room. It's busier now, than when we arrived.

But, no Shale.

Could she have recognized someone else who makes her nervous? I take another pass through the faces in the room, but there's nothing and no one who stands out.

Did she just want attention, for one reason or another, and she was maybe acting out because of it?

I know I dread the moments to follow. After lunch, I'm going to drop her off at Margie's. Maybe that's what's bothering her as well.

We started preparing her for this yesterday. Telling her ahead of time, and multiple times to try to ease her into it, so that it'll go better. She's gotten upset each time I've brought it up, but she has to go back.

There's a sense of impending doom that I can't shake. I know she's not going to take it well, but Rayleen has been attached to my hip for a whole week. I need a break, and I feel bad that I do. But, I just can't get as much done with her hanging around.

The kidnapping situation was just too much for her, especially so soon after losing Alexa. I feel bad about it, but life needs to start moving on.

I take another bite of my peanut butter sandwich. We'll take this slow and easy. I'll let her take her time. Maybe it'll be easier that way.

Margie won't be pleased if Rayleen's upset the whole time she has her.

I wonder if Jaiden's had lunch yet. I should use the time without Rayleen to go find her; I don't have anything else to do.

James likely has her working harder than she's supposed to be right now. She just got out of the hospital and is supposed to be taking it easy. If I had it my way, she'd be confined to a chair or bed wherever she would like to be. With, a promise not to work her brain too hard.

Maybe at the farm, since it seems more peaceful out there. It's too loud in here for her; I think. Chief mentioned noise and light have been bothering her.

But, maybe the sun might be too much for her still? I can try to keep her in the shade. Or, a hat? Would the hat be too much for her head? Maybe a sun hat? Neither of us have one. Maybe the farm or someone at the farm has one.

Or, maybe at the market? We could go to the market and see if they have anything there. If not, we could shop or window shop. It might be fun. Though, I wonder if it might be too much walking for her?

Either way, I can use lunch as an excuse to steal her away, and we can go from there. See what she's up for.

I should've thought about this before ordering, then I could have ordered an extra to go. There's a bigger rush now, so it would take a while just to get the order in.

Rayleen wouldn't eat if I went and stood in line for so long. Not that she's really eating now.

"Where's Jaiden?" A man outbursts through the lounge doorway. Everyone freezes after they look his way. He's quickly followed by two younger men on either side of him.

His eyes look black from here. Wrinkles accentuate the agitation around his eyes and between his untamed brows. Dark brown hair is slicked back. He wears a dress shirt tucked into dark wash jeans, with black dress shoes.

I don't recognize this man. He's cleaner and more well-dressed than everyone here. We're all dressed in comfortable, warm clothing and boots.

"Where's Jaiden? I know she's here somewhere." He practically snarls. His harsh darkened and hardened tone gives off dangerous vibes. Maybe he's a supply leader who turned hostile.

"Why?" I stand up from the chair. His eyes go to me.

He widens then narrows his eyes at me, and turns up his nose. "You don't need to know why. Where is Jaiden?"

"Who are you? And, why do you need to see Jaiden?" I repeat. I'm not just going to point this angry man in her direction without knowing his intentions.

"I don't have to explain myself to you." He snarls. "Where is she? I know she's here."

I raise my voice and harden my stance. He won't intimidate me. "You don't get to come in here and demand to see anyone without explaining yourself. Especially, when you look like you're ready to kill someone."

His eyes widen wildly. His nostrils flare. The man points his finger at me and shouts. His voice fills the whole room. "You're not going to keep her from me. I have an army ready to collect her if needed. You don't want it to come to that. None of you would survive."

Does he work for Sandra?

"We don't need to resort to violence, but I assure you your army doesn't scare us," James announces from behind him. He works his way around to talk to the man face-to-face. "I'm Councilman James Ellesworn and you are in my city. What is your name?"

"Jacob Kensington. You have my daughter." He declares. His wild anger has slipped under the surface.

My stomach drops. This man is Jaiden's dad? He's supposed to be dead.

No, he just claims to be her dad. He could just be someone claiming he's her dad, just to get access to her.

James pulls back slightly, taken aback by his announcement. He softens his tone. "You're her dad?"

"Yes, and I've been worried sick. But, I know she's here and I won't leave without seeing her." Jacob doubles down.

"Then, you won't mind if we confirm your identity with her," James says.

"I am who I say I am." He quietens now that he's getting somewhere with his demands. Jacob takes a wallet out of his back pocket and pulls a card out to give to James.

James examines the card and examines Jacob. He then gives it to someone behind him. They run off out of the lounge. "Still, we would like her to confirm that. He'll be back with the card, and your daughter, if she confirms you are her father."

I'd never seen him before. Jaiden never really talked about him much when we were meeting her. Her aunt, her mom's high school best friend, was the one who would drop her off and pick her up. No one's ever spoken to him directly. She never showed us any pictures; claiming he hates to be photographed.

But, the identification card he supplied James must've had the matching name and picture, or else James wouldn't have sent it off for verification. He really could be who he claims to be.

"Come inside. Sit. It'll take a couple minutes before we have an answer." Jacob and James sit at the nearest table to the door. His two guards go to the next one over.

Some people go back to what they were doing, while others barely function to keep watching what's happening. I sit down, now that they are.

"As you can imagine, we would prefer to exercise caution when a stranger demands to see one of our people." James sizes him up.

"I just want to see my daughter. Look. If I wasn't who I said I was, would I have this in my wallet?" He pulls out a picture from his wallet. I can't see it fully, but it's the right size to be a school photo, and I see a flash of highlighter blonde before it is turned.

"Dad?" Jaiden's voice exclaims from the doorway. "How did you find me?"

"Jaiden. Come give your poor old dad a hug." He booms brightly. His entire demeanour has changed. Relaxed, perhaps, from finally finding Jaiden.

Jaiden walks over to him. He stands as she gets close.

She stiffly gives him a quick hug, but he doesn't let her go when she lets her arms go. Jacob kisses the top of her head, then finally lets her go.

Jaiden backs away a couple of feet. She locks eyes with me. She seems like she wants something from me.

She looks back to Jacob.

I get up and walk over beside her. I look over to the man. Jacob's brown hair, up close, looks like a bad dye job; probably to cover up gray hairs. I put out my hand, to shake his. He doesn't lift his hand, so I drop mine.

"This is-" Jaiden starts.

I cut her off. "Hi, I'm Dominique. I'm her sister-"

Jaiden interrupts me. "She's my best friend; basically like a sister at this point. I met her when I went out for those therapy coffee dates with Auntie. She's the daughter of someone mom used to know. That's why we met. Auntie thought it would be good for me to meet some people that mom used to know. To have that connection, and help me feel closer to her."

I linger on Jaiden for a moment, processing her lie. Though, it's not entirely a lie, is it? More like a variance of the truth, and not the whole truth.

Did Jaiden lie to her dad about meeting her real family? Does he not know that she found her real dad? Does he even know that she isn't his blood daughter?

Why else would she lie? And, in front of all these people too. Some of which, know better. Maybe that's the point, so that anyone who knows better won't say anything.

I feel giddy at the drama I'm about to get; as soon as I can ask Jaiden alone. I will ask her about it later.

"Right." I continue her lie. "She's my best friend. I'm glad we happened upon each other after the attack. I wouldn't have survived this long without her."

"Really, Jaiden helped you survive? She's always been smart; gets that from me." He nudges Jaiden.

"How did you find me?" Jaiden repeats her unanswered question.

"A friend showed me some pictures on his phone. Said he recognized you and thought you might still be alive. So I came to find you." He tells her.

"That's great," Jaiden says. "Ah, have you eaten lately? Jules can get you something, on my tab. I just need to go finish something real quick, then I'll come eat with you. Five minutes, tops."

He sharpens his features and purses his lips. Jacob's eyes darken. "I come all this way, and you run off right away."

"I'm so sorry. I was just in the middle of something, and you appeared so suddenly. I just need to finish that real quick, and I'll be right back." Jaiden dashes off through the open doors, not leaving further room for argument.

I follow. Why is she running away so fast? It's highly suspicious.

She heads down the hall and ducks into the first room; Jerry's old room.

Jaiden jumps as I come into the room. I shut the door behind me. "Are you okay?"

Jaiden wrings her hands near her chest and puffs out a long whoosh of air. Her eyes are wide with stress. She looks like she's about to have a panic attack.

"Yeah, just, I thought he was dead. He was supposed to be dead, but now he's here. It's just a lot, and very sudden. I just needed a moment to breathe." She whispers as she wipes away a stray tear. "I'm sorry. I should have told you. We never told him we found you. We didn't know how he would react. He already- He probably wouldn't have reacted well with knowing what mom did. We were worried about how he'd react to me. And, we didn't want you to know that I was sneaking off to meet with you guys." Her words are rushed out.

"No, it's okay, don't apologize. A head's up might've been nice." I have a second thought as soon as I say it; I don't want it to cause her more distress. "Though, I guess that would have been impossible given the circumstances."

"Sorry." She apologizes.

"Stop apologizing. It's fine. Are you going to be okay?" I ask. That's the important thing. I know their relationship wasn't that great. It might be part of why she's panicking so hard.

"Yeah. Um, just please, be careful what you say around Jacob. He would use any excuse to steal me away. But, we should also go now. We shouldn't keep him waiting." She bolts passed me, evading my outreached arm.

I don't believe her.

Chapter 24

"Ah, Jaiden. There she is. My long lost daughter. Come over here and give your loving father a hug. I've missed you." Jacob stands up and spreads his arms wide open.

His display disgusts me. It's overkill.

I don't want to touch him, but I have to. I go over to give him a hug. I loop one arm awkwardly around him briefly. It's all for show, and I know it. He only hugs me in public; when he's playing the loving father.

People love it. They think that this is a touching reunion. A one-in-a-million chance that two people alive, but separated, find each other. It gives them hope; you can see it in their misty eyes and wavering smiles. They're imagining finding their own families and loved ones.

They don't know him like I do. He wants something from me or he wouldn't be here.

He always warned me about how I would be kicked out of the house to spread my wings as soon as I graduated school, or else I would have to pay a steep rent to stay.

My free ride would end, and I needed a sharp reality check. What's the difference between this and that? School ended and I moved out. The slight age difference wouldn't matter to him; not when there's no one to judge him.

He needs something from me.

Jacob sits back down in his spot. Jules got him a bowl of stew while I was gone. He shovels food into his mouth. I recognize this. He's not starving, he's eating like he does when he knows he doesn't have to pay, or how he eats at a buffet to get his money's worth.

He's eating like he did at Auntie's house, when he ate ten people's worth of mashed potatoes all to himself. Auntie explained to me, that he was the reason we weren't invited back the next years.

As she put it, he got there late, claimed to have to leave early to dish up first, got himself two plates of heaping mounds of food, ate it all like a pig, ordered people around like slaves, wrecked the toilet, and then left. All the while Mom and I ate quietly, politely and apologetically.

She said, looking back, that that was the first sign she saw that something was deeply wrong with him. But, he was rich and Mom had a prenup where she got nothing if she left him; not even me.

"Can I get more of this?" He points to the empty stew bowl. Jacob turns around holding the bowl up in the air. He points at the bowl when he sees Jules' attention on him.

Jacob turns back around when Jules exits into the kitchen.

"You must've had quite a hard time without me. I thought you were dead." He says in his brief food break.

"Not dead." I smile. I don't know what else to say about that without getting in trouble. It wasn't hard without him. It was easier without him. I didn't miss him at all.

I'd go through it all again, if it meant he never found me.

"I raced home from work, as soon as I heard about the attacks. I stayed as long as I could to wait for you, but you never came, and I had to leave." He lies. I know he lies because I was there.

School was out before the attacks started. I went home quickly and stayed for days. He was never there.

"Someone called a bomb threat on the school, before any of the attacks got going. So, they dismissed us all. I went right home, and you never came. I waited a week, but the house got attacked, so I left." I boldly call him out.

"No, no, no." He shakes his finger at me. "I searched the house, you must've been hiding, or not there. You must've stayed longer at school than you thought. I searched all over Leduc for you; trying to find you immediately after the attacks. Now you're here and all is well. We will take you back home with us."

I wonder if he's right. Maybe we passed each other. Maybe he left before I got back. Or, maybe he got back while I was napping, and he didn't see me in the bed.

How different things would have been, if I had been with him this whole time.

I shake the thoughts away. No. If he truly was there, he would have found me. I would have heard his heavy footsteps walking around. Or, at least, when he would come down the stairs; that always wakes me up. It doesn't matter how tired I was.

Wait, he contradicted himself.

Wait, he wants me to go with him. No!

"But, I'm here. I've made a life here. I have a job assisting Councilman James, house, friends and everything." I decline before James can. His instant frown and pointed look tell me enough. He's not going to just let me go. He came to get me, and he's not going to leave me without a fight.

"That's sweet of you to want to help these people, but you'd better come with us. I am still your father and you're a child. This is no place for you, not when we have a thriving community to bring you back to. Here, you won't even survive the winter." Jacob tries to argue.

"We have survived the winter though." I remind him. None of us would be alive if we hadn't.

"Of course, but you didn't have to struggle. You remember the vacation home in the Okanagan? We have a safe and thriving community there.

More food than, even you can eat. Running water; warm showers. Mild winters, with a longer growing season. Clean clothes. We can do laundry. We have dentists and doctors. Teachers." He trails off a moment. "You could have a real life, with real opportunities. You wouldn't have to wonder where your next meal is coming from, or fear for your life."

The way he explains it, it sounds like it would be great.

At one point, we had wanted to go south to escape cold winters. Winter sucked. And, they can grow more and longer in the Okanagan.

"That's all very exciting, but Jaiden has become an essential member of our community. To lose her," James snaps, "just like that would be devastating. I don't think we could survive another winter without her. She's very special, and her particular skills-"

I plead with my eyes that he doesn't continue and reveal more than that.

Jacob stares through James and saves me with an interruption. "Of course, you would be compensated. She's my daughter, and you brought her back to me; kept her alive for me. It would ultimately be her decision; as it should be. I recognize that she's made a home here, but she should also get an equal chance to decide to come live with her family.

No matter what she decides, I will help you survive the next winter. I can provide you tree saplings, fruit trees to plant. We have plenty of seeds you can grow, for your own vegetables. We have more than enough that we could provide you with fresh food through the summer. Help set you up to survive long term. Keep a trading route open."

"That's generous Mr. Kensington. Thank you. I agree, it should be up to Jaiden where she lives." Many thoughts race through my mind as James accepts the deal; some are dramatic, but others are more realistic.

Jacob doesn't do anything for free, and that's far too much compensation for me. He's doing this for some other reason.

There's more to this. It can't be because he missed me.

Like, maybe he won't deliver on any of the promises if I don't stay with him. He might not intend to deliver any of that in the first place, not unless he thinks James would be good to do business with.

I don't think we have anything Jacob would really want. Nothing he couldn't find for cheaper elsewhere. And, more conveniently located in relation to the vacation house.

And, he has nothing to lose by promising something to get what he wants, then not delivering on it. There's no police or bureau who will get him in trouble. And, James doesn't know where he lives exactly.

James won't let me go for good either. I'm too valuable to his safety and his war plan; my visions are too valuable.

I wonder if he regrets not listening to Niklas and sending me to a bunker when he had the chance?

"You'll join me on my trip back to the Okanagan. Then you'll be able to decide for yourself." Jacob tells me.

If I go, I won't come back; and not by choice. I panic internally. No, that might be an exaggeration; maybe.

I look between the two old men. There's no real choice in this. I'm just a child, and they are the adults fighting over my future. What I want truly doesn't matter.

If courts were still a thing, they'd send me with my dad. No question about that. I might even get in trouble and be labelled a runaway.

Something about it being important to have your parents in your life, no matter how they treat you; unless they put you in a hospital with severe physical injuries.

It's backwards considering all the terrible parents out there. It doesn't matter if you'd realistically be better off without them in your life; not if you're under eighteen.

Could I claim emancipation?

"She doesn't need to go all that way to make a decision." James insists.

Jacob holds up a finger to make a point. "She does if she is to make a proper decision. She needs to be able to see what I have to offer; see for herself."

The point itself I can agree with. I'm always an advocate for making a well-informed decision.

"I'll go with her." Dominique offers. "It would be fun to see your vacation home."

I do like that. At least I won't be alone over there, if I have to stay.

"Of course, the more the merrier." Jacob smiles.

"Great, I would need to take Rayleen with us too," Dominique adds.

"We do have a limit. We travelled by helicopter and can fly eight people maximum. We came here with three." One of his guards informs us.

"Great! You three, Jaiden, me, Rayleen, and John." Dominique counts out.

"And Cole," James adds.

Maybe I have a real chance at returning after all. Or, at least, I won't be alone. The group is a good group of people to have with me.

Who's to say I'll want to return? What if I like it there better?

Our vacation house would have all the amenities and orchards of fruit trees. Vineyards and fishing. Solar power and clean water.

No one would be using me in their war plans; I never did like fighting.

Unless, Jacob's got secret war plans. But, he doesn't know about the visions. Or rather, wouldn't remember or think I was serious.

"That's it. We can't take any more." Jacob says. His smile is tense and flat. He's upset. He didn't mean what he said. This wasn't part of his plan. He came here for me, and only me.

"Are you sure we can't take one more? Sara or DeAngelo should maybe come. If that's part of the reason why we're going?" John inputs.

Jacob looks over at one of his guys. "Depends on weight. And we don't have enough seat belts, but we could make it work. Someone could sit on the floor."

I don't want to push it anymore with him. I feel like we've gone too far as is. "If it's too much inconvenience, we'd be fine without either of the last two. I think we know well enough to be able to make any decisions if needed."

I don't think they'd be able to give much extra input to require their presence. I could always text them, if I'm unsure of something.

Besides, rules and regulations would cap the people in the helicopter at the number of seatbelts inside, just because some random guy says we could do more, doesn't mean we should.

Though, it might be based on eight men and we have Rayleen. Weights combined could be one man's worth.

I don't like the idea of a helicopter in the first place. I don't want to take any chance that having an extra person causes us to crash.

"We should stick with eight then." The man says.

"Wonderful!" Jacob exclaims. "We'll go now. We'll provide you with everything you need while you're with us. There's no room for packed bags, and I'd prefer to be back soon."

The sudden rush surprises me. I want to halt everything, but I feel it's too late now.

I should have asked James to take down the pictures of me, then Jacob would never have found me.

"I have to get John," Dominique says.

"Get him, and join us out near the park sign, across the road," Jacob says before she leaves with Rayleen to find John.

That's why we didn't hear them. Why there was no crowd and ruckus nearby; too far to notice.

Jacob holds his hand out to James. "Thank you for your hospitality, and for keeping Jaiden alive all this time. I will make sure we have an assortment of trees and seeds for you when we return in a few days."

"You've got a wonderful little girl there Mr. Kensington; very special. I look forward to Jaiden's decision in a few days, then." James looks between us.

Jacob gathers his crew with a wave and goes towards the exit.

James wraps me in a hug, and whispers, "I'm looking forward to your return. Don't take too long."

I nod and whisper. "Of course." I understand. He's telling me I have to return. I can't be gone too long.

His smile is strained when I pull away. I wave at the people in the lounge.

I duck my head to look at the ground, as I leave. I can't look at any more disappointed stares or gleeful smiles, or I might lose my nerve.

Fruit trees and seeds would ensure these people survive;

ensure I can survive if I return.

We get out the door before I check back. Cole and Rayleen follow shortly behind me.

I look back ahead, and up. The helicopter is being cautiously crowded by about a dozen people. The two crew guys go straight to the helicopter, and Jacob does crowd control; a big show of the long lost daughter who he is borrowing for a quick trip.

They congratulate him on finding me. They're going to miss me while I'm gone. I'm such a lovely girl.

I sweetly smile my way through it, nodding when necessary, until they disperse further away so we can go closer to the helicopter.

"We'll wait here until they get through flight checks," Jacob says.

I nod.

Cole sticks out his hand to Jacob. "We weren't properly introduced Sir, I'm Cole."

Jacob looks to me, then to Cole. He grasps his hand and shakes it.

"Nice to meet you, Cole. However, if I may, why are you joining us today?" Jacob removes his hand.

"I'm Jaiden's bodyguard." Cole starts.

"Oh, thank God." Jacob throws his hand over his heart. "I thought you were going to say you were her boyfriend. A little old for her. Almost gave me a heart attack." Jacob shakes his hand over his chest dramatically.

"No, Sir. I have no interest in your daughter that way." Cole assures him with a pat against his arm.

"Good. Though, this explains why James insisted on you joining us. I'm not going to hurt her. I'm not going to kidnap her. She'll decide to stay all on her own." Jacob states with an air of absolute certainty.

"Of course, Sir." Cole smiles. I can't help but think he's playing Jacob. He's laying the Sirs on a little thick to be natural. "I think it just gives James some peace of mind. As you can imagine, he likes to control situations, a quality many leaders possess, and this situation is quite out of his control. Having me join, could give him some peace of mind, that Jaiden will be safe during this exchange; even from events out of your control."

Jacob pulls his mouth to the side. "Can't fault him for wanting to protect her; I suppose." That conversation falls flat, so Jacob turns his focus on me. "You haven't barely said a word." Jacob points out.

Words catch in my throat. This is always a tricky balance with him; saying the right amount of words so that I'm neither too quiet nor too noisy. "I don't know what to say."

"Best to stay silent then. Wouldn't want to say something stupid." Jacob states.

"Yeah." I grin at his jest. Best to say nothing at all if what you would otherwise say is something dumb.

My head has a pressure in it. Stemming from the center to the top of my head. It takes a moment to recognize, it's been so long since I've had one, but I know the signs of an impending tension migraine.

It's close enough to where I was hit, that I question if it might be related to my injury. But, deep down I know, it's a stress migraine working itself up.

On that note, am I allowed to be flying right now?

Can people with concussions fly on a helicopter?

It's too late to talk to a doctor, and I don't want to give away that I have a phone.

I don't know if he would try taking my phone away. He was

always complaining about my old phone; the one I had to buy with my own money because he took away the one he provided me on his wild whims.

I'm sure a concussion would be fine on a plane, right? It's been about a week. Anything traumatic would have appeared by now. The increased pressure could, maybe, aggravate it though.

I don't know.

Are blood clots a risk in this?

I guess we'll find out.

I don't think Jacob would take it too well to know that I was injured either. It takes away the point of me being safe with James here.

The story behind it would do even worse.

Hey Jacob, I'm totally safe here. Except for that incident last week, where I was hit in the head by cannibals who planned to kill me and eat me.

Oh, and what about those people, we still haven't caught their killer, who were beheaded and put on a billboard?

Or, the other people who have been going missing?

What about the constant threat of Sandra coming back? Or, one of her spies deciding to take action?

Or, any of James' enemies deciding to come attack us at any point?

Let alone anything else that's happened to me since he last saw me.

Hey Jacob, I had to jump out the window of a building that was actively collapsing down on top of me. I've also shot at people. People want to kill me or use me for my visions of the future.

Jacob would…

Something bursts inside my chest.

Cruel Souls

A wave of nothing splashes over like sticky heavy molasses.

Chapter 25

The blades twirl around us making the ground vibrate. The machine comes to life to purr and rumble.

"We've just got to warm up, and we'll be on our way." The muffled voice comes through my headphones from the pilot.

Dominique rubs her thumb against the back of my hand.

My legs start bouncing, like they can't stay still. Everything catches up with me.

This is happening. I'm going to fly in a helicopter. It's so exciting!

I've never gone anywhere.

The plane crashed.

No Alexa. I shake my head; this isn't an airplane.

I've never gone anywhere on vacation before and this feels like a vacation.

I've heard of the Okanagan before. Julie from school, her family went there in the summer for a big vacation. They did a bunch of stuff on a boat with a tube.

That would be fun. I wonder if we could do that.

I should ask Jaiden's dad.

But, she said it took a whole day to drive there with their car. I wonder how long it'll take in a helicopter.

The voice comes through with a long bout of words. Some of them I can make out, but most of them blend together in indistinguishable mutters. I only really recognize and understand his last words. "And, up we go."

My seat in the middle moves side to side in each direction. The trees move down until I can see the tops of the trees, then nothing at all.

I look around as much as I can. John and Jaiden's dad are waving out the window. Dominique is beside me smiling, and watching me.

Jaiden is pale staring down at the floor. Cole watches out the window.

The helicopter tilts. I slam my hands to the open seat parts beside me to steady myself before I fall. But, I don't; not even close.

Jaiden has closed her eyes.

I don't think she's good with flying.

"Are you okay?" I ask.

She doesn't answer.

"Jaiden?" Dominique's word forces Jaiden's eyes open, and she comes upwards a bit.

"Yeah. Just really don't like this part." She smiles.

"Throw up on us and I'm throwing you out of the helicopter," Jacob says. He laughs to himself for a moment.

He wouldn't really throw her out of the helicopter, would he?

He continues with a story. "One time, we were flying to the Okanagan, she must've been four at the time. We're up in the air, and she just wouldn't stop throwing up. We used all the puke bags on board."

He stops to laugh at the memory. I don't get it though. Puking isn't funny; it's gross.

It feels weird that he finds it so funny. Maybe it's one of those things, like Alexa would say, that I'm not old enough to understand.

"So we run out, and we have nothing else to catch the puke anymore. So she goes to puke again, and all we've got is her mom's bag. I pulled it off the ground and opened it up just in time for her to barf inside." He makes the motions to show us, like it was happening.

Jaiden's dad laughs again. He wipes away a tear falling down his cheek. "God, her mom was so upset. I replaced everything of course. But, you should have seen her face when she realized what happened."

Jacob continues when no one says anything else. "Another time, we go to go on a commercial plane to Mexico. And this kid is puking so much, everyone on the plane knew to get out of her way as she'd run to the bathroom."

"Maybe we should change the subject before the thought of puking makes her puke," Dominique suggests.

"Did you bring any medication or puke bags for her?" John asks. That would be a good idea.

"No, she'll just have to try to keep it in. It's not a long flight. You can manage, right?" Jacob nudges Jaiden on the shoulder.

"Yeah, I'll try." Jaiden answers.

"See. She's good." He turns his attention back to us. "So you'll all have to tell me how you ended up together. I'm sure it's a fascinating story."

"I'll go first," Cole says. "Mine's probably the shortest. We just, my brother and I, went to the hotel lounge for food, and ended up meeting everyone."

John pulls out a baggy from his pocket with some dry cookies inside. He gives me one, and Dominique one, then hands the bag with one last cookie to Jaiden. She silently mouths a thank you to John, while handing him back the cookie.

She might not want anything in her stomach to throw up.

"None of it's too interesting." Jaiden starts immediately after Cole finishes. "I ended up finding Lucas, from next door. He was with a group that took me in at the Safeway.

Then we met James with a larger group and decided to stick with them. The idea being going south might be better for survival through the winter.

Then we found Dominique and Rayleen. John found us, he knew Dominique from before, and eventually we made our way to settle down in Red Deer."

"And, who do you belong to?" Jacob asks while looking at me.

"What?" I ask. Not understanding the question. Who do I belong to?

"Dominique is taking care of her," Jaiden responds.

"But, you're not her mom?" Jaiden's dad questions as he points at Dominique.

"No, her aunt passed away recently," Dominique says.

One thought hits me, all of Alexa's things are at the hotel. I panic for a moment. But, I remember in the next moment, they said we would be back soon; in a few days.

I don't know if I could handle losing all of her things forever. Then I wouldn't have anything to remind me of her.

We don't keep much, so what we do keep is very important.

I put my hand up to the string of my necklace. The orange crystal made its way inside of my shirt again. I pull the rock out and hold onto the warm gem.

I run my finger and thumb over all the edges. Memorizing every spec of space on the gem.

If nothing else, I have this. Alexa gave it to me when she found me. It was a present and a promise that nothing would happen to me again. That she would always find me and be there for me.

But, she isn't here here.

Dominique says that she's with me always now. But, James and Margie tell me she's not. That I have to shove her away when she comes up in my head.

I wish she was here here with me. Maybe she would tell me what's going on. Tell me whether she's here with me, or not.

I want her to be in here with me, if she can't be here here. I don't like it when people say she's gone forever.

I can pretend that she's here; in my head or in this gem. I can imagine her here next to me and guiding me through things.

But, only in secret or they might get mad.

My chest fills with a familiar ache

"Dominique," I say quietly. "I miss Alexa."

"I know Sweetie." She glares. But, the angry look isn't for me. Dominique looks over to Jacob.

She had told me to make sure I tell her my feelings, so that they don't stay bottled up. It's not good to bottle up feelings; she says.

The reminders pierce into my chest.

Dominique smiles sweetly when she looks at me. Her arms open and she tucks me into her side. She rubs her hand up and down my arm before she gives me a little squeeze.

I wriggle deeper into her side, as much as the seatbelt allows, and get comfortable. This helps soothe the ache; if only a little bit and only for a moment.

I wonder how much longer this is going to take. I don't want to be travelling all day.

This is much nicer than the dragon though. That was cold. And, I couldn't move around much. I was so sore after.

Chapter 26

Somehow, I was expecting more.

The view is still glorious; cities and houses bordering a long lake with mountains in the background. But, I was expecting monstrous mega mansions and super yachts as far as the eye could see.

Some of the houses we fly over look like they are barely bigger than trailers. The boats are simply just that.

Gigantic housing is far and few between.

One of those houses, we fly straight towards. An L shaped three story log cabin with stone work on the bottom level. Decking wraps around the lake side of the house for the second floor, with spiral stairs down to the first level.

Solar panels top the roof. I guess that's where their power is coming from.

As we get closer, I see that the building is really two stories, but the back of the building is made to look like it's three stories. The basement is a walk out from the back of the house, and the deck is on the main floor.

A large rectangular two story building off to the left of the house, must belong to them too. The buildings match aesthetic and design.

A whole rest of the community looks like they live beyond the second building in the existing smaller old houses, and cramped tents and RVs.

Tent city is a stark contrast to the ultra luxury mega mansion next door.

People come out to watch the helicopter arrive; emerging from all areas. The majority who don't come out of the two big buildings, come through a hole in the wooden fencing to get closer. Most make that journey over.

We hover above the large driveway, then drop slowly until we land on the ground.

"Please, stay seated until instructed." The pilot says through the headphones.

The helicopter powers down, and the blades slowly stop turning.

Jacob unclicks his seatbelt first. Quickly others and myself follow. Jaiden waits to unbuckle until she hears the pilot tell us we can leave.

The pilot and copilot leave the helicopter and open the side doors for us.

Jacob gets out and turns to give Jaiden a hand. He helps her out, then escorts her to the crowd. "My long lost daughter has returned. It's a glorious day!"

They cheer and clap. Jaiden tries to take a step back as the people descend unto them, but Jacob doesn't give her any room to go with his hand holding against her back.

The people crowd her, hug her, and give her things, while the rest of us receive odd looks and side eyes.

She must be hating this. I don't know how to help her.

We stand close to the helicopter while they go through the grand meeting.

I look over to John. We meet eyes and exchange an amused yet bored look; the clear difference in greetings is awkward and palatable.

I spend the time peering through the crowd. Looking at the people and their things.

While Jacob is dressed in business casual, the rest of his people are dressed rather the same variety as what our people are; with the same level of dirt covering most of them. Jacob is the only one with not a spec of dirt on him.

It reminds me of James' dinner party. The leader trying to make a clear point that he's better than all of the others.

But another thought hits me, we have more diversity in our group. There aren't any visible supernaturals. No visible minority groups at all. It's not exactly all blonde hair and blue eyes, but close enough.

"Dominique." At the sound of my name, I look down to the small red head. Rayleen continues, "I'm hungry."

I rub her back while telling her, "I'm sure we'll get food soon enough. We just have to wait until they're done this."

"But, they're taking forever." I resist putting my hand over her mouth to stop her from accidentally being rude. No one can hear her from here, I'm sure.

"It'll just be a little longer. They're giving Jaiden lots of fruit; I'm sure we can take some when she's done." That seems to be enough to calm her; I'm glad. I don't want to have to deal with a hangry tantrum in front of these people.

Rayleen goes back to watching the crowd.

I resist the urge to make a lesson out of this. I resist adding a, guess you should have ate your lunch when you had a chance, to the conversation. It wouldn't be helpful in this moment, but if it happens again then I might say something about it. I should maybe say something about it later.

We stand for forever, but probably just ten or fifteen minutes, as we wait for the crowd to settle and disperse.

Jacob shouts above the crowd, "Thank you for sharing this joyous moment with me. If you don't mind, I would like to take my daughter on a tour, then get her settled in before our grand feast."

Jacob takes the gifts from Jaiden and hands them to a woman who is as tall as he is. "Take these to her room, will you?"

She nods and says something I can't hear before she goes towards the house.

Jacob turns and claps, "shall we get going?"

I think about it too late to get a piece of fruit for Rayleen. The woman is too far away now to mention it. I just hope that Rayleen has forgotten about it.

She should have eaten more at lunch instead of playing with her food. You never know what's going to happen with your day, that you might need to have eaten your full meal.

At least, there is going to be a feast later.

Jacob turns and goes towards a large elongated building beside the main house. We rush to follow after him.

"This is our everything building. It used to be our toy garage, but we couldn't just let it sit collecting dust. So now we use it for everything; market, town hall meetings, feasts, anything we need." Jacob explains. "We'll go inside later. It's too busy, now. We wouldn't want to get in the way of hard workers."

He walks by the garage to a pathway in the fence. "We pulled down the fence here and down there a ways. Makes everything more accessible. We got tired of having to go around the whole fence every time we had something to do."

"Most of what's here is housing. Behind these RVs are," he holds his note until we come out around the RV, " tents."

Rows and rows of tents are set up in front of the small old houses; going down about six houses.

He's living in a grand palace, while most of the others here are living in tents. It leaves a sour note in my mouth.

"It'll take a while, but eventually you'll get to know who lives where and where to go if you need something," Jacob assures Jaiden, who nods.

He leads us around the tents and across the road. There are two fields with distinctly different plant growth.

"This is the vineyard. Irmgard and Ray make the best homemade wine around. You'll all have to try some. It's better when it's fresh and grown right in front of you." Jacob's swings his arm to motion to the trees. "These are the trees; mostly apples, cherries and peaches."

We walk towards them along the road, and back towards the house. There are rows of trees going down a long ways. Each tree has a plethora of flowers ready to become fruit.

This is what we need. A vast food supply that just grows itself. Something we could depend on each year to grow and give us food.

Jacob stops suddenly and turns to us. "I'll have to talk with Sal. She'll get the trees prepared for your people back in Red Deer."

"Should we find Sal now?" Jaiden asks.

"Patience. There's time for that later. You need to freshen up and get ready for the feast." Jacob starts walking again. "Come." He orders.

Jaiden and I exchange glances. We follow behind him, walking back to his house and inside.

Jacob takes off his shoes, so we all do as well. It's been a while since that's been the norm. My feet turn cool quickly, but it's not uncomfortable. The house is warm.

Jaiden lines up her shoes against the wall on a mat. I put mine beside hers.

The inside looks bigger than the outside. The entrance is large and open with stairs that lead upstairs. It looks cabin-like in here, and in the living room out towards to back right. However, the kitchen and dining areas look more like what you would find in regular housing; white flat walls.

The differences clash. It looks like two different minded people took sections of the house and got full control to decorate.

Rayleen leaves my side and rushes through to look at everything in front of us, ahead of us.

Gigantic windows let in loads of light and a view of the lake from outside.

Jacob shows us the bathroom off to the side of the living room, and points to a door to mention his bedroom suite. If this is it for the main floor, I imagine his room takes up half the level.

Jaiden quietly follows slightly behind and to the side of Jacob the whole time. It reminds me of how she follows James around.

She finally speaks a comment gone wholly ignored by her father. "The kitchen looks different." I'll have to ask her what she means by that later.

Jacob motions upstairs. "Let's see where you'll be staying."

We ascend the stairs to another smaller living room space. I imagine this one would have been for Jaiden, and the other was for her parents. But, then I remember Jacob said his room was on the main floor, so I don't know what the other room is for; guests maybe or a playroom.

I wonder about the basement. He hasn't mentioned anything about that yet.

Jaiden's room is across the way a bit. You can see her door from the main floor entrance, if you look up.

A trio of pictures display on the wall. I focus in on one picture specifically. Jaiden sitting on her mom's lap; she must've been four, or so. Her mom is beautiful. It's funny. Sitting next to her mom, besides the brightest blonde hair I've ever seen naturally, she looks like her mom. Her hair must've darkened with age.

Jacob stops for a moment with his hand on the door knob. "Unfortunately, I gave away all your things, and your room. You'll have to forgive me, because I thought you were dead. But, I was able to get your room back. You'll owe Anna a favour for giving you back your room."

Jacob lets us inside. The room is completely empty, except for basic furnishings.

I look to Jaiden. Her soft smile expression doesn't change. She's doing better than I would. If I disappeared or died, I'd still expect my parents to at least keep some of my things.

"You girls will stay here. Anna will be by with some clothes to try on and some girly things to get you ready. I expect you to shower so you don't get anything dirty.

The boys will have to come with me to the guest room. Wouldn't want any night time canoodling."

Jacob leaves with John and Cole, and shuts the door.

"Canoodling?" Rayleen asks Jaiden, then looks to me for an answer.

"He says some weird words sometimes." She shrugs then turns away to look over the room. I don't think she wants to explain canoodling to a six year old, but then again, neither do I. Weird words is a great non-explanation.

It's hard watching her open drawers and closets, and finding absolutely nothing.

"Sorry about your stuff," I say.

"I expected it." She shrugs again. "He didn't even wait for mom's body to get cold before he started throwing her stuff out. He's not sentimental."

"That's not-" I'm interrupted with a knock on the door and it swinging open. I still want to say something about it, but the moment to do so is gone with the new arrival.

"Hi, I'm Anna." The one who moved into her bedroom, that we subsequently kicked out of it. The tall woman from before in the crowd. "We met briefly outside, but it was so busy, I don't blame you if you don't remember my name. And, who are you?"

She looks like she's at least twenty years younger than Jacob. Why was she so lucky to get a room in this house? Jaiden doesn't appear to have any familiarity with her.

"Dominique." We shake hands.

"Hi, Dominique. Do you know what size you might wear for dresses?" She asks.

That's a hard question. I try to round about it, but so much depends on the outfit itself and the brand. "Between medium and large depending on the fit, or ten and twelve usually fits."

"That gives me a bit to work with." She goes over to Jaiden. "Stand straight." She orders.

Jaiden stands straight up as Anna pulls from her collection of dresses over her arm. She fumbles a bit before setting the dresses on the bed before pulling up a light pink silk dress.

She holds the dress up against Jaiden, but the waist doesn't meet Jaiden's edges. I can't really imagine Jaiden wearing any of these dresses willingly.

"We'll have to find you a bigger size. Your father had hoped you lost more weight than what you had, and this is the biggest one I brought." Anna leaves the room calling back, "I'll be right back."

I shut the door after her. "Well, that was rude."

"He never did like how fat I was." She shrugs.

She's doing entirely too much shrugging. She shouldn't be so nonchalant about all of this. I want to see some anger or sadness.

"You're not fat," I tell her.

"I'm not skinny." She shrugs.

I don't see it. She looks healthy; she's lost weight since we first met. But, even before, I wouldn't have called her fat. "You're solid framed. Built like your grandma, and all her sisters. Built like Auntie Dannie."

"Raised by a family where the women have small frames and great metabolisms, and that was the expectation." She explains.

So, it goes deep. I try to help. "You aren't built like that; you will never be built like that. So you can't be something you're not designed to be.

If you want to be healthy, you have to figure out what that means for your body type. And, just wear clothes to fit whatever your body looks like, whatever size that means."

"Yeah." Jaiden brushes it off. "We should get the showers done before she gets back."

"You go first." I offer. She nods and quickly retreats into the bathroom.

I watch the door for a moment. My heart is unsettled by her words and actions; by Jacob's words.

She's different with him, restrained, and I don't like it. This is worse than how she is with James, yet similar.

I sigh and close my eyes; taking them off the door.

Rayleen sits then lies down on the bed. She closes her eyes, and I wonder if she plans on going to sleep. Travelling has a confusing way of zapping all your energy despite not doing much at all.

Walking over to the big window, I look out to the lake.

For a moment, I imagine living in this giant cabin. A boat in our dock, we take it out to wakeboard and go fishing.

We'd know the people in the boats that are out there fishing. We'd wave and make plans for a game night.

Mom and I would cook up her homemade lasagna that takes hours to make, while Jaiden and Dad would read books by the fireplace.

We'd take an hour to eat because of all the talking and laughing. We don't have to rush, because there's no other place to be.

Jaiden and Dad would clean up and put leftovers away, then make popcorn for movie night. We'd watch any movie, maybe it's Jaiden's night to choose, then go to bed.

I'd sneak into Jaiden's room because I couldn't sleep and I know she wouldn't mind. We'd talk for hours. Mom would figure it out and come join us, while Dad slept unaware.

He'd figure it out in the morning, when everyone sleeps in until noon, and he'd laugh about it. Happy that we're all happy and love each other so much we'd lose sleep to talk and hang out.

Chapter 27

Smile.

Don't forget to smile. It needs to be a soft, natural smile; never leaving.

People will be watching; staring. Paying more attention to me than they ever would under regular circumstances.

More attention than I'd ever like to have on me.

Anna leads us through the half open garage door.

Rayleen and I walk right under, but both Anna and Dominique have to duck.

A medley of cooked food smell and subtle warmth hits us as we enter.

Two large food tables sit tucked to the back wall; filled with pots, jars, and plates of food. There are a few slow cookers, and warming trays.

An assortment of tables and chairs scatter the room. Two wine bottles sit atop each table; a red and a white. They're unopened, for now. I assume once everyone is here and ready to eat, they will be allowed to open them.

It might be an unspoken rule that it's rude to open them beforehand.

People fill the space. Mingling about before everything begins.

Some have taken their seats, while others are standing around talking.

A couple water coolers sit to the left of the food. There is a sign on the one, but I can't read it from here. My guess is it's labeling whatever they've got in it, because the liquid isn't clear. Maybe a juice or iced tea, or something.

A few people stop to watch us. I return every smile, nod and wave. I would be rude otherwise.

Please and thank yous are important. Be polite to everyone you see and meet.

Anna takes us to the right. We weave through the people and tables.

At the head table, the furthest to the side of the room, sits my father. John and Cole sit across from him, on the other side of the rectangular table. They have one chair open next to John. Two empty chairs are next to Jacob on either side of him

Sit up straight.

Don't cross your legs. But, legs need to be together, because you are in a dress.

Be polite.

"Thank you," I tell Anna.

"Of course. If you need anything else, just let me know." She smiles larger and nods her head.

"Thank you, I will." I won't.

I don't intend to, and I don't imagine she intends to as well. It's a nicety to offer, but not nice to accept the offer.

She smiles and waves at Jacob, before turning off to meet up with some people a couple tables away.

I know it wouldn't be acceptable to sit beside John, so I pick the open seat on the right of Jacob; closest to the exit.

"The other dress would have looked better, if only it had fit.

But, this doesn't look too bad." Jacob compliments as I approach.

"Thank you," I say. "You look nice as well."

Dominique and Rayleen have a quiet discussion about seats, while Rayleen looks at Jacob. She seems nervous, or shy. Dominique pushes her gently towards John, then takes the seat on the other side of Jacob. Rayleen smiles at John, as she sits next to him.

"At least you smell better now." He says quieter.

With the sound level in the room, I don't know if Dominique would have heard him, even if she had been paying attention. Jacob smiles with his right cheek.

"Yeah, the shower was great. It's been a long time, since I've been able to have a warm shower." I tell him just loud enough for him to hear; and likely John too.

Jacob reaches for his overfilled wine glass to take a drink. "You better have left some of the hot water for other people to use."

"Yes, don't worry. We had quick showers, and I didn't make it that hot." I know how it is.

"Not to worry. If it becomes an issue, I still have the shower timer." Jacob smirks into his wine glass before taking another drink.

"A shower timer?" Dominique asks.

She heard that one.

"I had a timer device installed on the pipes that will automatically shut the water off after a set time. Had to get it installed for her bathroom, because she used to use up all the hot water." Jacob explains to her.

I didn't though. My showers were never longer than five minutes, and averaged just two minutes. I know because I never set the timer off with my usual routine; which gave me only five minutes.

I never had that much time to spare.

Maybe he's confusing me with mom. Mom used to take forever in the shower, but he never used a timer on her.

Is sixty-two too young for Alzheimer's? It runs in his family, so he's bound to get that eventually.

Though his memory has always been terrible on certain matters, so it might just be that.

What happens when leaders get Alzheimer's in this world?

Probably not much, considering the amount of rulers in the past, who likely ruled with brain damage and no one questioned anything. They just accepted them as being off and cruel. Eventually, they might be assassinated or experience a life shortening twist of fate.

Would anyone question him and his decisions? Would anyone even think about him having dementia? Would it take a decade before anyone would question anything? How much could he get away with before that?

It's not worth arguing with him about it because, no matter what, I'd be wrong. He always said he'd never get it. He always liked to think that he was invincible and nothing bad would ever happen to him.

Jacob dismisses himself, by putting down his glass, and screeching his chair backwards. The room falls in decibels. Many stop what they are doing and look over to him.

He walks towards the buffet tables and addresses the crowd. "Thank you all, for making this feast, to help celebrate my daughter coming home to me. I won't make this long, I know everyone is hungry, so let's eat. Come on up."

Jacob ends his speech at the buffet table, plate in hand and reaching for the cutlery.

Some people race towards the food, but others stay seated. I try to get there quickly, yet politely, and end up in the middle of the initial line.

Dominique, John and Rayleen stick together and end up about a dozen behind me.

I don't spot Cole anywhere, but since he's not at the table, I assume he's in the line up somewhere.

The line goes relatively quickly, yet slow just the same, as we wait for people to dish up their food.

I wonder how frequent this situation is? How often do they have feasts like this? Is this special because of me?

How much leftovers will there be? Does a lot of their food go to waste this way? I assume some of it is reused, but not all of it could be perpetually.

When the lady in front of me reaches the plates, she turns around and hands me one.

"Thank you," I tell her.

She gets me cutlery as well. So, I thank her again.

"I've heard so much about you; it's nice to finally meet you. I'm Sal." She introduces herself.

My eyes light up.

"The one who takes care of the trees?" I half question and half exclaim. I wonder if that was rude a bit too late.

Sal smiles largely. She didn't seem to take offence to it. "Yes, amoungst a couple other things."

She turns to start grabbing food from the table.

The first item selections are buns and jams. She grabs a bun and moves on. I decide to save the plate room for other things later on, rather than fill up on bread.

Now that I've met her, I know what she looks like. I don't have to wait for Jacob to introduce me; and hope he introduces me.

Now that I've got her here, I should just talk to her now. That way I can ensure she knows what's been promised.

"Sal, sorry." I apologize for interrupting what she's doing. "Dad was going to bring me by later to talk with you." She turns her head to nod, and show me she's heard me, before she goes back to take some meat balls. "Dad graciously offered the group I was with, seeds and trees, to help them survive. To thank them for keeping me safe all this time.

And, he said you would be the one to talk to about that."

She looks at me and pauses. "Oh, he hadn't mentioned it earlier." Of course he didn't. It's why I'm mentioning it now. I don't know if he ever intended to actually follow through with the deal. But, I don't plan on staying long, and we need the plants. "But, of course. We have plenty of seeds stored, and I could start getting some tree cuttings set up and rooting for you.

When do you need them by?"

I don't know, but the sooner the better. "As soon as possible, I think.

My friends are only supposed to be here a couple days. Then, they're headed back. I'd hope to be able to send some things with them."

I grab up some meatballs and canned apples.

"I can get you the seeds tomorrow, and I'll cut the trees; start getting them in a rooting hormone and little pots or something. That's not much time to prepare them. But, it should be well enough." Sal offers and advises.

"That would be perfect; whatever you can do. Thank you, I really appreciate that." I tell her.

"Oh, it's no problem at all." Sal grabs some carrots out of a jar. "You were in Red Deer, right?

I'll have to see what can grow there. Not everything we can grow here would survive your winters."

"Thank you, that would be great." Anything she can do would be appreciated. Right now, were limited to small amounts of anything people hand in their homes, perennial plants, and the grains and things the farm museum had; if those will even grow.

"You're welcome." She says.

We gather the rest of our food in silence, until at the end she turns around. "It was nice to meet you."

"It was nice to meet you too," I repeat back.

I go back to my table and sit down.

Jacob dips his bun in the meatball sauce and takes a bite.

"Still love food, I see. Some things never change." He talks around the food in his mouth.

I look down at my plate. There is a bit too much food on it to be respectable. But, still enough food that I won't have a problem eating it all.

"It all looked great, I was just trying to get a little bit of everything," I say.

"Make sure you don't waste any of it. We don't waste food." Jacob reminds me.

We don't waste food has always been a rule.

"I won't," I promise.

Was it rude to take this much?

"If you keep eating like that, you'll never lose the chub." He says quieter.

I choose silence.

Holding the lump inside my chest, I look to my plate. The appetizing food, the excitement to try new foods, is gone. My stomach grows a lump in protest.

I no longer feel like eating, but I have to. I need food, and I don't want it to go to waste.

Dominique, Rayleen and John all sit back down at the table. I avoid John's pointed look. His extra hearing may have heard the conversation even from his longer distance away; or maybe not. Dominique and Rayleen certainly wouldn't have heard.

I hope he doesn't say anything if he had heard it.

Fixing the smile on my face, I look to Rayleen and hope she can provide a distraction. "What are you most excited to eat, Rayleen?"

"Apple crisp." She beams. I grabbed some of that too.

"It all looks delicious," Dominique says.

"Good. Eat up. There's plenty of it." Jacob encourages them.

Jacob shovels potatoes and gravy into his mouth. Inhaling his food; as usual. He talks around the food. "So, Rayleen, do you go to school?"

I start eating. The distraction seems to have worked well. Now to get through my food without any more comments.

"I used to." She answers.

"What grade are you in? Grade three?" Jacob guesses.

"Grade one."

He clears his mouth with a drink of wine. "How old are you?"

"Six."

"That's a good age," Jacobs says. "You don't need school anyway; just someone to teach you."

"She has Margie-" Dominique starts.

Jacob interrupts. "That's good. You need somewhere for her to go during the day to get a break.

School was good for that one thing. Parents need school so they don't murder their kids.

And, she's not even yours. That has to make it worse."

"What?" Dominique asks flabbergasted. I'm only slightly surprised he said that out loud; the audacity.

Jacob taps his fork in the air. "Secret to surviving parenthood; you'll understand this soon enough, if you don't already. Parents need breaks from their kids so they don't murder them.

That's why school was invented. Though, it's much easier to get a break when they're babies. You don't have to wait until school is open."

"What do you mean?" Cole asks.

"Oh, well, you know. With babies, they're just so easy. If you need a break, you just put them in their crib, and go out." I look to him for a moment, before remembering I shouldn't stare.

It's rude to stare.

I look down to my plate.

Is that what they did with me?

"Like, leave the house?" Cole asks for clarification.

"Oh, yeah." Jacob takes a drink of his wine. "Babies don't need much.

We used to leave Jaiden in her crib all the time, and go out.

That's how we did bed time for the first couple years. We'd put her in her crib and go out for supper. By the time we were back, she was out like a light; not a peep.

Worked well, until the little shit figured out how to climb out of her crib. Karen went to go get her in the morning, and found blood spread all over her room; with Jaiden sleeping on the floor; perfectly in the middle of the room.

She gave herself a nosebleed, and was just covered in it.

We had to get our cleaner to gut her whole room. Gave her a bed after that. But, that created a whole new problem.

The little fart just wouldn't stay in her room, so Karen would get worried she was going to leave the house while we were out.

So, I had to put a lock on her door, and locked her in her room at night."

The table sits in shocked silence while Jacob takes a long few gulps of his wine. His jovial tone, doesn't fit the words coming out of his mouth.

He hasn't told me the leaving me in the crib story before, but I can't say that I'm shocked. It fits with everything else I know and experienced.

I remember not being able to open my door. And, peeing my bed at night because I couldn't get out of my room to go to the bathroom. Then them screaming and yelling at me.

At some point they removed the lock. I don't know when. I don't remember figuring that out, or maybe they told me.

Then, my having accidents anyway.

I just remember being young, having an accident, and being terrified about getting caught out and about in the middle of the night. But, at least I was able to switch my bedding around with the door unlocked, then return to sleep; like nothing happened.

"Six is a good age. They don't cry anymore by then. You don't want to deal with that. We didn't last two days with a newborn, before we moved Jaiden to the basement so she'd stop waking us up at night."

"So, was Jaiden a good kid?" Cole asks.

Jacob brings up his finger to point at Cole. "An absolute angel if you ask anyone else.

I swear this kid loved to make people think we were crazy; talking about how much of a wild child she was. And, they'd all tell us that she's so quiet and well behaved. But, then she'd come home and she was loud and would make a mess. She'd eat us out of house and home.

No, she was a good kid. It's all just jokes. We joke like this all the time. She knows I'm just teasing her, right?"

"Right." I smile and nod. "Yep, it's just jokes."

I put an apple slice in my mouth as an excuse not to talk. The apple crisp is the last bit of food on my plate

It's not just jokes. He's had too much wine, and what little filter he has has eroded away. Jokes are never just jokes. They always have at least a kernel of truth to them; an inkling to the person's inner thoughts and feelings.

"Excuse me. I need to go for a smoke." Dominique announces. "I'll be back in a bit."

She gets up and quickly leaves out the open garage doors.

I thought she quit; maybe not.

I look around to the others full plates. Rayleen has made a dent in each of her food piles, but the others look like they've barely touched anything.

Jacob's plate is nearly empty now.

"You know we never had to worry about Jaiden. She always had her nose in a book, and a good head on her shoulders.

I like to think we did a great job in raising her right.

Must've done something right. You all seem to love her." He adds the joke to the end.

"She's pretty amazing," Cole tells him, while looking at me. It feels like he's directly trying to tell me instead. It hurts my chest a little.

My face turns hot with shame and embarrassment. I look down to my plate.

I'm definitely not amazing; just average. He's just saying that to make a point to Jacob.

"Thank you," Jacob says. He uses the napkin to wipe his mouth. "I'm going to go get seconds."

Jacob screeches his chair out. The loud noise joins the loud murmurs from the crowd. He takes his plate and goes back to the food table.

Without him here, I feel the heat of John and Cole's gazes as they train onto me and intensify.

Before they can say anything, I finish my own food and get up; taking the opportunity with Jacob gone. "I'm going to check on Dominique."

I don't wait for them to say anything.

I leave through the large doorway.

Looking around, I spot Dominique heading towards the back yard. She's taking a walk down to the beach area.

I jog to catch up.

"Dominique," I say as I get closer behind her.

She stops so I can catch up quicker.

 She turns around. "Hey."

"I thought you quit smoking," I say.

She nods once. "I needed the fresh air."

So not a smoke break, but a fresh air break. That's good. I wouldn't want her to start smoking again. "Yeah, it was getting a bit stuffy in there. I thought I'd join you."

Dominique slowly nods. "He always talk like that?"

"Yeah," I admit.

"I'm sorry." She apologizes.

She doesn't need to do that. I don't want her to feel bad about it.

"Don't be. It is what it is." I shrug. "He's just like that."

Dominique hits a hard edge with her tone. "He shouldn't be, and you should be pissed. I was. That's why I had to leave, or I was going to rage on him. But, I didn't because I know that would have upset you."

Thank you.

"He doesn't take well to other people's anger. He might banish you and refuse to help us." I admit.

She was right to leave if that was the alternative. I appreciate that.

"You're not staying, right?" She asks for reassurance.

The answer screams at me immediately. "Never, no."

"Good." She comes closer and puts her arm around my shoulder in a half hug. "Come. Walk with me. I'm not ready to go back and see him."

Dominique leads us through the back fence hole, and down a ways more to trace the shore line.

We walk in comfortable silence as we soak in the environment.

The soft water crashing is a nice ambient background noise for our walk. Crunching rocks and sand create a quiet rhythm.

Wind lightly sweeps around us in a warm hug.

Boats rock with the water a long ways down the lake. I wonder if there are other people living around this area. People who decided not to be part of this little town they've created.

How many people could be living around this lake? There are a couple larger cities that bordered the other side. How many of them survived?

Jacob might know. Though, they might also all be keeping to themselves. You don't know how people will react to someone who has plenty of resources to go around.

We circle around to walk closer to the houses on the way back. I wonder briefly if we should be walking around in people's back yards. I wouldn't have even dreamed about it in years prior.

It feels like I'm going to get in trouble.

A large tree's leaves sway with the breeze.

I should have known he'd be in charge of these types of people. The voice, my own thoughts, echoes through my mind.

A hanging tree. Three bodies hang lifelessly from the limb. Sara. John. Rayleen.

A rope around Dominique's neck tightens, and the men lifting her disperse. She kicks, and swings as the rope crushes her air pipe. Losing strength as the oxygen gets used up, and her body starves for air. Body twitching, and convulsing; I know the end is coming.

Hung for being a witch.

Hung for being werewolves.

Hung for being indigenous.

"Stop." I let out.

I take a deep breathe in, and let it out slowly. I will the memory out of my head.

"What?" Dominique looks out towards the tree after looking at me.

I shake my head. "Nothing." I don't want to panic you. "I just thought I saw something."

The kitchen. The ice cream. Both happened at night, so they should be safe tonight.

Sara was supposed to be here. But I insisted, she not come. I changed that without knowing I would.

But, what if they happened on the same night? Ice cream first, then later the lynching.

No, we have to leave today; tonight.

But, the seeds and the trees. We can't leave without those, or we might not have enough food to last us long term.

Jacob won't just let me go like that and so soon.

I was fine, and so was Cole. He was the one holding me back. They didn't know about us. They weren't murdering us.

No.

Everyone else needs to go. If the others aren't here, they might turn on Cole. But, I'm safe; I should be safe no matter what.

Jacob wanted me here for a reason. He wouldn't let his people just kill me; I think; I hope.

Okay. I breathe deeply, and try to gather my disjointed thoughts.

Dominique and the others need to leave immediately, or they will be murdered sometime between tonight and the upcoming days.

Jacob wouldn't agree to me leaving so soon, and we don't have a way to get back if he doesn't supply one, so he needs to be agreeable. I also can't leave until I secure the seeds and the trees or we will eventually starve.

The store houses are great, but no one is making the supplies anymore. We're going to run out whether it gets used or it expires.

So, I will create an emergency for them to return; Jacob would have to agree if I make a plea in public.

Then, I will gather up what we need, and figure out a way back home as a contingency plan for if Jacob refuses to let me go later on.

It should work.

I pull out my phone and look at it. It's how someone would communicate an emergency back at home. I need Dominique to believe something is happening too, or she might not leave me here.

We're just past an early supper, and the sun is still well in the sky, so there should be time to get them out of here before night. Lateness won't be an excuse they could use against us. I put the phone away.

"Sara says she needs everyone back home right away. There's an emergency." I rush out. I look her directly in the eyes.

"What's happening?" Dominique asks.

I didn't think about the details. "I don't know. That's all I got. We need to talk with Jacob, so he can arrange transportation. Come on." I hurry my pace.

Making it back inside, I go right up to Jacob at the table. With my heart pounding and my face hot, I hope it's enough to convince people that something is going on.

"There's an emergency back home. I don't know what's going on, we got a text, but no one's answering the phone. I don't know what's happening. Can you, please, get the helicopter to take them back right away?" I beg Jacob.

Quickly, the crowd starts to quieten. They're starting to pay attention to the scene I'm causing. It starts out in expanding circles, starting from the closest tables.

"Hold on." He puts down his fork. "What's happening?"

"I don't know. The message just said there was an emergency and that Dominique, John, Cole and Rayleen needed to return home immediately." I specifically state out names, so he knows that I'm not a part of them returning. That they aren't just making an excuse to get me back there.

"I don't want to make more trips that necessary. It's probably nothing." Jacob tries to brush it off.

"But, I'm just so worried." I waiver my eyebrows, and muster up some tears. I picture finding Mom dead. *Mom. Mommy.* The tears are ready and filling up my eyes. I blink hard to make what little of them there are fall down.

I swallow and choke up a little. "Sara wouldn't have sent me that message unless something catastrophic was happening. And, what if people are dying, and they need them to help save them. Please, can you take them home immediately? I'll stay, I just need to know that everyone back home is safe.

They've done so much for me. I don't know what I would do, if-"

Jacob puts both of his hands up to stop me from continuing on. "Tim, get the copter ready for a round trip to Red Deer. It sounds like my daughter's friends are needed back immediately."

"Thank you. Thank you, so much." I finish the show with a hug. I pull away and ignore the weird looks I'm receiving from everyone else from my group.

Jacob's people look in a mixed batch between concerned and proud. Jacob looks like the hero for allowing my friends to leave, to save our people from their emergency.

Jacob probably figures he won; this is what will get me to stay.

I tell my friends quieter. "You'll need to get your belongings, and change back into your regular clothes. So you can leave immediately. Quickly."

I leave. I have to leave before anyone starts asking questions that I don't have the answers to.

I duck around the corner of the building, and go around to the back of the building. Leaning against the cold wall, I clean up from my fake tears.

Rhythmic crunches of feet on the ground start up and quickly get closer. I look to my right, and watch John approach.

It's too late to run off.

Of course, he'd find me with his nose. He's alone though; which is good.

"What the fuck was that? I just texted Sara, and she said nothing's happening." Of course, he'd check with Sara immediately. And, of course, she'd answer immediately. At least he didn't call her for everyone to hear.

I decide to go with the truth and trust that he'll keep it to himself until they get home. He might help convince Dominique if she starts to put up a fight. "If you stay, you'll all die. I saw the spot it happens, in the neighbour's yard.

Dominique won't leave if it's not an emergency. We need those seeds to survive, so I have to stay. Jacob wouldn't have agreed if I was leaving right now too.

I'll be fine. I'll find my way home in a few days, and I'll have the seeds."

He takes the information in. John looks up to the sky and rocks back and forth a couple times. He looks back down to me, takes in a deep breath and puffs out his lips as he lets it out. "Are you sure?"

"Yes." I push out through a thick molasses feeling.

"If you're not back in a week, we're coming to get you." He warns me.

"No, the point is that you can't be **here** or **they are** going to kill you," I stress.

"But, not you," John asks a question in his statement.

"Hung for being a witch, being werewolves, being indigenous. I should have known he'd be in charge of those types of people." I recite from my thoughts in the vision. "They aren't going to kill me."

"Fuck." He squishes his cheeks, then lips with both his hands. "Okay. I'll do what I can to get her home, and stop her from coming back."

"Thank you."

"But, you have to promise me you'll come back home; safe and sound." John asserts.

"I'll try." I can't guarantee anything.

John shakes his head side to side then up and down. "What do I tell the others?"

"What I told you," I add more to make sure he knows exactly what I mean. "Not until you get back home and in private. Feign ignorance. And, avoid Cole until you're in the helicopter; in the air. Make sure to think, and tell him not to say anything until you're safe and in private. The pilot can't know anything."

"She's going to be pissed at me and you," John says.

"But, at least she'll be alive to be pissed off." I counter.

He raises his eyebrows. "True." John agrees. He sighs. "Okay, I'll go make sure everyone gets ready. I hope you know what you're doing."

"Me too," I tell him.

John leaves to help gather everyone and everything. I just hope he can help makes sure everyone leaves without a problem. Cole might be a problem. Dominique might be a problem.

I have to avoid them until they go to leave.

Maybe I should find Sal. See if we can quickly get some seeds before they go.

She was in the garage, and the others should be out of there by now; maybe. I'll be careful.

I set off to go around to the front once more. At each corner, I stop and look for any sign of John, Cole, or Dominique. But each time, the coast is clear.

"Jaiden." I jump at the sound of my name. Looking at where the voice came from, I relax when I see it's Anna. I stop and wait for her approach. "How are you doing? The emergency sounds scary."

"Yeah. I feel better knowing they're going back to go help out." I say.

Anna puts her hand on my shoulder for a moment. "Your Dad

is worried for you. He thought you might need someone to talk to." It clicks into place. I know what this is. Jacob's done this plenty of times in the past. "I just want you to know that you can always talk to me about anything. You need a friend here and we can keep it between us. Dads don't need to know everything."

She's telling on herself. Jacob told her to spy on me. It's what he does. He finds an adult to make friends with me, and pretend to be my confidant. But, then they just turn around and tell Jacob everything I said. Then, I get in deep trouble.

"Thank you, so much. I'll take you up on that later. But, I have to go now. Thank you." I rush away before she can say anything else.

I need to find Sal before they go. Maybe I can get them some seeds to take with them.

Chapter 28

The door closes with a bang.

I jump and spin around. Dominique closed the door hard; slammed it. Her foot steps are heavy and tense. She's mad.

The door opens back up and Cole slips inside, closing the door lightly behind him.

"Dominique." He says.

Dominique turns sharply. "Who was that? I've never seen her behave like that. That was a whole different person. Has she been like that around you?"

"No, I've never seen her like that," Cole answers steadily and quietly. "That's Jaiden in survival mode. Her father clearly has been mentally abusing her for years. Kids who go through that learn coping mechanisms, and manipulation can be one of those coping mechanisms.

She knew exactly how to act, and what to say, and what to do, in order for her to get him to do what she wanted."

"Then, why the fuck," Cole brings his finger up to his lips to shush her. Dominique continues quieter, "are we leaving her with him? I'm not going without her. There's no emergency big enough that they'd be calling us home without her."

Cole tips his hands up and waggles his head. "It could all be a plan from James; to get her back home. But, she knows we need those plants; the seeds. We won't survive years without an immense increase in food. Especially, with all the new people. We'll starve and lose everyone."

"We'll find another way." Dominique insists.

"She knows how to play him. Let her do it. We have to get back and see what kind of fire we need to put out. Then we get a car, and come back, and get her. But, until then, we take our cues from what Jaiden needs us to do. And right now, she is saying to leave her here, and go back home."

Dominique shakes her head. "What if something happens while we're gone?" She asks in a near whisper.

"Trust that she knows what she's doing." Cole puts his hand on Dominique's shoulder. "Do you honestly believe Jacob would let us leave with her, right now? She lived with him for years. She knows how to handle him. She can survive a few days longer, before we're back here to grab her. Now, get ready to leave."

Cole leaves.

Dominique sighs after the door shuts. She crosses her arms, then notices me watching from the corner of her eye.

She smiles at me, and softens. "Let's get changed, then go out to the helicopter."

Dominique changes in the bathroom while I change in the bedroom.

"I'm sad to see the dress go." She says when she comes out. Dominique lays the dress out on the bed.

Suddenly, I am too. It was so pretty and sparkly, and it's been so long since I've had a pretty dress. I like the cheetah spots and the golden colours. "Can I keep my dress?"

"No, sorry Sweetie. We were only borrowing these. They belong to someone else." She reminds me.

"Oh, okay." I put the dress beside hers. It isn't mine, so I don't get to keep it. I wish it was mine though.

"Maybe we can find you a nice dress when we get home?" I look over to her with the idea creating possibilities in my head. "Would you like that?"

Excitement bubbles up inside me. "Yes! Can it be just like this one?"

"Maybe. But, I have no idea what we'll find. Whatever it looks like, I'm sure it'll be just as pretty as this one. And you'll look just as beautiful in it." Dominique assures me.

Dominique takes a look around the room. "Do you have everything that you came with? We wouldn't want to leave anything behind."

I just came here with my clothing; shirt, jacket, boots, pants, and socks. I never took anything else off. Just to make sure, I reach up to grasp my necklace. As long as I have that, I don't need anything else.

"I have everything," I tell her.

"Ready to go, then?" I nod to her question. "Alright, let's go."

Dominique goes first. She opens the door for me to follow after her.

Cole leans against the wall on the other side of the door, while John stands opposite of him. They stare at each other's eyes.

I don't see Jaiden.

We leave the hall, then the house. I'm going to miss it. The house was so beautiful, and I didn't get a chance to fully explore it yet.

The helicopter waits for us with a small crowd. Jaiden and her dad are with a couple other people.

The pilot gives a thumbs up when we get close.

"You're all set. It was nice meeting you. Good luck with everything." Jaiden's Dad says.

He opens the door to the helicopter and holds his hand out for me. I take it and he helps me inside.

I think I'll miss him. He seemed very nice. Jaiden's so lucky that her dad found her.

I think Dominique is going to miss her though. Maybe, we'll get to visit her sometimes, so Dominique won't be so sad.

I buckle my own seatbelt.

Dominique hugs Jaiden, while Cole and John get inside, then her last.

The whole trip seems like a dream. I lean on Dominique and close my eyes as the engine builds up.

Chapter 29

Hair whips around my head. I use my one free hand to gather what I can out of my face.

Rayleen squeezes my other hand tighter. I pull her along and out from under the helicopter blades.

The pilot didn't want to stop the helicopter completely for the drop off. He instructed us to duck and run.

Once we're all clear, the blades pick up speed again. The wind blasts against us. I gather Rayleen against me so she isn't blown over.

He lifts off and quickly ascends. The helicopter turns and flies back off towards the direction we came from.

"Alright, everyone back to work. Nothing to see here." DeAngelo ushers the small crowd off. The larger crowd is scattered further away. They turn back to whatever they were doing before our arrival, once they see other people leaving.

"What's wrong? What happened?" I ask. Nothing looks out of the normal. Was it the hotels or the hospital that were affected instead?

Jaiden said that Sara said there was an emergency, so we assumed it was the farm that was in trouble. That's why we had the pilot drop us off here instead. But, maybe it was elsewhere.

"We'll talk inside." Sara turns and leads us to the house.

All along the way, I keep searching for something wrong. Searching for any sense of urgency or weariness, but I don't see anything.

People go about their business at a leisurely pace with smiles on their faces. They've wrapped up much of the work for the day, with it now getting darker out.

As we settle inside, once the door shuts and we're all here, I ask again. "What happened?"

"Nothing. Nothing's wrong." Sara reveals. I knew it didn't feel right. I knew this was a sham. She stares through John. "I texted John that. I told him. He didn't listen to me."

I whip my head towards John for an explanation. I choose to wait for an explanation before shouting at him for any wrong doings, but it's difficult. He knew nothing was wrong and still let us leave Jaiden behind. Maybe, Sara responded while we were almost here; benefit of the doubt.

"Jaiden had a vision that the people there were going to turn on us and kill us. She recognized the place where we died while she was walking with you." My mind goes back to our walk. She had gotten very still looking towards the lake, before she pulled out the phone. That must've been it. "She knew you wouldn't leave willingly, if you knew."

Jaiden orchestrated this. I'm torn between conflicted feelings and who to blame them on. "What about her? Are they going to kill her?"

"No, she's safe. She's white and human." He pauses a moment. It was a race thing. "She said she'll be back after she gathers the seeds and trees. It's our best chance for long-term survival."

"You shouldn't have left her." Sara glares. I share the same sentiment. We could have figured something else out. Why didn't she tell me?

The door swings open abruptly. James storms in. He looks

around. "Why isn't Jaiden with you? I never should have let her leave."

"We had to leave. She had a vision of us dying and made us leave. She promised she'll be back next week." John says.

James' eyes open wide and wild. "What if she isn't? What if she decides not to come back? Or, he won't let her come back? You were all supposed to make sure she came back alive."

"We'll go get her," Cole promises.

James storms out. John closes the door behind him, then looks out the window to watch him walk away.

"She said not to get her. She can't guarantee that our leaving completely fixes things. If the villagers turned on us once, they are likely to do it again; whenever we would go back. She said, one way or another, she would make it back to us." John tells us.

"So, we're just supposed to leave her?" I ask. Rage bubbles to the surface. How can she expect us to just leave her there?

"It's what she wants." John reminds me.

"No." It doesn't mean she's right in this. This is a decision we all should have been able to make. "We go back and get her; today. I'm not leaving her with him. Now that we know they want to kill us, we take weapons and back up with us so they can't."

"They've got a helicopter, what makes you think that they don't have better weapons? We go in with guns blazing, and you think they'd let us take and keep Jaiden? Even if we got her back, they know where we live. They could retaliate to take her back." John explains calmly.

I swallow my tongue. If we went in with force, they'd defend themselves.

"We could go spy on them," I suggest. "That way, they don't see us, but we could see Jaiden; make sure she's safe."

"By the time we get there, she could be on her way back. I've got a phone, you can text her, and ask. Make sure she's safe, and everything's going according to her plan. Keep in contact. Either way, we're a day's drive away from her." John suggests.

"You shouldn't have left her in the first place," Sara says.

"What were we supposed to do? Jaiden had a vision where she watched us die. Jacob wouldn't have let us leave, if we had tried to leave with her." John says. "We have to trust that Jaiden knows what she's doing."

"Then what makes you think, he'll let her leave in a few days?" Sara questions. We're going in circles.

"Enough. Enough." I interject. "John, keep texting Jaiden. Find out what's going on and how she is. How soon she thinks she can leave?

We get ready to go get her and leave as soon as possible. That way, if something happens, we'll be right there and ready to grab her, and not twenty hours away.

If everything goes well, then at least she has a safety net, and she'll beat us home. That's it, that's all. You can stay or come with me. I don't care, but I'm going."

I make to leave.

"Wait," Sara shouts. I stop and return. She goes into the other room briefly, coming back with a key she hands to me. "James lives across the road now. Said being near the farm made more sense. He kicked out a bunch of people so he could have the big house all to himself.

He moved Jaiden's stuff into the house next door. He wants her close." She goes to the window and points to the two larger houses across the street. "Jaiden's is the one on the left.

We changed the locks. Not that it matters. Locks are to keep honest people out. She'd probably want you living with her anyway. If you want. Would give her some semblance of protection."

DeAngelo adds. "Power, electricity, and sewer all work now too; by the way. Well, what doesn't have infrastructure damage."

I turn from the window to look at him in shock.

"What the Hell? We were just gone for a few hours." I exclaim.

DeAngelo shrugs. "He's been taking pictures and videos all over the place, and posting them. Have to admit this place sounds amazing when you start telling people we have working toilets, showers, and farmland. That's the deal, right? Make this place desirable so more people come."

I question. "How is it that we were gone for a few hours and suddenly, miraculously, James has everything running? We have electricity, water, sewage, everything? How does that happen? Is it magic? Or, did those things never really go down in the first place? They just shut us off from the grid? And, when convenient for him, he turns it back on again?"

The silence is deafening in the brief moment.

"There were supernaturals in every corner of every job industry. I wouldn't put it past them to have been control and just shut it down as a war measure." Sara agrees.

I shake my head and blink hard. "So many people died because they didn't have necessities. Heat for the winter. Fresh water."

"On both sides," DeAngelo adds.

"Don't say anything to James, because you never know what those in power are willing to do to conspiracy theorists; especially if they're right. Especially, if it could undo much of their good image they're trying to make." Sara instructs me.

I agree but swallow a hard lump in my throat. "That's disgusting."

Did he only turn it on because he wants to entice Jaiden to

stay? He didn't want to look bad in front of Jacob again?

I leave. I can't take anymore. My chest hurts, and eyes burn from unspent tears. Out the door, and towards the exit gate.

John quickly follows and steps in beside me. He doesn't speak; he doesn't have to. I hear more footsteps behind us. Glancing back, I see Rayleen following. We trek up the path.

James is out in front of his house, packing two bags into a car. He looks like he's leaving for somewhere.

"Are you going to get Jaiden?" John asks him as we approach.

"No, I have other things to deal with. I'll be back in a few days. We can discuss retrieving Jaiden when I return." James ends the conversation by going back towards the house.

John and I look at each other with a silent questioning look. What could he be leaving to go do? If we had asked, James likely wouldn't have told us.

I start back to go to the hotel. The long walk would do me some good. We could drive a car back when we have all of our stuff. But, Rayleen is joining us. She would get too tired on that long of a walk. I veer off towards a vehicle.

Chapter 30

A weight lifts off my shoulders the moment I'm alone, the moment the door shuts. I don't have to put on a show in here.

I don't have to hide the seeds I grabbed from Sal behind Jacob's back, while feigning going for a walk. Yet, I do still have to hide them another way.

I pull out the backpack I tucked under the bed. Unclipping the top and pulling open the string tie opens the bag enough for me to put the seeds inside. I close it up and shove it back under the bed.

I don't want to have the bag exposed for too long. Jacob has a habit of walking in without knocking.

I can organize it better tonight. The seeds, as a brick pack, should go to the bottom of the bag. The water and food I stole last night can go on top, and my change of clothes can settle in the middle.

I'll look for medicine tonight. Maybe some camping gear for Plan C. I still haven't figured out where they would have extra vehicles or vehicle gas. It's been long enough that the sitting vehicles might not have working parts anymore or the gas degraded too much.

They don't seem to have much for vehicles here in the first place. I didn't see anyone using any vehicles on my tours.

But, I suppose when you have everything you need, then you don't have to make regular trips out to other places. And, they do seem like they have everything they need. Everything seems ideal here for survival and living.

On the surface, it would be a perfect place to live. If Jacob wasn't here, if there wasn't the threat of death, then this could be a great place. Plenty of food, power, water and mild winters.

But, looking deeper there are cracks and sinkholes. It's only a matter of time before something happens. At least the others got out before anything happened to them.

All the main storehouses are in this house. Of course, they are. That gives him all the control of their supply.

But, convenient. Because, I was able to sneak downstairs and grab some things last night.

Got ice cream all by myself too. I missed the moment that Dominique will never get to experience. It didn't really happen.

I pull out my phone and check it. I have a message. I pull open the messages to find a couple texts from John.

I read through his new message, then back to last night's messages three times to let it all sink in and figure out how best to manage my immediate problem; Dominique.

John says Dominique isn't accepting my saying to stay where she is. I get it, with all that seems to be going on, but there's no point in putting them in extra danger, and we don't know for certain what's going to happen, yet.

Maybe if I text with Dominique, it might help reassure her? I text him. If I could message her directly, it might help better than John relaying the information back and forth.

I wait staring at the phone, glancing up at the door briefly. I don't have much time. I hope he responds quickly or this'll have to wait.

Just as I go to put my phone back in my pocket, a notification pulls up. I'll go get her.

That's good. Maybe I can get this done soon.

I move into the bathroom and lock the door. It's about the only place I could get reasonable privacy for an unsuspicious amount of time. I start typing out a longer message for when she texts me. I know she's going to ask me how I am or how things are going.

How are you? Dominique's message comes through.

I quickly wrap up my message to her and send it over.

Things are good.

John told me about your plan. Please wait.

Sal got me seeds. Waiting on the trees to be cut, and put in rooting hormone. Trying to figure out a good way to transport them. I guess after the rooting hormone the trees should be planted within two hours. Still looking for a good way to transport them.

Can you make sure a spot is prepped and holes ready to plant?

I should be home tomorrow or the next day. No point in coming.

I reread the message after having been sent. I don't know if I should add more or clarify anything. Maybe I should reassure her more that I'm fine. Or, would it be too much and suspicious?

Are you sure?

Yes. I respond immediately.

Okay, did John tell you James moved your stuff to the farm? We all moved to a couple of houses across the road. So go to the farm with the trees, and stay there. We'll show you your house.

Sounds good. I send back in response.

I don't think she's snuck a look at the previous messages. John's updated me on a few things. More things than I suspected would have happened since yesterday morning.

I miss you. Dominique says.

My chest flips. I didn't realize she would miss me. It hasn't been long. I type back. I miss you too.

Her next message comes through as soon as I hit send. I love you. Forever and always.

A smile bursts onto my face, the heat grows in my chest to unbearable levels, and a tear falls down each cheek. Three quick moments in quick succession of whiplash emotions.

She loves me? Why? I wonder if she means it, or if she's just saying it situationally.

I love you too. I respond in kind. She's my family, of course I love her, but I didn't expect that she would feel that way towards me.

That seems to be the ending to the conversation, so I put my phone away, flush the toilet, and run the sink for a moment before leaving the bathroom.

The alibi misdirect saves me. Anna waits for me in my room. I hadn't heard her enter.

"Hi," I say politely.

"Your Dad said to meet him on the driveway. There's another leader coming here, Mr. Smith. And, he wants you to be there to greet him." Anna announces then leaves; an abrupt end to the conversation.

I know Jacob has likely already been waiting longer than he would tolerate. I don't know how long Anna was in my room before I left the bathroom, but Jacob would expect an immediate arrival. Promptly after being told, by a woman who would have rushed to tell me.

I hesitate when I think about all the nitpicks Jacob made

comments about this morning.

"Your nails are long." As he stared at my hands.

"I'm going to have to hide the ice cream from you if I want to be able to eat any myself." After he found out I ate one small bowl of ice cream, then proceeded to take the ice cream tub to his room. "You don't need any more of that anyway. I'm doing you a favour."

"Your hair is shiny," as his lip twitched.

"I see you haven't lost your love of eating food in all this," as he looked down at my stomach with a frown.

"You should take advantage of having a shower as much as you can. How about you have another shower today?" Right after he audibly sniffed the air around me.

"I wonder if the women around here have that hair removal cream. None of them have hairy faces." As he stared at my lower face.

"You'll have to get used to being quiet again. I can tell you aren't used to being quiet anymore. Must have something to do with the group you were with. They were quite chatty, weren't they? We're quiet around here. We're not used to someone being so loud." He commented after I had a small good morning pleasantries conversation with Anna.

But, I don't have time to change any of them. I'll risk more comments and tell him I plan on fixing them later. Otherwise, maybe he'll make a comment about how he was just joking. And, then I don't have to change anything.

It would be more of an issue to be late; which I fear I already am. Nothing more rude of a person to do, than to waste someone else's time by being late.

Swiftly, I make my way out of the house. Jacob stands in the middle of the two closed garage doors.

He looks me up and down. His nose flares. He's upset with

how I look.

"You could have made yourself more presentable." He snips. "Put on a dress, at the least."

"Sorry. I got here as quick as I was told." I apologize.

"Stand next to me. We don't have time to get you changed." He looks over toward the driveway entrance, so I do too. A black limo is pulling up. I stand beside him.

"You're to make a good impression. I won't have you insulting our guest for any reason. It's important you behave yourself and don't cause any problems whatsoever. You are a Kensington and you will act like one." Jacob warns me quietly with a smile.

The driver gets out of the vehicle. They are possibly in hearing vicinity, so I know not to say anything incriminating about what was just said to me.

"Understood," I say vaguely and quietly.

Posture: check.

Smile: check.

Hands at my side: check.

Mr. Smith is let out of the vehicle by the driver. He makes his way over to us.

Mr. Smith is a short and stout older man with white hairs taking over from his natural black ones. He's dressed up in a business casual staple of a long-sleeved blue sweater over top of a blue dress shirt. His khaki pants are very bright and out of place.

He greets Jacob with a firm handshake. "Nice to see you again. And, this must be your daughter, Jaiden."

Mr. Smith looks me up and down. I put out my hand to shake his. "Nice to meet you."

"Is that any way to greet your Uncle?" Mr. Smith pushes my

hand to the side and wraps his arms around me for a hug. He squishes tight. I put my hands on the back of his sides awkwardly. "My have you grown into a lovely young woman."

I don't remember him. Why does he say he's my Uncle? Jacob doesn't have any brothers; does he? He's never mentioned any. Wouldn't they have the same last name?

I need to push him away, but that would be rude. His touch itches away at my senses.

Mr. Smith kisses my cheek before pulling away. I keep my smile unwavering, but the kiss burns at my skin, even more so, the saliva he left behind. I push down a shudder. Ew.

"You don't remember me do you?" He questions me.

"No, sorry." I apologize. I wish I knew, because I know I'm being quite rude right now. Hopefully, he doesn't take offence or Jacob will be mad at me.

He waves off my apology. "It's been years since we saw each other last, so I don't blame you."

I look over to Jacob for silent help. Between the two of them, I expect some sort of explanation to appear, but it seems like it would be rude to ask.

"I brought you a trinket." Mr. Smith tells me. His driver brings over a small black box and hands it to me before he goes back to the car.

I open the box at Mr. Smith and Jacob's silent insistence. The black velvet box contains a pink water drop-shaped gemstone encased in silver and clear gemstones.

"I was told pink is your favourite colour. It's a pear-shaped pink diamond encrusted in diamonds and white gold." Mr. Smith explains.

Pink isn't my favourite colour. I don't have a favourite colour; that custom never made sense to me. But, it seems like a colour Jacob would say is my favourite.

"Thank you so much. You didn't have to get me this, but I appreciate it." I look to Jacob for approval on my response. His face doesn't give anything away. This seemed like a moment where I have to accept the gift immediately and humbly. His mile-long stare has me questioning if I should have rejected the gift first, so that Mr. Smith could insist that I have it, and then I could accept it. "It's beautiful. Thank you."

"Put it on. Let's see it." Mr. Smith insists.

I fumble the packaging, trying to get the necklace out. Mr. Smith takes the necklace from me and instructs me to turn around so he can put it on me.

He pulls off my other necklace, the one the Kadiza alpha gave me. I grab it back in a quick motion; worried he might toss it away. I wrap it around my wrist to make a bracelet, as well as I can. It's loose, but it'll work for now.

I spin back around, when he let's go and backs away. Mr. Smith stares at my chest for a moment in approval. His gaze lingers too long.

"Now," Mr. Smith claps his hands together, "I was promised the best meal I've had in a long while. You know I like to be wined and dined before talking business."

"Yes, we'll get to that right away. Anna has been preparing for it all day. You won't be disappointed." Jacob assures him.

"I better not be." Mr. Smith huffs out a laugh. He pats Jacob on the upper arm.

"Then, let's go eat." Jacob waves his arm towards the front door. Mr. Smith and Jacob go side by side in front of me to the dining room.

They catch up talking about Mr. Smith's trip. Though, I would hardly call a short drive a trip. Unless I'm misunderstanding, he's just a bit south along the lake.

Jacob sent a messenger on foot to invite him out before supper last night, and he was back before the end of the night.

Mr. Smith pulls out a chair and looks expectantly at me. He shows me the palm of his hand, as he gestures towards the seat. "Thank you." I pull my smile wider for a moment, then take the seat.

He takes the seat across from me, while Jacob sits at the head of the table; his spot in reach to my right and Mr. Smith's left. Jacob faces to look out the windows.

"So you're, what, eighteen now? Graduated high school?" Jacob asks me.

I try not to be insulted, but I'm certain he doesn't even know when my birthday is. The only reason it was remembered last year was because of Kendra.

I haven't thought of her in so long. I wonder what happened to her and my brother.

Would Jacob be furious if I asked him where she is or what happened to her?

Would he even know? I always had the sense that she might've left him right before this all happened. Would he want to talk about the woman who disappeared with his beloved male heir?

I answer quickly. "No, I'm fifteen and I was set to graduate next year. Though, I would've had enough credits to technically graduate after the first semester."

"You'll have to forgive you're dad. You're so mature that you make him forget you're real age." Mr. Smith waggles his eyebrows.

"It's been a hard year. Must've made me think we were separated for longer than that." Jacob excuses.

"About five months," I tell him.

"Only that long? It's felt like longer." Jacob says.

Anna interrupts thick silence with the first serving of food; herbed bread sticks. She swiftly brings salmon covered in yellow sauce, mashed potatoes, and assorted vegetables.

I'm given a cup of bubbly brown liquid, while they get more red wine. Jacob tells Anna, "fill them up." She fills them almost to the top of the glasses; emptying the bottle between two glasses.

"It looks delicious. Almost competes for the top view of the night." Mr. Smith compliments before digging into the salmon with his fork.

I take his first bite as sign that I can start eating too. Jacob shovels his first mouthful in once he's done draining half his glass.

The food is delicious. It's been so long since I've had fish.

The butter based sauce is a surprise burst of flavour. I haven't seen any cows around here. I guess I should've had this query when I had the ice cream.

Where are they getting the dairy products?

Is that how Mr. Smith ties in? Maybe he's got cows where he lives, and there is a trade system between the two groups.

Something itches in my brain and tunes me into the conversation the two old men are having. "She's grown up since the days she would sit on your lap." Jacob finishes.

"I'm sure she's not so grown, that she couldn't still sit on my lap." Mr. Smith says. "It certainly made those dry meetings more tolerable."

I continue to eat my food, and look down at my plate. I gather together that they knew each other from before. Jacob and Mr. Smith used to have business meetings, and I guess I used to join and sit on Mr. Smith's lap.

I don't quite remember that. But, I do know that I used to sit in on meetings when I would be at the office. The other men he would be meeting were usually nice and I would sit with them while colouring; sometimes on their laps.

"You know Jaiden, if you ever get bored of this place, you are welcome to stay at my place. It would be nice to have a young woman around the house again. How about you come out in a week or two, and stay for a bit?" Mr. Smith offers.

"Oh, thank you, but I don't know how long I'm staying." Mr. Smith shoots a look to Jacob, who is staring through me. I shouldn't have said that. I have to clarify what I mean in an acceptable way. "I made a promise to my friends that I would get them seeds and trees; dad promised them. I need to go back to get them those. Not sure when, though."

Anna clears away the dinner plates, then comes back with three slices of black forest cake; Jacob's favourite.

I take spoon full after spoon full of the luscious dessert into my mouth; it may be my favourite too after not having it for so long.

My back teeth hit something long and gritty. The long hair bundled in the last spoon full.

I bite my lips closed and gag. My eyes water. I panic. Don't cause a scene. Don't be disrespectful. Don't be rude.

I can't spit it out. That would ruin the entire dinner. Jacob would be furious with me. I don't want to face the wrath that would come from embarrassing him like that; insulting Anna's cooking like that.

I gag again. Next time, I'm bound to throw up. I bound up the hair in the cake with my tongue, and swallow it down.

My stomach heaves. I wash down the, my throat lurches, with pop; finishing the whole rest of my glass in a few gulps.

I look to Jacob and Mr. Smith. Both appear to have completely missed the moment; that's good. It wasn't for nothing. I haven't disrespected our guest. I haven't embarrassed Jacob. I haven't insulted Anna's cooking; she's busy in the pantry and didn't see.

The rest of the cake might as well be mud now; for my lack of wanting to eat it.

Would it be insulting to not finish the cake? It's one of the things that Anna worked hard and long on for, and Jacob always warns against wasting food. We have a guest.

If there's another, I gag once more at the thought, hair, then I'll stop and claim I'm full.

I carefully dig more scoops of cake into my mouth. They are thin slices, unable to hide anything. I finish the rest of the cake without incident, however my stomach is queasy and my throat is tight. Each bite is forced down.

"Well, that was delicious. I couldn't possibly eat another bite. Well done." Mr. Smith leans back and sinks down a bit in his chair.

"Anna is the best chef we've got." Jacob compliments.

"Yeah, it was delicious." I compliment at risk of silence being rude and insulting.

"Well, I better get Jaiden off to do something else, so we can discuss business. If you'll excuse me, for a moment." Jacob rises up from his chair, and I promptly follow when it sinks in that he's trying to dismiss me. Any excuse to not have to socialize any more.

"Of course. It was lovely seeing you again, Jaiden. I hope to see you again before you head off to bed." Mr. Smith smiles largely.

"I might turn in early, I'm afraid. I've had a few exhausting days." I try to excuse politely.

"Of course. You're dad mentioned you had just arrived. It must've been exhausting trying to survive out there. So, in that case, sweet dreams. Don't let the bed bugs bite." Mr. Smith says.

"Thank you. Have a great night." I say.

Jacob waits impatiently for me to leave. We walk out of the dining room area and up the stairs. He puts a hand around my arm as I try to reach the last step.

"You don't want to stay with your poor old dad?" He grates quietly.

I play dumb. I know he's talking about me mentioning bringing seeds back to Red Deer. I match his level so Mr. Smith doesn't understand; if he can hear us. "I'm just going to bed. You said you had business to talk about?"

"You're planning on leaving, back to Red Deer." He accuses quietly.

"Just to get them the seeds and trees. I haven't made a decision yet about where I want to stay yet." I try to ease the incoming argument.

"You'll stay with me. You'll like it better here." He comes in closer and points his finger at me. "Don't worry, I still have a few surprises that'll convince you to stay."

"Like what?" I ask.

"Not yet." He shakes his head and smiles.

"Okay." He doesn't continue so I bid him goodnight. "Good night. Good luck with the meeting."

I start to walk away and up the last stair. He grabs my arm and pulls me back into a crushing hug. "You've gotten quite the attitude on you, from staying with those people. This isn't how you should behave. Your mother is rolling around in her grave." Jacob whispers. I try to pull away, but he won't let me. "Maybe your professional discretions will make up for what you lack in the wife department. You got to have something worth all this trouble you cause me."

Jacob lets go. His eyes are wide and wild before he fixes his face and goes back down to the table with Mr. Smith.

I walk the last bit slower than I would have liked, but fleeing won't do me any good. It would look suspicious and draw attention to me.

I don't want to draw attention to myself.

My heart panics relentlessly long after I'm safe in my room; showered and ready for bed.

I turn off the lights and go over to the window. Pulling it over, I open up the window fully.

The cool air refreshes the skin on my face. I close my eyes and focus on breathing; in and out. Clearing my mind as much as I can.

Trying to calm my stomach and fix the growing pain in my head. This one's targeting two spots on the back and front of my head.

Tension migraines; you get stressed then you get a migraine; stop being stressed and the migraine goes away.

Not immediately, but eventually.

I kick the thoughts out of my head again. Nothing, think nothing.

The biggest breathe of air goes into my lungs, then out. And again, and again.

Once I've decided I've had enough, I close the window to a centimeter space, and go crawl into bed.

If Jacob and Mr. Smith are still going at it, they give no indication. I haven't heard a peep out of them. All that tells me is that it wasn't one of those boisterous jovial kinds of meetings. I wonder what they are discussing down there and what matters of business and trade could be going on.

I bring my hand up to my forehead. I imagine the cold seeping in and soothing my headache.

It doesn't work.

I huff out a puff of air. I know sleep won't come easy.

Pulling the corner of the blanket to cover my eyes, I tuck it in on either side of my head. I roll a bit over and tuck the blanket underneath on that side, then repeat with my other side. I raise my feet up and capture the blankets beneath them.

Once cocooned in, I pull both my arms up around my head, and settle them on the pillow.

Maybe this'll work. Sometimes it helps.

I wait and wait for sleep to sink in as my brain swirls in thoughts and feelings that I can't control. The day's events slam into my forethoughts frequently.

As the pain blends into the background; ever persistent, yet more tolerable as the time passes.

The painful grip on my arm releases with a sharp push. My legs stumble as they fail to catch up with the sudden lunge of my body.

My arms swing forward, just in time, to soften the blow of the ground. Pain takes a back seat as I push it away to spring up and spin around.

The door slams shut. I try to door knob, but hit the locking mechanism.

"Guess we die together." A voice floats through the darkness.

"No." I deny. There has to be some way out of this.

I put my ear up to the door. Muffled cries and shouts drown out anything useful. I can't tell if they're gone; if they are still separating people and loading them up into different rooms.

The screams and cries increase exponentially. A glistening light creeps in from the space under the door. The door warms. Fire. My mind answers my unasked question.

"I'll hug you, if you want." She offers.

"I'm still trying to get out of here." The door might not be a good idea. The fire is right on the other side, but maybe a room beside us isn't lit up yet.

In theory, it's possible. I knock on the walls to hear the hollow space behind them. It all sounds the same to me, so I take the chance. Summoning the hardest kick I can, my foot goes through two sets of drywall. My ankle scrapes against the sides as my leg gets stuck.

I know in theory this is what I wanted, but there is still a dash of surprise that it actually worked. I pull my foot out of the hole.

People huddle in the bedroom on the other side, staring back at me.

I back away and kick at the wall again and again and again.

Chapter 31

It's a bit weird seeing so many lights on, in so many places.

Of course, we had the generators before, but we used those sparingly; we had bigger priorities than to light up every room in every building. We tried not using it for lights at all.

The sun is coming down. It's still quite early, about late supper time. Yet, each day's daylight is growing. And soon, the sun will reach into the later evening.

I can't wait for summer. It feels like this has been the longest winter on record, or at least since I've been alive.

We get inside, and hear the bustle of people in the lounge. Dishes are clinking. People are talking and laughing.

My stomach is still stuffed from the feast, and the soup medley that's likely for supper churns my stomach at the thought.

No one says anything, and I don't ask to stop for supper.

We go up the stairs and into Dominique's room.

It's oddly warm in here. The white square heater, radiator, under the window is rumbling loudly. How could anyone sleep with that going?

Outside the window, I see more lights than ever on at the hospital. The first two floors are almost completely lit up.

Dominique and John set to work gathering what they want to.

They don't have much for personal items, but they have collected a few things along the way.

I take a back pack and quickly pack the handful of things that I have in here. Clothing, hygiene stuff and my stuffy fit loosely in the bag.

A knock sounds at the open door. I jump around to look at who is there.

"Power works now," Miles says as he flips on the lights.

The light blinds me for a moment. I close my eyes to avoid the pain and brightness.

"Thanks. I think we just got used to nothing working." Dominique says.

"How was your trip?" He asks. "We weren't expecting you back for a few days."

I open my eyes a crack and find that the light isn't too bright anymore. Miles has moved closer into the room. He leans against the end of the hall with his arms crossed.

"There was a bit of an emergency, so we had to come back early. Jaiden stayed so she can get us vegetable seeds and tree saplings. She'll be back in a few days." John explains.

His smile drops. "Oh, what happened?"

Dominique shakes her head. "Honestly, nothing much. It was blown out of proportion and solved before we had even gotten back."

"But, James left in a hurry," I say. There must still be something happening if James had to leave.

Miles looks from me to ask the adults. "James left?"

"Yeah, we were on our way over here, and saw James was packing up a car. Said he had something to do, and would be back in a few days." Dominique reassures Miles.

"Where are you going?" Miles asks.

"Just to the farm," John tells him. He explains further, "James unilaterally decided to move all Jaiden's things over there, so we're going to live with her."

"Sounds like an upgrade." Miles uncrosses his arms and drops them. He places each hand into his pants pockets. "It's getting pretty empty in here; we're not going to have any neighbours left."

"There's plenty of people who can move in. James is doing a huge campaign to get everyone to move here. So it won't be empty for long." Dominique tells him. "Or, maybe you might want to move into a house?"

"Maybe. I'll put the vacancy on the board, and talk to Ted about it at the same time." Miles offers.

"Thanks." She says.

Miles smiles and pats the door frame on the way out.

"Can I bring my things- Alexa's things?" I correct myself immediately.

"Of course, sweetie," Dominique says.

My smile grows and I run out of the room and to our room.

It takes a moment to locate the light switch; I hadn't paid attention to it before. I flip on the light to be able to see fully.

The room is colder, somehow. More so, the further from the hall I get. It almost feels like how outside would feel. The heater isn't running in here or at least it's not making noise.

We didn't leave much. Dominique and I collected everything I would use earlier, and had moved it to her room. But, I want to collect my-Alexa's things, and take them with us too.

She didn't unpack much, and Alexa didn't have much more than I did. It won't take me long.

I check the all the drawers, and under and around things, to make sure I don't leave anything behind. Some of her clothes might fit me in a couple years. I check the bathroom and take the hygiene supplies from in there.

A voice escalates from behind the wall, then another. It sounds like two people are having an argument.

Curious, I walk over to the wall. Placing down the things in my hands, I turn and press my ear against the wall I share with Kelly and Miles. The murmurs turn a bit clearer.

"He's abandoning us again. Jaiden left, so he leaves!"

"He'll be back."

"Do we even want him to? He's been playing us from the beginning." Now that they both said something, I determine this muffled voice sounds more like it belongs to Kelly.

"He has his reasons." The other voice must be Miles.

"I'm starting to think we'd be better off joining Sandra, at least she's going to be honest with using us," Kelly says.

I gasp. I pull my ear away from the wall as the argument continues. I look at the wall, almost as though if I looked hard enough, I might be able to peer through.

Kelly is going to join Sandra.

I have to tell Dominique. Maybe she can stop Kelly from running away.

She can't join Sandra. She could get hurt. Sandra's mean.

Chapter 32

Rayleen bursts into the room, pale as a sheet of paper. "Kelly is running away to join Sandra!"

I look over to John in shock. He joins my gaze.

Kelly knows about Jaiden. She can't join Sandra, or she's going to tell her that Jaiden is the one who has visions of the future. Sandra might kidnap her to force her to have visions for her.

And, Jaiden isn't with us. She's far away and unprotected. Sandra would beat us there, and take Jaiden.

It's going to put Jaiden at risk.

"I don't-" John starts, but I run out the door before letting him finish; bumping slightly into Rayleen on the way out. "Dominique!"

I open Kelly's door, and rush in to confront her directly. Miles and Kelly break apart at the sudden intrusion. Kelly stops part way through shouting something to Miles.

"You can't leave!" I announce.

Kelly opens her mouth and scrunches her face. "What? Are you going to stop me?"

I cross the room in moments and get right up close to her; face to face. With my height, I look slightly down at her; using it to my advantage to intimidate her. "Yes! You're not leaving. You can't!"

Kelly presses something sharp against the bottom on my chin. I back away at the sudden pain.

A small knife is in her hand.

I put the back of my hand up against the bottom of my chin. Maroon liquid smears my skin. She cut me!

John lurches around me. He swipes at the knife, but misses. Kelly connects a punch to his cheek.

"Stop!" Miles shouts.

John grabs Kelly's wrist, with his left hand. Using his right forearm, he pushes Kelly into the wall. The air rushes out of her.

Miles approaches John from behind.

I'm too slow. I won't get there in time.

Panic bursts out. "John!" I try to warn him.

John keeps hold of Kelly's wrist, but frees his other arm. Twisting and grabbing Miles before he can do anything, then tossing him away.

Miles launches, tripping over his feet and skipping on one leg. His arms come up to protect his self.

The window immediately breaks on impact. The trash bags release from the sides, wrapping Miles up. His torso goes over first. Legs fly up, then slide down before disappearing.

Both my hands come up to cover my gapping mouth. My heart jumps to my throat. It all happened so fast.

John lets go of Kelly to rush to the open window. "Miles!" He shouts multiple times out the window.

Kelly pounces at me, but I'm frozen in shock. One hand wraps in my hair, as the other presses the knife to my throat.

Her body presses against my back and her breath tickles my

ear.

"Is he dead?" Kelly chokes out.

John doesn't answer.

That is the answer.

If Miles was alive, any indication that he would be alive and survive, John would be running to go help him. He wouldn't be staring down at him and saying nothing.

Hair rips from my head as Kelly yanks tightly backwards. The pain keeps me close with her; using me as a human shield.

My feet move with hers, as we back out of the room. My heart thunders in my ears.

Kelly pulls me down the hallway. We're passing our room, before John comes out of theirs.

"Stay back or I'll kill her!" Kelly threatens.

John puts his hands up, but keeps coming forward; though never closing the gap between us.

Kelly pulls us down the stairs and out of the hotel. We go around the front.

The sun is almost down. It's dark enough for the street lights to have turned on, but not dark enough for their light to make much of a difference yet. Dark enough Kelly won't burn up.

Miles lays crumpled on the ground. His head hit first, and broke his neck; obvious from the wrenched angle.

"You did this." She whispers breathily in my ear. I want to shout 'no', but denying it with a knife to my neck might not end well for me.

Kelly swings us around to put me in between her and John, and the others starting their approach to help.

"I was just venting. I wasn't going to leave. I was just venting to him. If you hadn't," her voice waivers, "I have no choice now! You killed him because you couldn't mind your own fucking business!" Her grip tightens and loosens as she screams out her pain through words.

Deep regret aches through me. I was trying to protect Jaiden. I didn't stop to think about it. If I had approached Kelly differently, then Miles would still be alive. They would have explained things, rather than having them escalate.

John may have physically pushed Miles, but I started the fight.

Rayleen said Kelly was leaving. I didn't think to ask questions.

Kelly throws me forward. The sudden rush takes me by surprise. I trip and crash to my knees. My hands and knees sear against the pavement.

John rushes by me. He gives chase to Kelly.

I brush off the pain, to stand up and give chase. But, it is clear very quickly, that I'm no match to catch up. The gap widens with each step I take.

John and Kelly get further and further away until they run out of sight.

I wrap my arms around myself to sooth the chill; to provide comfort.

Chapter 33

Normally, I don't mind silence when others are in the room. If I don't have to talk to them, that's usually a good thing. We each mind our own.

Sometimes, I'd even prefer it to them talking and me having to keep up a social conversation.

Coming from a morning of having to entertain Jacob and Mr. Smith with pleasantries, conversations, and smiles, has me craving easy social silence. Or, rather preferred, no unnecessary socializing at all.

However, this silence is sharp. Anna barely looked at me when I first came into the kitchen. She didn't even smile to greet me, or acknowledge in any way that I had said hi. Though, I suppose looking up is a sort of acknowledgment, and everything after that is intentional.

Her long brown hair is the likely culprit to the event last night. I had initially thought it was an accident, but given Jacob's comments about professional discretions, and how cold Anna is being now; it makes me wonder if it was intentional.

Anna's silence could be from knowing what happened. It could be guilt, and she doesn't want to bring it up.

It could be distain. If she sees past Jacob's initial charm, then she could hate him, and that could extend to me by association.

It could be from reluctance to follow Jacob's orders to put a hair in my cake, but having to do it to prevent his ire.

It could be because she thinks I'm mad at her over it, or she feels ashamed. She would fit the blame being the one who made it and having super long hair.

I swallow a lump in my throat, and try not to shudder visibly. Don't think about it.

I hope I didn't personally do something to offend her. Could I have done something, or not done something that offended her?

I search through the past couple days, and all our interactions; which are small and few. Maybe that's why. Maybe she's offended because we haven't spoken much. Maybe she's offended that I didn't confide anything to her when she offered.

Then again, I did also steal her room; inadvertently. It could stem from that too.

Anna pulls out a stone bowl with a stick of the same stone material inside of it. She puts little brown spheres she had drying by the sink inside the bowl, and starts hitting them with the stick.

I put down the spoon and finish my bite of ice cream and strawberry rhubarb jam. "What are you doing?"

Anna looks at me through the corner of her vision without moving her head from what she's focused on. "I'm grinding some nuts for extra flavour and vitamins for the cherry pie."

"Oh, I've never had nuts in cherry pie. Is it good?" I ask.

Anna stops grinding to look at me. "Some people, before, would have put almond extract in, so you wouldn't have really noticed. You shouldn't really notice this either. The dust will be baked into the crust."

She goes back to grinding the nuts. I recognize that she didn't answer my question, but I don't want to chance angering her by asking it again. The answer is sort of in her response anyway. It might be good, if that's a normal thing to put in the pie.

Anna goes into the pantry and comes out with a bag of chips. She opens it up and pops one into her mouth. She wipes her hands on her apron, and then goes back to grinding the nuts.

I finish my ice cream to silence, then put the dirty dishes into the dishwasher.

After our poor interactions, I still try to say a quick good bye and wish her a good day, but she doesn't say anything back. I don't dwell on it. Maybe she didn't hear me; I'll give her that benefit of the doubt.

Something nags at me as I walk up to my room. The pieces click together as I go over our interaction.

Cherry pie and chips. My vision comes back to me as a memory flash. Anna stood close and was hushed. I didn't pay attention to the background. But, she was eating chips and warned me not to eat the cherry pie tonight.

Was she wearing the same clothes? I can't remember. I don't think I cared enough to pay that close of attention to them; in either the vision or just now.

What was she wearing?

If this was that moment, something changed so that she didn't warn me. If it's not that moment, then maybe we have pie again and that's the pie I shouldn't eat. Maybe, the moment will just come a bit later in the day.

I don't think I should take any chances.

My brain pulls me back to the nuts. She had just finished washing them when I had come into the room. They were small round balls; too small to be hazelnuts.

What kind of nuts were they? What kind of nuts could they get around here? The grocery stores would likely only have the regular nuts, if any remained by now, so it would maybe be something grown here.

No, wait. The answer might be in front of me. They might've looked like nuts, but they also look exactly like cherry pits.

The same cherry pits that you aren't supposed to eat, because of the arsenic levels inside of them. When the shell is cracked open, or grinded to a powder, the something inside the cherry pits interacts with a person's digestive juices to create arsenic.

So, I'm most certainly not going to eat the pie tonight. At any chance that my suspicions are correct, I can't take the chance.

I'll just have to find a way to politely decline dessert tonight. Maybe I could fake a sickness.

I don't know how I could spare Mr. Smith. There would be too many coincidences for me to have him avoid the pie altogether. Jacob, the world might be better off with him dead.

I don't know how many times I wished that he had died instead. How many times, since, have I hoped that he would die?

Then again, Anna poisoning the pie while Mr. Smith is here means that she wants him dead. Or else, she would do it when he's not visiting. Maybe there's a good reason for that. He might be just as bad, or worse.

Then again, now she wants me dead. Or at least, she thinks that I'm necessary collateral. Or maybe, she thinks that I'm not worth the risk of a warning.

I need some air.

Momentarily, I entertain the idea of a walk, but I don't want to interact with the amount of people that I would come across.

I settle on going out to the deck. Maybe I could scope out the yard, and if no one is there, then I could go to the lake shore.

I would have to bypass Anna. Maybe that's when she would warn me. It would give her another opportunity.

I go back down the stairs, and slowly walk by the kitchen. I wave at Anna, but she doesn't notice or chooses not to acknowledge me. It did look like she had looked my way.

The lock sticks for a moment, but I try again and it unlocks. The moment I open the door, I hear someone shouting, faintly from the distance, but I can't make out the words.

I slide the door shut behind me.

The noise tickles my right ear, so I walk to the edge of the deck to see if I can see anything.

I look all around. The ocean just has some people fishing, but they seem fine. They're sitting in their boat calmly.

There's no one in our yard.

I move closer to the right-most side of the deck.

A growing crowd half circles the hanging tree. Four bodies dangle from its limb.

I dash to the railings and crash in to it hard. Is this it? Did they come back? It was supposed to happen at night.

But, the bodies aren't the same. From here, I can see two shorter bodies and two longer bodies. Two children sized bodies and two adult ones.

Jacob is there, near the bodies, and so is Mr. Smith. He's shouting stuff to the crowd while Jacob stays back and nods now and then. The crowd is too loud to hear anything said. Too many people are shouting, and I'm too far away, for anything clear to come across.

Maybe I should go down there. I nix the idea just as soon as I have it. It seems much safer to stay up here.

I don't want any part of what is happening down there.

Watching from a distance seems much safer. I don't know what happened. I don't know what the crowd wants.

Did the crowd hang the people, then Mr. Smith and Jacob came upon it? Or, did they instruct it to happen?

I don't know the people here well enough to recognize who

was hung, especially from this far away. Were they strangers?

I don't think the crowd is turning on Mr. Smith and Jacob. Or, they might've hung them by now too.

Why would they do this? Was it Mr. Smith's idea?

The crowd's noise dies down as Jacob lays his palms out towards the ground, raising and lowering his hands.

Mr. Smith can finally be heard over the people. His voice carries on the wind in bits and pieces. One word pierces my ears, "Demons."

I saved my friends, so they found someone else to target.

With this act, at least, I won't have any qualms about letting Mr. Smith die tonight too. I hope they both die.

Is this why Anna seemed tense in the kitchen? Maybe the sharp silence wasn't because of me.

Has this happened before? Does it happen every time they suspect someone of being a supernatural?

Is that actually why they hung everyone? It had nothing to do with Dominique being part Dene, and everything to do with her pretending to be a supernatural. Or, maybe it was both.

Cole somehow avoided it. Did he say he was human?

Did this only happen because Mr. Smith was here? Or, is this something that Jacob initiates too?

Knowing that they're complicit, I'm certainly not going down for a closer look. I'm sorry to the family, or whoever it is, but I'm not risking Jacob turning this into a daddy-daughter moment.

I certainly can't go down there and show any sign I don't agree with what they did. With these types of leaders, you agree, or you're likely to wind up rotting in jail or dead.

Focus.

I need to leave; sooner rather than later. And, it's for sure not going to be in the helicopter. There's no way he's letting me go back. I'm not going to be able to convince him to let me go back; not even under the guise of getting them the seeds and tree saplings.

I used my one public plea on getting my friends back. His people won't be responsive to too many of those.

I need to make a plan. I need to make a list of everything I would need. I need to make contingency plans for a variety of situations.

I need more food. More water, or ways to get clean water easily. I need warmth. Transportation. I need to get out of here with no one catching me.

Cole should be here by now; theoretically the timeline is possible. I could have a friend watching from the shadows. How could I alert him? How could I let him know when I leave? Would he notice? I don't have any clue where he would be.

He might not even be here yet. Just because someone could make the trip in a day, before this, doesn't mean he could now. Anything could have happened to delay him.

I duck down when the crowd starts dispersing. Something inside of me thinks I might get in trouble for watching.

There's too many people around. I could never leave now, not without attracting attention and confrontation. Not without people immediately trying to hunt me down as they quickly notice I'm gone.

It will have to be later, tonight, after they've been killed; or after everyone is asleep. And, unfortunately, without the trees.

I'll text the others later, after I get out of here safely. I wouldn't want to tell them, then not be able to leave yet.

They can't come here again.

Maybe they can let Connor know, who would then maybe let Cole know. He's never said that they have a phone, but he might.

Maybe Cole will see me leave, and come find me. I just know that I can't risk staying around to look for him.

Chapter 34

Dominique comes through the door first, then John.

I worry. The words catch in my throat. I want to ask what happened, but I can't bring myself to.

There was too much yelling and thumping. I know there was a fight. It's been so long since things turned silent.

John holds his hand out for me to take. He helps pull me out and up off the floor under the desk.

I watch John and Dominique carefully; waiting for one of them to explain.

John stands by me, watching Dominique stiffly. While, she sits down at the edge of the bed. Something happened to her, but what?

Dominique puts her hands on her knees, then quickly pulls them off to look at them. There are bloody torn holes in her pants. She pulls something out of her hand and drops it to the floor. It's too small to see what it was. But, I think she fell, so maybe a rock.

Dominique takes a deep breath in and lets it out slowly. A tear trail begins to fall down her cheek, but she doesn't cry out.

What happened?

The words catch again.

Dominique drops her head, her hair falling to hide her face. Her hands come up to her head. Fingers slide into her hair, then make a fist around them.

She pulls her head up, and lets go of her hair. Dominique grabs at a portion of her hair, and looks at it.

"I need scissors," Dominique says quietly.

"Why?" John asks.

She drops her hair. "I don't ever want someone to be able to grab my hair like that; ever again."

"Are you sure?" John asks. She wants to cut her hair?

Dominique turns her head to look John in the eye. "Yes."

"Do you want to take a moment to process this?" John asks for reassurance. "You could cut it tomorrow, if you still feel the same way."

"It's hair. I can always grow it back out if I want to later." Dominique answers.

"Alright. Let's find you scissors." John says. He pats Dominique's shoulder on his way out the door.

"What happened?" I choke out.

"Kelly left to join Sandra." Dominique pauses. "There was a fight. Miles-" She cuts herself off, and stops altogether.

I'm too scared to ask her for more information. Something bad happened to Miles.

Chapter 35

The sun warms my skin despite the still cool breeze. The sun has started winning in the war for spring versus winter. Short periods of time are tolerable without a coat on; though I still wear a heavier sweater.

John's phone vibrates in my hand.

I open my eyes and pull the phone up to see Jaiden's response. That was fast.

Things are good.

John told me your plan. Please wait.

Sal got me seeds. Waiting on the trees to be cut, and put in rooting hormone. Trying to figure out a good way to transport them. I guess after the rooting hormone the trees should be planted within two hours. Still looking for a good way to transport them.

Can you make sure a spot is prepped and holes ready to plant?

I should be home tomorrow or the next day. No point in coming.

If what she says is true, there wouldn't be a point in going. We'd waste more gas getting there, just for her to come back, maybe before we even got there.

It's enough that Cole up and disappeared without saying

anything to anyone.

I assume he went to go get her. Connor feigned ignorance, if not actually knowing for certain. He said Cole left as soon as the sun was up, but didn't say where he was going; packed for a few days trip.

Connor didn't say no when I asked directly if he thought Cole went to get Jaiden. He just shrugged.

For someone who was so righteous about the truth, he sure didn't hesitate to blur the lines about this. Maybe that's just an act.

We went through this all last night; John and I did, with Jaiden on the other end of his texts.

John said Jaiden doesn't think Sandra would show up immediately. Kelly doesn't have a phone, not that she's ever revealed, so she can't look up online where Sandra might be or contact someone that might know; maybe even Sandra herself.

Sandra went into hiding, and no one knows where she is exactly. It could take a long while, weeks or months even, for Kelly to find her; if that's even what she's actually going to do. There's a chance Kelly might avoid Sandra, and just start a life elsewhere.

And, Kelly didn't know where exactly Jaiden was. It's a long lake. There would be plenty of time and warning before Sandra would likely figure out which of the thousands of homes belong to Jacob. By then, Jaiden could be long gone.

Jaiden said she'll watch the sky for dragons and the surrounding areas for signs of her.

Are you sure? I ask; just to be sure that she's sure. I'm still not even certain myself.

Yes. She answers quickly.

I bite my lips together, then let them go. On to better things, I guess. Okay, did John tell you James moved your stuff to the farm? We all moved to a couple of houses across the road. So go to the farm with the trees, and stay there. We'll show you your house.

I'm excited to show her the new house. Sucks how we got it, but it feels like a good thing. A new start is something we all need.

I hope James doesn't ruin the farm.

Sounds good. Her curt responses are hard to converse with. Maybe, she can't really talk right now. I'm a bit disappointed at that, but I understand that she might not be able to talk for long periods of time.

I'll let her go right away here.

I miss you. I tell her. An ache in my heart has settled, and I know it won't leave until she's back home safe.

I miss you too. Jaiden echoes back.

I love you. Forever and always. No goodbyes. She's the last family I've got. I don't want to lose her too.

I love you too.

I smile and close my eyes; relaxing back to sink into the chair, and taking a deep breath to calm my nerves.

For just a moment, things feel like they're going to be alright.

But, it doesn't last long. My brain catches back up with me to push all my current issues back to the front of my thoughts.

I should give John his phone back. He went into the house to find something to drink, after he passed me his phone to talk with Jaiden.

He's been distant. Choosing to exhaust himself in the fields, or by doing whatever other physical labour people need done today.

I reason that he must be processing what happened. It has nothing to do with me.

Well…

It does have to do with me, but not in a personal way; sort of.

He killed Miles. It might've been an accident, but it still happened.

He's going to have to deal with the guilt from it.

I don't know how I feel about it either. The time apart might be good for me to process my conflicting feelings about it too.

I understand how it happened, but it didn't have to happen like that.

Everything happened in mere moments. I accused Kelly, intimidated her, she fought back, John came to my defence, Miles came to Kelly's defence, and then John pushed him away.

If I hadn't picked the fight, then nothing would have happened.

But, John chose to push him away hard, and that choice led to Miles falling out the window.

In the moment, I don't think I would have been paying attention to where I was trying to push a person off of me to.

I certainly might not have even thought, had time to think, that the window would break under the pressure. There might've been something wrong with the window itself.

Tires crunch against the rocks on the road. I open my eyes to spy on whoever is moving about. A car pulls up next door. I don't recognize the red car.

James comes out of the vehicle. He left in a different car yesterday. I frown and crease my eyebrows.

I thought he wasn't going to be back for a few days.

He's the whole reason the fight started. If he hadn't of left, Kelly wouldn't have even been talking about leaving for Sandra. Rayleen wouldn't have over heard and told us she was leaving. And so on, and so forth.

If he was more reliable, then none of it would have happened. Heated frustration slips out with my breath.

I decide jog over to meet him. He needs to know everything that happened. He needs to assume some fault for it; before something like this happens again.

I catch him right before he hits the steps for the entrance.

"James," I call sharply. He stops and turns, with a box in his hand. "You missed some things. Kelly ran off to Sandra because you left. Miles is dead. He died in the fight trying to stop Kelly from leaving.

There's talk now about how invested or not you are into making this work. You're going to have to stop disappearing if you want people to trust that you have their back. That you actually want to make this community work."

I make up the last part. I don't know if people are talking, but I bet they are.

Besides, I know it'll get the point across. Maybe he'll take it more seriously if he knows his beloved project is at stake because of his actions.

James turns around and walks inside his house.

I have half a mind to follow him, but I doubt it would do any good. I'm not looking to pick a fight with someone who doesn't care, today. I simmer the boiling heat in my chest.

I walk across the yard, and back to my house.

Going inside, I pull off my boots. John isn't in the kitchen and living room. I follow noises to find out where people are. Making my way to stand in Rayleen's doorway.

John is moving the bed per Rayleen's instructions.

She gets her own room, and we told her she could decorate it however she wanted. For her, that meant removing everything except the furniture from the room. Then, moving around the furniture, and then she'll think about what to put back in the room, and what will be redistributed.

She called it a move out/move in cleaning. One of her foster family's did it for her, and it helped her feel more at home in the room.

I have had half a thought to do it myself to John and my room, and Jaiden's room. That way we can make it our own.

It will be nice to have something fully our own, permanently.

I watch the scene in warmth. This could be good for us. A good start to our family. This feels right.

We're just missing Jaiden.

Chapter 36

Anna brings in the whole pie and sets it down on a cork pad on the table. The smell of sugared baked cherries reaches my nose.

"It looks great," I add to a chorus of praise.

The pie does look and smells fantastic. She leaves the pie spatula for us to dish ourselves up portions, and then she leaves for Jacob's rooms.

She knows the best way to make sure plenty will be eaten, is to leave it on the table for those who are dishing up to get seconds; for them to cut larger than average slices.

Especially, Jacob. Leave a dessert dish in front of him and he's bound to gobble up half of it; like he didn't even eat dinner at all.

Jacob stands up to dish up the pie to his plate then to Mr. Smith's. They each get a quarter of the pie.

When he goes to dish me up too, I decline. "No, thank you. I honestly couldn't eat another bite."

"Probably for the best," Jacob says without a fight. He turns his head to Mr. Smith. "More for us."

I had rehearsed several responses for a number of his possible reactions, but I guess I don't need any of them.

With their conversation topics used up for the night, and

attention on dessert, they finally stop talking. Though I'd almost prefer the noise to the loud smacks and slurps. Like nails on a chalkboard, the noises scratch at my brain.

It's like holding a breath too long waiting for the two of them to finish the pie on their plates.

Jacob dives in for another quarter and Mr. Smith takes the other.

They both appear exactly how they did before eating the pie. Neither looks in dire straits.

I wonder how long it takes for the food to get to the stomach?

How long would it take for the arsenic to transform and soak into their systems?

Would the food they ate dampen the effects of the arsenic to nonlethal levels?

Would the chemical required for the chemical reaction have been cooked out with the oven?

There seems like entirely too many variables to rely on this as the way to kill them.

Unless, there is need for plausible deniability. If this doesn't work, you could get away with no one knowing anything, or blame it on food poisoning. There's not going to be any testing done to determine the cause of death; that's not possible right now. There's no hospital or police forensic testing for arsenic poisoning.

The long breath hold starts again.

My mind boils down all the questions to one simple one.

Will it kill them?

Mr. Smith slows eating about half way through, then stops altogether. He leans back in his chair and closes his eyes. A lazy satisfied smile upon his lips.

Jacob finishes his pie piece with smacking lips and finger

licking.

Neither show any signs that they are poisoned. Not, that I would entirely know exactly what that would look like. My gauge for poisoned errs on the side of more extreme reactions; dead.

Maybe the pie wasn't poisoned. Then, I guess there was no harm done.

I give Jacob a chance to dismiss me again, right after dessert, just like last night, but he doesn't.

Silence follows dessert for entirely too long, while they sink in their chairs to digest their gluttony.

I contemplate if I can ask to be dismissed without seeming rude to our guest.

I don't know if I want to chance being rude to him, if he sends those he hates to get hung. There is zero chance of Jacob trying to save me, if a business partner offers enough compensation for it, or has enough leverage against Jacob. I'm fairly certain he'd kill me if he thought it would benefit a crucial business dealing.

Jacob has always skirted around the law, and pushed as much as he could without being caught and reprimanded. Now that there is no law, he's free to do anything he wants.

That, is a dangerous thing.

Mr. Smith seems exactly the same, possibly worse. Or, at least, more dangerous to me. There's absolutely no attachment to me, keeping him from doing anything.

Mr. Smith opens his eyes and seesaws his shoulders. "I'll miss Anna's cooking. Are you certain I couldn't persuade you to let me borrow her?"

"You're already getting the good end of the stick on this one, you don't need more," Jacob tells him.

"Hm," Mr. Smith looks at me. "Do you know how to cook?"

"Not like this." I can't make fancy sauces and pies; though

I've also never tried.

"You'll have learn. It's an important skill; a necessary skill you should know by now" He reprimands me.

"I've learnt a bit along the way. I took a foods class. But, we didn't make anything too fancy; lots of cookies. We made lasagna once. And I've helped make a few stews recently." I try to defend myself. I'm not completely useless in that category. "But, it would be good to know how to make more."

It's always good to learn more.

"Anna should teach you. I'm sure your father you be amenable to that." Mr. Smith looks to Jacob for a response.

I look for Jacob's reaction.

Jacob stares through Mr. Smith for a moment. He's thinking his way through his response. "I could be persuaded. Otherwise, there are always cook books. She's always done well enough with book learning."

"Bah." Mr. Smith scoffs. "I'll throw in a jar of honey for her to take some cooking lessons with Anna."

"Five." Jacob bargains.

I don't know why this is something to be bargained over. But, old business men will be old business men sometimes.

Everything is a deal, and nothing is done for free.

"Those better be some good lessons if you're going to get five jars." Mr. Smith surmises.

Jacob tilts his head and shrugs up his shoulders. "It's a valuable life time skill."

"Deal." Mr. Smith puts out a hand to seal in a shake.

Jacob obliges.

None of their bargaining means anything if Anna won't teach me, or won't teach me properly. I don't think she'll want to teach me, if she's trying to poison me.

Though now, she won't get a choice.

Bad teaching will instead, get blamed on me for being a bad student.

"Jaiden, open the door. It's gotten a little warm in here." Jacob orders suddenly.

"If you'll excuse me," Mr. Smith stands up using the table for support, "I have to use the washroom." He leaves.

I get up and open the door in the outside wall. I pull back the screen door, to make sure the bugs don't get in.

I take my seat again.

Excuse to leave on my lips, when my voice catches. Jacob looks pale and glistening. And, he's complained about being hot. Mr. Smith excused himself to the bathroom after being slightly unsteady.

Maybe there was something in the pie.

"Excuse me, I'm going to go to the washroom," I say, as I rise up in my chair a bit. Stopping halfway up in case Jacob denies me. I'd have to use the upstairs one; since this one is full, and Jacob's is forbidden. It's the same distance to the basement one.

Jacob's hand shoots out to grab my wrist. He pulls me closer.

"Are you unwell? Maybe there was something wrong with the fish? Salmonella?" Jacob whispers.

"You don't feel well either?" I ask.

"Hot. I've got a headache. Only a matter of time before I'm the next one in the toilet. Go. Before you make a mess." Jacob dismisses me.

I rush up the stairs in a quick, but not too quick of a pace.

I go into my room and shut the door. Letting myself into the bathroom, and closing the door, before I feel like I'm okay to relax.

It doesn't last. My fingers tingle in the need to do something.

My mind runs laps.

What do I do?

The question runs through my head many times. I question myself if it's really happening.

Are they really poisoned or was it a coincidence?

Are they poisoned enough to kill them, or just enough to make them sick?

I bounce back and forth between what to do next.

I dash out of the bathroom and to my bed. Kneeling on the floor, I grab out the bag. But, as soon as it's in my hands, I have second thoughts.

What if they aren't poisoned?

How can I leave where they won't see me go? Every way out involves some degree of going by them or being in their view.

I can't chance that.

I push the bag back under my bed. Pulling myself to stand, I go over things again.

Maybe I should go back down to see how they are? If no one is there, I could go.

But, they might also come back by the time I come back to grab my bag.

What about Anna? Is she going to come back to see if the job is finished? She'd normally be doing the dishes after supper is done, so she should be coming back quickly.

I can't go out there with a backpack without knowing if the area is clear.

Walking back through my door, I take a peek at my bed to make sure I pushed the bag under deep enough.

Quietly, I tiptoe out of my room and to the railing. I can't quite see the table, but I can see the light is still on in the closed bathroom door.

I take the stairs down to the main level.

Jacob isn't in his chair. Maybe he went to the bathroom.

It takes a moment to spot Jacob crumpled on the floor, curled around my fallen down chair.

A flash of mom pulls up in my memories and brings tears to my eyes.

"Dad," I say his title three times as I approach him.

His breathing is shallow, but still there. His body still moves.

I reach to check his pulse, but pull my hand back like it was burned. I don't know what I'd be looking for.

I know he's alive by the breathing, but I don't know what different pulse speeds would mean at this point. Other than nothing means he's already dead.

His breathing doesn't seem right either; slower and shallow. Beads of sweat cling to his forehead. His skin is paler than it should be.

"Dad." I shake his arm.

He groans softly. If not dead, he's incapacitated.

I have to go. Now. Unnoticed and on foot.

I rush upstairs and to my room. I change out of the dress into my, now clean, clothes that I had arrived in.

Pulling the bag out from under the bed, I swing it to put it on my back.

That one vision I had, I was travelling, walking back home. At least I know I'll make it. I was excited about being close to people I knew.

But, I have a better plan; one that doesn't involve a large amount of travel. I'll find somewhere safe, then text Dominique to come get me or meet me somewhere. To get a message to

Cole for him to pick me up somewhere; if they're able to contact him.

"Are you leaving?" Anna asks from the doorway. I jump at her sudden appearance. She looks flushed.

"I thought I'd go for a hike," I say. It's the only thing that could explain the backpack. But, I know it's a flimsy excuse.

"It's late." She reasons.

"Not too late. I won't be gone too long." I try to get passed her, but she doesn't move out of the way.

"Did you like the pie?" I recognize this. She's fishing for what I know.

I smile apologetically. "I didn't eat it. I'm sorry. I was too full from supper. Dad and Mr. Smith looked like they were enjoying it though. They practically ate the whole thing all by themselves."

"Where are Jacob and Mr. Smith?" She asks.

"Still eating pie, I think." I lie. "If you didn't see them, maybe they went out to the deck? Or, maybe the garage to smoke some cigars. Mr. Smith was in the bathroom when I had left. And, dad was at the table still eating."

"You should have eaten the pie too. I could go grab some for you?" Anna offers.

Should it concern me that she's insisting I eat the pie too? Is it personal, or is she trying to tie up loose ends?

"No, thank you. I don't really like cherry pie." I excuse.

"I don't believe that." Anna closes in on me. "Just like I don't believe you're going for a hike. Should we go find your father and ask him what he thinks about this?"

"He already said yes; said I could use the exercise," I say.

"Then you wouldn't mind if I confirm that with him. You're too young to be walking out there by yourself."

I know what we would find. We both know what we would find. If you know what you're looking for, you should be able to spot Jacob pretty easily when coming into the house, certainly by the time you get around to entrance of the stairs, and certainly when coming out from Jacob's rooms.

I don't know, at this point, if she's decided to kill me by any means possible. Poison in the pie is one thing, but another messier method is another.

"I know what you put in the pie, but I won't tell anyone." I blurt out. If ignorance won't work, maybe this will. "Just, please, let me leave and go back home. I won't cause any trouble for you."

"Why?" Anna blocks the doorway more, moving into the middle of the frame.

"We won't return. We have no reason to. I just want to go back to my life before Jacob uprooted it. I miss my friends. I was never planning on staying."

"Why don't you care that I killed your dad?" Anna asks. I wonder if that was her original question.

"Jacob was going to kill my friends; that's why I sent them away. Just like he had that other family hung. I might be human, but my friends are all supernaturals.

And, he was going to sell me to Mr. Smith; already had in their latest deal." I don't know if he was, but it helps add to my case. And, honestly, it doesn't feel like that hard of a stretch. "That's just the end to a very long list of the abuse he dealt me my whole life.

I never wanted to be here. I never wanted him to find me in the first place. I knew he would never let me go, so I was going to sneak out one of these nights, once I had enough supplies to last me the trip back. That's why this bag is all packed up." I hope all of this helps my case.

Anna mulls it over. "Okay, leave. But, I'm going to tell

everyone that you did it. That you killed them. So you better leave, and never return. We'll kill you if you come back."

"That's fine with me," I tell her. I don't want to push my luck in asking her to make sure no one tries to retaliate.

"I'll watch you go." Anna and I leave my room, after the doorway, I try to keep her to my side or front. You never know when you could get a knife in the back.

She forces me to be the first one down the stairs. I try not to look back at her. I go down quickly while skirting the railing with my hand. She might miss with a knife, or hit the back pack. And, if she tries to throw me down the stairs then I might be able to catch myself.

I go towards the front entrance.

"This way, out the back so no one sees you. Follow the lake shore north to town." I turn my head to look at her. She points towards the right direction so I know where to go. It's off to the left of the house. To the right would be towards Mr. Smith's. So, maybe she does want to give me a chance after all.

"Just getting my shoes." She nods and lets me gather and put on my shoes.

We get back to the dining area. The bathroom light is still on, but the door is cracked open. A leg lies across the opening. Jacob has moved onto his back. He's completely still now. I bite my question back.

"They're both dead." My eyes snap to Anna's. "I can see the question whirling around in your head. I had to finish the job; to be sure. Suffocated them both. We suffered long enough."

I nod. I don't know what I could say to that.

I open the back screen door and leave. It doesn't seem like the type of moment to say goodbye.

The chill of the air is still warm, but it won't be for long. Night is settling in and so will a colder chill. I walk quickly to the corner edge of our property. Keeping half an eye behind me to make sure no one is following me.

Anna watches me the whole way. I know she's watching to make sure I leave the right way. She's taking a chance on me; I could very well turn her in. I wouldn't, but she doesn't know that for certain.

I pick up the pace once I'm out of view. Jogging for a bit, but the shore is too rough to keep going at any good pace; not without risking a twisted ankle.

I look behind me again, sweeping the area around me just in case they come from another direction.

At the same time, I half look for Cole's familiar face. He's the least of my concerns at the moment, though.

Pulling out my phone, I make sure it's still on silent. I wouldn't want an ill-timed text or call to reveal my location to anything hunting me. I push the volume button down. It flashes the silent symbol. I click the power button and push the phone back into my pocket.

I'll text John later. Once I'm safe. Once I'm far away from here. We can come up with a plan from there.

Maybe I should go into the trees. Anna knows where I am. If she sends people after me, they'll know where I'll be.

But, animals might be in the woods. When it gets darker, I won't be able to see far away.

Don't cougars hunt mostly at dusk and dawn? Bears too, I think. If one of them decides to attack, I wouldn't know until claws and teeth were already sinking into me. I'd have no chance.

But, humans might have guns and long-distance attacks. I'd have a better chance in the woods of escaping bullets.

The humans finding me might be worse than the animals.

I have to be loud so that the animals don't attack me. They

won't come near me if I'm loud. At least, that's what I've heard about bears. But, I have to be quiet so the humans don't hear me and find me.

I will be quiet.

I veer off into the woods and hope for the best.

Chapter 37

Once upon a time, there was a little boy named Jeremy. He loved dragons and unicorns so much!

He was very fortunate to live on a farm that had dragons and unicorns.

Every day, Jeremy would eat breakfast then go out to the dragon barn with his mom.

While she was cleaning the stalls, Jeremy would play with the baby dragons.

They would run, and hop, and skip, and jump. But their most favourite game to play was fetch. Jeremy would take a rope and he would throw it as far as he could. The baby dragons would run, and hop, and skip, and jump after the rope.

When they got it, they would bring it back to Jeremy so he could throw it all over again. They would play this game over and over and over again because it was so much fun!

When they got tired, it would be breakfast time for the little dragons.

Once they were done their breakfast. Mom and Jeremy

would take the baby dragons to the training arena. They attached harnesses to the small dragons. The harness was attached to a rope, attached to a column in the middle of the room.

Jeremy would run, and hop, and skip and jump all around the room. Trying to get the dragons to follow him. And eventually, the baby dragons would try to learn how to fly.

Once they were done flying training, they would go outside where all the bigger dragons were.

Jeremy and Mom would grab a saddle and put it on the biggest dragon. They would go onto the saddle and go up, and up, and up, and up.

They fly over a field, over a forest, over a road, over a river, over some flowers, and over a city.

And over a highway, over a hill, over a pond, over a road, and over a town.

They flew around the town, so Mom could show Jeremy all the places she used to live, and work, and play, and learn.

Then, they would circle back around and go over the town, over the road, over the pond, over the hill, over the highway, over the city, over some flowers, over a river, over a road, over the forest, and down, down, down, down, down into the dragon field.

Mom would take the saddle off of the biggest dragon and put it on the oldest dragon. And, they would hop on and go up, and up, and up, and up, and up.

Over the field, over the forest, where they would take a sharp turn and follow the tree line over to the neighbour's house.

The neighbour's griffins would fly all around the property with them, and when it was time to go back home, the griffins would leave.

Jeremy and Mom would fly over the farmhouse, over the unicorn field, and down, down, down, down, down into the dragon field. They would take the saddle off of that dragon, put it away, and say goodbye to the dragons.

Next, they would go to unicorns. Mom would clean out the stalls, while Jeremy had a very important job to do. He had to shine the unicorn horns and brush the unicorn's fur and hair. He loved this job because the unicorns came in such pretty colours.

They were black, gray, white, brown, red, orange, yellow, green, blue, indigo, violet, gold, and silver.

Some of them were two colours, three colours, four colours, five colours.

Some of them were rainbow colours.

Some of them were all the colours.

He had so many unicorns. He wanted to name them all. So, he picked out names for them.

A, B, C, D, E, F, G, H, I, J, K, L, M, N, O, P, Q, R, S, T, U, V, W, X, Y, and Z.

When he ran out of letters, he started wondering exactly how many unicorns he had. So he lined them all up and started counting.

1 unicorn, 2 unicorns, 3 unicorns, 4 unicorns, 5 unicorns, 6 unicorns, 7 unicorns, 8 unicorns, 9 unicorns, 10 unicorns, 11 unicorns, 12 unicorns, 13 unicorns, 14 unicorns, 15 unicorns, 16 unicorns, 17 unicorns, 18 unicorns, 19 unicorns, 20

unicorns...

"Mr. Chris, there's a dragon outside!" A male voice exclaims.

I bound up from my cushion on the floor; boring book now abandoned. Any excuse to get out of reading for a few minutes. Since everyone else is now distracted, I know I can too. I won't get in trouble if I do the same thing that everyone else does.

I rush to the window with everyone else. Bumping shoulders with some of the other kids who are trying to get a look.

I wonder if anyone would think it's cool that I rode on a real-life dragon? I almost say it out loud, but I don't think anyone would listen.

What if they didn't believe me? What if they think I'm making it up for attention? What if they asked me to explain? What would I even say?

I look all around in the air for the flying dragon. Echoes cry all around me asking where it is.

"Down there!" A couple people shout above the rest. I watch someone point down to the ground and follow their finger.

A large dark red dragon stands on its four legs in James' hotel parking lot. It paces back and forth in an oval. Someone sits on the back of it, on a saddle, like you would a horse.

I know that dragon.

It's Sandra's dragon. The one we rode on when Sandra had taken us.

The person riding on the dragon is probably Sandra. But, whoever it is, it's too far to see exactly who it is to confirm it.

I try to back away from the window, but there are too many people behind me to move anywhere. I feel squashed. It's hard to breathe.

"Everyone stay here. Don't leave. I'll be right back." Mr. Chris orders us right before he leaves through the doors for the stairs.

"Alright, let's go!" One of the older boys immediately says, once the teacher has gone out of sight and hearing.

"Mr. Chris just said-" a girl starts to say.

The older boy interrupts her. "Haven't you seen the movies? You stay, you die. It's always the main characters who don't listen to the people in charge, who go off to try to save themselves, that end up being the only people alive in the end. And, I don't know about you, but I'm not going to die here."

"No one said we were going to die. We don't even know who they are and what they want." She disputes.

"You can stay and die if you want, but I'm going." He goes first, then a small group of other boys follow him. One brother drags his sister along. Quickly, more and more children leave, as others do.

Since everyone else is going, I'm going too.

I don't want to be the only person left behind. And, I have no idea what Sandra is going to do, but it can't be good.

A couple kids stay behind. They are going to listen to the teacher. They don't want to get in trouble for going against his orders.

For a moment, I wonder if I should do the same. But, there is something else inside of me telling me to run.

I need to find Dominique.

Hopefully, she's at the big hotel.

She was supposed to be going back and forth with food and supplies between a few places. But, she also said she had some meetings today at the big hotel.

The winding stairs aren't as long going down as they are going up, especially in a hurry. Gravity helps pull us down faster. I watch my steps to make sure each foot lands on the stairs. I wouldn't want to fall and knock others over.

Security is pushed aside by the wave of children bursting out of the building. I duck to avoid an adult's arm. Others aren't lucky. They get grabbed and taken back inside.

We scatter in a few directions. Most run towards the big hotel. Either, because they live there, or because that's where the dragon is.

They want to see the dragon. They don't know how dangerous Sandra is. I wonder if I should warn them, but I don't know why she's here.

I rush forward towards James' hotel to get to Dominique. If she's not somewhere else, then she'll be there. Everywhere else is too far away to get to on my own.

I slow down as I get to the front corner of the building. Most of the other kids break off to join the crowd. Pushing their way to the front, to get a better and closer look.

The dragon has stopped pacing to sit back with his side facing the entrance. Sandra sits in the saddle. The dragon's wings tuck into his side, blocking part of Sandra; shielding her. Her head pokes out from where I'm at though.

The closer I get to the front door, the more of her that gets visible. I duck down and hide behind people as much as possible.

I don't want Sandra to notice me, or she might kidnap me again; or try to kill me again.

I weave in and around the growing crowd of people coming out the front doors. I look at each person in the crowd, searching for Dominique.

I glimpse someone, through the spaces between bodies, approaching Sandra and the dragon. I stop and watch; holding back a warning against getting too close.

"I'm here for Jaiden," Sandra shouts for all to hear.

"She's not here." Someone, Shale I see now, shouts back at

Sandra and all to hear. He's too close to her. "Her dad collected her, and she hasn't come back yet."

Could Shale be going back to Sandra? Why would he get so close to her after everything she's done? Was he a spy? Was he the one who Dominique was searching for; the one who vandalized that billboard?

Traitor!

"Liar!" Sandra screams.

The window closes as people move. Screams and gasps jolt my body. I shrink in on myself. Once I can get a good look at Sandra again, the dragon moves into the opening instead.

The dragon has Shale by his stomach, up in the air. The body whips up then down to the ground with a sickening thump.

I scream a little, but cover my mouth to stop it.

"Where's Jaiden?" Sandra shouts.

"She's not here. You're welcome to look for yourself." Someone from the crowd yells back at her.

I wish they wouldn't give her ideas. If she searches everywhere, she might find me.

I have to get out of here.

Run!

"Give her to me!" Sandra pulls on the dragon's reins. The dragon stands back up and squares up to look at us. Fire bursts out of its mouth and into the crowd right in front of the entrance; hitting people and the doorway.

I sprint back the way I came and hug the wall around the side of the building.

"Give her to me, or I'll burn it all down!" Sandra's voice gets deeper and growly.

"She's not here. She never came back!" Someone cries out.

It's true. But, Sandra wouldn't know that. She would think we're lying to save her.

Cole returned without her. There was a fire. We thought Sandra did it. It wiped out everything. There was no one left to ask where she had gone. He searched the area for her, but he never found her, or her body.

He was too late. He blames himself for not getting there sooner. We should have known Kelly would find Sandra immediately, and Sandra would immediately go find Jaiden.

Everyone assumed she'd make it back to us eventually; if she's alive. That she'd call us soon. Or, maybe, text us to rescue her from somewhere. But, that hasn't happened yet.

Dominique says she's alive and out there somewhere. That she'll make her way back to us; alive.

But, I hear the others' doubts. Sandra killed or took her. The fire killed her. She died escaping, or on her way back. She would have called or texted if she was alive.

No one else knows what happened; with the fire.

Dominique blames herself for leaving Jaiden behind.

Screams cry out again. I cover my ears and crouch down, yet still watching for danger. The rough wall catches on my jacket.

The dragon starts off, quickly running, then lifting off. The dragon opens its mouth and bursts flame at the market, and trails a line of flame hitting apartments and the back of the hospital.

It circles back, to set fire to the small hotel and the butchery.

The dragon flies further up, and circles around again. I brace for another round of fire, but Sandra flies off over the market.

He was right, if we had stayed in the tall windowed building, we would have died. Sandra didn't hesitate to set it on fire. She didn't even hesitate before targeting the hospital.

My arm yanks me up on my feet. I screech.

A woman grabs me around my waist. I don't know her. "Let's get you out of here." She tells me as she grabs my hand and starts pulling me away from the wall.

I dig my heels into the ground to pull down my whole body. "I have to find-"

She cuts me off and turns to talk to me as she continues to pull me. "No one. We need to get you safe. This truck will take you and all the other kids back to the farm. Your family can find you later." The woman yanks and pulls me successfully with her. She grabs me up and sits me on the back of a truck. "Get in."

I look into the truck with a bunch of my classmates, then back to the hotel. I'm torn on what I should do.

The adults are telling me to go to the farm and wait for Dominique there.

But, I want to find her now.

The woman goes back to get some more kids, or to help in other ways. I lose track of her when another adult blocks my view.

A bunch of adults are piling kids into the back of this truck and another. They force me to move closer to the inside.

The kids here are only a small amount of what made up my learning class. I don't know what happened to the rest.

Maybe I should go.

Dominique might be at the farm. Maybe she isn't here.

John would be there, for sure. He could help.

I look around; searching the crowd for her, but there are too many people and too much chaos.

Some of the adults jump onto the back of the truck right before the truck starts moving.

"Everyone alright?" One woman asks. The kids don't say anything. Crying takes the place of words. "We'll get you guys safe, then get you back to your families."

The woman looks over to one of the men. Tears betray the fear and worry she tries to hide. She looks back towards the buildings on fire.

I look beyond her to the flames rising into the sky.

My breath shortens. My leg starts hurting underneath my nails scratching at them with my right hand. I look down at my hand. My leg itches, and my hand twitches.

It's an oddly familiar ache, though not to me.

I slap my hands together and fold the fingers in between each other.

My stomach sickens.

No! I scream internally to Alexa. Stop!

I'll never do that! I don't do that. You did, but I won't. I hated it when you hurt yourself.

I won't do that!

Chapter 38

The lounge is full up with people, but I don't see much for food. It is too late for breakfast, yet too early for lunch. People are using the lounge to get in some music and socializing. If they have anything, it's a drink.

We've grown so much that we might need to get more socialization zones going, so we aren't so crowded in.

We are starting to need things to do that go beyond survival; entertainment things. I don't know what we could do first. A bowling alley would be hard to set up, but maybe we could set up a volleyball net. Maybe we could look and see if we could find a basketball net or two.

Some sports areas might be the easiest to set up. Then, we could look at some other things. It would be nice to be able to go to a place to do some arts and crafts. Or, maybe, somewhere we could play board games with groups of people.

Maybe we could set up a movie theatre. That certainly helped morale through the winter. Maybe, if we could find a projector, then we could set up and outdoor theatre for the summer.

Maybe it'll help once the warmer weather is, for sure, here to stay. It's never a guarantee until May long weekend has come and gone; even then… May long has passed. Though it's been warmer and no snow for a couple weeks, I still don't believe it's fully gone.

People might naturally gravitate to the outside. We could easily make a fire pit like at the farm. Maybe set up a little park area.

I take a deep breath in and let it out slowly. I guess I'd have to figure out who to talk to in order to arrange all of that. Set up more meetings to discuss things and more meetings to get things done.

I yawn.

Two meetings down, and one to go today. I stave off another yawn. How did Jaiden get through all of this without dying from boredom? My brain hurts from the mind-numbing hours focusing on the same cycled information.

Why do they always talk in circles? So that they can bill by the hour, instead of getting the job done in five minutes. I answer my own question.

Hectre wipes down the counter top near the till. He's using his time to clean, while people are in between meals and not asking much of him. "Hey, do you have any coffee left?"

"No sorry. Only water or juice right now." He offers. My shoulders slump down. "Long day?" He asks.

"Very."

"I might have tea. I'd maybe have to make a pot, so it would take a bit. It's got caffeine though." Hectre offers.

"No, thanks." I've had more tea, than I would like to drink for the rest of my life.

Hectre motions with his finger to get closer. I lean over the counter a little. "Jules is making some coffee cake for lunch. I might be able to get you a sip of espresso."

"Yes," I say without hesitation. Even just a sip, that'll do the trick.

Hectre goes in through the doors and comes back out just a moment later. In his hand holds a small glass with some brown liquid scaling the sides. He hands me the glass. It's the smallest sip of what's dripped back to the bottom of the cup, after the rest was poured out.

I shoot the remainder into my mouth, tasting the bitter energizer, and feeling a zip of energy coursing through me. I know that it's too soon, and not enough caffeine, but it helps anyway.

"I love you," I say as I pass the glass back to him.

Hectre chuckles. "You better."

Gasps of horror and excitement interrupt our jest. Whipping my body around, my gaze scans the room for something happening. But, the people seem to have their attention on the outside.

Déjà vu feelings pull up instant dread.

"I'll go talk with her. See what she wants." Shale volunteers before I comprehend what's happening. He's gone before I get to the window to see Sandra circling the parking lot with the dragon.

I won't stop him; I couldn't stop him. If he wants to risk it, he can go right ahead. He used to be on her side, maybe Sandra will talk with him.

Shale walks outside and quickly gets to the parking lot. A crowd of people follow him out and start collecting outside.

I should go out there. Demand to know what she did with Jaiden; if she did something to Jaiden. I'm crowded in from behind, or I would go.

She might know something. Sandra could have been the one to set the fire. I don't care what James said.

The more people that go, the less view I can watch from. I get on top of the table. I can see above everyone's heads this way.

Shale and Sandra talk.

The dragon lunges forward and grabs onto Shale.

My hand instantly slaps over my mouth in shock.

He goes up and then down, as the dragon goes for the kill. Shale doubtfully survived the slam to the ground, if he survived the teeth through his sides.

When the dragon snaps at his stomach again, I know he's dead, or will be very soon.

The dragon lifts its head up, and opens its mouth. A bright spot is the only warning, before the dragon heaves fire onto the people standing in front of me.

I stumble backwards. Catching my balance to jump on the ground, I don't stop when my feet hit the ground.

Rayleen!

I have to get Rayleen.

We have to get out of here.

Hectre shouts above the chaos. "Emergency exit this way!"

He directs us towards the back of the lounge. People run in a wave down the hall and towards the back of the hotel. We go through a door, into a stairwell, and out another door.

I see the fire blast before I see the dragon. My heart drops.

The dragon sets fire to the third and forth floors of the market. Rayleen was on the fourth floor; the school was on the fourth floor.

The kids! We have to get them out of there.

I sprint across the street.

There are people struggling to get out of the doors; lugging their belongings with them.

The back of my jacket is yanked hard away from the doors.

"No one's going in!" I twist around and the security guard lets go.

"The kids are up there!" I exclaim.

"No, they aren't. They left!" He swings his arm back towards the hotel. Pointing towards the front of the building. My stomach drops.

"Did you see Rayleen?" He raises his face in confusion and shakes his head. He doesn't know who that is. "Red head girl about this tall?"

"No, sorry." He says.

I need certainty. "Are you sure they all got out?"

"The hospital!" Someone screams.

I need to know for sure. "I need to check." Even if she got out, what if another kid stayed behind?

"No one goes back in! That building isn't safe. It's going to come down with you in it. You want me to tell her you died because you went in a burning building while she was out here safe?"

"You don't know that she's out here!" I scream in his face.

"You don't know that she's in there! The whole batch of kids came out, no one would have stayed in there by themselves. Either way, you're not going back in there." He sizes himself up; puffing out his chest and standing taller. He's willing to use force to keep me out. "A bunch of kids were driven off towards the farm. Maybe she was with them?"

Why didn't he start with that?

Would she have gone with them?

I look back to the hotel. Three fires burn in front of me. The market burns behind me.

The hospital, someone shouted about the hospital too. Oh God, did she set the hospital on fire too?

There's too much fire. It's all going to burn down. We can't save it. There's no firefighters around to put out the flames.

James. Where is James? I haven't seen him yet today. He's

powerful. He might be able to fix this. Or Margie, where is she? Was she in the hotel? Did she get out?

With all this chaos, I don't know if there's a way to find anyone easily.

We need to get people to the farm.

I have to make sure Rayleen is safe. I have to trust that she got out; that she went with the truck of kids to the farm.

We need to get James here. Find Margie, and other magic users. Maybe they can put out the fires.

With a new mission in mind, I run to the small hotel's parking lot. People are already packing up vehicles; over filling them with as many people as possible. A batch of kids in a truck takes off, but I can't see if Rayleen is with them.

They're already sending more people to the farm. People are abandoning here for safety.

I see a few people getting inside another car. Sprinting over to them, I jump inside the door, and sit on the lap of a woman. Mine is the last open spot in the car. The woman I'm on closes the door.

Ted pulls out of the parking spot and screeches forward. He speeds off down the main road.

A moment of guilt strikes me, as I watch everything burn behind me. Maybe I should have stayed. I could have done something useful. I could have helped people get away. I should have looked more for Rayleen. I should have insisted on looking inside the market for her. I should have gone to help patients escape the hospital.

"What is that?" Ted shrieks.

I whip my head forward, but can't see anything with my head near the roof. I lean forward to look out the side window, drawing the window down when that still isn't enough.

The ground shakes and a roaring rumble fills the car. Grey

clouds of dust plume the air in the distance.

I send the window back up when the dust rolls towards us.

What is happening? Is this Sandra? Is this a full on war attack? Maybe the Sandra and dragon thing was just a diversion.

Ted turns down a road towards the farm.

"The buildings are falling." A man gasps. He panics as he hits Ted in the chest with his open hand. "Drive. Drive. Drive!"

I lean and twist just in time to see a building collapse. The ground swallows it up. When it finishes, the ground starts shaking once again.

Tires squeal at the force of the breaks, when we slow abruptly to turn. We pull forward along the front of the farm. Ted parks the car in the long line up of vehicles outside the fence.

I push the door open and leap out. I cover my mouth and nose with my sleeve, but quickly see that the dust isn't here. I look behind me. The dust comes our way to a certain point, then it gets thrown back.

James sits on the ground in the middle of the road, seemingly watching this all go down. But something tingles in the air, and I feel like it's him.

Another building crashes down, the next in the line. This time, the dust hits an invisible dome around where the building was.

"Dominique!" Sara shouts before grabbing onto my arm.

"What is he doing? We need him to go put out the fires." I shout.

"They're making a fire break. We protect the farm first, then we go put the other fires out." She explains.

"But, Sandra left. We don't need to do this. People are dying over there." I stomp over to James, and repeat those things for him to hear. "You need to go to the fires and put them out. Sandra left. People are dying over there."

"We'll all die if we don't handle this correctly. Take her away so I can concentrate." James says.

"We don't have to do this. You're wasting time. People are dying!" I shout.

Arms wrap around me. A whisper in my ear tells me, "You aren't going to win this argument with him. We'll go help them. Do what we can."

I turn in his arms. "Have you seen Rayleen?"

John nods shortly. "I just sent her off to our house with some other kids. They were the first ones back."

With everything else going on, my relief only lasts a moment before my dread focuses back on everything else.

I break away from John, yet stay within reach. With all that's going on, too many people stand and watch the buildings fall. Too many watch the flames growing in the distance.

But, what could they be doing? Without the magic users James controls, we can't put out the fires. He's putting them all to use here.

No major injuries have come in. There's no medical area, just some people buzzing around with bandages and salve.

Pulling down the buildings makes travelling back and forth dangerous. I peer back the way we had just come through. The road is destroyed; or covered, at least. We couldn't go back that way if we wanted too.

The way in passing the Bower Mall is still open though. They haven't pulled down any of the buildings down that way; yet. "We have to go back."

"I'll get a truck," John says. He takes off.

We're so far away that the fire break won't mean a thing. If they would just put it out, all this could be stopped now.

Never mind that we could have used those buildings, or the things inside of them. I don't think he's thought this through.

The air magic people could blow it out like a birthday candle. The water magic people could put some water on it. Fire magic users could control the flames, and put it out like that. James could pull down the buildings that are actually on fire and would be coming down anyways. Margie could throw some dirt on it.

It could be over right away, but they're wasting time.

John takes some keys from a guy. He holds them up so I can see. He presses a button. Some lights flash on a silver truck in the line up. They flash again.

We both take off for the truck in a run. Meeting inside the cab, John starts up the truck, and quickly turns us around to leave. I grab the seat and the door as my body lurches with the force. I put on my seat belt.

John speeds the truck along the road.

My eyes flicker towards the Bower mall. No one is out. They might be completely unaware of what's happening.

No, they'd have to know by now. They're too close to the farm not to notice the rumbling, if they can ignore the noise of it all.

They're choosing to hide instead of helping.

John turns the corner for the straight shot to the hotels. We approach more carefully as we get close.

I take off my seatbelt the moment John slows to stop. Taking off out of the immobile truck, I get outside and freeze.

The fire has grown and spread to nearby buildings and trees. More fires, separate fires, blaze in the distance across the river. She must've set fire to more buildings as she was leaving; if she did leave completely.

"Don't run into any burning buildings and I won't either, deal?" John places his hands on my shoulders, then kisses my temple.

"Deal." I agree.

John takes off for the parking lot in front of Jerry's. I wander between the choices.

I could help John. He talks with someone kneeling beside someone else on the ground.

Other people are going in and out of the buildings with rescued people and things. Some are throwing supplies out of windows.

Then, there's whatever chaos is happening at the hospital. They'll need help too.

We ultimately need to get people to the farm.

The people running in and out of buildings are choosing their risk. Deciding to go back for things and people. They are capable adults.

Some of the injured, some of the people tucked away watching everything from their sheltered spots, don't have a choice.

Away from the main buildings, across the road are some people leaning against the butcher's building. I decide to start there.

"Is everyone okay?" I ask as I approach.

"Some minor burns, if that's what you mean." A man answers for the group.

"Are you from around here?" I ask. Do they have homes they could go back to?

"Not anymore." He responds; eyeing up a spot behind me.

"We used to live in those apartments." Another man clarifies. He points to the enflamed apartments behind the market.

"Let's get you off to the farm then. Hop in the back of the truck." I tell them.

"The farm's under attack." The one man says.

Oh, of course people would think that. I defend James' choice, if only to convince people to get to safety. "That's James pulling down the buildings for a fire break. Just incase they can't put out the fires. We just came from there. It's safe."

A couple looks are exchanged before they lift off from their spots and agree to get into the truck.

With one set of people taken care of, I look around for some more. The next closest bunch of people are in the hotel parking lots. I walk that way.

With all the people we should have, in the number of buildings on fire, there should be way more people out here; let alone those in the nearby buildings.

I can only hope they're safe somewhere else; having gone off to somewhere safe behind other buildings and out of view. Otherwise, the other possibility means they're hiding within buildings.

We don't have the people to search all the buildings.

I cover my ears at the impossibly loud first groan of the rectangular building.

My eyes snap to the market.

Someone runs out of the front door with a chair in arm. Items and people fall out of multiple windows with a tossed speed. People gather items and move them into the back of trucks.

The middle of the building claps down on the next level, sending that one and the next one down. As it hits the ground level, the rest of the building crashes down in a roar.

A breeze turns into a wave. I crouch and tuck my face into my shoulder. Closing my eyes before dust irritates them. I try not to breathe in.

When the noise stops.

When the wind stops.

John shouts, "Dominique!"

I unravel and look out towards where I had last seen him.

"Here!"

We're safe, but I know others weren't so lucky.

326

Chapter 39

The sun is going down faster than I would like. When there are no street lights and no town lights, the sun going down can mean complete darkness.

I should stop for the night. It could be dangerous to keep going, but it could be more dangerous to stay.

This is the most likely first stop for anyone looking for me. The fugitive is going to run to the next town and stay the night. So, I shouldn't do that. I need to keep going.

Even if it could mean that Cole doesn't find me.

The problem with keeping going, is the possible animals, lack of light, and how to keep going.

I can easily solve one issue with my flashlight, and I can't do much about the animals, but the other is proving harder.

I also have to risk being seen because of the light.

There is a distinct lack of working vehicles and gas in this town. Jacob and his people have left their mark all over town. Everything was raided and up for grabs.

I manage to find a tall bicycle and it's about the best I figure I'm going to get.

I lean the handle bar against the side of a building, and get myself between them.

With my shoulder against the building, I put my right foot on the pedal. In a smooth motion, I kick up and put my leg over the bike. Transferring the bracing point from my shoulder to my arm, then hand. The handle comes off the building. I push off of the building to balance the bike in the center, and push the pedals in their circle.

The bike wobbles as I take off, but quickly balances out with speed.

I ride out of town on the main road. If I can get one town over, maybe that would be safe enough to find a spot to sleep. That might be safer than traveling at night.

The ride is nicer than walking, but I still make sure to keep an eye out. The trees move with each sway of the wind. The evening creatures are making their noises.

It's the unnatural noises that I would mostly need to worry about.

My mind starts wandering to the darkness. Eyes could be watching me, and I wouldn't know. I stop myself with a shake as the hairs on the back of my neck start prickling.

Stop that. You'll just freak yourself out over nothing.

I shoulder check to look around and behind both ways; there's nothing there. I pick up speed either way after officially freaking myself out.

With the extra speed, I reason, I will get away faster. And, whatever is out there, won't be able to catch me.

A whistle stings me in the ears. I slow quickly, yet quietly. Stopping the bike completely, and falling to one foot, as I wait a moment to figure out the whistle. It caries a tune; up and down in a circling rhythm. Not natural and not the wind. It has to be a person.

The noise is coming from the woods on the left, yet still in front of me. It wouldn't be any of Jacob's people; shouldn't be any of them.

Something else could be trying to lure me into the woods.

I contemplate zooming by on the bike. It would be safer. I don't know who the person is, and what they want.

Whistling in the dark, isn't a great way to gain trust.

It could be a trap.

No, it wouldn't be a trap. No one would set a trap out here randomly with the miniscule traffic they would get, especially in the middle of the night. Maybe a trap of opportunity?

I set out to go. The position I stopped in was awkward. Having to lean the bike to the side, and balance it all on one foot, but trying to get going without a prop will be much more awkward.

Moving the pedal into position, I figure I can immediately start going once I kick the bike to center with my other foot.

My foot fumbles on the peddle, then hits the ground hard. The seat digs into my back hard, and the bike tilts to the other side. The back wheel skids.

I curse myself for stopping. It's going to be hard getting the bike back going, especially if I have to do so quickly.

"Hello?" A female voice calls out.

"Hello?" I answer automatically. It's a girl. The edge of danger dulls slightly.

"I'm in the ditch. Help me, please! I crashed my bike and wrenched my ankle. I can't walk. I've been here a few hours. My home's not far." She explains from the darkness.

I hesitate. This could still be a trap. If her home's not far, she could have crawled back.

"Hello? Are you still there?" The voice calls out.

"Yes, I'm here. Where are you?" I get off my bike. It's pretty much useless anyways, without something to help me get going.

"Crawling up the ditch." Just as she says that, something moves onto the road up ahead. The shadowed figure doesn't look human.

My heart pounds in my chest. I've made a terrible mistake.

I pull out my phone and turn on the flashlight towards the creature.

She appears human enough, but not quite. The light pulls an iridescent green from her light skin before she shields her face with a black gloved hand.

"Sorry." I sweep the phone light towards the ditch she said she crashed in. A black motorcycle with purple accents lays in the crevice. A few black panel pieces and a mirror lay separately.

Her story checks out, so far, at least. "Are you alright?"

I wave the light back towards her, but not at her face. I look over her, but it's hard to see any damage. The black leather outfit doesn't give much away.

"Hurt my ankle pretty bad. We're not terribly too far from my home, but a lot further than I could get by myself." She explains. She smiles nicely.

"Right, okay. So let's get you up, and we'll start walking you home." I tell her. I offer my hand to help her up. She grabs on and we heave her up to one foot.

She hisses when her other foot touches the ground. "I can't put any pressure on it."

"We can use my bike. You can sit on it and we'll push you along." She is about a full head taller than me, so maybe she'd fit the bike better.

"Good idea." She lets go of my hands when she's balanced out on the one foot.

I leave her to grab the abandoned bike. We get her on it and she rests her heel on the pedal. We work together to walk the bike in the direction of her home. She walks her one foot on the ground, while I support and push the other side.

"I'm Alette." She bursts through the silence.

"Hi Alette, I'm Jaiden," I answer her unasked question.

"What were you doing out so late?" Alette asks.

I quickly figure out that I shouldn't overshare. I don't know her. She seems nice enough, but she might not be. She could be fishing for information to use against me later. "Long story, but I'm trying to find my way back to my friends. What were you doing before you crashed?"

"I just went out for a ride. I like the view. We can help you get back to your friends, as thanks for rescuing me." Alette offers.

It could be risky, but it could also work out better; possibly safer to travel with a group.

"We?" I ask.

"Bike club. Don't worry everyone is super sweet. I promise no harm with come to you, and we'll return you to your friends just as we found you." She promises.

"You don't need to go too far out of your way. My friends live far away." I give her the chance to back out. She doesn't understand what she's offering.

On the other hand, in the back of my mind, I worry that her biker gang might just want to steal our city, our things, or make us pay for protection, or something terrible.

"How far?"

"Central Alberta." I generalize.

Alette clicks her tongue. "So far away from home."

I wonder if that was bad to say. Now she knows I have no one nearby to help me.

Don't tell strangers that the parents aren't home, type of idea. I failed that test. But, I didn't want to lie.

"My dad found me a few days ago, after we were separated from when everything happened before." I clarify vaguely.

"The Reset?" She asks.

"The Reset?" I repeat the words to a different question intonation.

"That's what we've been calling the start of this; with the attacks. When the supernaturals rebels first started attacking the world." Alette explains.

"Yes, then," I confirm her original question. "We were separated at The Reset, but he found me a couple days ago and brought me back here to live with him."

"But?" She emphasizes to ask for continuance. But, why am I not there? Why am I on my way back to my friends?

"But, I didn't get a real choice until tonight, and I decided to leave and go back home," I answer.

Alette grunts an acknowledgement.

We walk and ride a ways in silence, until we come upon a travelled dirt path into the trees. Alette has us turn to go into the woods.

"How old are you?" She asks.

I hesitate. I don't know what the right answer is.

I still don't know Alette well enough. Saying my true age could help me or hurt me; depending on the people. But, people don't usually ask unless they already have suspicions.

"Fifteen." I decide to go with the truth.

"That makes sense." She clarifies. "You're still technically a kid, and your dad would still want to make those big decisions for you. Well, we definitely can't let you go alone now. Who knows who you'll run into out there? We'll get you back to your friends; safe and sound. I promise."

"Thank you," I say. Maybe I did run into the right person; helped the right person. The pit in my stomach starts to lessen.

"Hng." Alette sounds. "Right, so you know how when you're family is great, but you invite a friend over so you give them rules and a rundown of how to act or not to act? We need to do that now.”

“Okay, sure.” I guess so. I did the same whenever someone would meet Jacob.

“Keep in mind that, I promise you, my friends are sweet and won’t harm you in any way.” Alette tries to reassure me.

“Okay.” I drag out the word suspiciously.

“Our kind, have intense rules that we follow. It’s tradition. So, don’t tell anyone your real name, we only go by nicknames. You’ll call me Potato; it’s a long story. You’ll introduce yourself as Blondie.” What is she? Why nicknames?

I open my mouth to ask questions and comment, but she continues quickly.

“Be polite, but never apologize. We don’t believe in apologies. We believe in an eye for an eye. And an apology means you owe someone an eye.

On the reverse side, nod deeply to acknowledge something, instead of thanking someone for that something. We don’t give thanks, never say thank you or thanks. You can be grateful.

What is done for you and what you do for others is a given, because we are family. So you don’t say thank you.”

I interrupt at a natural pause. “But, you thanked me?”

“I did and I gave you my real name. I acknowledge that your culture doesn’t follow the same rules and etiquette.

However, now you are coming into my home. It’s a different culture and I will need to follow my cultural rules while in my home and you need to respect my culture while in my home.” Alette explains.

It makes sense.

“Of course, I’m sorry. I didn’t mean to offend you.” No apologies! I quickly internally shout at myself.

“You didn’t, and don’t apologize. Just follow the rules while at the clubhouse and you'll be fine." Alette says.

I'll try my best. No real names. No apologies. No thanks.

"Don't worry." She continues after a moment's pause. "You're bringing me home to my family, and with us, family is everything. This, what you are doing, makes you family too.

They won't hurt you; they won't bother you. Though they might appear a bit intimidating in the beginning, most of them are actually the sweetest, more caring people you'll ever meet.

You only have to worry about them wanting to keep you forever." Alette chuckles. "It's a joke, sort of."

I hesitate, but don't show it. I keep pace with the bike.

With the rules and bike gang, it's a lot. I worry that I made the biggest mistake of my life helping Alette.

We walk a ways further. The worn path starts to show signs of more when we come up to an archway. Someone has woven trees together to give personality to the way.

The path widens afterwards, with smaller offshoots in other directions.

It reminds me of a campground. The woodsy entrance with a worn dirt path that leads off to a handful of locations and cabins.

"We're here!" Alette says as the corner of a building peeks out from behind trees. There's a distinct lack of lighting in the area and at the house.

Is this her house, or the clubhouse? A clubhouse should be lit up, at least inside; I would think. She kept talking about multiple people, a biker club, mentioned as 'we'. There certainly are enough motorcycles, dirt bikes, and bicycles lined up to elude to the amount of people there should be.

Would they just be asleep? Are they somewhere else? Is it all in her head? Is it a trap?

We dump the bike when we arrive at the wooden structure's front porch.

As soon as we step up, the door swings open. The warm fire light from inside takes a moment to adjust to. Light music and chatter fill the air.

Relief floods me knowing she's not making up people.

"Potato!" Arms from a wide man stretch open. "You brought a friend!" He's loud and bold, decked head to toe in a black leather suit.

"I'm hurt. I crashed, but Blondie found me and decided to help, in exchange for bringing her back to her friends; safe and sound." I wish she didn't put it like that; it makes it sound like I wouldn't have helped her otherwise.

I don't want them to get the wrong impression.

"Oh shit!" He exclaims.

"Language! She's a child." My cheeks warm. I feel like I'm the one who got scolded, not him.

"I will watch myself in the future." He half bows with his hand on his chest.

I nod. I don't know if I can say it's fine, but I know I can't apologize or thank him. Alette said I could nod to acknowledge, so that's what I feel safe doing.

"I can take her from here. She's heavy for you." He takes up Alette's other arm. Once he's got her, I let her go. My shoulder aches from the exertion. It feels good to stretch it out. "Come inside. Let's get you warmed up."

"She can't stay long," Alette tells him quietly.

He doesn't answer, but nods.

I follow the two inside.

With a view from behind, I spot large patches on their backs. At first, I see a flying butterfly. But, that's not quite right. It's a person attached to the wings. It's a fairy. They've got fairies as their club logo.

Less scary than if it were skulls. I much prefer fairies to skulls. It makes them seem more like an after-work parent's bike club, than a murderous gang.

The music stops once people catch on to something abnormal happening.

People stare at me and Alette. The fire brings out the slightest glimmer in their skin when the light parts hit them. They don't all shine green, but other colours too. So lightly, it takes focus and a moment to realize it.

What are they? Is the answer obvious?

I stop staring back quickly; it feels rude to stare. Though, they don't have the same reservations about me.

I understand why; a stranger brought back one of their people. They're sizing me up and trying to figure me out.

Or, maybe they're springing whatever trap I walked into.

Alette, Potato, catches them up. She has to repeat herself a couple times as more people come and pay attention. She introduces me as Blondie and ensures they know that they'll be returning me to my friends.

One of the men brings an intricately carved wooden box to help patch Potato up. It has bandages and glass vials of different earthy things.

"Are you hungry?" Another man asks Potato.

"Yes! I ran out of food at breakfast, and that was just some dehydrated apples. And, get Blondie something too, from out and about." Potato demands.

"Out and about?" He scrunches his face up and he looks me up and down. "Do I have to? We don't have much left."

"Yes." Potato insists.

"I have some things I can eat in my backpack, if it's too much to much trouble." I offer to ease the inconvenience. "I ate supper, so I'd be good until tomorrow."

"It's not any trouble." She turns her head from me to him. "He's happy to do it for our honoured guest. He wouldn't want to be rude to our guest."

"Anything for our guest." He echoes, while staring at Potato.

I bite the thanks on my tongue and nod instead.

He leaves to go into another room, but comes back quickly with a jacket. "I'm going to see what Frankie has. I don't have anything snacky left."

I nod again, while biting my tongue.

I should've asked more questions about appropriate responses to thank someone. I don't want to offend anyone by seeming ungrateful. Nodding doesn't seem like it is enough.

He leaves out the door we came through.

I watch as Alette finishes getting patched up. The man and her have a conversation beyond my reach.

My eyes start wandering around, now that the attention on us has given way, and people are going back to their business; going back to whatever they were doing before our interruption.

It reminds me of Jules' lounge; the music, the laughter, comradery, warmth and food.

The clubhouse is a log cabin in the woods. We're just missing the camp councillors; I muse.

No dead animals hanging on the wall, which is nice. They always creeped me out with their stares. To each their own, but it's not for me.

The fireplace is the main focal point of the room. Right in the middle of the back wall is a giant stone inset fireplace. Couches and chairs face toward the fireplace to focus on gathering around it.

Where we sit, there are a few high chairs at a ledge attached to an island. Behind the counter is a mini kitchen bar.

The dark woods and dark furniture add to the deep cozy feeling of the room.

They aren't using the lights in the ceiling. I wonder if that's because they lack the power to have them on. Or, they might be conserving energy for other things.

The music player is a round machine on a side table in the corner. I can't see if it's attached to an outlet from here. But, I bet it could be battery-powered for its size.

Loud boisterous laughter pulls my attention to a curly-haired blonde woman. She has the loudest laugh I've ever heard. The noise fills the room with a catchy glee. She laughs with her whole soul put behind it.

The door opens and the food guy returns. He has a prewrapped brown disk in hand.

I nod my appreciation as he passes it to me, then goes on by. I'm not even sure he saw my nod.

Alette looks between my food and the man, nods her approval, then goes back to paying attention to talking to the medic.

I open the plastic covering to the dessert inside. I take a bite and discover a chocolate-covered chocolate cake. It has a white icing between layers.

Overall, it's a delicious and incredibly sweet treat.

Almost too sweet, which is weird to say. But, after months of not having anything like this, even including the cake Anna made, it seems like it could use about half the sugar it contains, and still be too sweet.

Snacking and talking give way to singing and dancing.

Alette gets up so I do too.

She puts her hand out to stop me. "Stay here."

I want to ask to come with her, but I refrain. I don't want to be alone here, and she's the only person I know. But, she said to stay here, so that's what I have to do. I sit back down and watch her go to the other side of the room; near the kitchen.

I settle back up on the tall chair and make sure I don't swing my legs.

Alette talks with someone about me; I'm certain of it. They both keep glancing in my direction. It's a sure sign that people are talking about you. I can't tell if it's a good or bad topic. Both their expressions are mostly neutral, if a bit positive.

A woman rushes up to them, and each of them drops their expression as they talk it through. Something serious is happening and it concerns me; both ways. Alette and the man both glance over to me. The only reason the woman isn't, I'm sure, is because her back is to me.

Alette picks up her smile and hops over to me. The two she left stare my way.

I wait expectantly as Alette works out how to talk to me, and say what she needs to say.

"Looks like we won't be able to leave right away. So, we'll get a good sleep and head out in the morning." She announces.

"That's fine," I tell her.

I wasn't expecting to leave immediately. A good night's sleep, in a safe space, is much appreciated.

"You don't mind?" She watches me warily.

I smile slightly larger and place up both my hands. "Not at all."

"It's going to delay how fast we can get you home." She reiterates.

"It's fine. No worries. I figured it would take a while either way. I expected it. As long as I make it back eventually."

It's just a bit of a delay. I figured it was too late to leave now.

It only makes sense that we'd get some sleep, and head out tomorrow.

I'll update Dominique when I get a moment alone.

Chapter 40

The warm breeze rustles the curtains. It's the only noise in this room, maybe in this house.

I doubt Dominique is awake yet; she never is. Even with my morning lounging routine, I'm always up before her.

You were right, Alexa. Relaxing in bed and taking a moment before the day starts is much better than bouncing out of bed; I can admit that now.

But, there is a limit.

I pull myself up and out of bed, then quickly get dressed into my working clothes and brush my teeth.

I imagine Alexa still sleeping in the bed. I won't need her for this morning; maybe for the whole day.

Leaving the room, I stick my arm out to cling to the door; stopping myself quickly.

Walking back into the room, I close the window and the curtains. Open windows at night help keep the room cooler, but if it's open all day then my room is insufferably hot by evening.

Making my way to the kitchen, I open the fridge. There is more open space than not; we'll need to go to the market soon.

What day is it? Oh, doesn't matter. I'm sure Dominique would let me know if it's Monday or Thursday.

We always go to the market, even if it's just to look. But, usually we're out of fresh stuff by then, and we're running on empty now.

I scowl at the pale goop in the glass jar on the top shelf. Maybe one of these days the yogurt will be better; definitely not today. There's not enough sugar to cancel out the sour from this batch.

Dominique and Jules say I just have to deal with it and use natural sugars when we can find it. Maybe the next batch will be better.

The raspberries should be good to eat soon. Maybe that'll help when it's sour like this.

Or, maybe we could buy some more jam.

My hand touches the cold pitcher of milk, once I decide I'll just eat an oatmeal bar again. Milk and an oatmeal bar are good enough for an easy breakfast.

I place the milk on the counter, then go back to grab out a chunk of the baked goods.

The fridge beeps at me to close it, just as I swing the doors shut.

I forgo a plate. I don't want to make more dirty dishes than necessary; less I have to wash.

The bar is eaten and gone before I get my glass of milk poured anyways, so I don't need it. I drink the milk while putting the pitcher away, and grab another oatmeal bar chunk.

The cup goes by the sink, before I wrap the bar in a reusable container.

I fill up my water bottle from yesterday with water.

Prepped to go, I walk to the front door. I set the food and water down to get on my work shoes. They're a muddy brown colour despite having originally being blue.

I should clean them one of these days, but there's almost no point. I'll either grow out of them soon, or they'll just get dirty again quickly.

I pull on my gray hoodie too. It's still a bit cooler out this early, and I can just take it off when I get too warm.

Gathering my things, I leave the house; locking the door behind me.

The cooler fresh air fills my lungs. Tweeting and chatters greet me. I start walking towards the barn.

Only the birds and David are out this early; I muse. Though, not completely true. I can see others out and about, and I'm up and out. It's not even that early.

Although, I'm certain that no one is up as early as David is. He seems friendly. He's always happy when I see him.

His brother explained that he's still a child in his head, even though he's an old man. He starts his day earlier than anyone else, gets all his chores done, feeds and takes care of his creepy goat, then goes to have a nap. I don't see him any other time of the day.

I spot him in the field with a few others.

Some prefer to get to work early, before it gets too hot out. Which works great, because others like to work when it's hotter out.

I like to get my chores done first thing. Get it out of the way before too many people get up.

Do it before it's too hot out.

Do it before I have to go to school.

Dave is already up and with the egg-laying chickens.

"Morning," I say.

He jumps a little at my sudden greeting but quickly relaxes when he recognizes me. "Morning Ray of Sunshine!"

I beam at the nickname.

"How are the chickens this morning?" I ask as I join him in the cage.

I pull the basket off the hook and start my morning chores by gathering the chicken eggs. Then, I'll clean the cage, and change their water.

"Looking great! All are happy and healthy. We've got a small batch for cooking tonight. So make sure you head to supper early." Dave recommends.

"Good to know. Thank you." I doubt we'll actually have any of these in recognizable egg form. At most, I've seen bits in stir fry before. I'm told egg makes some broths and sauces creamy. It's used in baking mostly.

Or, wait, does he mean we'll have some chicken for cooking tonight? That would be a change. We haven't had any fresh chicken in months. I'll definitely make sure to get to supper early. Something like that would go fast, even with ration control.

"Sure thing." He responds.

We work in silence as we move from animal to animal. We work in silence, even when someone from the kitchen staff comes to collect the milk and eggs.

I hear the hooves on the ground before I see her. I stand up and wipe my forehead with my arm. "Almost time for school," Claire warns me in a motherly tone.

"Morning!" I greet her.

"Good morning," She answers.

"Claire." Dave walks up to the horse his wife rides on and grabs her hand.

"The boys are at school. I'm headed out. Going to see if I can find the brown one." Claire is determined to catch a brown wild horse that's been spotted wandering around.

"Again," Dave says. He's told me he's not too fond of Claire going out by herself. But, Claire is determined, and no one can keep up with her on the horse.

"Maybe one of these days we'll get lucky. We've had three sightings in the last two weeks. Maybe one of these days I'll get lucky. Would be nice to have more than one horse." Claire argues. It's the key argument that helps her win each time they have this conversation.

"Not for me. More poop to clean up." I joke.

Maybe that'll save us from another round of this. Save everyone from whatever mood Dave might fall into until she comes back safe in the evening.

She smiles largely. "Well, there is that." Turning back to Dave she promises, "I'll be safe. I won't catch the other horse if it puts up a fight. But, chances are, it was someone's pet, and it's just looking for a new home."

I leave them to go put back my rake and dump the wheel barrel.

With some of my chores done, I go home, clean up and switch my outfit before running off to school. The relaxed opening time, means even if I'm the last to arrive, I'm not in trouble for it.

They know I work beforehand, many of us do. That's why we always have a free period first thing. People can read, catch up on other work, ask the teacher questions, or work on their life skills projects.

I've already done so much work today, that I decide to pretend to read a Dragon Island book. It'll give me a little bit of a break before I have to do more.

I stare at the pages blankly. Making sure to turn them now and then to keep up the pretense.

"We're switching things up today." Mrs. T announces from her desk. "We're going to start today with Life Skills.

Megan was able to free up her morning to be with us, to help us with a project. So we'll be doing Life Skills this morning, and bookwork for the afternoon. Let's tidy up, and then we'll get started."

I hadn't noticed Megan when I arrived. Though, I hadn't really looked around much. She might've come afterwards.

Mrs. T and Megan walk to the front of the classroom to get closer to the door and get everyone's attention.

I put the book back to where I had just grabbed it from, then go take a seat on the orange and brown flower couch.

As everyone settles, Megan begins. "Good morning class, thanks for having me. Are you excited to build things today?"

The yeses groan through the class. I don't say anything.

"It's early. Let's try that again. Who is excited to build things today?" Megan tries to rally the crowd.

We all follow through with a clearer, "me!"

"That's better!" She says. "Today we're going to build birdhouses, bee boxes, and bat boxes for the community. Let's start with the easy one. Can anyone tell me why bee boxes help the community?"

"Honey." A couple of kids shout out at the same time.

"Yes, bees make honey. Honey is delicious. What's another reason?" She asks.

"Wax?" Kate asks.

Megan taps her finger over in Kate's direction. "Wax. We can use the wax for some useful products like candles, lip balm, and sealants."

Megan picks Winston's raised hand so he can answer. "Pollination. More bees around to pollinate our crops."

Megan nods and points at Winston for a moment. "Bees are very important to our food chain. If we didn't have bees, some of our plants wouldn't give us food. Good. What about birds? How do birds help us?"

"They eat the bees." One of the older boys shouts.

"Maybe. Bees are a part of other creatures' food chains, yes. But, how do birds help us?" Megan tries to get us back on track.

"They poop on us." The same boy shouts.

The class roars in laughter.

"Okay, enough." Mrs. T reprimands us. "Birds help us by eating pests and providing fertilizer through their poop. Can anyone think of another way they might help?"

"They spread seeds," Winston answers.

Megan continues. "Yes, birds can help spread seeds from one place to another. It grabs a sunflower seed from one place, drops it, and that seed has the potential to grow.

Birds can also help loosen the soil a bit as they walk and peck at the ground. What about bats?"

"They get in your hair," Kathy answers.

"Potentially, but not as likely as TV or books would want you to believe. They aren't aiming for your hair; they want the bugs that are attracted to your body heat.

Bats help eat mosquitoes. I know you all hate mosquitoes.

They eat all sorts of bugs that could cause harm to us and to our plants. They also help with fertilization and seed spreading."

"So, if you'd all like to follow me, we'll go to the woodwork shop and get you started." Mrs. T wraps up the discussion. "Before we go, when we get there, we'll split off into our Life Skills Groups and I will assign you a project.

Older ones or the more skilled ones of their groups, are not going to be doing all the work. This is meant to be a life skills lesson, we need everyone to help and learn. We need to remember that when you do everything for someone, they won't learn anything.

So, let's share the work this time, please." She claps her hands. "Alright, let's go."

About Jacey K Dew

Jacey is an author and mom who was raised in Leduc, Alberta by her adoptive family.

She took inspiration from familiar locations to set the scenes. Asking the question, what if supernatural beings took over?

Jacey started writing stories when she was sixteen and continues to have a passion for creating tales. Writing across genres in whichever story needs to be told next.

Jacey can be found at a multitude of social sites under the handle @jaceykdew and her website hub jaceykdew.ca

Her link page can quickly sort you to social sites, merchandise and book shop, blog, fan club, and a few retail stores her books are available at.

You can also sign up for her newsletter on the links page to receive the occasional email about on goings, book releases, bookish news, discounts and freebies.

jaceykdew.ca/about/links

Subscribe to SuperData to immerse yourself in the Three Souls Universe. Choose between free and paid levels to customize your reader experience. Free to access forums, emails, customizable profiles, freebies, discounts, behind the scenes information, and Ask the Author discussions. Or, choose a paid subscription to add physical mailed items.

jaceykdew.ca/superdata

Other Books by This Author

Vacation Romance

Skylar Bryson goes on the vacation of her lifetime. Tasting freedom and stepping out of her comfort zone while meeting interesting new people and gaining a different perspective. Will Skylar find more than adventure in Mexico? Once Skylar returns home her world is turned upside down. Will Skylar find her support system in her new companion, or should well enough have been left alone?

Coming of Age, Life Lessons Novella

Anna's parents had strict rules for life. Suddenly, at eighteen, her parent's deadly accident throws her life in turmoil. She has nothing more than her parent's rules to go by, but she soon learns that maybe her parent's beloved rules may be wrong for her.

Small Town Drama Novella

She never thought she'd have to return to the city in the crux of a mountain. When her mother falls ill, Kara is beckoned home and thrust into the world she left behind.